Praise for Grace Burrowes

'Grace Burrowes is terrific!'
Julia Quinn, *New York Times* bestselling author

'Sexy heroes, strong heroines, intelligent plots, enchanting
love stories ... Grace Burrowes's romances have them all'
Mary Balogh, *New York Times* bestselling author

'Wonderfully funny, moving romance, not to be missed!'
Eloisa James, *New York Times* bestselling author

'Grace Burrowes is a romance treasure'
Tessa Dare, *New York Times* bestselling author

'Grace Burrowes writes from the heart – with warmth,
humour, and a generous dash of sensuality, her stories
are unputdownable! If you're not reading Grace
Burrowes, you're missing the very best
in today's Regency Romance!'
Elizabeth Hoyt, *New York Times* bestselling author

'An extremely touching love story ...
My One and Only Duke is her most vivid,
compelling portrait of the Regency era yet'
BookPage, 'Best Books of 2018'

'Skilfully crafted and exquisitely written, Burrowes' latest
is pure gold; a brilliant launch to a promising series'
Library Journal

Also by Grace Burrowes

The Windham Brides Series

The Trouble with Dukes

Too Scot to Handle

No Other Duke Will Do

A Rogue of Her Own

Rogues to Riches Series

My One and Only Duke

When a Duchess Says I Do

Forever and a Duke

A

DUKE

BY ANY

OTHER NAME

GRACE BURROWES

piatkus

PIATKUS

First published in the US in 2020 by Forever, an imprint of
Grand Central Publishing, a division of Hachette Book Group, Inc
First published in Great Britain in 2020 by Piatkus

1 3 5 7 9 10 8 6 4 2

Copyright © 2020 by Grace Burrowes

The moral right of the author has been asserted.

A CIP catalogue record for this book
is available from the British Library.

ISBN 978-0-349-42505-4

Printed and bound in Great Britain by Clays Ltd, Elcograf S.p.A

Papers used by Piatkus are from well-managed forests
and other responsible sources.

Piatkus
An imprint of
Little, Brown Book Group
Carmelite House
50 Victoria Embankment
London EC4Y 0DZ

An Hachette UK Company
www.hachette.co.uk

www.littlebrown.co.uk

To those contending with chronic,
intermittent infirmity

Chapter One

"Lady Althea Wentworth is, without doubt, the most vexatious, bothersome, *pestilential* female I have ever had the misfortune to encounter." The hog sniffing at Nathaniel Rothmere's boots prevented him from pacing, though the moment called for both pacing and profanity.

The sow was a mere four hundred pounds, a sylph compared to the rest of the herd rooting about in Nathaniel's orchard; nonetheless, when she flopped to the grass, the ground shook.

"Have you, sir?" Everett Treegum asked with characteristic delicacy. "Encountered the lady, that is?"

"No." *Nor do I wish to.*

Another swine, this one on the scale of a seventy-four-gun ship of the line, tucked in beside her herd-mate, and several others followed.

"They seem quite happy here," Treegum observed. "Perhaps we ought simply to keep them."

"Then Lady Althea will have an excuse to come around again, banging on the door, cutting up my peace, and disturbing the tranquility of my estate."

Two more sows chose grassy napping places. Their march across the pastures had apparently tired them out, which was just too damned bad.

"Is it time for a Stinging Rebuke, sir?" Treegum asked, as a particularly grand specimen rubbed against him and nearly knocked the old fellow off his feet. Treegum was the Rothhaven estate steward. Swineherding was not among his many skills.

"I've already sent Lady Althea two Stinging Rebukes," Nathaniel replied. "She probably has them displayed over her mantel like letters of marque and reprisal." Nathaniel shoved at the hog milling before him, but he might as well have shoved at one of the boulders dotting his fields. "Her ladyship apparently longs to boast that she's made the acquaintance of the master of Rothhaven Hall. I will gratify her wish, in the spirit of true gentlemanly consideration."

"Mind you don't give her a fright," Treegum muttered, wading around the reclining swine to accompany Nathaniel to the gate. "We can't have you responsible for any more swoons."

"Yes, we can. If enough ladies swoon at the mere sight of me, then I will continue to enjoy the privacy due the neighborhood eccentric. I should have Granny Dewar curse me on market day. I'll gallop past the village just as some foul weather moves in, and she can consign me to the devil."

Treegum opened the gate, setting off a squeak loud enough to rouse the napping hogs. "Granny will want a fair bit of coin for a public curse, sir."

"She's partial to our elderberry cordial." Nathaniel

vaulted a crumbling length of wall one-handed. "Maybe we should leave the gate open." The entire herd had settled on the grass and damned if the largest of the lot—a vast expanse of pink pork—didn't appear to smile at him.

"They won't find their way home, sir. Pigs like to wander, and sows that size go where they please."

Running pigs through an orchard was an old Yorkshire custom, one usually reserved for autumn rather than the brisk, sunny days of early spring. The hogs consumed the dropped fruit, fertilized the soil, and with their rooting, helped the ground absorb water for the next growing season.

"Perhaps I should saddle up that fine beast on the end," Nathaniel said, considering a quarter ton of livestock where livestock ought not to be. "Give the village something truly worth gossiping about."

Treegum closed and latched the gate. "Hard to steer, though, sir, and you do so pride yourself on being an intimidating sort of eccentric."

"Apparently not intimidating enough. Tell the kitchen I'll be late for supper, and be sure the hogs of hell have a good supply of water. They will be thirsty after coming such a distance."

Treegum drifted in the direction of the home farm, while Nathaniel turned for the stables. He preferred to serve as his own groom, and Elgin, the stablemaster, having been on nodding terms with the biblical patriarchs, did not object. He did, however, supervise Nathaniel, as he'd been doing for nearly a quarter century. The other stableboys referred to their supervisor as Elfin, and in all the time Nathaniel had known him, Elgin's looks had remained true to that description.

"Fine day for a gallop," Elgin remarked. "Please do avoid the field nearest the river, sir. Too damned boggy yet."

"I'm paying a call. Wouldn't do to arrive at her lady-ship's door with mud-spattered boots."

Elgin took his pipe from between his teeth. "A *social* call?"

Nathaniel led Loki from his stall. "Shocking, I know."

"A *social* call on a *fe-male*?"

Loki shied and snorted at nothing, then propped on his back legs and generally comported himself like a clodpate.

"Are you quite finished?" Nathaniel inquired of his horse when the idiot equine had nearly banged his head on the rafters.

"Spring is in the air," Elgin said, clipping Loki's halter to the crossties and passing Nathaniel a soft brush. "Which ladyship is to have the pleasure of your company?"

"My company will be no pleasure whatsoever." Nathaniel started on the gelding's neck, which occasioned wiggling of horsey lips. "I am to call upon Lady Althea Wentworth, our neighbor to the immediate south. Her swine are idling in our orchard, and I have every confidence she had them driven there in the dark of night precisely to annoy me. While I commend her ingenuity—grudgingly, of course—I cannot continue to humor her."

Loki was five years old, and at more than seventeen hands, he *looked* like a mature horse, bristling with muscle and energy. He was a typical adolescent, though, both full of his own consequence and lacking in common sense. Robbie had made Nathaniel a gift of him, claiming that even an eccentric duke needed some entertainment.

Nathaniel hadn't had the heart to refuse his brother, given the effort Robbie must have expended to procure the horse.

"And you are entertaining," Nathaniel murmured, paus-ing to scratch Loki's belly.

"Lady Althea has pots of money," Elgin observed. "She put that house of hers to rights and made a proper job of it too. She's a handsome woman, according to the lads at the Whistling Goose."

"From whom all the best and least factual gossip is to be had." Nathaniel moved around to Loki's off side. "When a woman of considerable wealth is described as handsome, we may conclude she is stout, plain, and cursed with a hooked nose."

"You have a hooked nose," Elgin said, setting a saddle on the half door to Loki's stall. "Yon gelding has a hooked nose. I used to have a hooked nose until it got broke a time or three. What's wrong with a hooked nose?"

"Loki and I have aquiline noses, if you please."

Loki also had a temper. He objected to the saddle pad being placed on his back, then he objected to the saddle being placed atop the pad. He objected strenuously to the girth—the horse was nothing if not consistent—and he pretended he had no idea exactly where the bit was supposed to end up.

Until Nathaniel produced a lump of sugar. Then the wretched beast all but fastened the bridle on himself.

"Shameless beggar," Nathaniel said, gently scratching a dark, hairy ear. "But standards must be maintained, mustn't they?" How often had the previous Duke of Rothhaven intoned that refrain?

"If Lady Althea's so plain," Elgin said, "and you aren't interested in her money, then why must you be the one to inform her that we have her pigs?"

"Ideally, I will inspire her to pack her bags and retreat all the way back to London. Even our formidable Treegum isn't likely to produce that effect." Her ladyship did spend some months in the south every year, though she always

came north again, like some strange migratory bird helpless to resist Yorkshire winters.

"And if she's not the retreating kind?"

Nathaniel led his horse out to the mounting block, took
up the girth another hole, pulled on his gloves, and swung
into the saddle. "Then I will settle for impressing upon her
the need to leave me and mine the hell alone."

"You're good at that," Elgin replied, giving the girth a
tug. "Maybe too good."

Loki capered and danced, his shoes making a racket on
the cobbles. Then he bolted forward on a great leap and
swept down the drive at a pounding gallop. Every schoolboy in the shire knew that His Grace of Rothhaven galloped
wherever he went, no matter the hour or the season,
because the devil himself was following close behind.

And the schoolboys had the right of it.

* * *

Althea heard her guest before she saw him. Rothhaven's
arrival was presaged by a rapid beat of hooves coming
not up her drive, but rather, directly across the park that
surrounded Lynley Vale manor.

A large horse created that kind of thunder, one disdain-
ing the genteel canter for a hellbent gallop. Althea could
see the beast approaching from her parlor window, and her
first thought was that only a terrified animal traveled at
such speed.

But no. Horse and rider cleared the wall beside the drive
in perfect rhythm, swerved onto the verge, and continued
right up—good God, they aimed straight for the fountain.
Althea could not look away as the black horse drew closer
and closer to unforgiving marble and splashing water.

"Mary, Mother of God."

Another smooth leap—the fountain was five feet high if it was an inch—and a foot-perfect landing, followed by an immediate check of the horse's speed. The gelding came down to a frisking, capering trot, clearly proud of himself and ready for even greater challenges.

The rider stroked the horse's neck, and the beast calmed and hung his head, sides heaving. A treat was offered and another pat, before one of Althea's grooms bestirred himself to take the horse. Rothhaven—for that could only be the Dread Duke himself—paused on the front steps long enough to remove his spurs, whip off his hat, and run a black-gloved hand through hair as dark as hell's tarpit.

"The rumors are true," Althea murmured. Rothhaven was built on the proportions of the Vikings of old, but their fair coloring and blue eyes had been denied him. He glanced up, as if he knew Althea would be spying, and she drew back.

His gaze was colder than a Yorkshire night in January, which fit exactly with what Althea had heard of him.

She moved from the window and took the wing chair by the hearth, opening a book chosen for this singular occasion. She had dressed carefully—elegantly but without too much fuss—and styled her hair with similar consideration. Rothhaven gave very few people the chance to make even a first impression on him, a feat Althea admired.

Voices drifted up from the foyer, followed by the tread of boots on the stair. Rothhaven moved lightly for such a grand specimen, and his voice rumbled like distant cannon. A soft tap on the door, then Strensall was announcing Nathaniel, His Grace of Rothhaven. The duke did not have to duck to come through the doorway, but it was a near thing.

Althea set aside her book, rose, and curtsied to a precisely deferential depth and not one inch lower. "Welcome
to Lynley Vale, Your Grace. A pleasure to meet you.
Strensall, the tea, and don't spare the trimmings."

Strensall bolted for the door.

"I do not break bread with mine enemy." Rothhaven
stalked over to Althea and swept her with a glower. "No
damned tea."

His eyes were a startling green, set against swooping
dark brows and features as angular as the crags and tors
of Yorkshire's moors. He brought with him the scents
of heather and horse, a lovely combination. His cravat
remained neatly pinned with a single bar of gleaming gold
despite his mad dash across the countryside.

"I will attribute Your Grace's lack of manners to the
peckishness that can follow exertion. A tray, Strensall."

The duke leaned nearer. "Shall I threaten to curse poor
Strensall with nightmares, should he bring a tray?"

"That would be unsporting." Althea sent her goggling butler
a glance, and he scampered off. "You are reputed to have a
temper, but then, if folk claimed that my mere passing caused
milk to curdle and babies to colic, I'd be a tad testy myself. No
one has ever accused you of dishonorable behavior."

"Nor will they, while you, my lady, have stooped so
low as to unleash the hogs of war upon my hapless estate."
He backed away not one inch, and this close Althea caught
a more subtle fragrance. Lily of the valley or jasmine.
Very faint, elegant, and unexpected, like the moss-green
of his eyes.

"You cannot read, perhaps," he went on, "else you'd
grasp that 'we will not be entertaining for the foreseeable
future' means neither you nor your livestock are welcome
at Rothhaven Hall."

"Hosting a short call from your nearest neighbor would hardly be entertaining," Althea countered. "Shall we be seated?"

Lynley Vale had come into her possession when the Wentworth family had acquired a ducal title several years past. Althea's brother Quinn, the present Duke of Walden, had entrusted an estate to each of his three siblings, and Althea had done her best to kit out Lynley Vale as befit a ducal residence. When Quinn visited, he and his duchess seemed comfortable enough amid the portraits, frescoed ceilings, and gilt-framed pier glasses.

Rothhaven was a different sort of duke, one whose presence made pastel carpets and flocked wallpaper appear fussy and overdone. Althea had been so curious about Rothhaven Hall she'd nearly peered through the windows, but Rothhaven had threatened even children with charges of trespassing. A grown woman would get no quarter from a duke who cursed and issued threats on first acquaintance.

"I will not be seated," he retorted. "Retrieve your damned pigs from my orchard, madam, or I will send them to slaughter before the week is out."

"Is that where my naughty ladies got off to?" Althea took her wing chair. "They haven't been on an outing in ages. I suppose the spring air inspired them to seeing the sights. Last autumn they took a notion to inspect the market, and in summer they decided to attend Sunday services. Most of our neighbors find my herd's social inclinations amusing."

"I might be amused, were your herd not at the moment rooting through my orchard uninvited. To allow stock of those dimensions to wander is irresponsible, and why a duke's sister is raising hogs entirely defeats my powers of imagination."

Because Rothhaven had never been poor and never would be. "Do have a seat, Your Grace. I'm told only the ill-mannered pace the parlor like a house tabby who needs to visit the garden."

He turned his back to Althea—very rude of him—though he appeared to require a moment to marshal his composure. She counted that a small victory, for she had needed many such moments since acquiring a title, and her composure yet remained as unruly as her sows on a pretty spring day.

Though truth be told, the lady swine had had some *encouragement* regarding the direction of their latest outing.

Rothhaven turned to face Althea, the fire in his gaze banked to burning disdain. "Will you or will you not retrieve your wayward pigs from my land?"

"I refuse to discuss this with a man who cannot observe the simplest conversational courtesy." She waved a hand at the opposite wing chair, and when that provoked a drawing up of the magnificent ducal height, she feared His Grace would stalk from the room.

Instead he took the chair, whipping out the tails of his riding jacket like Lucifer arranging his coronation robes.

"Thank you," Althea said. "When you march about like that, you give a lady a crick in her neck. Your orchard is at least a mile from my home farm."

"And downwind, more's the pity. Perhaps you raise pigs to perfume the neighborhood with their scent?"

"No more than you keep horses, sheep, or cows for the same purpose, Your Grace. Or maybe your livestock hides the pervasive odor of brimstone hanging about Rothhaven Hall?"

A muscle twitched in the duke's jaw.

Althea had been raised by a man who regarded displays

of violence as all in a day's parenting. Her instinct for survival had been honed early and well, and had she found Rothhaven frightening, she would not have been alone with him.

She was considered a spinster; he was a confirmed eccentric. He was intimidating—impressively so—but she had bet her future on his basic decency. He patted his horse, he fed the beast treats, he took off his spurs before calling on a lady, and his retainers were all so venerable they could nearly recall when York was a Viking capital.

A truly dishonorable peer would discard elderly servants and abuse his cattle, wouldn't he?

The tea tray arrived before Althea could doubt herself further, and in keeping with standing instructions, the kitchen had exerted its skills to the utmost. Strensall placed an enormous silver tray before Althea—the good silver, not the fancy silver—bowed, and withdrew.

"How do you take your tea, Your Grace?"

"Plain, except I won't be staying for tea. Assure me that you'll send your swineherd over to collect your sows in the next twenty-four hours and I will take my leave of you."

Not so fast. Having coaxed Rothhaven into making a call, Althea wasn't about to let him win free so easily.

"I cannot give you those assurances, Your Grace, much as I'd like to. I'm very fond of those ladies and they are quite valuable. They are also particular."

Rothhaven straightened a crease in his breeches. They fit him exquisitely, though Althea had never before seen black riding attire.

"The whims of your livestock are no affair of mine, Lady Althea." His tone said that Althea's whims were a matter of equal indifference to him. "You either retrieve them or the entire shire will be redolent of smoking bacon."

He was bluffing, albeit convincingly. Nobody butchered hogs in early spring, for any number of reasons. "Do you know what my sows are worth?"

He quoted a price per pound for pork on the hoof that was accurate to the penny.

"Wrong," Althea said, pouring him a cup of tea and holding it out to him. "Those are my best breeders. I chose their grandmamas and mamas for hardiness and the ability to produce sizable, healthy litters. A pig in the garden can be the difference between a family making it through winter or starving, if that pig can also produce large, thriving litters. She can live on scraps, she needs very little care, and she will see a dozen piglets raised to weaning twice a year without putting any additional strain on the family budget."

The duke looked at the steaming cup of tea, then at Althea, then back at the cup. This was the best China black she could offer, served on the good porcelain in her personal parlor. If he disdained her hospitality now, she might...cry?

He would not be swayed by tears, but he apparently could be tempted by a perfect cup of tea.

"You raise hogs as a charitable undertaking?" he asked.

"I raise them for all sorts of reasons, and I donate many to the poor of the parish."

"Why not donate money?" He took a cautious sip of his tea. "One can spend coin on what's most necessary, and many of the poor have no gardens."

"If they lack a garden, they can send the children into the countryside to gather rocks and build drystone walls, can't they? After a season or two, the pig will have rendered the soil of its enclosure very fertile indeed, and the enclosure can be moved. Coin, by contrast, can be stolen."

Another sip. "From the poor box?"

"Of course from the poor box. Or that money can be wasted on Bibles while children go hungry."

This was the wrong conversational direction, too close to Althea's heart, too far from her dreams.

"My neighbor is a radical," Rothhaven mused. "And she conquers poverty and ducal privacy alike with an army of sows. Nonetheless, those hogs are where they don't belong, and possession is nine-tenths of the law. Move them or I will do as I see fit with them."

"If you harm my pigs or disperse that herd for sale, I will sue you for conversion. You gained control of my property legally—pigs will wander—but if you waste those pigs or convert my herd for your own gain, I will take you to court."

Althea put three sandwiches on a plate and offered it to him. She'd lose her suit for conversion, not because she was wrong on the law—she was correct—but because he was a duke, and not just any duke. He was the much-treasured Dread Duke of Rothhaven Hall, a local fixture of pride. The squires in the area were more protective of Rothhaven's consequence than they were of their own.

Lawsuits were scandalous, however, especially between neighbors or family members. They were also messy, involving appearances in court and meetings with solicitors and barristers. A man who seldom left his property and refused to receive callers would avoid those tribulations at all costs.

Rothhaven set down the plate. "What must I do to inspire you to retrieve your *valuable* sows? I have my own swineherd, you know. A capable old fellow who has been wrangling hogs for more than half a century. He can move your livestock to the king's highway."

Althea hadn't considered this possibility, but she dared not blow retreat. "My sows are partial to their own swineherd. They'll follow him anywhere, though after rioting about the neighborhood on their own, they will require time to recover. They've been out dancing all night, so to speak, and must have a lie-in."

Althea could not fathom why any sensible female would comport herself thus, but every spring she dragged herself south, and subjected herself to the same inanity for the duration of the London Season.

This year would be different.

"So send your swineherd to fetch them tomorrow," Rothhaven said, taking a bite of a beef sandwich. "My swineherd will assist, and I need never darken your door again—nor you, mine." He sent her a pointed look, one that scolded without saying a word.

Althea's brother Quinn had learned to deliver such looks, and his duchess had honed the raised eyebrow to a delicate art.

While I am a laughingstock. A memory came to Althea, of turning down the room with a peer's heir, a handsome, well-liked man tall enough to look past her shoulder. The entire time they'd been waltzing, he'd been rolling his eyes at his friends, affecting looks of long-suffering martyrdom, and holding Althea up as an object of ridicule, even as he'd hunted her fortune and made remarks intended to flatter.

She had not realized his game until her own sister, Constance, had reported it to her in the carriage on the way home. The hostess had not intervened, nor had any chaperone or gentleman called the young dandy to account. He had thanked Althea for the dance and escorted her to her next partner with all the courtesy in the world, and she'd been the butt of another joke.

"I cannot oblige you, Your Grace," Althea said. "My swineherd is visiting his sister in York and won't be back until week's end. I do apologize for the delay, though if turning my pigs loose in your orchard has occasioned this introduction, then I'm glad for it. I value my privacy too, but I am at my wit's end and must consult you on a matter of some delicacy."

He gestured with half a sandwich. "All the way at your wit's end? What has caused you to travel that long and arduous trail?"

Polite society. Wealth. Standing. All the great boons Althea had once envied and had so little ability to manage.

"I want a baby," she said, not at all how she'd planned to state her situation.

Rothhaven put down his plate slowly, as if a wild creature had come snorting and snapping into the parlor. "Are you utterly demented? One doesn't announce such a thing, and I am in no position to..." He stood, his height once again creating an impression of towering disdain. "I will see myself out."

Althea rose as well, and though Rothhaven could toss her behind the sofa one-handed, she made her words count.

"Do not flatter yourself, Your Grace. Only a fool would seek to procreate with a petulant, moody, withdrawn, arrogant specimen such as you. I want a family, exactly the goal every girl is raised to treasure. There's nothing shameful or inappropriate about that. Until I learn to comport myself as the sister of a duke ought, I have no hope of making an acceptable match. You are a duke. If anybody understands the challenge I face, you do. You have five hundred years of breeding and family history to call upon, while I..."

Oh, this was not the eloquent explanation she'd

rehearsed, and Rothhaven's expression had become un-readable.

He gestured with a large hand. "While you ... ?"

Althea had tried inviting him to tea, then to dinner. She'd tried calling upon him. She'd ridden the bridle paths for hours in hopes of meeting him by chance, only to see him galloping over the moors, heedless of anything so tame as a bridle path.

She'd called on him twice, only to be turned away at the door and chided by letter twice for presuming even that much. Althea had only a single weapon left in her arsenal, a lone arrow in her quiver of strategies, the one least likely to yield the desired result.

She had the truth. "I need your help," she said, sub-siding into her chair. "I haven't anywhere else to turn. If I'm not to spend the rest of my life as a laughingstock, if I'm to have a prayer of finding a suitable match, I need your help."

Chapter Two

Lady Althea sat before Nathaniel, her head bent, her fists bunched in her lap. Ladies did not make fists. Ladies did not boast of breeding hogs. Ladies did not refer to ducal neighbors as *petulant, moody, withdrawn,* and *arrogant,* though Nathaniel had carefully cultivated a reputation as exactly that.

But those disagreeable characteristics were not the real man, he assured himself. He was in truth a fellow managing as best he could under trying circumstances.

I am not an ogre. Not yet. "I regret that I cannot assist you. I'm sorry, my lady. I'll bid you good day."

"You *choose* not to assist me." She rose, skirts swishing, and glowered up at him. "I am the only person in this parish whose rank even approaches your own, and you disdain to give me a fair hearing. What is so damned irresistible about returning to the dreary pile of stone where you bide that you cannot be bothered to even finish a cup of tea with me?"

Nathaniel was sick of his dreary pile of stone, to the point that he was tempted to howl at the moon.

"We have not been introduced," he retorted. "This is not a social call."

She folded her arms, her bearing rife with contempt. "That mattered to you not at all when a few loose pigs wandered into your almighty orchard. You do leave your property, Your Grace. You gallop the neighborhood at dawn and dusk, when there's enough light to see by, but you choose the hours when other riders are unlikely to be abroad."

Lady Althea was unremarkable in appearance—medium height, dark brown hair. Nothing to rhapsodize about there. Her figure was nicely curved, even a bit on the sturdy side, and her brown velvet day dress lacked lace and frills, for all it was well cut and of excellent cloth.

What prevented Nathaniel from marching for the door was the force of her ladyship's gaze. She let him see both vulnerability and rage in her eyes, both despair and dignity. Five years ago, Robbie had looked out on the world from the same place of torment. What tribulations could Lady Althea have suffered that compared with what Robbie had endured?

"You gallop everywhere," she said, a judge reading out a list of charges, "because a sedate trot might encourage others to greet you, or worse, to attempt to *engage you in conversation*."

Holy thunder, she was right. Nathaniel had developed the strategy of the perpetual gallop out of desperation.

"You travel to and from the vicarage under cover of darkness," she went on, "probably to play chess or cribbage with Dr. Sorenson, for it's common knowledge that your eternal soul is beyond redemption."

Nathaniel's visits to the vicarage—his sole social reprieve—would soon be over for the season. In December, a Yorkshire night held more than sixteen hours of darkness. By June, that figure halved, with the sky remaining light well past ten o'clock.

"Do you *spy* on me, Lady Althea?"

"The entire neighborhood notes your comings and goings, though I doubt your Tuesday night outings have been remarked upon. The path from Rothhaven to the village skirts my park, so I see what others cannot."

Well, damn. Vicar Sorenson was an indifferent chess player, but he was a good sort who believed his calling demanded compassion rather than a sacrificial duke.

"I will hold your sows for a week," Nathaniel said. "After that I make no promises."

He strode for the door, lest the lady attempt to prevent his egress.

"I am poor company," she said to his retreating back, "but I will not bore you. I must learn how to deal with local society on my own terms, and you have perfected that art. Nobody laughs at you. Nobody dares suggest that your foibles merit ridicule. You have taken a handful of peculiar behaviors and turned them into rural legend. Your life is exactly as you wish it to be and nobody would dream of gainsaying your choices. Our neighbors accept you, foibles, eccentricities, and all. I must learn to make them accept me as they do you, and you are my only possible tutor."

Nathaniel's common sense, the internal lodestar of all his decisions, shrieked at him to keep walking. To ride his horse straight back to Rothhaven Hall and lock himself in the walled garden until autumn.

But he was not an ogre. Not yet. He half turned. "Who laughs at you?"

"Everybody."

"I am not laughing, thus your answer is inaccurate. Does Vicar laugh at you? Does Granny Dewar?"

Lady Althea picked up his plate of sandwiches and brought it to him. "Everybody in Mayfair. If I make any attempt to move in the circles expected of a duke's sister, I am a walking joke. Even my sister-in-law's good offices were not enough to protect me from ridicule, and she is a duchess. I have hope that I will do better here in Yorkshire—guarded hope. Good food should not go to waste."

The sandwiches were not merely good, they were delicious, a reminder that chicken went down well with a dash of curry, and beef benefited from a light application of basil and black pepper. At Rothhaven Hall, old Cook rarely served fowl of any kind. Half a century ago, he'd been a potboy, then a baker's apprentice. Now he was a cook of limited patience and even less imagination.

Lady Althea clearly employed a *chef*.

"Have you a dancing master?" Nathaniel asked, finishing his sandwich. "A music master? A tutor who can teach you to dabble in watercolors?"

"Do not patronize me," she said, returning to her chair. "My brother saw to it that his siblings were exceptionally well educated. I can embroider, tat lace, dance, sing, draw, paint, plan a menu, ride, drive, manage a budget, engage and sack servants, and otherwise comport myself competently in three languages, but with polite society, I am a perennial figure of fun."

On the table beside her chair lay an etiquette manual,

A Lady's Guide to Correct Deportment by Mrs. Harriet Norman.

"And you seek to improve your grasp of proper behavior by reading that drivel?" The third sandwich was cheese and butter with a hint of dill and coriander. Nathaniel adored cheese that had a personality. He'd forgotten such delicacies existed.

"That *drivel*," Lady Althea said, "is intended to aid the shopkeeper's daughter who seeks to marry a squire, the squire's niece who longs to wed a cit. I have searched the length and breadth of the realm. No manuals exist that tell a woman how to comport herself when she's..."

Her brows drew down, her gaze fixed on Nathaniel's empty plate.

"Good food shouldn't go to waste," he said. "My compliments to your kitchen. You were saying?"

"If you agree to hear me out, I will stuff you with sandwiches until it's dark enough for you to risk a mere trot back to Rothhaven. Your horse might thank me."

"Loki is a stranger to gratitude. An obliging hostess would excuse herself at this point, have a word with the footman under the guise of ordering a fresh pot of tea, and tell the kitchen to send a wheel of this cheese over to Rothhaven."

Extraordinary how satisfying a few sandwiches could be when they were prepared with some skill.

"An obliging hostess might," Lady Althea said, setting two more cheese sandwiches on a plate. "I am a jumped-up gutter rat draped in Paris fashions, according to a certain marchioness. Her sister the countess declared me an unfortunate oddity and amusing in a sad sort of way. If I sent you a cheese, you would likely rebuke me for my generosity with another one of your epistolary scolds. I would be the first in the shire to collect three of those setdowns, and that would only add to my notoriety."

She held the plate out to him, and Nathaniel lacked the fortitude to refuse it. The glowering, articulate woman who'd cut him down to size with a few words was sounding more and more bewildered.

More and more defeated.

He took the chair opposite her and accepted the plate. "I don't know as I've ever met a gutter rat before, much less one who can be described as 'jumped-up.' While I do justice to the tray, perhaps you can provide a few details regarding your unusual provenance?"

Nathaniel would listen to her tale, polish off a few more sandwiches, then gallop home. Or perhaps—Loki was young and his stamina limited—they'd travel the distance at a smart canter instead, just this once.

* * *

Wilhelmina, Duchess of Rothhaven, ran her finger over the signature inked at the corner of her son's latest epistle. In the first paragraph, Nathaniel would inform her that a generous sum had been transferred to the London accounts for her use.

In the second, he would report on the health and well-being of the Yorkshire staff, nearly all of whom had been at Rothhaven since Wilhelmina had arrived as a bride thirty-odd years ago. If a trusted retainer had to be pensioned off, those remaining took up the slack, or—in a very few cases—Nathaniel hired a grandchild, niece, or nephew of the departing employee.

The boy was nothing if not loyal. Unlike his idiot father.

"Every time I see my son's signature franking a letter, I rejoice, Sarah."

Sarah looked up from her cutwork. "Because His Grace thrives, Cousin?"

"Because he thrives, because he's so conscientious regarding his duties, because if he's minding Rothhaven, we can continue to kick our heels here in the south." Wilhelmina hadn't any particular fondness for London, but she loved her offspring very much. Better for all concerned if she kept her distance from Yorkshire and let Nathaniel go on without her meddling.

"You earned your freedom," Sarah said, adjusting the angle of her scissors. "An heir and spare in less than three years."

The late duke had bestirred himself to leave his wing of the family seat to congratulate Wilhelmina on that feat, the only time His Grace had thanked her for anything.

Sarah offered her a smile. As girls coming of age in York, they'd dreamed of a London Season. The great day had arrived, and of all the ironies, after traveling hundreds of miles from Yorkshire, Wilhelmina had caught the eye of a Yorkshire ducal heir. She and Sarah both had, actually, but he'd offered for Wilhelmina, and an offer from a future duke was not to be refused, even if his family seat lay at the edge of the world's most desolate moor.

And even if that future duke had had about as much personal warmth as a January gale.

Sarah worked the little scissors at her paper, leaving a pile of trimmings on the tray in her lap. "Yorkshire is beautiful in spring. I wouldn't mind seeing it again."

Wilhelmina gave the same reply she'd always give. "Perhaps next year." She set aside Nathaniel's letter and held up her embroidery hoop, debating whether to add another spray of leaves to the handkerchief she was working on. "The Season is all but upon us, and that is the best time to bide in London."

Sarah snipped away. "Don't you ever grow homesick?"

"I miss my offspring. I do not miss Rothhaven."

Sarah peered at her over gold-rimmed half spectacles. "Meaning you do not miss the ancestral pile, or you no longer miss your late husband? He was certainly a handsome devil and quite vigorous."

Oh, he'd been a devil. Thank the heavenly powers Nathaniel hadn't turned out anything like him. "Who could miss a dwelling that has all the charm of an icehouse? The Hall is a magnet for dust and cobwebs, and nobody can live there for long without risking rheumatism. I really do wish Nathaniel would let the dratted property out."

Though he couldn't. Wilhelmina knew that.

"He needs a duchess," Sarah said, putting down her scissors. She unpeeled the folds of the paper, her movements as always patient and careful. "He's not getting any younger."

"He'll marry in good time. Nathaniel has his hands full with Rothhaven." Another response that hid a world of heartache. Nathaniel *could not* marry, and for that too, Wilhelmina blamed her late husband.

"Rothhaven Hall holds unhappy memories, doesn't it?"

Unhappy memories were inevitable in the course of a long life. When a woman had borne two children to a man undeserving of love, and then seen both of those children treated terribly, her memories bordered on hellish.

"Rothhaven Hall holds creeping damp and mildew, as best I recall. What is that supposed to be?"

Sarah's cutwork was a chain of barely connected figures, far more of the paper having been snipped away than remained.

"I intended it to be a replica of the lace pattern you devised for the curtains in the music room."

"Best give it another go, my dear." Paper was expensive, but Sarah well deserved her little pastimes. She'd been a friend, companion, and occasional shoulder to cry on for decades. What mattered the stationer's bill compared to loyalty like that?

"What does Nathaniel have to say?" Sarah asked, up-ending her tray into the dustbin beside her chair.

"Spring is arriving—always a relief. The flocks and herds thrive, Vicar Sorenson sends his regards." That was the third paragraph of the letter, but it was the postscript Wilhelmina treasured most.

Nathaniel missed his mama, he wished they need not dwell so far apart. Over the past year, the postscripts had become more elliptical, like Sarah's cutwork. What went unsaid far surpassed the few sentences jotted on the page, but that could not be helped.

The larger situation was entirely hopeless. Nathaniel would never marry, and the ducal line would die out. If anything gave Wilhelmina satisfaction, it was knowing that her late husband's most desperate ambition would never be realized.

The Rothhaven succession would end thanks to the previous duke, and well it should.

* * *

Don't leave me. The words welled up from an old, miserable place in Althea's memory. A violent father inflicted one sort of pain, a mother who'd died too young another, and loneliness yet another.

Quinn, as the oldest of the Wentworth siblings, had gone out looking for work from a tender age, leaving Althea to manage Constance and Stephen. Papa would disappear for days at a time, then stumble home reeking of gin, his mood vile. Althea dreaded to hear him pounding upon the door, but as a child with only one extant parent, she'd dreaded to hear of his death even more.

Then Quinn had found steady work that meant he no longer dwelled with his family, and Althea had learned to dread every moment. Thanks to Quinn's wages, she, Stephen, and Constance had had more to eat, but she would have traded her food for an older brother's protection in an instant.

Now she dwelled alone amid splendors unthinkable to that girl, and Rothhaven was deigning to share a cup of tea with her. He had asked her to explain her unusual pedigree, which suggested a degree of isolation on his part that surprised even Althea.

"If you haven't heard of the Wentworth family's improved fortunes, Your Grace, then you truly are a dedicated recluse."

He paused, a cheese sandwich halfway to his mouth. "I like my privacy, but even I know Wentworth is the family name associated with the Walden dukedom. Your brother is the recipient of that title?"

Did nobody feed this man? "He is, and with the help of a devoted duchess and three darling daughters, he's bearing up manfully."

"No heir?"

"My brother Stephen, as yet unmarried." Jane was growing impatient with Stephen, and Althea wished Her Grace the joy of finding a bride who could tolerate Stephen's many peculiarities.

"Titles devolve to unlikely heirs all the time. What about those circumstances renders you unfit for polite society?"

Rothhaven's plate was empty again. Althea tugged the bell pull, and when Strensall stepped into the room, she gestured to the tray.

"Real sandwiches this time, Strensall, not the decorative kind, and have a wheel of the Danish dill sent over to Rothhaven Hall, please. A few bottles of the Pinot as well, and some of the pear torte from last night."

Rothhaven peered at his tea. "Generous of you."

"Consider it an apology for my wayward sows." Also a lure. Monsieur Henri's pear torte was food for the gods and goddesses.

Rothhaven waited for Strensall to depart before resuming the conversation. "Now that you have dodged my question twice, my lady, perhaps you'd favor me with an honest answer: Why are you so unfit for the station that's befallen you?"

Althea rose, though a lady never paced. "My branch of the Wentworth family wasn't merely humble, we were destitute. Many decent families fall on hard times, but my father fell upon the gin cask and never let go. He expended more energy avoiding work than many a hod carrier has spent plying his trade, and he was nasty."

Such a tame little word for the evil that had been Jack Wentworth.

"You've described half the peerage, though port figures more prominently among their vices than gin."

Althea went to the window. Sunshine fortified her, as did fresh air and quiet. In the cramped, twisted warrens of the slums, those commodities were nonexistent.

"If my father was no worse than any earl of your acquaintance, then why am I made the butt of one insult after another? *Never let it be said that Lady Althea carries the smell of the shop with her, when the stench of the alley is so much more distinctive.*"

Rothhaven helped himself to more tea and this time he added milk and sugar. "Somebody *said* that?"

"And four other somebodies found it uproariously clever."

"Did you offer them the cut direct?"

"I pretended not to hear them."

Strensall returned carrying yet another tray, this one laden with food. Monsieur had included a few slices of pear torte, and Althea battled the impulse to prevent Rothhaven from gobbling them all.

Old habits died hard, when they'd been the difference between survival and starvation.

"One learns," Rothhaven said, inspecting the offerings, "to never ignore an insult. Will you sulk over by the window or attend your guest? Considering the measures necessary to lure me into your parlor, the least you could do is preside over the tray."

Althea returned to her seat. "I thought a lady never took unnecessary offense? If I gave the cut direct to everybody who whispered about me behind a potted palm, I'd cease speaking to half of Mayfair. Besides, I don't know how to deliver the cut direct. Jane says it's a look in the eyes, a public dismissal, but I haven't seen it done, and I'm not Jane. I lack a proper aristocratic nose for the cut direct."

Althea piled two sandwiches on one plate, and a fat slice of pear torte on another with a square of vanilla tablet to the side.

"Who is Jane?"

"Her Grace of Walden, my sister-in-law. She has majestic height, a splendid nose for looking down, and this…this *presence* that inspires equal parts respect and liking. She *manages* my brother, a singularly contrary man, and he *likes* it. She is also a preacher's daughter and genuinely kind. Jane has no sense of how to wage a war of petty slights and mean innuendo, and the last thing I want is for her to become tainted by my problems."

"The cut direct isn't complicated." Rothhaven set down his plate, inhaled through his nose—another splendid fixture—and slowly turned his head to regard Althea with a disdain so glacial she nearly squirmed in her chair. He held her gaze for an excruciating eternity, then pointedly looked away.

"You see?" he said, picking up his plate. "Not complicated. You notice, you hold in a contempt too vast for words, you dismiss. Try it."

"Don't be ridiculous. One doesn't rehearse such a thing."

Those green eyes that had chilled Althea to the heart a moment ago crinkled at the corners. "Coward."

"No wheel of cheese for you. A gentleman doesn't insult a lady."

"You all but declared war on my privacy, but you won't practice giving me a dirty look? I thought you were made of sterner stuff."

Had Althea been at table with her siblings, she would have pitched her napkin at him. "I don't want to look silly."

His Grace munched the first sandwich into oblivion. "I will kidnap your cook on the next stormy, moonless night. This is quite good. As for looking silly, when you ignore an obvious slight, *that* is when you look silly. And don't tell yourself that some slights are too small to notice. When you deliver a setdown to even the pettiest malefactor, the real bullies leave you alone. Come, my lady. Pretend I'm the last bounder to speak ill of you. Put me in my place."

Althea mentally chose a bounder among bounders, the Honorable Pettibone Framley. "He said, *'I feel sorry for it.'* He smirked at me as if I were a beast in the menagerie, too stupid to comprehend the taunt."

"A truly vile excuse for a man. Summon his memory and deliver him the cut direct. Chin up, gaze bold. Acknowledge, disdain, dismiss. Don't sneer. Let your eyes speak for you."

Glaring at Rothhaven was difficult, and dismissing him was impossible, but Althea gave it her best effort.

"That was quite good," he said, popping a square of tablet into his mouth. "When you are truly offended, the effect will be magnificent. Be offended easily and often, and the fools will soon learn not to trifle with you. What *is* this?"

"A Scottish sweet. Monsieur Henri adds a dash of vanilla, and the effect is quite rich."

Althea had ingested a sweet of a sort too, the delicious treat of learning how to respond to an insult. Turning the head slowly was an important part of the impact, both before and after that bit with the eyes. Acknowledge, disdain, dismiss.

"I must have the recipe," Rothhaven said. "And I must be going. Is there a reason you do not commend the idiots and gossips to your brother and sister-in-law's devices? A duke of indifferent origins doubtless has vast experience putting the gossips in their places."

"Several reasons, my pride first among them. I must learn to make my own way. If I can wedge past all the whispers and jests, I might find a local gentleman whom

I can esteem. I cannot rely on Quinn and Jane to search out such a fellow for me when they have little familiarity with Yorkshire society, and their efforts on my behalf in London were disastrously unavailing. Then too, Quinn won't merely issue a setdown, he'll ruin anybody who insults his family."

"I might like this Quinn person. I adore this sweet."

Althea didn't always like her older brother, but she respected him immensely. "His Grace of Walden won't merely start talk in the clubs, he will destroy, unto the nineteenth generation, any who offend him. He's obnoxiously wealthy, he cuts a wide swath in the Lords, and he all but owns two banks. He can make his competitors tremble before he pours his morning tea."

Rothhaven dusted his hands over an empty plate. "Some people need ruining, but I take your point. If you are already seen as having the mannerisms of the back alleys, then returning annihilation for a slight only confirms the impression."

A duke expressed himself in those succinct, sophisticated terms. Althea could only nod. "I must find my own way to manage polite society, particularly here at Lynley Vale. Jane was raised in and around London. She has no connections this far north, and no idea how things are done in the country, while I haven't anywhere else to go. In this neighborhood, no one's standing exceeds your own. Will you help me?"

He already had. Althea would practice the cut direct before her cheval mirror, and to perdition with dignity.

Rothhaven rose, looking much less severe than when he'd stalked into the parlor. "Alas, my lady, I cannot. Spring planting is around the corner, and my estate would fall to pieces if I took my hand from the reins for even a figurative instant. My thanks for a pleasant hour, but please promise me that you and your staff will put it about that I am thoroughly disagreeable—if you must mention that my path has crossed yours at all."

His eyes were crinkled at the corners again. Why did he have to have such lovely eyes?

"You cannot plough and plant every hour of the day, Your Grace."

He took her hand and bowed. "You would be surprised. Please do retrieve your errant swine, and I'll look forward to that wheel of cheese."

Dismissed, though without the disdain. Althea did not care for the experience even so. She walked with him to the front door and passed him his hat and spurs.

"I will revile your execrable manners in the churchyard if you like, and assure all and sundry that your breath is sulfurous. Mightn't you pay a call or two on me when planting is finished?"

He opened the front door, letting in a gust of fresh, peaty air. "Could you intimate that I was fearsome rather than malodorous?"

"Very well." Althea accompanied him down the steps to the mounting block. "I will inform any who care to listen that the measure of your step is ominous and that a lift of your eyebrow inspired me to paroxysms of terror."

"I'd settle for a frisson of dread. One doesn't want to shade into melodrama."

One didn't want to part from Rothhaven never to see him until autumn, when he'd gallop past Althea's park at dusk on Tuesday evenings.

"I would appreciate even a proper morning call," she said. "A mere quarter hour of your time."

A groom walked the duke's gelding along the path that led from the stables, and Althea felt a sense of having come desperately close to attaining a goal, only to have it slip through her fingers.

That would not do. Not at all. Rothhaven was clearly the right resource for the challenge she faced, he simply needed more motivation to assist her.

"Never beg," Rothhaven said, buckling on his spurs. "Never give quarter, never beg. With time and determination, I'm sure your situation will improve. My thanks for your hospitality."

Don't leave me. Please, don't leave me. That heart-cry belonged to a young girl watching her mother's still form being carried from the cramped, dank quarters that had qualified as home. The same girl had thought those words when Quinn had left York to take a job in service at a country manor. As a woman, Althea had again bit back that plea when Quinn had been led off to Newgate.

Rothhaven was barely an acquaintance, but Althea had pinned her hopes on his cooperation—how much trouble would it be for him to pay a few morning calls?—and now he was leaving too.

He checked the snugness of the horse's girth, let down his stirrups, and swung into the saddle. The great black beast began capering around on the drive, clearly ready for another dash across the countryside.

"I play chess," Althea said, "and backgammon and cribbage. You could come here on Tuesday nights, and nobody in the village would know. Nobody would know anywhere."

The horse danced in a little circle, then propped on his back legs.

"Settle, imp," Rothhaven growled.

The horse gave one halfhearted buck, then stood like a lamb.

"Please," Althea said, gazing up at the duke. "The cut direct is helpful, but there's so much more…"

He touched his hat brim. "Never, *ever* beg. Good day, my lady." And then he was off down the drive, galloping as if the devil were at his heels.

Chapter Three

"The days grow longer," Nathaniel said. "I enjoy these evenings at the vicarage tremendously but must turn my attentions to the estate for the nonce. Spring has arrived at last."

Dr. Pietr Sorenson set aside the chessboard, the scene of a pleasant if uninspired match all around.

"And when spring arrives," he said, "you are off to tend your herds and acres, consigning me to the dubious comforts of Leviticus. I would rather not end the winter's play on a note of defeat. Can't you spare me one more week?"

Sorenson was a widower, and he'd once remarked that evenings were the time when sorrow hung most heavily.

"This is my second one-more-week, Pietr. I cannot argue with the sun." To emphasize the point, Nathaniel began putting his pieces away.

"Defeat it is, then. I did not see your rook, you naughty

fellow. I absolutely did not see him prowling about there at the periphery. You grow more subtle in your stratagems while I bumble about like a hog rooting through the middens."

Sorenson had a subtlety all his own, as any good vicar did. "You saw her ladyship's prodigal pigs returning to the fold?" Hannibal crossing the Alps with his pachyderms would have been less of a spectacle.

"I was out for a ramble. Hard to miss so much splendid livestock on the move."

In the three days Lady Althea's swine had tarried in Nathaniel's orchard, he'd grown accustomed to seeing them there, accustomed to their happy grunting and sighing. Pigs were in truth tidy creatures, and her ladyship's herd was well behaved. They didn't tear up roots or burrow under the orchard walls, and Treegum swore the orchard would be healthier for having entertained callers.

Nathaniel tossed his queen into the box with her court. "Her ladyship apologized for her errant sows. Sent over a wheel of cheese the like of which I would pay handsomely to keep in my larders."

"With the dill? Delicious stuff. She's an interesting woman."

Another lure. Nathaniel told himself to stand up, shake Vicar's hand, and ride back to the Hall. The same instant he would have risen, Vicar uncorked the brandy bottle and poured them both another two fingers.

"This is an excellent vintage," Nathaniel said. "Shall we drink to good harvests and brilliant sermons?"

"Why not, and to shorter evenings in which to brood and ponder away the hours. She offered to put a new roof on the vicarage, you know."

So much for changing the subject. "Her ladyship?"

"Of course, her ladyship. The Wentworth family doesn't have mere pots of filthy lucre, they have lakes and rivers of the stuff. She could put Rothhaven Hall to rights with her pin money."

"The Hall is sound enough. If you need a new roof, you will apply to me, sir. I thought her ladyship went south for the Season?"

Rothhaven Hall was being allowed to deteriorate insofar as appearances were concerned. The old pile was built to last through the ages, but Nathaniel purposely neglected anything that would give the place an inviting air.

And Sorenson well knew why.

The vicar nosed his brandy. "Lady Althea and her sister, Lady Constance, have gone south in spring for the past several years. My curate is a cousin to her butler, though, and Strensall says Lady Althea intends to enjoy springtime in Yorkshire this year."

Well, damn. Nathaniel had hoped his neighbor would remove to London, where a well-rehearsed cut direct would serve her in good stead. He sipped his brandy—delightful stuff—and told himself to bring up the benefits of running pigs through orchards.

"Polite society is brutal to her." Nathaniel set down his drink, clearly having imbibed more than he'd realized.

"New money and lots of it can bring out the worst in those with older pedigrees. Her ladyship is better off rusticating with us up here in Yorkshire, where we treasure our eccentrics and treat them with the respect they are due."

Sorenson winked and saluted with his glass. He was a man approaching mid-life but had the sort of vigor that would see him into an active old age. Like many in the area, he was blond, blue-eyed, and rangy, and his sense of humor was never far from the surface.

"Her ladyship plays chess," Nathaniel said. "Also cribbage and backgammon. You might consider calling upon her from time to time. Take your curate and he can visit with his cousin while you enjoy a game with her ladyship."

Sorenson began putting the white army away. "And how does the Dread Duke know such interesting details about a woman who can't be bothered to make small talk? I've tried charming her in the churchyard more times than I can count, and while she's never quite rude, she never engages in friendly chatter."

She doesn't know how. "Does she attend the assemblies?"

"Maybe one or two a few years ago. Not lately."

Because she had no escort, very likely. What was wrong with her family that they all but banished her to the moors and dales?

"Perhaps you ought to invite her, Sorenson. You're the vicar, the professional good Samaritan."

"Oh, right. Then I'd be seen singling out an unattached lady for special attention. The pastoral committee would soon be taking wagers on my marital status. In theory, I could offer for such a woman, being nominally a gentleman, but the match would be considered a mésalliance, and besides, Lady Althea isn't at all drawn to me. Why don't you court her?"

The question was offered half jokingly, so Nathaniel dredged up a smile. "Take a wife? A dread duke rather loses his cachet if he's been snabbled by a duchess, don't you think? If ever I give up my freedom, I'll need far more inducement than a wheel of cheese."

Sorenson paused in his tidying up, the white army still half on the field.

"Is it freedom to limit Your Grace's company to the

retainers who've known you since boyhood? Is it freedom to seldom leave the grounds of your estate by day, and always at a dead gallop? Is it freedom to deny yourself an occasional jaunt down to London, where you might speak for Yorkshire in the Lords? How long has it been since you've seen your mother?"

Nathaniel could put Sorenson in his place with a single look—acknowledge, disdain, dismiss—but the *effort* of posturing as an unapproachable duke was simply too great at such a late hour and for so little purpose.

"Her Grace and I correspond regularly, and the Hall was not a happy abode for her. And for your information..."

I paid a call on Lady Althea and enjoyed her company tremendously. If anything made Nathaniel want to *jaunt down to London*, it was the notion that her ladyship rode into battle alone, year after year, against a legion of petty bullies. How would any prospective husband get to see the wit and determination in her if she remained a target for polite society's poison arrows?

"For my information?" Sorenson prodded.

"Lady Althea is lonely," Nathaniel said, rising. "When you decline to call upon her, you slight your duty to a member of the flock. She wasn't raised here, she has no friends in the neighborhood, and her family apparently neglects her. You can spare her an hour over a cribbage board, Pietr. She'll stuff you with excellent fare and probably trounce you to boot."

Sorenson rose as well, his drink in his hand. "I do so benefit from being on the receiving end of a sermon from time to time, and you aren't wrong. You have a flair for a scold."

Lady Althea was a prodigy at delivering scolds, did she but know it. "The next time Squire Annen and his lady invite you to dine, suggest they invite her ladyship. You know how to introduce the newcomers, and yet you've been remiss with Lady Althea."

"Now you're my social conscience, Rothhaven?"

Now Nathaniel was angry. Contrary to his reputation, his temper seldom bothered him. He played a part—the growling, arrogant master of the Hall—and he did so for good reasons. He was careful never to confuse the role with the real man.

But on Lady Althea's behalf, he was angry, and that was reassuring. "Some people choose solitude. Others are banished to it. Lady Althea has done nothing to deserve banishment."

Sorenson took a leisurely sip of his drink. He wielded agreeableness with the same skill Nathaniel applied to ill humor and hauteur, and the vicar was a shrewd man.

"What did you do to deserve banishment, Rothhaven? A man who truly sought solitude wouldn't put up with my chess, much less make a weekly pilgrimage across the fields for it."

Sorenson had never come this close to overtly judging Nathaniel's choices before. "I won't be making that pilgrimage again until autumn," Nathaniel said. "And to answer your question, I have been banished as punishment for the great transgression of having been born, as you well know. I'll bid you good night and see myself out."

He collected Loki from the little stable and carriage house at the back of the vicarage grounds. Loki tried shying at a few moonshadows on the way home, though his heart wasn't in the mischief.

"You needn't cheer me up," Nathaniel murmured. "We can enjoy a pretty spring night for once if we please to."

The horse apparently agreed. Thus it was that as the

path curved past Lady Althea's park, Loki sauntered along at a tired trot, while Nathaniel pretended to ignore the single illuminated window on the corner of Lynley Vale's second floor.

* * *

"Who could that be?" Constance paused in the rearrangement of her shawls long enough to cock an ear toward the park. "Sounds like a lone horseman."

"The Dread Duke going home from his weekly call upon the vicarage," Althea replied. The hoofbeats echoed across the darkened park in a slow, even pattern. Perhaps His Grace was in a contemplative mood. "More brandy?"

"No, thank you. I must moderate my consumption in anticipation of the ordeal ahead." Constance tossed back the last of her drink and set the glass on the table. Althea and her sister were enjoying their nightcap on the balcony off Althea's sitting room, swaddled in shawls against the evening chill.

"Why go to London at all?" Althea asked, leaning her head back against the cushions. "Why subject yourself yet again to ridicule, gossip, and slander?"

"I subject myself to our nieces. Twitting Quinn by spoiling his daughters is the most fun I've had since learning to ride astride. Besides, Yorkshire is pretty, but it's desolate."

And London—where few unmarried ladies worth the name had ever ridden *en cavalier*, much less learned to enjoy good brandy—was something even worse than desolate. Constance also painted with oils, another transgression against London's version of propriety.

How in perdition did she stand the place? "I'm considering traveling to Italy," Althea said.

"I thought people traveled the Mediterranean in winter."

"When have I ever done what's expected of me?" Althea set her drink aside, the lassitude fine spirits could impart having become too much of a temptation lately.

"A medicinal tot now and then is hardly scandalous, Thea. If you do go to Italy, bring me back some daring art, would you?"

"Of course, dearest." Though that assumed Althea would be coming back soon.

They fell silent, and the hoofbeats came closer, still muffled by the evening dewfall. Althea had sent the wine and cheese to Rothhaven Hall, also the tablet recipe, but she didn't expect His Grace would call again. With a man like that, a decision was a decision, and he'd said no quite firmly.

"Do you ever consider taking a husband?" Althea asked.

"I do not. Our mother took a husband. Look how that turned out."

"Quinn became a husband. I'd say that's turning out rather well." For Quinn, Jane, and their offspring.

Constance took up Althea's glass. "Quinn became a husband to Jane. They were extraordinarily lucky to find each other. If you're looking for a fellow, the wilds of Yorkshire aren't likely to offer much of a selection."

"The wilds of London offered no choice at all. I can't go back there."

"That sounds dire, Thea. Do you mean you cannot go back there *ever*?"

"Not to socialize. Do you recall the Honorable Mr. Pettibone Framley?"

"Pretty-boy, to his familiars. He makes quite an

impression. The blond Byron is another one of his sobriquets. Tell me you weren't foolish."

The chill was deepening, though the stars were spectacular. "I was foolish. He was charming. I let him steal a few kisses, and within a week, Stephen told me that in the clubs, I'd become the Strumpet of Birdsong Lane."

Constance muttered an epithet unbecoming of a lady *or* a gentleman. "Quinn could ruin him for you, though Stephen ought not to have been bearing tales. Our baby brother exercises questionable judgment sometimes."

"*Jane* could ruin Framley for me, but what's the point? I'd be the Strumpet of Birdsong Lane if I'd permitted him no liberties at all. The year before, I was accused of trying to steal Miss Faraday's fiancé. The year before that, Appolonius Warton stepped on my hem and landed me on my backside before half the world. Jane could do nothing about any of it, because to stir the pot is to spread the stench."

"They go after you," Constance said. "You threaten them and they close ranks. I'm harmless by design, because I have learned from your example. I sit with the wallflowers, dress as plainly as I can, and never flirt, so they ignore me."

Althea suspected Constance's determined plainness had other motivations, though now was not the time to investigate them.

"All I wanted," Althea said, "was to make a few friends, to have a gallant or two." Rothhaven had been right: Comporting oneself like a puppy left on the back stoop, begging to be taken inside to a place by the hearth, had been the greatest foolishness of all. *Never beg.* Even if once upon a time begging had been your only means of surviving.

"What do you want now, Thea?"

I want a family, people of my own to love and argue with. "My bed, I suppose. I'll be awake to see you off in the morning, and I will look in on Thorndike Manor from time to time while you're gone. Your people know they can call on me if anything should arise?"

"Nothing has arisen in the vicinity of Thorndike since Prince Rupert lost the Battle of Marsten Moor. Are you certain you don't want to come to London with me? Quinn and Jane will wonder at your absence."

"I have never liked London. Quinn dragged us south because his banking business required him to set up a household there, but my memories of London are tedious."

Constance rose, her shawls wrapped about her like so many furs. "And your memories of Lynley Vale are so much better?"

"I've met His Grace of Rothhaven, Con. My sows went a-viking and paid a call upon his orchard. He was so incensed he left his property in broad daylight to scold me. He nearly called me out."

"And does he have a squint and crooked nose?"

He has a lovely smile and kind eyes. "He's personable when he's not in a temper. I invited him back for a game of chess if he's ever so inclined."

Constance bent down and hugged Althea about the shoulders. "I looked him up in Debrett's. He's the nearest lofty peer to either of our properties, and I was surprised that he hasn't married. An older brother died before succeeding to the title, and I couldn't find any cousins. My housekeeper, who knows everything about everybody, doesn't think the current duke *has* an heir. All very odd."

She straightened and drained the last of Althea's drink. "Your sows have to be the most valuable pigs in all of Yorkshire. Have they ever escaped before?"

"They didn't escape. I was curious about Rothhaven and did what was necessary to inspire him to pay a call. I doubt he'll call again." And that was disappointing. Very disappointing.

"His loss," Constance said. "I'll make your excuses to Quinn and Jane, but don't be surprised if they dispatch Stephen to look in on you."

"Forewarned and all that." Stephen was a good brother. He'd ride over Althea's tenancies with her, flirt with the squires' daughters, and threaten to install another lift in some corner of Lynley Vale that had managed splendidly without a lift for three hundred years.

Then he'd be on his way, and neither meddle nor bear tales.

"Are you coming in?" Constance said. "The night grows downright nippy."

"Soon. Pleasant dreams."

"Why doesn't a personable, relatively young, unmarried duke have a duchess, Althea? Why does he tear about the shire on horseback at odd hours as if the excisemen are after him? That cannot be a happy existence."

"No, it cannot, but that is what he has chosen, and his neighbors respect his choice."

Constance retreated indoors and the silence deepened, save for the sound of hoofbeats fading in the darkness.

* * *

"The time has come to separate the irises." Robbie made that announcement as if it portended marching armies and deposed kings.

"I thought separating irises was an autumn activity," Nathaniel replied, spooning overcooked eggs onto a plate.

"Early spring works too. It is still early spring, isn't it?"

A man who seldom went out of doors in the winter months had little sense of the advancing season. "We're weeks away from our last frost, so yes, I'd say early spring yet reigns. More eggs?"

"Please."

Nathaniel exchanged plates with Robbie and took a smaller serving for himself. While Nathaniel would never, ever resent having Robbie home, conversation with his brother could be something of a burden.

What topic would I suggest to Lady Althea if she wanted to foster pleasant talk over a meal?

Robbie tucked into his eggs. From long experience, Nathaniel knew the man felt no compunction to maintain any discussion whatsoever at table. For years, Robbie apparently hadn't been permitted to converse with his fellow diners.

"Where will you put the separated flowers?" Nathaniel asked. "Your garden is splendidly full of blooms as it is."

Robbie downed another forkful of what had to be the most uninspired dish ever to issue from an English kitchen. "Old Mac can toss the extra on the rubbish heap. The whole bed will choke if I don't thin them. Flowers need air, sunlight, water, and space to breathe. The garden has no more room."

So plant them outside of your bloody garden. "You could dig a new bed, Robbie."

"I have dug all the new beds the space will hold."

"Hanging pots?"

"Hang them from what, Nathaniel? The garden has no trees."

"Pot them for the back terrace."

"Irises can't thrive for long in pots."

Nathaniel was no sort of gardener, and Robbie determined on a course was as unstoppable as a herd of rambunctious pigs.

"The rubbish heap it is, I suppose." Another household would have planted those flowers along the front drive, offered them to the tenants, or given them to the neighbors. Rothhaven's extra flowers would die beside the muck heap.

"You went out last night," Robbie said. "Your usual Tuesday call upon the vicarage?"

His tone was casual, but Nathaniel nonetheless heard the worry. Robbie had been abandoned by their father, and still—years after Robbie's return to Rothhaven—Nathaniel's loyalty was not a given in Robbie's mind.

"My last call on the vicar for the season. Planting and shearing approach." And the staff wasn't getting any younger, meaning every able-bodied man was required to pitch in.

"Last week you paid a call. *In the afternoon*, if I'm not mistaken."

And Robbie, in his usual fashion, had brooded on that development for days without saying anything. Now he was asking a question, and doubtless dreading every possible answer because dread had become part of his very nature.

"A neighbor's breeding sows got loose and took a notion to inspect the walled orchard. They are a valuable herd, and I didn't want her ladyship to worry about their whereabouts."

Robbie rarely offered a direct gaze, but he did now. "You might have sent Elgin with a note. Were they Lady Althea Wentworth's hogs?"

How did the true recluse of Rothhaven Hall know that?

"They were, and they are back where they belong now, none the worse for having taken a constitutional."

"Tell me about Lady Althea."

When Robbie had first come home, he'd barely spoken. He hadn't left his room by day for nearly a year, and he'd not gone outside for two. He'd read as if the printed word was food for the soul, until his room could hold no more books or newspapers. The library had been his initial destination beyond his room, but at first he'd ventured forth only at night and after being assured all the curtains were drawn.

His conquest of the walled garden had begun three years ago, and he'd confined his activity out of doors to that space ever since. At first, he'd sat out there sketching briefly on overcast days. Then had come the oils—a more complicated undertaking—and finally, the gardening by the hour. He'd left the house in the past year only to tend his flowers. Other than that, he never so much as went for a drive in the closed carriage or sat on the front steps with a morning cup of tea.

Now he was asking about a neighbor, and Nathaniel dared hope that was a positive sign.

"Lady Althea is a singular female. She manages her own household, though she's neither widowed nor married, and from what I saw, she manages it very well."

"What did you see?"

Elegance, an eye for beauty, spotless housekeeping. "Light, Robbie. Her home is full of light. Lots of windows, none of them boarded up or bricked over. The draperies pulled back, the mirrors abundant and polished to a high shine. Not so much as a smudge on the chimney lamps or brass fenders."

Nathaniel had forgotten what that much light felt like inside a house.

"The opposite of Rothhaven," Robbie said.

"Rothhaven is elderly compared to Lynley Vale. Keeping a shine on this place would take effort beyond what Mrs. Beaseley can spare us. Toast?"

"No thank you. Have we any more of that cheese?"

The last of the wheel Lady Althea had provided sat on the sideboard. Nathaniel fetched the plate and set it on the table. "This is Lady Althea's cheese. She sent it over by way of apology."

"A fine quality, to apologize when one has caused inadvertent hardship for others. What are her other attributes?"

Nathaniel waited until Robbie had taken as much cheese as he pleased—most of it—and speared one of the three remaining slices for himself.

"To be honest, I think she's somewhat lost on the moors, Robbie. She wasn't raised in the country, she has not enjoyed her London Seasons, and yet, she's a duke's sister. The squires and their ladies won't presume to call on her, and she's not quite sure how to call on them." Like young people at their first tea dance, though Nathaniel couldn't say that, because Robbie had never attended a tea dance.

Or a dance of any variety.

Robbie aimed another direct gaze at Nathaniel. "The moors are dangerous."

That lesson was drummed into the head of every Yorkshire child from infancy. Every village had a tale of some toddler disappearing into a peat bog or a tippler wandering off into a snowstorm.

"Lynley Vale is quite safe," Nathaniel said, "and in her way, Lady Althea is formidable. She not only raises the finest pigs in the shire, she's well educated, employs a master chef, and is competent at both chess and cribbage."

The curtains were drawn, as they were in every room save Nathaniel's personal sitting room, which looked out over the endless sea of heather, gorse, and broom that covered the moor. A shaft of sunlight managed to steal into the breakfast parlor nonetheless. Robbie was Nathaniel's elder by not quite two years, though he looked younger. His air now was that of a newly fledged scholar puzzling out a difficult translation.

"You *liked* her," Robbie said. "You enjoyed calling on her."

Robbie would never make accusations, but his observations could nonetheless have a challenging quality. That too was progress.

"I admire her fortitude, though that very trait is likely why polite society has been so cruel to her. She also offered a tea tray to make the gods weep."

Robbie's gaze went blank, and Nathaniel at first thought his brother was having one of his staring spells, but no. Robbie's eyes were intently focused rather than empty, and he wasn't blinking.

"You should call on her again."

"I can't." *You know why I can't.* Except that Nathaniel wasn't sure exactly how much Robbie comprehended. He was a singularly intelligent man, but his experiences had left enormous bogs in his mental terrain. He grew muddled, his memories colliding and blending in odd ways. His staring spells took a toll, and he'd suffered at least one blow to the head in childhood that had had disastrous and lingering consequences.

"Pay a call on her, Nathaniel. You did it once, you can do it again." Robbie flung out those words with all the glee of one sibling hoisting another on his own petard. Nathaniel had frequently invoked the same logic to inspire

Robbie to repeat accomplishments such as leaving his room, opening a window, or venturing to sit on a bench in the walled garden.

"Robbie, such an overture could be misconstrued."

"By whom? You won't misconstrue it. If she's as bright as you say, she won't misconstrue an occasional chess match. You have extolled the virtues of fresh air and sunshine to me for years, Nathaniel, until I had no choice but to take Mama's garden in hand. Now I suggest you trot a mile down the lane, and you haven't the courage for it."

Robbie speared another slice of cheese as if landing a touch on an opposing fencer's breast. Clearly, he was pleased with himself, while Nathaniel was torn.

For Robbie to confront anybody about anything was unheard of. He was painfully agreeable, a trait learned at the hands of well-paid jailers professing to act in the captive's best interests. To suggest that Nathaniel leave the estate on a social call...

That went so far past unheard of as to be suspect.

"Why should I call on Lady Althea? She could well think to reciprocate the courtesy, and then we must turn her away. Rudeness causes talk."

"You've already turned her away—twice. Tell her the usual tale: The Hall is falling down around your ears, your staff has more than enough to do, and you are out of the habit of entertaining. *You haven't a hostess.*"

Long, long ago, Robbie had been a normal boy. He'd teased Nathaniel, been his only playmate, and his partner in endless mischief. That had all but ended when Robbie had turned eleven. Papa had insisted his heir graduate from a pony to a full-grown horse. A bad tumble had followed, and life had changed for all concerned.

Not for the better, but now a glimmer of that confident,

mischievous boy showed through in Robbie's words: *You have no hostess.*

"You know why I have no hostess." Why Rothhaven would never again have a hostess.

"Indeed, I do, but that does not explain why you must deny yourself even a game of cribbage, Nathaniel. The moors are dangerous when we attempt to navigate them alone. You and I ventured out there regularly long ago. We took the dogs, we had walking sticks, we were careful. Lady Althea is alone, and people can be nasty. Go play the duke and let her win a few hands of cards. The neighbors will call on her just to quiz her about you, and you can get back to being the curmudgeon in residence."

Nathaniel considered that scheme—raising Lady Althea's standing by paying her a visit or two, imparting a bit of the guidance she was so keen to gain from him, and for once allowing Robbie to be the older brother dispatching the younger on an errand.

From those perspectives, another call on her ladyship made sense, and would even be gentlemanly. She sought a husband, and Nathaniel could boost her a few steps along the path that led to her goal.

He could and he should provide her that assistance, but like Robbie locked in his windowless room, Nathaniel did not want to depart from the safe and narrow way he'd been treading for years. He'd spoken the partial truth when he'd told Robbie he admired Lady Althea's fortitude.

The rest of the truth was that he found the woman attractive, and that was a sentiment more dangerous than all the bogs and moors in Britain combined.

Chapter Four

In the three days since Constance's departure for London, Althea's usual solitude at Lynley Vale had taken on a curious weight. When she and Constance had first returned to the north and they'd both been busy with households to put to rights, visits back and forth had been frequent.

As Constance had become acquainted with Thorndike Manor's neighbors, time spent with Althea had figured less prominently, until this past year, when Althea had bided with her sister over the Yuletide holidays and not since.

"Perhaps she has a special friend." Althea offered that suggestion to Septimus, the pantry mouser. He regarded his duties belowstairs as purely honorary. Witness, he'd wandered into Althea's sitting room, after following her around the manor for most of the day.

"Shall we read our evening away?"

Septimus leapt onto a hassock and commenced his ablutions.

"No reading, then. Shall we pen a letter to Jane explaining that expiring of boredom in Yorkshire is preferable to expiring of mortification in Mayfair?" And how could a lady *be* bored when running an estate meant she always had more to do than the day allowed?

The cat curled at an angle to undertake an indecent maneuver involving its nether parts.

Jane was owed some explanation for Althea's decision to avoid the social Season, and a letter sent tomorrow would arrive in London before Constance did. Althea had taken the chair at the escritoire by the window and was casting about for an innocuous way to begin her epistle when something clicked against the glass of the French doors.

The wind this time of year could be fierce, and an occasional twig or acorn might be blown against the windows. Birds, confused by reflected sunlight, had been known to dash themselves against a pane, but the sun had set an hour ago.

The sound came again, a cross between a ping and a thwack.

Althea opened the door and got smacked on the shoulder with a pebble. "Ouch."

"Good evening, my lady." The voice rumbled softly from deep shadows below the balcony. "Might you be interested in a game of cribbage?"

Althea had thought much on her previous encounter with Rothhaven and had decided she'd been a fool. The duke had the right of it: Never beg, and especially don't beg eccentric neighbors who refuse to aid a damsel asking for a bit of social guidance.

"Rothhaven, I employ both a butler and a night porter. Have you a reason for eschewing the front door?"

The privet hedge rustled. "Piquet or chess. Choose, or I'll disappear back from whence I came."

Never to be seen again. He needn't say the words for Althea to infer them. "In a puff of black smoke no doubt. I choose cribbage. Best of three hands."

He vaulted onto the balcony more lightly than Septimus leaping onto the chaise. "If you're subjecting me to cribbage, then I'll have another wheel of that cheese for my trouble."

No scent of horse or leather clung to him, meaning he'd come on foot. "Did you travel the lanes looking for stray children to snack on, Your Grace?"

"I traveled the fields and half-ruined my boots. I have a suggestion. Rather than remove to more commodious surrounds, let's stand out here half the night waiting for lung fever to overtake us."

"You disdain to use the front door, but expect the hospitality of my private sitting room at an hour bordering on indecent. And women are supposed to be the gender in want of rational processes." She returned to the parlor, a room small enough to be kept cozy on even frigid nights.

Rothhaven followed her and crossed to the fire, unbuttoning his greatcoat. "Will we be disturbed?"

"I am expecting the ghost of the first Viscount Lynley to walk in the next hour or so. Perhaps you and he are acquainted. The viscount was famous for riding the shire at all hours too, though his inspiration was the fine ale brewed by the local publican's daughters."

"I am not troubled by the company of ghosts, my lady. Gossiping servants are another matter entirely."

Oh. *Oh.* "You are concerned for my reputation should we be discovered debauching at the card table."

He draped his coat over the back of Althea's reading

chair and commenced a circuit of the parlor. "Even a man of my prodigious imagination is stymied by the notion of debauching over a hand of cribbage. Nonetheless, you are an unmarried female, and I am a similarly unencumbered gentleman. Conclusions will be drawn if we are found alone together after dark, and your campaign to land a bachelor will be over before it begins."

He paused before a sketch Constance had done of Quinn. Both Constance and Cousin Duncan enjoyed significant artistic talent, while Stephen was a prodigy with mechanics. Quinn could make money multiply with a snap of fingers.

While I can age a good cheese and hold conversations with my cat. "If you think my brother would force you to marry me, you need not worry. Quinn isn't that sort. Brandy?"

"Please."

With Rothhaven inspecting the appointments, Althea wished she'd thought to bring a shawl with her to the parlor. She wanted to cover herself against a slight chill, for the sake of both modesty and comfort. He examined each frame on the wall, drew the curtains over every window, and peered closely at her bookshelves.

She poured two brandies and handed him one. "Will you open the drawers of my writing desk next, Your Grace?"

He passed the brandy under his nose. "When you are shown into a guest parlor, how do you comport yourself?"

"Civilly. One sits and either accepts or declines a cup of tea, and hopes the tea cakes aren't stale." Which they all too often were.

"How does an obedient child behave upon entering the schoolroom?"

Althea had never been a child in a schoolroom, but she

took his point: Walk in quietly, sit at the indicated desk, remain in the appointed chair until given leave to stand. Expect a rebuke for wandering about the room or showing undue interest in anything but the day's lesson.

"Isn't it rude to peer at my every sketch and sniff my brandy?"

"Why do people display art on the walls if it's not to be admired? Why is the nose considered the most delicate aspect of any high-quality spirit? You never did answer my question: Will we be disturbed by a chambermaid bringing up a last bucket of coal?"

"We will not." Althea took a sip of her brandy. "Shall we to the cards?"

"Not yet, my lady. If you're determined to ignore propriety to the point that you drink spirits, then at least drink them properly. This is excellent brandy and it deserves proper respect."

So do I. Though to be fair, Rothhaven had already passed along a useful insight: Don't sit if, where, and when you're bid to sit, like a child in the schoolroom, always in fear of a birching. Wander and investigate like a predator beginning the evening's hunt.

"How does one respectfully drink brandy, Your Grace?"

He lifted his glass with a slight, circular flourish of his wrist that caused the liquid to slosh gently. "I shall demonstrate and then we will settle to the cribbage. Consumption of high-quality spirits involves three phases. Attend me, for I shall not repeat myself for the laggards in the class."

Rothhaven explained that one first evaluated the appearance of the drink. How quick or sluggish was the liquid to run down the sides of the glass? How deep was the color, how clear? Then the aroma was to be savored by holding the glass at chin level and nosing the scent. First

impressions mattered, but some brandies evolved thereafter into a more complex fragrance—or a worse stink.

The second phase was the experience on the tongue—
his words—and that involved sampling a small taste, rolling it about in the mouth, and pausing before actually
swallowing. He delivered his lecture seated at the card
table, demonstrating as he expounded, and Althea was
reluctantly enthralled.

His hand cradled the glass just so—casually cherishing
fine crystal without a hint of affectation.

He spoke with the confidence of an expert and yet his
explanations were simple and clear. He focused on his topic
with a controlled relish that brought Althea's attention not
to the brandy, but to the man holding forth.

And to his mouth as he sipped, considered, and expounded.

"The finish is not to be overlooked," he said. "The
entire experience, no matter how lovely, can be sabotaged
by ignoring the finish or rushing it. Rather like"—he took
another slow, considering sip, eyeing Althea over the rim
of his glass—"a kiss."

Althea's imagination had gone to an analogy even
naughtier than kissing. This whole digression had taken
on untoward overtones, and she suspected Rothhaven had
done that on purpose. More behaving as he pleased rather
than as he ought.

"I find a rousing argument also needs a good finish,"
she said. "A quip, a cut, a double entendre, but either I
think of those clever words as I'm retiring for the night
hours later or what comes to mind is more vulgar than
even I am willing to say in decent company."

"The French call that the wisdom of the staircase. We
are very clever and well spoken in our heads as we either

go down the steps to climb into our coaches or up the steps to seek our beds. Shall we to the cards, my lady?"

"I would rather you delivered another lecture." Althea swirled her drink experimentally, then brought it to her nose.

"I never lecture. Don't rush your evaluation of the brandy's appearance. Hold it up to the light, mentally compare it to others you've sampled."

She complied, though the brandy looked like brandy to her. Garnet liquid with amber fire in its depths when examined by candlelight. Quite pretty, actually.

"Perhaps the next time you're not-lecturing, you could impart a few insights about those witty retorts at which I fail so regularly."

"Look at me."

Never accede to a man giving orders. Never. Althea continued studying her brandy. "For a fellow who professes not to lecture, Your Grace, you certainly—"

"I am imparting an insight. As you nose the brandy, *look at me*. Convey with a glance that you take your time evaluating what's on offer, that your judgment is neither hurried nor ill-informed regarding any matter of substance. Look at me as if you'll take the same care evaluating *me*, should I ever be worthy of your whole attention."

Althea regarded him, realizing that this little discourse on proper consumption of spirits applied to tea, chocolate, wine—any social occasion where a beverage was served. She sipped, and found that the brandy had acquired subtleties of taste, sensation, and aroma for being more carefully considered.

Just as some people became more interesting upon closer acquaintance.

"I daresay you have a talent for this," Rothhaven

muttered, taking up the cribbage board and extracting the pegs from the compartment on the end. "Do we cut for the first deal, or shall the lady go first?"

Althea stalled by taking another sip of her brandy—a lovely potation, now that she bothered to notice. Warming rather than fiery, sunshine and fruit with a hint of sweetness instead of the syrupy banality of a cordial.

Rothhaven's question—whether to cut for the deal or observe the inane ladies-first protocol—was another test of some sort. Althea could bow to good manners and have the advantage of the points in the first crib, or she could flout convention in one detail and open the game without respect to gender niceties.

She might not have the first crib in that case, but she would imply that convention did not always control her.

"It's always like this, isn't it?" she said, setting her drink aside. "Every moment in company is an opportunity to either conform to or conflict with expectations. The choice is mine." Why hadn't she seen this more clearly? On an intuitive level, she'd known that breaking rules carried consequences, but she'd not considered that breaking rules could have *benefits*.

Interpreting rules opened up worlds of opportunity for gaining the upper hand in society.

"Precisely," Rothhaven said, setting the deck before her. "You choose, and others can either accept your choices or find someone else to bore with their small-mindedness."

Interesting point of view for a man who chose to hole up in his manor house like a fox in his covert.

"So what is your pleasure, Lady Althea? Shall you have the first deal or do we cut the deck?"

"You are my guest," she said. "Why don't you decide?"

He snorted, whether with humor or derision Althea

couldn't say, and she probably wasn't supposed to care. He picked up the deck and began dealing, which hadn't been one of the options under discussion.

* * *

Ladies did not take strong spirits as a rule. Nathaniel's mama, however, had been very clear that what applied to delicate flowers in the south of England was inapplicable to the hardier specimens contending with northern winters. Even her companion, the formidable Cousin Sarah, took an occasional nip.

Lady Althea made sipping brandy into a feminine production. She combined grace, daring, self-restraint, and a subtle sensuality that proved ladies should not take spirits because gentlemen got ideas merely observing the process.

Nathaniel tried to focus on his cards, though the game was going badly. Lady Althea played with assurance, and she made prudent choices.

"You are enjoying a run of luck," he said, discarding an eight and a seven. In the next instant, he recalled that the crib—the third hand that alternated between the two players—belonged not to him but to her ladyship this round. He'd just put very valuable cards into her lady-ship's crib.

Who named this wretched game anyway?

"I like cribbage," she replied. "No other two-handed game comes close for balancing luck and skill."

Nathaniel could think of at least one other *two-handed game* where luck and skill were in even greater demand.

He lost. He lost not because he was the victim of bad luck, but because he liked watching Lady Althea shuffle the deck, because he'd had a bit too much brandy too quickly for a man who typically abstained, and because he wanted to watch her enjoy her victory.

He narrowly beat her in the second game and went down to defeat again in the third.

"I have earned my cheese," he said, draining the dregs of his drink. "And enjoyable labor it was too. You have a head for probabilities."

She collected the pegs and returned them to their compartment. "I thought I was merely lucky."

"In the first and third games, you were lucky. In the second, you evidenced good mathematical skill, but alas, not quite good enough."

She gathered up the cards and tidied them into a stack. "I never know when somebody is teasing me or making a jest at my expense. Were you insulting me just now?"

Good God, she was so *earnest*. Of course polite society had no idea what to do with her. "If I insulted you, I am no gentleman, am I?"

"If I am a lady, I give you the benefit of the doubt—up to a point. Ladies are gracious and kind. Nobody ever says *why* they are, but it's expected of them."

Not expected of *us*, but rather, expected of *them*. She did not see herself as a lady. She saw herself as a woman impersonating a lady.

"I do not see myself as a duke," Nathaniel said slowly. "I am a man impersonating a duke. I do the best I can, but I often fail."

Her ladyship gave him that intense, blue-eyed perusal that made him want to provoke her to smiling. Anything to give her a reprieve from the unrelenting seriousness that she wore like a widow's black veils.

"You might consider receiving the occasional guest,"

she said, putting the cards into a drawer. "Dukes entertain. The occasional smile might enhance your chances of
pulling off this impersonation. I know several other dukes
and can claim one as a brother. I have seen him both smile
and entertain guests"—she closed the drawer and leaned
closer—"*at the same time*. Dukes do."

"Regardless of how *dukes* behave in the general case,
I do not entertain." Nor did Nathaniel quite know how
to react to her teasing, if that's what she was about.
"The hour grows late and I should take my leave of
you." The brisk Yorkshire night breezes would slap
some sense into him and snatch away useless fancies
about earnest women who played a good game of
cribbage.

Nathaniel rose and so did her ladyship.

"Why did you come here tonight?" she asked, holding
up his coat for him.

He slid his arms into the sleeves and faced her. "Because I was out for a ramble and saw your lamps were still
lit." In fact, he'd been debating this visit for three days.
Her ladyship's raised brow suggested she knew a bouncer
when she heard one.

"I'll walk you to the front door."

Nathaniel did not relish the thought of vaulting over the
balcony, but neither could he risk being discovered with
her. "I would prefer not—"

"The staff has long since gone to bed," she said. "Come
along."

He followed rather than argue, mostly because he
wanted to see more of her house. The appointments were
exquisite, the housekeeping ruthlessly thorough. Every
mirrored sconce was polished to a gleaming shine, and not
a single cobweb clung to the gilt of the picture frames

or pier glasses. Even the wood floors bounced candlelight into a mellow sense of order and peace.

Not like Rothhaven Hall, where the maids were old enough to be Nathaniel's grannies, and the footmen even more venerable.

"Your house wants flowers," he said as they approached the front door.

"I haven't a conservatory, Your Grace, and the garden has yet to yield much in the way of blooms. Thank you for an enjoyable evening."

Nathaniel waited for the words that would put a crimp on the whole excursion—*you must come again sometime*—but her ladyship remained with one hand on the door latch, her expression merely pleasant.

"My thanks as well," he said, "and I'll bid you a good evening." He possessed himself of her free hand and bowed over it, but rather than allow that gesture to remain perfunctory, his tired, somewhat brandy-soaked brain instead noticed the hand he held.

Her nails were clean and neatly trimmed—no surprise there—but the pads of her fingers were rough, and minute scars crisscrossed her knuckles. A serious gash had healed at the base of her thumb, without benefit of stitches if the irregular scar was an indication.

"You see the evidence of picking oakum," she said, "among other unladylike endeavors. I never go out without my gloves." Her gaze had grown wary, her posture straighter.

Nathaniel stood for a moment more or less holding her hand while he pondered an appropriate rejoinder. She was braced for a setdown, and he wanted to put out the lights of any man who'd ever delivered her one.

Lady Althea withdrew her hand. "If you'd like to call

again, Your Grace, please do send a note. Be punctual and I will receive you myself at the front door."

"And if I don't care to use the front door?" He honestly didn't care for skulking along hedges and hoisting himself over balustrades.

"Then I will not receive you at all. Enjoy the walk home."

He'd hoped for a smooth, urbane conclusion to the evening and was instead on the receiving end of a chilly dismissal. What fool had announced that the finish *mattered*? Though her ladyship had the right of it: He was better off adhering to the routines that ensured privacy at the Hall, and this departure had been unwise, for all he'd enjoyed it.

Enjoyed it very, very much.

He took her hand again, and this time kissed her knuckles, an enormous breach of protocol. He held her hand one moment longer and looked her directly in the eye.

"Exquisitely done, my lady. *Exquisitely* done. Good night."

He left her smiling, her right hand grasped in her left. The flame in the sconces created a halo of fiery highlights in her dark hair, and her blue eyes were for once devoid of wariness.

A lovely image to remember her by.

* * *

Sleep refused to oblige Althea, but then, she'd never needed much sleep.

Poverty forced a distance between creature needs—for rest, safety, sustenance, companionship—and the realities of life. Working exhausted, functioning when terrified, thinking clearly in the midst of horrendous anxiety became normal for any child cursed to have Jack Wentworth as a father.

"Old Jackie is dead," Althea murmured, giving up the battle for rest. Dawn would arrive soon, though by summer, dusk and dawn would be within kissing distance of each other. She climbed from her bed, changed into two shifts and an old walking dress, and put on her most disreputable half boots.

What the boots lacked in style they made up for in sturdiness.

Wandering at dawn was another habit left over from girlhood. The world was quiet and innocent at dawn, full of hope and good smells. Baking bread, scrubbed front steps, freshly mucked-out stables. The odors of abundance, domestic industry, and order had been a comfort to a child who later in the day would not have dared to venture into the better neighborhoods.

"But first thing in the day, the world belongs to those willing to wander." She gave Septimus a pat on the head and left the bedroom door cracked for him.

The garden called, though it wasn't much of a garden. Some previous owner of Lynley Vale had seized about half an acre from the surrounding moors to level into parterres, added a fountain and a buffer of rolling lawn, and then gone back to raising sheep.

"It's enough." Althea stole into the misty gloom by way of the library terrace. Rothhaven had come this way the previous night, and from there he'd invaded Althea's dreams.

"Or my nightmares." Althea walked the crushed-shell path that ran around the garden's perimeter, though the wilder terrain beyond called to her.

Rothhaven would like knowing he'd disturbed her sleep. A brooding recluse who galloped free in the evenings and strode the fields by night wasn't entirely content to remain behind his castle walls.

"So why pretend otherwise?" And why—why, why, why?—plant that sweet, tender kiss on her less-than-ladylike knuckles?

That thought sent her to the foot of the garden, where somebody had left a bucket of muddy tubers. Irises, from the looks of them, very recently dug up and in need of replanting. Althea's gardener was a conscientious soul, and irises would make a nice addition to the staid privet hedges and empty urns.

"So would daffodils." She left the garden by way of the groundskeeper's shed and retrieved a trowel and bucket, then ambled along a foggy track toward the river. Closer to the water, the mist was thicker, imparting a half-eerie and half-enchanting fairy-glen quality. A lanky hare loped across the path, then stopped several yards on, wiggling its nose in a fashion that suggested Althea had brought an unwelcome scent with her.

"Good day to you."

The hare hopped away, not in any particular hurry.

She found her quarry—a bank of daffodils not yet in full bloom—and proceeded to soak her hems and get her hands filthy filling her bucket with robust specimens. Activity felt good, just as putting Lynley Vale in order had felt good, but realizing that her home had no flowers—Rothhaven had seen that in one casual glance—was daunting.

"When will I learn?" she asked the dewy morning air. "When will I feel as if I'm who and where I'm supposed to be?"

Something twitched at the edge of her vision, another hare perhaps. Foxes could thrive near moorland as did game birds, but this movement felt...less benign.

Althea rose and stuffed her trowel into the bucket of uprooted flowers. "Is somebody there?"

She was on her own land, and a scream would bring help, but if she screamed over a nesting grouse she'd feel quite the fool.

The mist swirled on an unseen current of air and revealed the outline of a man, bareheaded, his greatcoat brushing the tops of field boots. He stood a good twelve yards away, so utterly still Althea might have missed him, but for the darkness of his attire against the pale fog.

"Good morning." Althea was ready to hike her skirts and run, but nothing about the fellow was menacing—nor did he seem friendly.

He turned and strode off, the mist swallowing him up before he'd gone six strides.

Had it been Rothhaven? The height hadn't seemed quite impressive enough, the walk not as decisive as Rothhaven's, but then, she'd not seen His Grace previously in pre-dawn half-light. Perhaps the vicar had gone for a constitutional to help compose one of his lofty, articulate sermons and hadn't wanted small talk to interrupt his train of thought.

Though the man had taken the path that led to Rothhaven Hall, the opposite direction from the vicarage.

Althea collected her flowers and made her way back to her own garden, no longer quite as charitably disposed toward solitude at such an early hour.

The encounter had been odd. Very odd indeed.

Chapter Five

The night air had failed to slap any sense whatsoever into Nathaniel. Instead he'd wandered home by way of the lanes, in deference to his boots and also because he'd been reluctant to return to Rothhaven Hall.

The manor had sat like a black hulk against the moonlit sky, the sight melancholy rather than menacing. Without a single lamp glowing in a window, Nathaniel's home had looked more like a prison than the haven it was meant to be. Sleep had been elusive after that unhelpful thought had taken root, and Nathaniel had tormented himself with second thoughts.

The wisdom of the well-punched pillow suggested he ought not to have kissed Lady Althea's hand. Perhaps he should have kissed her cheek, or perhaps he should have let himself out through the French doors and bolted across her garden hotfoot.

Or—in for a penny, in for a pound—he might have

kissed the lady herself and got a proper dressing down for that presumption.

Robbie joined him in the breakfast parlor, his hair a bit windblown, the toes of his boots damp.

"Have you been in the garden already?" Nathaniel asked.

"Good morning, and yes, I have been in the garden. Spring and autumn are the busiest times for a gardener, and I smell rain in the air."

Robbie liked rain, liked the dreariness and the steady patter. Rain meant people were less likely to be abroad, to his way of thinking, and that was a good thing.

"I've been seized by a notion," Nathaniel said, dabbing marmalade onto his toast. "We could connect the orchard walls to the walls of our existing garden and double the garden space we have to work with."

This scheme had occurred to him in the small hours of the night, as he'd ruminated on the way Lady Althea's lawn blended into her back garden. Not much maintenance required, and the scheme set off Lynley Vale nicely and made sneaking up on the place by day impossible.

Not that Nathaniel would be sneaking up on Lynley Vale ever again.

"Can you afford the labor this time of year?" Robbie asked, taking the place to Nathaniel's right. "I know your home farm is busy now too."

As were the tenancies, the brewery, the dairy, the kitchen gardens, the stables... The weight of a sleepless night abruptly doubled.

"If we order the stone now, we'll have it on the property when the labor is available." Rothhaven Hall almost never hired additional workers, not unless an employee was pensioned off and could personally vouch for the discretion of his or her replacement.

"To run walls all the way to the orchard will take a lot of stone," Robbie said, tucking into his eggs. "You'd have to raise the walls around the orchard by another three feet at least as well."

To ensure privacy. Always, always to ensure privacy. "We can take it in stages. First add on to our existing garden, then complete the work on the orchard as time allows."

"Have you a mason among your employees?"

This pleasant, unremarkable conversation was familiar terrain on a battleground Nathaniel had been fighting over for years. He used plural pronouns to discuss projects such as this—*we, us, our*—and Robbie returned fire with the ammunition of the second person singular—*you, your, yours*.

Nathaniel sat at the head of the table even when dining alone with his brother, and if Robbie was feeling particularly unhappy, he used proper address—*Your Grace, Rothhaven, His Grace.*

"We surely have somebody whose skills are adequate for building a wall." Nathaniel set down his toast, only a single bite taken from one corner. The marmalade was bitter, but then, marmalade at Rothhaven was always bitter.

"Is there any more of that delightful cheese?" Robbie asked, pouring himself a cup of tea. "I would not want to suggest that Cook's efforts are in any way lacking, but an omelet might be a nice addition to the breakfast buffet."

Coming from Robbie, that was tantamount to open rebellion. He never criticized the staff, never suggested change of any kind. He believed that rigid routine helped minimize his *incidents*, and who was Nathaniel to argue with that logic?

"We haven't any more of that cheese," Nathaniel said,

"though Lady Althea might be willing to send some our way. What exactly are you getting up to in the garden?"

Robbie went off on a flight about arranging colors in a pattern consistent with the rainbow—red, orange, yellow, green, blue, violet—which would never in eighteen eternities have occurred to Nathaniel. Robbie had of necessity become a genius at defeating boredom, while Nathaniel...

His problem was worse than boredom, and it had dogged him without pity since last night. He'd sat at a card table for less than two hours and conversed with another adult about politics, brandy, books, and music. Even more than the warmth in Lady Althea's sitting room, even more than her most excellent libation, the sheer companionability of the evening spent with her had swaddled Nathaniel in comfort and ease.

If his problem had been simple sexual frustration, he was acquainted with ladies in York who were amenable to a casual encounter with a fellow they knew only as Mr. Nathaniel Debenham, a wealthy squire from west of Durham.

Nathaniel hadn't been to York in months, because those encounters didn't help with what ailed him. In fact, they made his affliction worse, and the time spent with Lady Althea had rendered him nearly sick with his malady.

He was *lonely*. The word had taken years to emerge from between lists of duties, worries, and hopes, but having admitted itself to the broad light of awareness, it refused to resume a life in the shadows.

Robbie kept up a stout wall between himself and all of life beyond Rothhaven Hall, and most especially between himself and the ducal role. That meant Nathaniel was also kept at arm's length. The servants had learned to maintain a distance as well—proper respect, they called it—and

they worked hard enough without the burden of befriending eccentric aristocrats. Sorenson never presumed past
cordial games of chess, but then, he had an entire parish
to befriend.

And then there was Lady Althea, full of intensity
and purpose, bright as a new penny, and ferocious as a
mother cat.

Also damnably kissable. "I could easily make an ass
of myself."

Robbie paused, the marmalade knife in his hand. "I beg
your pardon?"

"Just thinking out loud. I'm off to confer with Elgin
about the state of our broodmares. Foaling will soon be
upon us, and Elgin must boast of the accommodations he's
prepared for the new arrivals and their mamas."

Would the Rothmere family ever again welcome a
brand-new arrival? A ducal heir? An equally precious
sister or cousin to that little boy? Nathaniel could see no
way to accomplish that feat, not as long as Robbie refused
to venture beyond the garden walls.

"I will see you at dinner," Robbie replied, slathering
preserves on his toast.

"Not luncheon?"

"The garden calls, Rothhaven, and rain will soon be
upon us. I must do what I can when I can."

That was a subtle scold, and Nathaniel was in no mood
to be scolded. He left the breakfast parlor and stopped by
the library, thinking to shuffle through the morning post
before dealing with Elgin.

The penmanship on the third letter caused a vague
unease to roil in his gut. He'd seen that hand before or
something very like it....

And he'd read the few words the note contained as

well: *I know your secrets, Your Grace, and you will pay for my silence.*

Nathaniel had ignored the same warning when it had arrived a month ago, because really, what was there to do? No demand for payment had been made, no specific action threatened. He shoved the letter into the desk drawer, dropped the rest of the damned mail onto the blotter, and left through the nearest door.

* * *

"You issued a summons." Rothhaven made a simple statement of fact into an accusation.

"You turn away all callers," Althea retorted. "How else was I to ensure your cheese found its way to you other than by putting it directly into your keeping?" She snatched his walking stick from him the better to ensure he didn't do an about-face and let himself back out into the night.

"The first cheese found its way into my kitchen readily enough," Rothhaven replied, making no move to unbutton his greatcoat. "The second was assured of safe passage if its quality was anything like the first."

"And how was I to know that?" Althea set his walking stick amid the parasols and umbrellas by the porter's nook. "It's not as if you sent a note thanking me."

Rothhaven drew himself up, then leaned near, like a dragon examining the morsel it would soon toast for a snack.

"Allow me to impress upon you, my lady, the distaste I have for being hailed by royal decree to retrieve cheeses from my neighbor."

Something had him in a temper, not merely in the usual state of annoyance he wore like a highwayman's cloak.

"Do we stand here in the foyer, Your Grace, arguing over a cheese like a pair of dockside streetwalkers, or shall we repair to my parlor, where we can have a fire to warm us while we bicker?"

"Surrender the damned cheese and I'll be on my way."

"The damned cheese is wrapped and waiting for you in my parlor."

He unbuttoned two buttons. "You weren't sure I'd use the front door."

"You pride yourself on eccentricity. For all I know, you'd attempt to stuff yourself down the chimney purely for the sake of novelty. Come along."

He stalked at her elbow, his boots thumping against the carpets. For a man bent on remaining undetected, he made a deal of noise when in a pet. The parlor was warm, the sconces lit. Septimus had been curled on the sofa but he was nowhere to be seen now.

"You were having tea," Rothhaven said, sampling a jam tart. "These are good."

"Monsieur Henri regards the kitchen as a vocation, not simply a job. *Do* help yourself, by all means."

Rothhaven went wandering around the room again, though he put his tarts—all three of them—on a plate before settling at Althea's desk. He shrugged out of his coat between bites and then picked up a sealed note Althea had spent the better part of an hour writing.

"You are corresponding with Lady Phoebe Philpot?" *Munch, munch, munch.*

"You have crossed the line, Rothhaven, from flouting convention to outright rudeness. That is my personal correspondence, and I did not invite you to examine it."

"No," he said. "You issued an imperial summons, and having conjured the Demon of Rothhaven Hall, you must now suffer his company. If you take exception to rudeness, then how do you tolerate Lady Phoebe?"

Althea poured him a cup of tea, added a dollop of honey, and brought cup and saucer to the desk. "I won't be tolerating her company, as it happens. She sent the first invitation I've received in months, and I must decline it."

He finished his tarts and dusted his hands over the empty plate. "You are disappointed to decline an invitation from the biggest gossip between here and London?"

"It's an *invitation*, Rothhaven. Beggars can't be choosers, even when those beggars grow up to acquire a title."

He peered at her note again. "You don't have a beggar's penmanship, but then, you were speaking metaphorically."

Althea would have taken the seat opposite the desk, but that was where a guest would sit and this was *her* parlor in *her* home. She took the wing chair by the fire instead.

"I spoke literally. From earliest memory, I did whatever work I could find, but when there was no work, my father would send his children out to beg. My brother Stephen lost the use of a leg early in life, and his job was to look wan and pathetic, leaning on his crutch. My job was to do the actual pleading."

Rothhaven remained seated at the desk, tapping the note against the blotter in a slow, quiet rhythm.

"Your father *sent his children out to beg?*"

The note of horror was predictable, though disappointing nonetheless. "Quinn was older and usually away from home because he was large enough to take on serious manual labor. He also knew that as soon as he came back to the house, Papa would demand any money he earned. I learned from Quinn's example."

Tap . . . tap . . . tap . . . "What did you learn?"

"First, if I made any money begging, buy Papa some

gin, or be prepared to dodge a very fast, mean set of fists. Buy food second and be sure we children had eaten most of it before arriving home. Give Papa the gin and the remaining food. Save a little coin to give Papa as well, and if the day was particularly lucky, save the last coin to hide somewhere outside the house. Rather than discuss this, might we resume arguing over the cheese?"

Over anything.

"So Phoebe Philpot extends you an invitation, and you are again that hungry girl, willing to brave the cold for hours in exchange for a morsel of acceptance."

I will always be that hungry girl. "I cannot have what I want without learning to manage the Phoebe Philpots in this life. She's nothing compared to the brood of vipers at Almack's or the gantlet of Hyde Park's carriage parade." She should be nothing, rather.

Rothhaven broke the seal on the note, donned the spectacles in the pen tray, and read Althea's polite regrets. "This will not do. Why aren't you attending her infernal dinner?"

"Rothhaven, my own brothers do not open my correspondence. My sister at her most obnoxious—"

He crumpled up the note and glowered at Althea.

For the first time in her acquaintance with him, Rothhaven looked genuinely angry. Wearing her spectacles did not lessen his ferocity one bit, but rather, gilded his ire with a hint of scholarly scorn. Ye gods, he'd be a terror if he ever voted his seat in the Lords.

"My companion is in York visiting her sister," Althea said. "If I admit I'm dwelling here alone, I'll cause talk. When I show up at Lady Phoebe's without Mrs. McCormack, Lady Phoebe will ensure the news is all over the county before my coach brings me home."

He tossed the balled-up missive straight into the fire. "You've never mentioned having a companion."

"Why would you assume I lack one? I'm an unmarried female living apart from my family. Of course I have a companion. Unlike you, when I ignore the rules, I do not endear myself to my neighbors. Drink your tea before it grows cold."

"You're not having any?"

Althea wanted a brandy, or several brandies, but drinking spirits to deal with frustration was a dangerous practice.

"Perhaps you'd be so good as to pour out for me, Your Grace?"

To her surprise, he prowled over to the low table, poured her a cup, added a dash of milk and a drizzle of honey, put a jam tart on the saucer, and brought it to her.

"My thanks. If you ever give up duking, you might do as a butler."

He settled into the opposite wing chair. "Tell me about your companion."

"Why?"

"Because when I ignore the rules, it's endearing—according to you. When you ignore them, you are judged and ostracized."

The tea was good. Hot and fortifying. "The last time I called on Lady Phoebe, she'd placed on the mantel in her formal parlor your refusal of her invitation to a musical soiree. At first, I thought she was making a point—she invited the local duke to her affairs, but did not invite me, a duke's sister. I would be received if I called with Mrs. McCormack at my side, but my call would not be returned."

"Be grateful. Lady Phoebe is insufferable."

How did he know that? "She is an earl's daughter, Your

Grace. Insufferable or not, she is the hostess of highest rank in this area. I am unmarried, a relatively recent addition to local society, and without connections here. She is the citadel I must storm."

Rothhaven aimed a look at Althea over the rims of the spectacles. "*You* are the hostess in this area of highest rank. Your younger sister is the second-highest-ranking hostess. Lady Phoebe has been doubly deposed from top-hostess honors."

If Rothhaven had tossed his tea over Althea's skirts she could not have been more dumbfounded. Firstly, because he'd stated the obvious, and secondly, because she'd never noticed this herself. Could this be part of Lady Phoebe's hostility? She *resented* anybody who outranked her?

"I haven't dared to invite anybody to anything," Althea said, "lest they decline."

"They would accept out of vulgar curiosity if nothing else."

"I must correct myself. I invited you—my nearest neighbor—to an informal dinner. You declined my invitations twice."

That retort merited a second visit to the tea tray, which Rothhaven relieved of another jam tart. "I decline everybody's invitations."

"Which is why Lady Phoebe had your regrets displayed on her mantel, like a mark of royal patronage. You ignore the rules and are nearly venerated for it. I observe the rules as carefully as possible and get nowhere. I want one-tenth the cachet you have with the neighbors when you don't even show up."

Rothhaven resumed his seat at the desk and uncapped the ink. "No, you don't. My cachet, as you call it, comes at a high price. This is the reply you send, but wait until at least next week to have it delivered." He scratched at a piece of foolscap while holding his tart in his left hand.

Althea rose to read over his shoulder:

On behalf of herself and Mrs. McCormack, the Lady Althea Wentworth accepts.

AW.

"I'm to refer to myself in the third person?" And in the somewhat formal third person, using the written version of address that would appear on the outside of a letter.

"Third person implies your correspondence secretary wrote the reply at your behest. My own steward very early in my tenure as the titleholder explained the niceties of this fiction to me, and it has served me well."

"I have a *behest* and a correspondence secretary?"

He waved the paper gently to dry the ink. "Not to be confused with your amanuensis, whose responsibilities relate largely to managing the estate and handling communication with your London merchants and suppliers. You will have to copy this in a feminine hand, but make sure the writing differs in a few particulars from your natural penmanship."

"In case I ever have occasion to actually write to Lady Phoebe as myself." Rothhaven's gift for strategy put Althea in mind of Quinn, who'd learned shrewdness early and well, and from a very hard school. "Do I beg off if Mrs. McCormack isn't back before the date of the dinner?"

"No, you do not *beg off*. You send a note worded as this one is, expressing the Lady Althea Wentworth's regrets that Mrs. McCormack will be unable to attend, and apologizing for the late notice. Offer no explanation at all.

Have your regrets delivered about four hours prior to the occasion."

"Because," Althea said slowly, "that is barely enough time to find a replacement guest if the numbers are to match, but a savvy hostess will be able to produce another lady guest on even that little notice. What a diabolical mind you have. I will have challenged Lady Phoebe before I step down from my coach."

Rothhaven removed the glasses and set them on the blotter. "Just so. Now about that cheese, my lady?"

Althea went to the sideboard and retrieved a parcel wrapped in brown paper. "Before you dash off over the balcony or leap through a window, was that you I saw wandering down by the river at dawn? It looked like you, but perhaps you didn't hear me when I called a greeting. Fog distorts sound, I know, though I'm almost certain it wasn't the vicar."

Rothhaven shrugged into his coat and fairly snatched the parcel from her hands. "You shouldn't be out wandering alone at such an hour."

"You, who wander alone everywhere at all hours, often at a gallop, lecture me to have an escort on my own property?"

"Precisely. If you aspire to have one-tenth of my cachet, you must develop your own crotchets. No fair stealing mine. My thanks for the cheese."

He bowed, and Althea should have curtsied. Instead she seized him in a hug. "Thank you, Rothhaven. For an eccentric, reclusive, crotchety demon, you really are a lovely man. Enjoy the cheese."

He muttered something that sounded like "Oh, for God's sake" and did not hug her back. Perhaps that was because he held a sizable wheel of cheese in one hand, or perhaps an aversion to hugs was another one of his crotchets.

* * *

"I used to love the evenings," Everett Treegum said, settling into a rocking chair. "The sun rose on new opportunities and, with my energies refreshed from a night of sound slumber, I went about my tasks grateful for my blessings. By the end of the day, I was tired and satisfied, pleased with my efforts, usually, or confident that tomorrow would be better."

Elgin blew the foam off his ale, the flecks spattering the worn planks of the servants' hall floor. "Now we want nothing so much as to stay warm and comfy under our quilts until we have to piss so badly we venture forth. At least winter's behind us."

In Yorkshire that was never reliably the case. "I don't know how much longer I can do this, Elf."

Treegum and Elgin had been trading that confession for the last few years. Mrs. Beaseley would likely echo the sentiment, had she not already sought her bed. Thatcher, the butler, had fallen asleep in his rocking chair, as had become his habit of an evening.

"We will man our posts as long as need be," Elf said. "We promised Her Grace."

"Her Grace hasn't bothered to look in on the Hall in five years."

"She's getting older too." Elf shifted the pillow at his back, having completed his half of the usual exchange. Sometimes Elf took on the part of the grumbler and left Treegum the role of philosopher.

The rocking chairs that sat in a semi-circle around the

wide hearth had shown up two years ago, doubtless a gift from His Grace.

"Our duke is trying to do his best," Treegum observed. "Miss Sarah informs me he writes to Her Grace every month without fail." Such a pretty hand she had, and she wasn't too proud to drop an occasional note to an old friend either.

"His Grace and Her Grace try hard, and we manage."

"But I never expected to be *managing* for years on end."

Elf took a long swallow of ale. "I didn't expect to *live* this long."

"Exactly my point. I almost wish Lady Althea's hogs would come calling regularly. That livened things up a bit." Those wayward sows had livened up the duke himself— even Treegum thought of him as the duke now—and His Grace was becoming a positively grim fellow.

"Lady Althea has trouble written all over her, Treegum. She's not a woman to do as she's told."

"Then maybe some trouble is what we need. We tend to our tasks, we keep our mouths shut, Master Robbie reads away the winter and gardens through the summers, but without an heir, what's to become of the Hall?"

The fire was dying and the night air brisk, so Treegum added half a bucket of coal to the flames. In some households, the coal was tightly rationed, but not at Rothhaven Hall. The dukedom was in excellent financial health, even aside from the investments Master Robbie found so diverting. Without expensive Seasons in London, lavish dinner parties, or the usual vanities expected of a ducal home— flaming torches to light the drive, extensive landscaped grounds, floral displays to enhance the main façade— expenses were modest.

Then too, the staff was small and getting smaller.

"Something has to change, Elf, and soon. We can all dodder into our graves, but those lads deserve more than a house haunted by lies and arrogance." Treegum and Elf had both served under the previous duke and, as youths, under his un-lamented father. Hard, proud men who had wanted hard, proud sons.

Idiots.

"I can still recall the last duke," Elf said, "shouting at the boy when the poor mite was shaking himself half to death. Calling him names and ordering him to get up."

"He's not had a shaking fit for some time." That they knew of. Master Robbie kept to his rooms for much of the day reading newspapers, or he puttered alone in his walled garden.

"So you'd see them ruined?" Elf asked. "Master Robbie sent back to a madhouse, His Grace in the dock? A pack of vultures would likely take over running the Hall, and that would kill the duchess, that would. Kill me too."

"His Grace has seen his mama well set up. She'd manage." The duchess rarely even sent a letter to the Hall anymore.

The conversation usually wandered on to a discussion of changes that might help the situation at the Hall. Another trip into York for His Grace. Maybe a pretty maid or two hired from the village. Sensible women, not too young but not too plain either. Ladies who could lift a man's spirits, so to speak, and whose loyalty would be to the Hall. Even hiring a true cook might have had some positive effect, not that the present kitchen tyrant showed signs of retiring or that hiring anybody would sit well with the duke.

But Treegum truly was tired, too tired to revisit pointless talk yet again. "I'm off to bed," he said, pushing to his feet. "Don't stay up too late."

Master Robbie liked to roam the Hall at night, and the staff did him the courtesy of allowing him solitude for his rambles. That was the least they could do for a man who'd spent years unable to venture forth from his own home.

"Sweet dreams," Elf said.

Treegum didn't bother replying. Nobody at the Hall had had sweet dreams since Master Robbie had come off his horse all those years ago. Perhaps they'd never have sweet dreams again.

* * *

When the seasons shifted, Althea's sleeping patterns shifted as well. The full moon also had the power to disturb her rest, as did thoughts of a certain duke.

"More daffodils," she informed Septimus as she laced up her old boots. "One bucket at a time and a few years from now, we might even have enough to cut some bouquets for the house."

She'd avoided the river for the past few mornings, but she hadn't been able to avoid recollections of the time spent with Rothhaven.

"Is he angry?" she asked the cat, who was busy sniffing the bedcovers. "And if so, why? Or is he frustrated?"

Some unhappy emotion drove Rothhaven, but what could a duke have to be unhappy about? He owned sizable acreage, he was respected if not beloved by the local populace, he lived life on his own eccentric terms, and he never had to trouble himself about the good opinion of the Lady Phoebes of the world.

"He should be a more cheerful fellow," Althea said, pinning her braid into a haphazard bun.

But then, she herself was sister to a duke, lavishly

well provided for, in blooming good health, and far from content.

"Perhaps Rothhaven longs for a family too," she suggested to her reflection. She really ought to redo her braid, but the morning damp would only make a mess of her hair anyway. "Besides, nobody will see me."

She declined to leave through the library and instead went out the front door, pausing only to retrieve Rothhaven's walking stick from the porter's nook. If she ran into any more strange men lurking by the river, she'd have a weapon other than her bucket and trowel.

And if carrying an item personal to Rothhaven afforded her a sense of emotional fortitude too, well, that hardly mattered. She still hadn't sent off her acceptance to Lady Phoebe. Rothhaven had said to wait, so wait she would.

Even if waiting was driving her nearly daft.

The grass was wet with a heavy dewfall, and when Althea crossed paths with the hare, his progress through the bracken was visibly marked in damp paw prints. Close to the river, the mist again thickened, and the yellow of the daffodils took on a muted, watercolor quality.

So pretty. So peaceful, with only the occasional leap of a fish or plop of a frog to break the dawn stillness.

Althea bent to her task, digging up the plants that had already bloomed. Such a patch of flowers, stretching for yards along the bank, had to be quite venerable, but who had started it? Had some gardener of old dumped a wheelbarrow full of thinnings here, only to find the discarded stock did better in the wild than when confined to a garden?

Had the lady of the manor asked for a planting to beautify her riverbank?

Between one thought and the next, the back of Althea's

neck prickled. Rather than bolt to her feet, she merely sat back, and there he was again, several yards off, her man of the mist. His stillness was uncanny, the stillness of an ancient tree or perfectly calm lake. Deep, fixed, focused.

"Good morning." Althea spoke calmly but not too cheerfully, for she did not want to appear nervous.

And she wasn't, oddly. Rothhaven's walking stick lay at her side, a stout length of serious oak. Her common sense told her that if this man was intent on doing her harm, he would have sneaked up behind her while she mused about knights of old and prodigal daffodils.

"I'm so glad spring has arrived," she said, putting a final specimen into her bucket. "More than the cold, I find the bleakness of winter oppressive here in Yorkshire. What of you, sir? Have you a favorite season?" *Have you a name?*

He bore a resemblance to Rothhaven, in his posture more than anything else. His collar was turned up against the morning chill and the brim of his top hat obscured his eyes, but his height, broad shoulders, and leanness had something of Rothhaven about them.

A cousin, perhaps. Many families gave management of the home farm or the post of land steward to relatives. Witness, Quinn doled out estates for his siblings to manage.

"I love the spring flowers," Althea went on. "By this time of year, I'm so hungry for natural beauty, I could—"

The man took a step back. This was different from Althea's last encounter with him, when he'd simply turned and walked away, disappearing into the mist.

"Would you like to take some daffodils with you?" she asked, getting to her feet with the aid of Rothhaven's walking stick. "The blooms are abundant here. You could take an armful and leave twice that many."

He took another step back. He regarded Althea as he did so, as if his gaze alone could communicate as effectively as words.

"Perhaps you'd like some of my transplants?" she asked, shaking out her skirts. "I already have plenty, and because this is my land, I can fetch more whenever I please."

If he tarried much longer, the sun would begin burning off the mist, and Althea could get a good look at him.

He took another step back.

She advanced two steps.

He moved again, his progress in the direction of Rothhaven Hall.

A sensible woman would wish him good-morning and get back to her gardening. Althea wasn't feeling particularly sensible. She picked up her bucket and advanced two more steps.

Her visitor turned then, and in no particular hurry at all, continued ambling down the path.

Althea debated with herself for perhaps two entire seconds before she stripped off her muddy gloves and laid them over the edge of her bucket, then followed in the wake of the man who had something of Rothhaven about him.

A lot of Rothhaven.

Chapter Six

Nathaniel had been haunted by the damned note. Of the few who knew the family's secrets, who among them would send threats through the mail? Why send threats? Why not simply spout a tale to some London tattler about a mad ducal heir, unable to travel in a coach, unwilling to leave his property even on horseback, and likely to stare off into space for entire minutes, oblivious to all around him?

To distract himself from those worries, Nathaniel had stayed up late estimating costs and cubic feet of stone for extending the walled garden to the orchard. The project would serve many purposes, not the least of which was expanding the space available to Robbie for wandering, puttering, painting, and gardening.

Nathaniel sat on the bench nearest the house as the morning mist swirled and danced across the fields. By the river, the fog was still a downy cloud come to earth, softening the transition from night into day.

Here in the garden, pearlescent twilight prevailed, a peaceful place for a man to argue with himself over all manner of trivialities.

The staff, though aging, would benefit from having the garden expansion project to focus on. They needed to know the Hall wasn't stagnating, despite the reclusive habits Nathaniel cultivated of necessity. The new walls could be built at a snail's pace, if need be.

Nathaniel himself could lend a hand and work off any foolish temptation to again call on Lady Althea. If last night had proved nothing else, it had proved that his acquaintance with her was at an end. She had revealed an affectionate aspect to her nature—*had hugged him*—and that was not to be borne. But for the stupid cheese he'd held, he would have comported himself like the world's largest barnacle and hugged her right back.

Would still be hugging her right back.

Lady Althea had a vitality that brought to mind trite analogies—moth to flame, warbling sirens, and so forth. Her lively mind, her outspokenness, her courage, they drew him. The image of her as a child, forced to beg, forced to protect herself from the one man who should have been protecting her...

Paternal evil was apparently not limited to ducal families, but that Lady Althea had been its victim wrecked Nathaniel's hard-won composure.

"And the worst transgression of all," he murmured to the fresh morning air, "is not that she stirs my sentiments, but that she is so very damned *desirable* as she does."

Somewhere outside the garden, a door latch clicked, probably a maid off to fetch the day's milk from the dairy or honey from the apiary. The estate was all but self-sufficient, by design. Rothhaven Hall was close enough to York to acquire any necessity in a matter of days, but Nathaniel had to plan for the time when Robbie would be left alone, no brother to buffer him from the demands of the outside world.

Something as simple as a tumble from the saddle could change everything.

Movement across the garden stopped that dolorous line of thinking. Somebody had entered from the far gate.

Nathaniel remained unmoving on his bench. If the under-gardeners sought to scythe the grass, they asked Nathaniel's permission first, and he scheduled an afternoon to review the books with Robbie. Robbie either didn't notice or didn't care to mention that the grass seemed to scythe itself.

The staff took the order to avoid this place seriously, so who...?

Nathaniel knew that walk, knew that purposeful swish of skirts. His reactions to seeing Lady Althea marching about his garden at dawn went in all directions.

Sheer shock, to see somebody striding along with that much purpose in a space given over to tranquility and repose.

Delight, that she would come to the Hall for any reason.

Sorrow, that he must turn her away, and do so decisively.

And beneath that bleak sentiment, a stirring of resentment. He did not *want* to turn her away. *Far from it.*

He rose and approached the intruder. "What the hell has the world come to, when a duke's sister must entertain herself by trespassing on her neighbor's property?"

She jumped, swinging the walking stick to her shoulder as if preparing to take a turn at bat on the cricket pitch. "You startled me."

"How inconsiderate of me," Nathaniel said, ambling

closer, "to linger in my own garden at dawn. Have you come to peer through the windows in the tradition of nosy, prying, neighbors from time immemorial?"

She flicked a gaze at the façade of the Hall. "Is attempted peeking a crime?"

Nathaniel dared not come any closer to her. "Trespassing, my lady, is a crime. I will not hesitate to turn you over to the magistrate." If Nathaniel did such a thing for the sake of making a show, he'd also notify the magistrate that no charges should be pressed, for a reclusive duke must not testify at the parlor session. Or at the assizes. Or anywhere.

When had his role become so suffocating?

"Fine," Lady Althea retorted. "Turn me over to the magistrate, and I will explain to him that I was simply returning my nosy, prying neighbor's walking stick. The same neighbor who apparently feels free to roam my riverbank first thing in the day. The same fellow who lurked in my garden in the dark of night."

She poked him in the chest, three times: In the—*poke*—dark of—*poke*—night—*poke*. Then she smoothed her palm over the same smarting place and Nathaniel had to grab her hand simply to get her to stop touching him.

Or something. "You should not be here, my lady. You know better."

"You should not have left your walking stick at my house, Rothhaven. You know better. Some beady-eyed footman would notice that no gentleman's walking stick has ever graced my porter's nook before, and yet, yours appeared between sunset and sunrise. We can't have that, now can we?"

She smelled of damp wool and honeysuckle, her hems were soaked, and her hair...her hair was a positive fright.

Tiny beads of moisture clung to a halo of errant strands. Her braid was half-down and half-up, not so much a coiffure as a battle lost to the elements.

"In my experience," Nathaniel retorted, dropping her hand, "no footman is half so astute. Women use walking sticks when they take a notion to hike the countryside. I'll thank you to return mine."

She held the stick away from him. "Apologize first."

The lady was in deadly earnest. She'd clobber him with his own walking stick if he failed to abide by her command, and she'd make the blow count.

He scowled to keep from smiling, not for the first time in present company. "Apologize for . . . ?"

"For startling me, for being so inhospitable to a guest, for threatening me with criminal charges when you have behaved with even less regard for the law. What if one of your pebbles had broken my window? Should I have had you tried in the Lords for destruction of property *and* trespassing?"

She'd do it too. "You invited me."

"Not to lurk in my garden, I didn't. Not to come and go like a thief in the night. Not to pounce upon me at dawn when all I sought was to leave this walking stick where you'd find it."

Nathaniel had the suspicion she'd been intent on no such errand, but the gleam of righteous ire in her eyes said otherwise. And she was correct: He'd been not simply unfair, but ridiculous. Increasingly, he was ridiculous and the whole charade had passed tiresome years ago.

"I am sorry, my lady, for startling you. For indulging in the bad though effective habit of solving as many problems as possible by being somewhat disagreeable. For receiving you so uncordially. Now may I have my walking stick?"

She considered the handle, which was plain silver, but good and heavy, and sized to fit Nathaniel's grip.

"My brother Stephen has a pair just like this one," she said, passing the walking stick over, "serviceable and elegant. Too good for hiking the fields, Rothhaven, and not as much of a weapon as some others would be."

Nathaniel set the walking stick against a statue of St. Valentine. At one time, decades ago, this had been called the lovers' garden, because it was safe from the world's eyes. Now it was simply the walled garden, Master Robbie's retreat.

"You could make that apology convincing by inviting me to breakfast," Lady Althea went on, strolling along a border of red, white, and yellow tulips.

Nathaniel fell in step beside her, the better to monitor her snooping. "My staff would have a collective apoplexy if I invited anybody to breakfast." Robbie might have an apoplexy in truth. The provocations for his illness were mysterious, though he'd apparently outgrown the worst of the violent fits.

"Then replace your staff. You are entitled to entertain as you please, Rothhaven. Another plate at breakfast is no trouble at all."

"My staff does not deal well with change."

"Neither do you, but then, I have been known to treat my first supper invitation from Lady Phoebe as if she's dropped a sovereign in my begging bowl, haven't I? I should be *bored* of accepting invitations by now. Beyond bored, though I never thought to receive any invitations, except perhaps the invitation to rot my life away in the poorhouse."

Sweet thundering Valkyries. What was he to say to that? "Revising one's outlook takes time. In all of history, how many beggars have had to adjust to the constraints of ducal expectations?"

She stooped to disentangle a pair of tulips that had yet to bloom. "Not enough of us, apparently. Polite society is the most ossified, pointless, ridiculous excuse for a human institution ever there was."

Such bitterness in those words, and such truth. "Then why work so hard to gain polite society's approval?"

She subsided onto a bench that faced another border of tulips. Pink and white, though a stray yellow specimen bobbed among the others like a sheepdog amid its flock.

"I don't care for polite society, Rothhaven, but I have nieces. Please do have a seat."

Nathaniel could not fathom what nieces had to do with enduring an evening of Lady Phoebe's sniping and braying. He took the place beside Lady Althea, the bench faintly damp.

"Explain yourself."

His lack of manners earned him a peevish look.

"Won't you be so good as to explain yourself, rather."

Her ladyship's gaze fixed on the errant yellow tulip. "My nieces are precious and trusting and unpredictable, and they have brought my brother revelations nobody else, not even his dear Jane, could have brought him. He reads them stories, he walks at a child's pace the length and breadth of Kew Gardens, one daughter on his back, another holding his hand. He pretends to be a bear, down on all fours, prowling about the nursery as the children hop away like bunnies, laughing uproariously. It breaks my heart."

That last was said softly, an honest admission of pain.

"And this man is a duke?" When Nathaniel's father had roared, nobody had laughed, ever.

"First, Quinn was less than nothing. He was Jack

Wentworth's worthless get, though there's apparently some doubt about Quinn's actual paternity. His mama ran off and died. Then Jack married my mama, who died before she could run off, alas for her. Quinn worked himself to exhaustion trying to keep his siblings fed. Thank the kind powers Jack Wentworth expired of too much bad gin, and Quinn's luck shifted. He has a head for business, and our fortunes steadily improved."

A relief to know Althea's brother was dutiful where his sister was concerned. "Go on."

"We were managing quite well, then some old title had nowhere else to go, and Quinn got stuck with that too. He became a duke, he married Jane, and she became a duchess, and they...they are happy despite their lofty status. Polite society has to take them seriously, for they are a formidable couple. I was simply dragged along, like a branch caught in the axle of a post chaise. It's almost as if, having been forced to accept Quinn and Jane, the biddies and lordlings are doubly determined not to accept me, though I know that can't be the case."

Very likely, that was exactly the case, and now Nathaniel ought to join the ranks of those who condescended, slighted, and subtly insulted Lady Althea Wentworth. Nothing could come of her neighborliness, not with Nathaniel, not ever.

"And your nieces?"

"They have given Quinn a reason to put up with all the nonsense, somebody to love and protect. For him, being a papa is a far more compelling challenge than being a duke. In their way, those little girls have guarded his spirit, just as Jane has guarded his heart. I want that, Rothhaven. I want that badly."

Nathaniel did not dare admit his own thoughts on the

fraught topics of family loyalty and unguarded hearts. "Wait here," he said. "I won't be long."

He retrieved his walking stick from St. Valentine and left Lady Althea alone to prowl about unsupervised in his walled garden.

* * *

The walled garden was a revelation to Althea.

As an edifice, Rothhaven Hall was no more forbidding in appearance than a tipsy dowager napping off her cordial among the wallflowers. The old dear would awaken in a bad humor, not a kind word for anybody, but mostly, she'd be embarrassed to have lapsed in public.

Rothhaven Hall, from the front drive, was lapsing. Winter-dead weeds clogged what had once been flower beds, rain and snow had pitted the lane with potholes. The flagstones of the front terrace were buckling and heaving with the changing seasons, and the windows Althea had been able to see on her previous non-visits needed a thorough cleaning.

Years of neglect had turned the exterior of the house crotchety, but the walled garden told a different story.

Here, nature's whimsy and man's order were in gracious harmony. A bed of roses had been neatly pruned and mulched the better to snuggle through the cold months. The Holland bulbs were everywhere, tidy rows of color that bobbed this way and that in a slight breeze.

The garden had no fountain, but rather, two birdbaths, each a chubby, smiling Cupid with a giant clamshell balanced on his shoulders and wings. No lichens blighted the angels' gleaming white stone, no chips or cracks marred their cheerful perfection.

Somebody loved this place. Somebody spent hours here, turning a rectangular patch of Yorkshire sod into a private paradise. The landscaping was more formal than Althea preferred, but later in the season, as the borders burst forth on long sunny days and tender annuals bloomed in the central beds, the look of the garden would evolve toward something more carefree.

"You did not flee." Rothhaven stood on the terrace near a statue of some old fellow holding a crosier with one hand and an enormous quill with the other. The duke carried a tray, and such was his gravitas that he still managed to look like a duke even when doing a footman's job. "A sensible woman would have departed."

"Who would want to leave this place?"

Consternation flickered across Rothhaven's features, or perhaps exasperation. "You should. But first I will offer you tea, and then you must be on your way." He came down the steps and set the tray on Althea's bench.

"Tea would be delightful. Do you often break your fast out here?"

"Do I start my day lazing about on damp stone benches when there's work to be done?"

The teapot was a delicate porcelain affair wreathed in flowers and butterflies. It suited the garden, but did it suit the grouch who was pouring out?

"Do you often start your day amid peace and beauty, Your Grace?"

Rothhaven apparently recalled how Althea liked her tea. Steam curled from her cup—more pastel flowers—and His Grace put half a slice of buttered cinnamon toast on her saucer. He passed it over with an air that said "There, I've been gracious. Now, get ye gone," then took a seat on the bench himself.

"Do you maintain this garden?" Althea asked.

"Not personally. What will you wear to Lady Phoebe's gathering?"

Althea took a sip of good China black. "If you meant to disrupt the peace and beauty of my morning, you've succeeded admirably." She dreaded even thinking about what to wear.

Rothhaven poured himself a cup of tea and dunked his toast in it. "You will be tempted to wear some Paris creation, complete with matching jewels. Silk and velvet, because the evenings are nippy, and pale colors will emphasize your youth."

"I have little enough youth left to emphasize." Althea dipped her toast because Rothhaven had, and because she liked doing it.

"You don't need youth. Youth will eventually abandon us all. Lady Phoebe's youthful charms departed before Wellington served in India, and yet, you consider her a social authority. Does this Jane person you admire so much wear pastels and lacy confections?"

Somewhere beyond the walled garden—the orchard perhaps—a lone bird piped a greeting to the sun.

"Jane is statuesque. She wears...her consequence." Jane would not see thirty again, and yet, she grew more gorgeous with each year. When she and Quinn smiled at each other down the length of a formal dinner table, Althea had to look away.

"Jewel tones," Rothhaven said. "Blue to bring out your eyes. Eschew the pallid schoolgirl colors and avoid the quarter-mourning hues of older women trying not to outshine their daughters. Luminous semi-precious gems will do—pearls, nacre, and opals rather than anything with a hard glitter to it."

"Quarter-mourning?"

"My mother's term for the drab attire women settle for later in life."

A good description, because later in life, every woman had something to mourn, even if she hadn't lost loved ones. "No sapphires? They go with my eyes too."

"*You* will provide all the sparkle required. You needn't rely on gems to catch the candlelight, as some women do."

Althea helped herself to another triangle of cinnamon toast and passed one to Rothhaven. "When you are complimenting a woman, Rothhaven, try not to sound as if the exercise vexes you past all bearing."

He gazed out over the beautiful garden, his profile far too stern for such a lovely place on such a beautiful morning. "You should not have come here, Althea."

"You should not hide behind these walls, Rothhaven. A garden party in this little patch of heaven would be talked of for years."

He set his teacup down rather too hard on the tray. "When you are vexing a man past all bearing, my lady, try not to sound as if you're paying him a compliment."

Althea took her time with her tea and toast, while Rothhaven sat beside her, as silent and stoic as the nearby stone saint and not half so cheerful. Something truly difficult lay at the heart of his unsociable behavior.

Something painful.

"You are welcome to walk along my part of the river whenever you wish, Your Grace. I will inform my staff that you have the freedom of the property, and I'll not disturb you on your rambles should our paths cross again."

"I do not *ramble* like a truant schoolboy."

"I ramble," Althea retorted, finishing her tea. "I ramble because Yorkshire is breathtaking, spring is wonderful, and exercise is good for the mind. I ramble because as lovely as Lynley Vale is, I have no aspiration to spend my every waking hour entombed behind its walls. I ramble because walking the bounds of my property is one way to meet my neighbors, with whom I would be on cordial terms, if possible. I've seen you twice down by the river, Rothhaven. You need not lie to me about that."

"You've seen Sorenson."

"No, I have not." The longer Althea considered what she had seen, the more convinced she was that Rothhaven had been trespassing on her land. "Today you all but led me back here to your garden. I know your stride, Your Grace, know how you move. I was pleased to think you might be relenting, even a little, in your isolation. I am not luminous or brilliant, contrary to your flattery, but I do try to be friendly."

Rothhaven turned the full force of his gaze upon her, and Althea saw a storm raging in his eyes. Not fury, precisely, but bewilderment so intense as to fell all other emotions in its path.

"You must not..." His expression shifted and shuttered, and he studied the door through which Althea had entered the garden. He was silent for a moment, as if a voice only he could hear was presenting evidence only he could consider. "I would appreciate your discretion regarding any sightings of the odd man on foot by the river."

"Of course. I will ask my staff to avoid going near the river at dawn and dusk. I will avoid it myself at those times if you wish."

"I do so wish."

Four words, but how they disappointed Althea. Rothhaven would apparently make no more exceptions for her, and her good cheer was choked by the knowledge that she had blundered *yet again* into a situation where she was not welcome.

Except that wasn't quite right. Rothhaven had played cribbage with her—three games—and he'd taken tea with her in his own garden. He'd also been enormously helpful to her where the Lady Phoebes of the world were concerned. Just as Althea was certain nobody else had taken tea with him at dawn, so too, nobody else had been half so insightful regarding her social ambitions.

And all he wanted now was to be free of her company.

"It's time I was on my way," she said, rising. "Thank you very much for the hospitality, Your Grace."

He stood and offered his arm, something of a surprise, but then, a proper host escorted guests to the door.

"Aren't you ever lonely?" Althea asked. "Don't you ever want to drop by the posting inn and have a pint with the lads?"

"The lads would back away in horror."

"No, they wouldn't. They'd boast of your company all the way to York."

"Exactly why the posting inn will do without my custom." Rothhaven unlatched the garden door, bowed her through, then joined her outside the garden walls. "You must not come back here, my lady. It serves no purpose and does your reputation no credit. You should not be wandering alone even on your own property."

"Balderdash. If Lady Phoebe heard I'd taken tea with you, she'd become my dearest friend."

Rothhaven closed his eyes as if assailed by a megrim. "Althea, please promise me that you will never, not for any provocation or bribe—"

Althea pressed her fingers to his lips, and he opened his eyes. "Never, *ever* beg. A wise man told me that.

Friends respect each other's confidences, Rothhaven. You have been a friend to me, and I don't abuse the trust of my friends. I never saw this magnificent garden, I did not encounter you down by the river, and I have never entertained you in my home. I understand."

He caught her hand in his, his grip warm and firm. "You do not understand. You cannot possibly. I barely comprehend my situation myself at times."

Althea wanted to understand, but all she knew was that Rothhaven would lock that garden door behind her, and she was unlikely to speak with him again. She'd see him galloping breakneck under a moonlit sky or stealing off to the vicarage once the days grew short.

But speak with him? Laugh with him? Break bread with him? He would not allow it.

Very well. Friends respected each other's decisions. Never, *ever* beg.

"Do you know what else friends do?" Althea asked, stepping closer.

Rothhaven's eyes were bleak and wary. He'd clearly already locked the garden door in his mind.

"Having known few who merit the term *friend*, the answer to your question eludes me."

"Sometimes"—Althea closed the remaining distance between them—"friends kiss each other good-bye." She was being bold, but then, His Grace's every admonition and instruction to her had been about boldness, about seizing control of a situation and bending it to her will. She had no wish to bend Rothhaven to her will, though she did very much want to leave him with something to think about, something personal to her.

She felt rather than saw the surprise flare through him, but he didn't flee behind his walls, didn't step away or laugh. In fact, he bent his head the merest fraction of an inch closer.

"Do they, my lady? Do they indeed?"

* * *

"This isn't right." Lord Stephen Wentworth could not stalk about in high dudgeon, but he nonetheless crossed the breakfast parlor, a cane in each hand, as his siblings regarded him warily.

More warily than usual, rather. "Althea should be here with us," he went on. "She always spends the Season in Town, and if you lot believe the charms of Yorkshire in spring—which temporary blessing won't *arrive* to Yorkshire until July—have seduced her from the blandishments of our company, you are fools."

Quinn took the bait, as Stephen would have predicted. Quinn was head of the family and more of a duke with each passing year.

"When you are through insulting the only people to regularly put up with your rudeness, *my lord*, you might consider that Althea is an adult. You have no use for polite society, so why would you expect her to travel hundreds of miles for the privilege of tea with a lot of gossiping viscountesses?"

"Because she has a use for us," Stephen retorted. "We are her family."

Jane, buttering her toast at Quinn's right elbow with every appearance of placid calm, glanced at her husband. Quinn captured his wife's hand and kissed her fingers, then let her go when she smiled at him.

How nauseatingly domestic.

Constance, sketching down at the corner of the table

that received the first rays of morning light, pretended to ignore this exchange. She excelled at pretending to ignore anything she didn't like or comprehend. She'd waft away to her studio after breakfast, though, and sketch joined hands and marital glances by the hour, her means of taking a mystery apart.

Stephen had no patience with such subtleties when a sibling's well-being was at stake.

"We should do Althea the courtesy of respecting her decisions," Quinn said, pouring Jane another half cup of chocolate. "If I could avoid Town in spring I would, but Parliament is sitting, and thus I am expected to bide here."

Five years ago, Quinton, Duke of Walden, would have told Parliament to bugger itself. Now he chaired committees, directed charities, wrote reports, and hardly ever swore in the presence of ladies. Having daughters did that to a man.

Being an uncle was having a similar though muted effect on Stephen. "What if Althea is unwell?" he asked, hooking both canes on his left wrist so he could spoon eggs onto a plate at the sideboard. "She'd never say a word, and we'd go waltzing off to Almack's, while our sister battled consumption or gout or some damned ailment with no family at her side."

Quinn offered Jane a bit of ham on the end of a fork. "So you delighted in having family hover about as you contended with your bad leg?"

Stephen had wanted to murder anybody who showed him the least consideration. He still regarded pity as a deadly sin. Witness, he insisted on filling his own plate, and managing both the plate and two canes over the short distance to the near side of the table.

He made it to his chair without incident. "We cannot allow Althea to retire from the field in dishonor, Quinn."

Jane took a sip of her chocolate. "While you were off larking about the Continent, Althea endured five London Seasons, Stephen. She's been presented at court, she's been fawned over by the fortune hunters. If Mayfair is not to her taste, she should be allowed to do as she pleases."

I am related to a pack of nincompoops. "I spend enough time in London to know that the hostesses are cruel to her. They pair her with the worst dancers, the leering buffoons without fortune or manners. At all those lovely, formal dinners, they sit her beside the gouty barons with agile, naughty hands. The biddies and beldames gossip about her in the retiring room no matter how carefully she dresses or how correctly she comports herself. She's not doing as she pleases by rusticating in Yorkshire. She's admitting defeat."

Quinn glowered over the rims of the spectacles he wore for reading the morning papers. "How do you know this?"

A silence grew, while Stephen anticipated having to verbally arm wrestle his older brother. Quinn would never attack him physically—more's the pity—but he could cut with words more deftly than Stephen could wield a knife.

Constance put down her pencil. "How could you not know it, Quinn? It's been going on for years."

Jane peered at her cup of chocolate. "One strongly suspected. One did not precisely know and one did not want to insult Althea by prying. Then too, if Althea was seen to hide behind my skirts, matters could go even worse for her, though the hostesses are always pleasant to me. Who must I ruin?"

Constance got up to serve herself some coffee and tipped the contents of a flask into the hot brew before returning to the table. Both sisters imbibed spirits when among family, which was more cause for concern. Would Althea become a sot, gazing mournfully out across the bleak moors? Stephen occasionally flirted with sot-hood, and might yet succumb to its lures.

"Better to ask who has treated Althea decently," Constance said. "The she-wolves mostly leave me alone because I hide behind my sketching and content myself with the company of wallflowers. Older sisters typically marry first, so Althea has borne the brunt of the match-makers' spite. Without her here this Season, I expect I will become the butt of more ill will."

And yet, Constance had come south anyway, her version of sororal loyalty.

"It's like this, Quinn," Stephen said, holding his coffee cup out to Constance, who obliged with a meager serving of spirits. "When Jack Wentworth sent his younger children out to beg, Althea stood before me, so nobody could see me with my pathetic little crutch and twisted leg. If she got a few pennies for her humiliation, she made sure Con and I had something to eat before we returned home.

"When we did go home," Stephen continued, "Althea went in first, to deal with Jack. If we'd earned little—or nothing, which was often the case—she endured his displeasure and she forbade us to go to her rescue, not that we could have done much."

Quinn took off his spectacles, folding the earpieces slowly, right then left. "I knew Jack was dangerous, but why wasn't I told that Althea purposely drew his fire? We agreed none of you three was ever to be alone with him."

Constance held her coffee cup beneath her nose. "Tell you, so you could do what? Scold Jack into reforming? He would have killed you for trying. You were earning what you could, and that's why Jack let you live. The problem with Althea isn't that she's accustomed to putting up with bullies, it's that she remembers our mama."

"Althea is very good with the girls," Jane said. "She knew that Bitty was afraid of dogs when I had no inkling."

Elizabeth—Bitty—was no longer afraid of dogs because Althea had jollied her niece past that fear.

"Althea wants a family," Constance said. "She recalls what it was like to have a mama, she sees how happy a family can be, and she deserves that. She would never choose a spouse who'd bring gossip down on the rest of us—a sheep farmer or wainwright, no matter how lovely he was—so Stephen has the right of it: Althea has given up on the one dream she's longed for."

Quinn wrinkled a splendid ducal beak. "York has a few eligibles. She might simply be shopping in a different market or taking a breather between rounds."

"Because for Althea," Stephen said, "finding the right spouse must be akin to horse trading or pugilism? Is that how you think in-laws should be acquired, Quinn?"

"We don't know why Althea has chosen to remain in Yorkshire this year," Jane said. "Writing to her is of no use. She replies conscientiously, all platitudes and pleasantry. We must send a competent spy."

Well, thank God for Jane's common sense.

"Very well," Stephen said, adopting an air of martyrdom. "I can forgo the pleasures of Almack's in favor of two hundred miles of travail on the Great North Road. I have no use for the dance floor and it has no use for me."

"A spy," Constance said, sipping her drink. "A fine idea. How soon can you leave?"

Chapter Seven

Althea's kiss was as contradictory as the woman herself. Her grip on Nathaniel's lapels was ferocious, while the press of her lips to his was delicate. She invited with her mouth, she demanded with her hands.

He could refuse neither the demand nor the invitation, and took her by the shoulders to guide her two steps, such that her back was against the garden wall. Nathaniel managed this without breaking the kiss, for there would be only this one foray into madness, and when it was over he could permit no others.

Althea settled back against the hard stones with a sigh that feathered past Nathaniel's mouth. She slipped one arm around his waist, inside his jacket. The other hand went to his nape, as if to hold him still for her exploration.

Cinnamon and sweetness flavored her kiss, and when she took a taste of Nathaniel he wrapped her close. Arousal should have been a foregone conclusion when a man had been without intimate pleasure for so long, and yet, it wasn't.

He could have ridden into York any evening during the past six months. Instead, he'd galloped Loki like a madman, stayed up all night reading the philosophers, and become too fond of the brandy decanter, but he'd felt no inclination to seek out a woman.

He was becoming in truth the recluse he sought to present to the world, and that realization honestly infuriated him.

Althea's kiss stirred long-dormant desire even as it soothed years of unhappy emotion. She pressed herself nearer and urged Nathaniel closer too. His senses awoke, not like a man rising from a night of slumber, but like a creature coming out of hibernation after months of torpor in some cold, dark cave.

The scent of mossy stones, rosy woman, and dewy grass blended with the song of a single bird, and the rays of a sun determined to burn away the night mist. The sheer sweetness of the kiss gilded desire with tenderness, and when Althea at last sank against him, her cheek pressed to his chest, Nathaniel could not step away.

She remained in his arms, her back to the wall, her fingers stroking his nape. He seized more details to savor when the company of brandy and philosophers had paled, as it inevitably did.

Her ladyship wore no stays, and her figure was natural and full. When Nathaniel grazed his nose along her cheek, she shivered a bit, suggesting he'd found a sensitive spot. The floral scent of her soap concentrated where her neck and shoulder joined, and he resisted—barely—the urge to taste her there.

That, he must not do. His body would have happily

turned the moment into an interlude for which his honor would never forgive him.

"You ought to be going," he said, making no move to let loose of the lady. Had five words ever torn a larger hole in a man's heart?

Retrieving Robbie from the hell the old duke had consigned him to hadn't been a choice. When Nathaniel had pieced together the truth, he'd simply acted, certain that Robbie would have done the same for him had their circumstances been reversed. No loving sibling left his ailing brother to rot upon the moor in the care of strangers.

Only gradually had the consequences of that choice become apparent. Robbie hadn't been prepared for rescue, and while he'd longed to return to Rothhaven Hall, he'd imposed conditions that Nathaniel had agreed to too readily.

Anything for my only brother.

And now, anything had become everything.

And everything had expanded to include dealings with a woman who, in the space of a single kiss, could bring back to life a heart that had become as shuttered and bleak as Rothhaven Hall itself.

Althea stroked a hand over Nathaniel's chest. "I know something now."

While I have been rendered nearly witless. "What do you know?"

She gave up the support of the wall and purely held Nathaniel. "You do not want to be alone. Not really. You choose it, though I haven't a clue why and I dislike this decision of yours exceedingly."

He endured her caresses as he would strokes with the lash, and he held still lest she cease petting him. "Interesting. I dislike the thought of you currying favor with gossips and tabbies. Any man worthy of you won't like it either."

Althea kissed his cheek, sighed, hesitated, then slipped from his embrace. "I have learned something else, something about myself."

She looked a fright, her hair half-undone, her hems damp, her boots muddy, and yet, she was the loveliest sight he'd ever beheld.

"What else do you know?" He tucked a curl dangling behind her left ear back among its kin.

"I know that I will never curry favor with anybody again. I will socialize, I will favor my neighbors with my company, I will condescend in the most gracious sense of the word, and in a few worthy cases I will offer friendship, but my days of currying favor are over. Thank you for that, Rothhaven."

His was not a worthy case. She stated her conclusion politely but clearly, as a lady ought. "I am pleased to hear it." He could not tell her to go, not again.

"Farewell, Rothhaven. If ever you have need of me..."

He shook his head. The cruelest cut of all would be to leave matters between them unresolved—cruel to them both. He could not offer to be her friend, not now.

"Good day, my lady, and my thanks for your many kindnesses."

She looked up the path, which led around the walled garden and onto the portico off the estate office. She looked down the path, where the last of the mist was drifting away from the fields and pastures.

Then she turned without another word and walked away. Nathaniel ducked back into the garden and stood alone until long after her footsteps had faded.

* * *

"Well, here I am," Mrs. Millicent McCormack said, bustling into Althea's informal parlor with a workbasket over her arm, "and I don't mind telling you, my lady, I was relieved to get your letter."

Althea had summoned her companion home, but she hadn't expected her back quite so soon. "Relieved, Milly?" She remained seated at her desk, Milly having established early in their relationship that they needn't stand on ceremony.

Millicent McCormack was that perennial social conundrum, the wellborn widow fallen on hard times. Althea had met her at a meeting of the York Charitable Association, liked her humor and candor, and liked even more that a woman with limited means would still try to better the lot of others. Althea had offered Milly a post as her paid companion and had never had cause to regret that decision.

"Sister is a dear," Milly said, settling on the cushions with as much grace as a heifer flopping into fresh straw, "but she's set in her ways. Every other word out of her mouth is 'When Harold was alive...' or 'Harold used to say.' Harold was my brother-in-law for nearly twenty-five years. I well recall his opinions and pronouncements, though he wasn't a bad sort. How have you been keeping?"

Difficult question. Since leaving Rothhaven outside his walled garden three mornings ago, Althea had been unable to focus on much of anything.

Except his kiss. The sheer fire and sweetness of Rothhaven's kiss had haunted her waking and sleeping imagination. She'd sensed hidden depths in him, and a moment in his arms had attested to hidden *universes*. He was passionate, tender, subtle, bold...

And he was determined to remain beyond her reach.

"I am well, thank you," Althea said, marveling at how smoothly the lie came out, "and I am happy to report that we are to dine with Lady Phoebe Philpot on Thursday."

Millicent was past fifty and had been widowed nearly ten years ago. She dressed in quarter-mourning, as Rothhaven had called it, and sat with the wallflowers and dowagers at any gathering. She was pretty in a plump, genial way, and as the daughter of a baronet, she was acquainted with good society in all its tedium.

"Lady Phoebe is having us to snack on," Milly said, threading her needle with red silk. "She must have run out of gossip now that the truly prominent families have flown south. She'll want to know why you didn't go to London this spring."

Whether from experience or native wit, Milly had a sense of strategy that Althea lacked. Such a question from Lady Phoebe, for example, would have caught Althea unaware.

"If she asks, I will reply that I expect to follow my sister south...." Well, no. Althea did not expect to follow Constance south. Possibly not ever again. "London has quite honestly grown tiresome."

Milly took up an embroidery hoop that held a pillowcase. "You'd *say* that to her?"

How would Rothhaven reply to such a rude inquiry? "I will ignore the question. Why doesn't *she* go south to London each year?"

Milly stabbed the linen with her needle. "My guess is, she lacks the connections. Her husband is a wealthy solicitor, but only a solicitor. He must work for his bread, and some say his methods are not always above reproach. What will you wear?"

That was easy. "The blue velvet with my pearl choker and opal earrings. Ivory gloves, my peacock shawl, and the fan that matches it."

"Not the sapphires? The sapphires are exquisite, my lady."

"If I wear the sapphires, Lady Phoebe will intimate that I'm trying to outshine my neighbors and that I have no taste."

Milly held up her hoop, which was abloom with bright red roses and satiny green foliage. "I hadn't considered that. Excellent point. The sapphires are a bit much for rural Yorkshire. Any news from your family?"

"None—yet."

Althea had sorted each day's post with a mixture of dread and hope. Nobody had written to scold her for hiding away in the north, and nobody had applauded that decision either. Perhaps Constance had led the family to believe Althea would journey south later in the year.

Constance was an adept liar, when needs must, and even more skilled at serving up difficult truths. "What would you think of having some of our neighbors to dine at Lynley Vale, Milly?"

Milly's needle paused. "That's starting small, never a bad idea, but you might be criticized by those not invited to your first entertainment."

"What if I hired the assembly rooms in the village?"

"The local folk have their four assemblies a year, my lady. What would you hire the assembly rooms for?"

"I am the ranking hostess in the parish. I have an obligation to socialize." The words didn't feel as outlandish as they might have a fortnight ago. Besides, how was a woman to meet eligible parties if she never entertained? Titles might not litter northern shires in abundance, but

Yorkshire had its share of venerable lineages and substantial fortunes.

Though Althea's motivation to *meet* such parties had suffered a considerable setback outside Rothhaven's garden three days ago.

"In theory," Milly said, "the Duchess of Rothhaven is the ranking lady in the parish, not that she's set foot at Rothhaven Hall for more than five years. You are, however, one of few who can claim a ballroom among your assets. Pity nobody ever uses it."

Oh, *that* was subtle. "Did you know the duchess?"

"As it happens, I knew her quite well long ago. Our families were neighbors, back before she went off to London and snagged herself the local duke. Seemed a shame she had to go all that way just to marry a man she might have met in York. What are you doing, my lady?"

"Sketching out a few ideas for the garden. What is the Duchess of Rothhaven like?"

Milly snipped off her red thread and took out a spool of golden silk. "Our paths diverged long ago, but when I saw her after her marriage, she never appeared happy. One can't complain about having married a duke—if memory serves, he'd been considering both Her Grace and a cousin—but I suppose marriage is often not what we expect it to be.

"Her Grace certainly didn't drag her feet about putting an heir and spare in the nursery," Milly went on, "but even that didn't seem to give her much joy. She and the duke lived very separate lives, even for the times, and then there was that accident. What mother wants to see her son suffer so dreadfully?"

Althea pretended to consider her garden sketch, while mentally scolding herself for the question she was about to ask.

"What happened?"

"Nobody was quite sure. The staff at Rothhaven Hall, if they even knew, were very discreet. The oldest boy came off his horse and was never quite right after that. He did go away to public school, but at some point he expired from natural causes. Influenza or a putrid sore throat, perhaps a lung fever. The details were vague. One must pity the current duke, for losing a sibling is always a miserable way to come into a title."

Althea felt many things for the current duke—exasperation, affection, attraction—and pity was not among them. He'd scold her into next week should she disrespect him to that extent, but what did it say about her that she'd enjoy even his scolds?

* * *

Nathaniel had given himself several days to plot and plan, to doubt himself, and to change his mind, but the fact remained that he needed to confront Robbie. He chose his moment in the quiet hour after dinner, when the staff was unlikely to venture abovestairs, and when Robbie could not retreat into his garden.

"Do you recall how to play cribbage?" Nathaniel asked, giving the fire on the library hearth a poke.

Robbie looked up from some treatise on the propagation of Holland bulbs. "Of course. Dr. Soames allowed me to play cards and chess with the other residents on occasion."

"Might I interest you in a game now?" And why hadn't Nathaniel thought to play cribbage with his brother previously? They had had years of quiet evenings in the library, years of winter afternoons and summer mornings.

"I suppose so."

Nathaniel fetched the board and cards from the cupboard and set them up on the reading table, which was closer to the fire. Robbie brought his pamphlet and sat quietly while Nathaniel got out the pegs, counted the cards to ensure the deck was complete, and cast around for something to say.

Robbie was a restful companion, if a complete lack of conversation could be considered restful.

But then, a boy who'd been subjected to bloodletting, ice baths, hours of uncomfortable postures, restraints, purges, blistering, laxatives, and strange diets had learned to hold his tongue for weeks at a time.

"Shall we cut for the first deal?" Nathaniel asked, shuffling the cards.

"I forget how to do that."

"How to shuffle the cards?"

"Yes."

Robbie had educated himself about agricultural terms, he'd learned to describe meteorological phenomenon, including the different types of clouds. He'd studied musical forms, articles of fashion, and so much else that Nathaniel had known simply because he'd been at large in a young gentleman's world. And still, more than five years after coming home, Robbie's vocabulary of skills and knowledge had odd gaps and blanks, much like his ability to attend the world.

And yet, he read newspapers by the hour and handled the ducal investments more deftly than a street urchin juggled oranges.

"Shuffling is simple." Nathaniel demonstrated a few times. The deck was old, worn, and easily riffled. Robbie watched closely—he was keenly attentive to anything novel—and soon had the knack.

He set the deck in the middle of the table. Nathaniel cut and turned up a three.

Robbie pulled an eight. "I forget whether the low card deals or the high card?"

"Usually the low card, but that varies by agreement of the players." Another tiny gap. "I'm happy to have the first crib."

Robbie pushed the deck at him. "Was that Lady Althea taking tea with you in the garden the other morning?"

Had Robbie also been biding his time, waiting for the right moment to broach a difficult topic? His patience made Job look like a whiny toddler.

"Her ladyship followed you back from the river, apparently." Nathaniel shuffled again and began dealing.

"Did she?"

"She's seen you there twice, though I suggested she saw me rather than you."

Robbie watched the cards piling up, six in front of each player. "Will she believe that?"

"Likely not, unless she missed the fact that my boots were absolutely dry immediately after I'd supposedly wandered through the dewy grass at length. I did not know she'd followed you up from the river, else I would not have confronted her in the garden."

Robbie picked up his cards, his expression unreadable. "Because your dry boots gave away the game."

"Because she is an intelligent woman possessed of natural curiosity, and now she has seen your garden, and she knows that Rothhaven Hall might look like a moldering pile from the drive, but the garden tells another tale. A tale she will wonder at, and one I made no effort to explain, for obvious reasons."

Nathaniel held a good hand. He could discard points

into his crib and keep a good combination of cards in his hand as well, an ideal way to begin the game.

"Are you angry, Rothhaven?"

Call me Nathaniel. "I am concerned."

Robbie had the sweetest smile, precious in its rarity and warmth. "You want to plant me a facer, but you can't because I'm frail."

"You ceased being frail five years ago, but you are still vulnerable, as am I." Robbie worked with weights, he spent hours in the garden, and now he was apparently hiking the countryside. Frail, he was not. Though he had been, he'd been very frail for a very long time, thanks to the *excellent care* inflicted on him at Papa's expensive madhouse.

"I only go out on foggy mornings," Robbie said as he began the pointing phase of the hand, "when nobody's about."

"Somebody was *about*, twice. A very observant somebody."

"Fog makes it easy to disappear."

"So why didn't you? You all but led her ladyship to our doorstep." Nathaniel ended the hand with a nine-point lead and passed the deck across the table.

"I hadn't realized she was behind me until I was halfway home. Then I slipped around the corner of the wall, hoping she wouldn't realize where I'd gone. I had no idea she'd let herself into the garden. Nobody else ever has."

Robbie shuffled as if he'd been doing it for years, then dealt Nathaniel an indifferent hand. Was Robbie also shuffling the facts about, engaging in the nearest thing to deception?

And if so, why?

"Nobody else has sent their breeding sows to invade the orchard either, Robbie. Her ladyship is not going south for the spring as she has in previous years, and she didn't spend much of the winter with her sister. We must accept that we have a neighbor now. Our vigilance should increase rather than relax."

Though how much more vigilant could Nathaniel be? He had no wish to become the jailer the previous duke had arranged for Robbie.

Robbie racked up a tidy advantage even before counting the cards in his crib. "I like the fog, Rothhaven. Just as you must have your gallops at dusk, I am ready for something beyond the garden walls. I should have told you sooner, but I wasn't sure...."

He counted his crib and found six more points.

"You *weren't sure*?"

"When I win back a part of what I've lost," Robbie said, "I never trust the gain, for fear it soon once more will elude me, and then you will be disappointed in me. With the fog, there is no far horizon, no great gaping sky to make me anxious and uncertain. I can see but a few yards into the mist, and yet, I still know the path. Years later, I still know that path."

Robbie had gone off to "school" a bright young boy whose accident had left him moody and prone to shaking fits, staring spells, and twitches. By the time Nathaniel had brought him home years later, he'd no longer been moody. His outlook, from what Nathaniel had observed, was the flat calm of a Highland loch on a summer's day.

Robbie had learned not simply to ignore his emotions, but to will them out of existence.

He still had the staring spells and the occasional seizure, and while away from home, he'd acquired a host of other problems. His digestion had become delicate, the result of years of odd dietary restrictions and tinctures forced upon him by his minders. He'd become unused to any human touch at all, leaping back if Nathaniel casually brushed his brother's hand while passing over a book.

The worst affliction was a fear of open spaces. Robbie had asked to be dosed with laudanum for the journey back to Rothhaven Hall, and had insisted even then that all the coach shades be drawn for the duration of the trip. He'd spent months in his room, with the drapes again pulled tight against any glimpse of the open sky or vast rolling moors.

Then one day he'd opened the drapes and found he was *unable* to clearly perceive the far horizon. What followed had been two years of swinging between fear of the outdoors and a fascination with the limits of slowly improving distance vision.

Since his return home, nothing with Robbie had happened quickly, and as he'd noted, little progress had been made without multiple setbacks.

"You weren't sure you'd be able to leave the garden," Nathaniel said, collecting the cards. "That's understandable."

Though, God help Robbie, what if he'd become lost in the fog?

"I was doing my usual pacing of the perimeter walk one autumn morning, and the mist was so thick I could not see the manor itself as I passed the garden door. I opened the door, knowing that if you or Treegum were lurking at a window, you could not see me tackling that challenge. The privacy was...sublime."

Robbie was awash in privacy. He had acres and eons of privacy, but he'd wanted yet still more, and ironically, the out-of-doors had provided that.

"You opened the garden door."

"We don't keep it locked. I don't recall making the decision to open the door. I just did, and beyond it lay…" He completely ignored the cards Nathaniel dealt, his expression enraptured by a memory only he could see. "A soft, white nothingness. The quiet was wonderful, the peace….I took a step through the door and the fog welcomed me. I didn't go far, I could still smell the garden, but I traveled a new world that morning, Nathaniel. A new universe."

Entirely by himself, when he could have fallen to the ground in a shaking fit at any moment and in a place where nobody would have thought to look for him.

"And you've been making that same trek on foggy mornings ever since." Nathaniel picked up his cards and found another hand that could prove advantageous. He sorted out two cards for the crib and waited while Robbie did likewise.

"I went a little farther each day, and it's as if I was trav-eling not only to the river, but also back to my boyhood. To the time before the accident, when I was mostly happy and healthy. My feet still knew the way, and the river is so beautiful on a misty morning."

When had Robbie ever called anything beyond the walls of the Hall beautiful? Nathaniel was torn between rejoicing that his brother had taken yet another step toward freedom, and terror, because with freedom came horrendous risks to every member of the household.

"I'm glad you've found a reason to leave the garden, and Lady Althea has promised to warn her staff and tenants away from the river early in the day. She'll find someplace else to walk at that hour, so you needn't worry that she'll come upon you again." *Though please God do not venture near the water.*

Nathaniel would save that admonition for when the discussion was less fraught.

Robbie arranged his cards, the light in his eyes dimming as if an overcast had rolled across a sunny sky.

"I don't suppose we could buy that patch of land by the river, could we, Nathaniel?"

Now I'm Nathaniel. "The timing is delicate, given certain considerations with which I'll acquaint you, but her ladyship might be agreeable." Though where would this end? Robbie's penchant for investing had made them wealthy, but buying half of Yorkshire wasn't a solution if they hadn't the staff to look after all that property.

Robbie tossed out a card. "What circumstances, Nathaniel?"

"I've ordered an enormous load of stone for extending the garden walls out to the orchard. The stone itself as well as the expense of transporting it and raising the walls will be significant."

"And you've also purchased seed for planting, a new plough, and a new seed drill. I know. That's all well within our means. What else?"

Nathaniel had debated whether to mention the notes to Robbie, but this conversation took the decision from him.

"I expect we are about to be blackmailed." He searched through the cards in his hand and found that he'd once again discarded the wrong ones into the crib and tossed away a significant number of points with them.

"Blackmailed?" Robbie's usually serene gaze narrowed. "By whom?"

"I was hoping you might have some ideas."

* * *

"Lady Althea, what a pleasure to welcome you to my humble home." Lady Phoebe Philpot, a-twinkle in diamonds and malice, offered a shallow curtsy after the butler had announced Althea to the guests gathered in the formal parlor.

"The pleasure is mine," Althea replied, returning the curtsy at a depth intended to be so unassailably respectful as to convey amusement. "I do apologize for Mrs. McCormack's absence, and on such late notice. She was desolated to miss tonight's gathering."

As luck would have it, Milly's digestion truly had acted up that afternoon, and Althea's companion had remained at Lynley Vale, drinking weak tea and trying to look crestfallen.

"Spring is a time for indispositions," Lady Phoebe replied, taking Althea by the arm. "Perhaps that's why you haven't yet removed to London? My mama was prone to the worst rheumatism in spring. When I was a girl, we never went south before mid-April."

Her ladyship wore a pleasantly curious expression while implying that Althea was old enough to suffer rheumatism.

Althea donned a similarly bland smile. "Don't you find the same old London gossips and scandalmongers tedious year after year? Perhaps that's why you yourself bide here in the countryside rather than go racketing south. I vow there is nothing more distasteful than people who cannot mind their own business. Mayfair during the Season boasts more than its share of such souls, don't you agree?"

A gentleman by the window snorted. He was youngish, fashionably dressed, and holding a glass of claret.

"Then you don't care to stay abreast of what polite society is about?" Lady Phoebe asked. "Don't care to know whose son has gone out to India to make his fortune, or *who* has become engaged to *whom*?"

Althea gently disentangled her arm from her hostess's and moved off a few steps to sniff at a bouquet of daffodils. She rearranged two of the flowers so the one with the tallest stem stood in the center of the bouquet.

"Unless one of the parties to the engagement is myself or an immediate family member, such news isn't urgently relevant to me, is it, Lady Phoebe? Of course, I wish all couples contemplating matrimony much joy, but then, I wish all mankind joy." She peered at some cutwork yellowing behind framed glass above the daffodils. "Shall we be about the introductions?"

The guests watched this exchange with as much subtlety as spectators ringing a prize fight. Althea knew that her ensemble showed her to good advantage and made Lady Phoebe's finery overdone by comparison.

Rothhaven had been right on so many counts.

The introductions proceeded without further skirmishing, and the gentleman holding the claret turned out to be William, Viscount Ellenbrook. He was enjoying Lady Phoebe's hospitality on the way to his own estates in the West Riding. Unlike several of the guests, his manner was genuinely cordial, and Althea was relieved to find him seated to her left at table.

"Did you answer her ladyship honestly earlier?" he asked quietly as footmen tended to the first remove.

"Regarding?"

"Why you are avoiding London. I myself am dodging at least three heiresses whom my dear mama has declared would suit me wonderfully. I'm sure they are lovely young ladies, but Mama married Papa. Her judgment in marital matters is not to be trusted. More wine?"

"Please." The wine was unremarkable, the fare equally so, but at least Ellenbrook was good company. He kept his hands to himself, he did not gossip, and he did not over-imbibe. Althea was on the verge of declaring the evening a qualified success when the ladies rose to take their tea in the parlor.

"Might I call upon you, your ladyship?" Ellenbrook asked, as he stood politely with the rest of the gentlemen.

Lady Phoebe clearly heard the question, as had her niece, Miss Sybil Price, seated on Ellenbrook's other side.

As had half the table, while Althea hadn't seen his lordship's request coming.

She had three choices. She could accept Ellenbrook's overture, which would be polite, and also consistent with her wishes. Ellenbrook was good-humored, intelligent, and handled himself well in company. He merited a cordial reply.

Althea's second choice was to politely refuse, making some vague reference to renovations in progress, Milli-cent's ill health, or another excuse for turning away callers. This was the choice she should have made, given the despair in Miss Price's eyes, and the venom in Lady Phoebe's. In London, Althea had resorted to all manner of fictions to placate the Miss Prices and Lady Phoebes lurking beside every potted palm.

And what had that accomplished, other than to encourage the same women to slight her and talk about her behind their fans?

"I am always happy to receive my friends and neighbors at Lynley Vale," Althea replied. "Lady Phoebe can give you my direction, but I will warn you: If you make any attempt to steal my cook, you will be escorted from the property."

That general invitation—Althea's third option—should have been less upsetting to Miss Price. If the young lady had any initiative, she'd accompany Ellenbrook on the call.

As Althea made her way to the drawing room, she realized she honestly did not care how Lady Phoebe regarded the exchange.

"Aunt, I do believe you've forgotten to offer Lady Althea a spot of tea," Miss Price said, when every other female guest in the parlor had been served.

"Did I? Oh, my lady, I beg your pardon. Let me send for a fresh pot."

"That won't be necessary," Althea said, certain the fresh pot would be tepid and weak, when it eventually arrived.

"I must insist. Tell me, what do you hear from your family these days?"

Lady Phoebe's question felt like the handshake offered before a champion pugilist pounded an upstart challenger into the dirt. "They are keeping well, thank you."

"You must miss them terribly. Do come sit beside me and tell me the news from your dear sister-in-law. Has Her Grace been blessed with a son in her nursery yet?"

Nasty, nasty woman. Althea moved closer to the sofa, there being nowhere else to sit, and consigned her hostess to the ranks of verbal brawlers. No science to her meanness, no subtlety.

"Their Graces count their three daughters foremost among their many blessings."

Her ladyship took a slow sip of tea, which was rude in the extreme when a guest had not yet been served. "A peer needs an heir, though, you must agree. Such a pity when a title goes *begging*. One never knows who the College of Arms will turn up when they grow desperate." Her tone said that a wealthy and honorable banker inheriting a ducal title—as Quinn had—was the worst insult the peerage could have suffered.

A few weeks ago, Althea would have tried to change

the subject, or worse, she would have agreed with Lady Phoebe's bile in the vain hope her ladyship would be placated. Since then, Althea had made Rothhaven's acquaintance, had kissed him, and had left him to his walled garden and his somber hall.

She dreamed of him nightly, she missed him by day with a hollow, hopeless ache. Compared to those sentiments, dealing with Lady Phoebe had become like swatting at a persistent housefly. Her ladyship was impossible to ignore and utterly undeserving of attention.

"Fortunately," Althea said, "my brother Stephen is heir to the Walden title, and my cousin Duncan serves as the spare."

Lady Phoebe stirred her tea. "Lord Stephen is the lame fellow?" As if Stephen were a foundered coach horse.

"An injury sustained in childhood means my brother uses two canes rather than one. He is far from lame."

A footman arrived with the fresh teapot, which necessitated a pause between verbal rounds. Althea imagined the other ladies quietly placing bets.

"How do you take your tea, Lady Althea?"

"Plain will do."

"Here." Lady Phoebe set the cup and saucer on the low table. "Sit with me and enjoy your tea."

"Will you be going south later this spring?" Althea asked, taking another sniff of the daffodils.

"I haven't decided. Some of that depends on Miss Price. Sybil is positively deluged with invitations from all the best families in York and one doesn't like to ignore neighbors no matter how delightful the blandishments of the capital. Tell me, Lady Althea, is it true that His Grace of Walden now owns *two* banks? What could one possibly need with a second bank?"

Two piles of filthy lucre, two blatant associations with trade, two blots on the Walden escutcheon.

Althea wandered near the sofa rather than broadcast her reply to the whole parlor. "I would not know, Lady Phoebe. His Grace's business dealings are certainly no concern of mine." *Or yours.* "I'll have that tea now."

Lady Phoebe lifted the cup and saucer and Althea extended her hand. Had Althea not been watching Lady Phoebe's eyes—every pugilist knew to watch an opponent's eyes—she might have ended up with tea all over her favorite blue velvet dress. Instead, Althea saw her ladyship's gaze narrow an instant before Althea would have taken a hold of the saucer.

Tea spilled all over the sofa and carpet, but not a drop landed on Althea's clothing. "Oh, I am so sorry," Althea said. "So clumsy of me. I should have been more careful."

"No, no," Lady Phoebe replied, rising quickly. "The fault is entirely mine. I do apologize, my lady. Thomas, deal with this."

The footman hurried over and applied a linen table napkin to the damp sofa cushion, while Miss Price looked as if she wanted to weep.

"Aunt, perhaps we should send someone to look in on the gentlemen? We don't want to keep our guests too late. The moon does eventually set, you know."

The moon would not set for hours, but Althea's hopes for the evening had slipped far, far below the horizon. When the gentlemen joined the ladies, she sought the company of Vicar Sorenson, who could be trusted to be civil. He proved an able conversationalist regarding Dutch landscapes—a riveting topic, indeed.

For the next hour, Althea smiled and nodded and tried

not to glance at the clock too often, but by the time she was tucked up in her coach and trotting toward Lynley Vale, she considered the evening anything but a success.

She had followed Rothhaven's brilliant advice in both spirit and letter, and still, she had failed to favorably impress her neighbors, and they—more to the point—had failed to impress her.

Chapter Eight

"Would you please let Treegum know I'd like a word with him in the estate office after breakfast?" Nathaniel had raised his voice to pose the question because the butler, Thatcher, was somewhat hard of hearing.

"Of course, Your Grace. Will do, straightaway, Your Grace. Treegum. Breakfast in t' estate office. At once, sir." Thatcher shuffled off, neglecting to bow before taking his leave.

Nathaniel suspected Thatcher would have forgotten his jacket half the time but for the housekeeper's vigilance. Thatcher should have been pensioned off years ago, though finding a replacement was a delicate undertaking. The front door needed no tending, and thus Thatcher also functioned as a first footman and general factotum.

Last night Nathaniel had tarried in the library until late, though Robbie hadn't had any great insights into who might be sending threatening notes. He'd ruled out Dr. and

Mrs. Soames, the couple who had had primary responsibility for keeping him all those years when he'd been "at school." Dr. Soames was in poor health, and Mrs. Soames had died the previous autumn. That Robbie remained informed regarding his former jailers was interesting.

Other than that pair, nobody beyond the Rothhaven staff should have grasped that Robbie was alive and dwelling at the Hall.

Well, nobody but Mama, Vicar Sorenson, and possibly Althea Wentworth.

Nathaniel had entered the breakfast parlor, prepared to resume the conversation with Robbie, but the room was empty.

"Is my brother in the garden already?" Nathaniel asked, as Thatcher shuffled toward the door.

"Nowt in t' garden, Your Grace. Have yet to see t' young master."

Nathaniel had overslept—the waxing moon typically disturbed his sleep—and Robbie was an early riser. "You're sure he hasn't come down?"

"Always up and about, that one, but have not seen him this day. Shall I fetch more toast, Your Grace?"

Not only was the rack Thatcher had delivered full, another full rack sat by Nathaniel's teacup. "No more toast, thank you. But a word with Treegum in the estate office within the half hour would be appreciated."

"Aye, sir." Thatcher left, muttering about no rest for the weary.

Robbie's place setting was untouched and a glance out the window confirmed that he wasn't in the garden. Nathaniel's first thought was that Robbie had started the day with a seizure and was still abed.

Except Robbie wasn't in his room, and his bed was

neatly made up. His painting supplies were in their usual cabinet in his sitting room, his newspapers neatly stacked in anticipation of several hours' reading.

Robbie wasn't in the garden, he wasn't in the orchard or the cellars, or anywhere Nathaniel or the staff could think to look.

"Grown men don't just disappear," Nathaniel said when Treegum reported that Robbie hadn't been sighted at the stables or the home farm, not that he'd ever ventured either place in adulthood. "Did we check the kitchen garden?" That space was also walled, though reaching it would mean crossing the back gardens and the deer park.

"I did, sir," Treegum replied, "and nobody has seen Master Robbie out of doors since yesterday."

Old memories, of being told that Robbie was too busy to write, too far away at school to come home for holidays, or too ill to travel home, clouded Nathaniel's ability to think.

Where the hell is my brother? "Did you know Master Robbie had taken to walking down to the river?"

"To the river? No, Your Grace. I can't think a man given to the falling sickness should be wandering anywhere near water."

The worry in Nathaniel's gut swirled into dread. "God help us." He took off across the garden at a dead run.

* * *

Althea at first thought the man was asleep. He looked like a younger, more studious version of Rothhaven, though he was tall and trim, and his clothing well made. His hat had tumbled aside, and he lay curled amid the daffodils like a cat having a good nap in the morning sun.

But who chose to nap with a fine pair of boots in the water? "Sir?"

He was deathly pale and deathly still.

"Sir? Can you hear me?"

A shiver passed over him.

Not dead, then. Althea had seen dead bodies as a child, sots who'd breathed their last on the steps outside a locked church doorway, stick-thin orphans who'd succumbed to consumption in a dank alley.

She pulled off her glove and put her fingers to his neck. A steady pulse greeted her touch.

"Time to wake up," she said loudly, giving his shoulder a shake, or trying to. He was sturdy, though perhaps he'd hit his head on a rock when he'd slipped off the path. A specimen in good health did not routinely sleep away the morning in the damp bracken.

No odor of alcohol came from him, and nothing about the grass or flowers looked as if a fight had brought the fellow low.

Althea reached to shake him again and found herself looking into wary green eyes. "Good morning, sir."

He stared back at her. No blood matted his dark hair, but he might have suffered a conk on the noggin nonetheless, poor fellow.

"You've taken a tumble, and I can't imagine lying in the damp is good for anybody. Shall we try to get you to your feet? Your boot boy will not thank you for the state of your footwear." His breeches were soaked past the knees, but a lady didn't mention a gentleman's breeches.

She reached for him again, and he scrabbled back, away from the water.

Althea slowed her movements and retrieved his hat. "A knock on the head is never pleasant, is it? I believe we've met, though we haven't been introduced. I'm Lady Althea Wentworth, if you'll forgive my forwardness, and you must be related to His Grace of Rothhaven." She slowed her words too and focused her gaze on his hat.

He ought to have introduced himself. Instead he scrubbed his hands over his face and glanced upward.

Had Althea not known better, she would have thought him a mouse caught in an open field as a pair of hawks soared overhead. He hunched in on himself and shivered again, though the mid-morning sun was gaining strength and the day was bright and mild.

"A lovely day to be out for a stroll," she said, batting the last of the damp from his hat. "Shall I walk you back to the Hall? It isn't far, and I was enjoying a constitutional myself." She'd waited until mid-morning, determined to leave the dawn hours at the river to Rothhaven.

Or to this fellow. An odd silence ensued, during which he ignored the hat Althea held out to him.

"I have to go." He tried to stand, but could not get purchase on the bank. He was clumsy, as if drunk or exhausted, which also suggested a blow to the head.

"I'll help you." Althea set his hat aside. "You've had a shock and ought not to attempt heroic measures. Of course, after a bad moment, that's when we're most tempted to over-exert ourselves, isn't it? To prove the moment wasn't so terrible after all."

Another pause, as if English was not the man's first language, though the only accent Althea detected in his speech was a hint of the Yorkshire tendency to linger softly on vowels.

The man plucked a wet blade of grass from his coat sleeve. "Nathaniel will be concerned."

Nathaniel was Rothhaven's given name. "Good. His

Grace is far too self-involved. Let him worry about somebody else for a change."

Althea's companion took another peek at the sky and
then fixed his gaze on the daffodils. "I must return to
the Hall."

"My brother has an unreliable knee. He used to fall
frequently. The easiest way to get up is to start on your
hands and knees, and then we'll get you to your feet.
Take your time, but I would appreciate the courtesy of
your name."

"Everybody calls me Robbie." He heaved to all fours,
then to one knee. Using Althea as his cane, he levered to
his feet and stood for a moment, his breath coming heavily.
"I hate this."

Althea picked up his hat. "You should have seen me
learning to dance. The waltz was simple enough, but the
quadrille utterly defeated me. I'd never seen it danced, and
as often as I turned the right way, I turned the wrong way. I
ended up on my bum more than once. My younger brother
found it hilarious, and I'd pretend to laugh too."

"Then," Robbie said, brushing at the muddy patch near
his elbow, "you went back to your room and cried."

"Bitterly."

His smile was like Rothhaven's, but sadder, more weary
and defeated. "I will thank you for your assistance and
leave you here, Lady Althea." He attempted a bow, lost his
balance, and yelped when he tried to right himself.

"Careful," Althea said. "Have you wrenched your
ankle?"

He swore in French, something about a damned body
that might as well be in the grave. "Apparently, I have at
least wrenched my ankle. If you'd be good enough to alert
the Hall, His Grace will send somebody for me."

Another shiver passed over him, and despite his apparently robust frame, he had yet to regain any color.

"I don't like to leave you here alone," Althea said. "Do you suppose, if we found you a stout walking stick, and I offered my shoulder, you could travel back to the Hall with me?"

He stared at the path wending its way between boulders, blooms, and undergrowth. "I would rather not remain here at this time of day. The sun is out."

What that had to do with anything Althea did not know, but a blow to the head could scramble the wits as effectively as any quadrille ever had. She wasn't about to leave him here by himself, with a turned ankle, an addled mind, and no means of defense.

"Give me a moment," she said, striding off to look beneath the trees for a suitable walking stick. She happened on a six-foot-long piece of oak, swung it hard against a tree trunk to whack away two feet, and passed it to Robbie.

"Will that do?"

"Remind me not to oppose you on the cricket pitch."

"Ladies are not supposed to excel at cricket, more's the pity, but I do fancy the occasional round of pall-mall. Shall we be off?"

She got an arm around his waist, and he took a firm hold of his makeshift staff. Progress was slow and brought to mind the many, many times Althea had assisted Stephen in a similar manner. What an odd time to realize she missed her brother.

Robbie took a bad step, lost his length of oak, and pitched against her.

"Sorry."

"No bother," Althea muttered, though she was certain the bother to his dignity was considerable. They were halfway sorted out when a commotion came from up the path.

Rothhaven panted to a stop three yards away. "Thank God," he rasped. He took in a few more breaths, suggesting he'd exerted himself past the ability to speak.

"Rothhaven," Althea said. "Good day. Forgive me for failing to curtsy, but Mr. Robbie has gone top over tail and wrenched his ankle. He might also have taken a rap on the head and I'm concerned that his ordeal will leave him with an ague or a lung fever. Your assistance would be appreciated."

All manner of emotions flitted across Rothhaven's features. Incredulity, consternation, annoyance, and then...a slight, resigned smile.

"Of course, my lady." Rothhaven positioned himself on Robbie's other side and they made good progress back to the Hall. By the time they'd gained the back terrace, Robbie had suffered two more passing shivers.

"Mr. Robbie should take to his bed with a hot water bottle and peppermint tea until the physician can get here," she said.

"No doctor," Robbie said, making an attempt to stand on his own. "I refuse to be quacked."

Something passed between him and Rothhaven. An old argument, an entire debate, such as Althea often had with Stephen about using two canes at all times. But Robbie wasn't merely being stubborn. His gaze had acquired the same haunted look he'd turned on the blue morning sky.

"We can stand here arguing," Althea said, "or we can put you to bed. I am competent to wrap a sore ankle and I know my way around an herbal. We'll want comfrey salve or arnica, both if you have them. Willow bark tea, ice water, clean linen, and if the pain grows too great, some poppy syrup."

"No laudanum," Robbie said. "No quacks, no laudanum, Nathaniel. Promise me."

Rothhaven touched Robbie's shoulder, the gesture so personal Althea wished she hadn't seen it.

"I promise, Robbie. You're safe. Shall we get you comfortable in the estate office? I'd like to spare you the stairs for now if I can."

Robbie—apparently that was a first name—nodded, the inclination of his head regal despite his bedraggled state. "The estate office will do."

They shuffled into the house with Althea minding the door and trailing behind.

An older fellow came up from the steps that led below-stairs. He was spare, white-haired, and looked out on the world through vivid blue eyes.

"Master Robbie, so glad you're home."

Master Robbie?

Rothhaven kept moving. "Treegum, please fetch bandages and the usual medicinals from the herbal. We're dealing with a sprained ankle. We'll be in the family parlor."

Treegum gave Althea such a thorough visual inspection she might well have been a felon escaped from the hulks come to steal the silver. Then the old fellow was off down the steps with surprising speed for one of his venerable years.

"The difficult part," Althea said, when Robbie was sitting on the sofa, "will be getting that boot off, though perhaps time spent soaking in the river will have made the leather more forgiving."

Rothhaven stood over Robbie, hands on his hips. "You *fell* near the river?"

Robbie nodded. "Apparently so."

Rothhaven glanced at the clock on the mantel. "And you left the house *at dawn*? I thought you said—"

"The fog was thick, Nathaniel. I simply wanted one last ramble."

"But that was *hours ago*. And the whole morning—"

"Stop fussing the poor man," Althea said. "Time enough for recriminations and lectures later, though in my experience, grown men with any dignity generally lecture themselves mercilessly in such situations, all the while pretending they are immortal and invincible. Help me get this boot off."

Robbie's smile was more mischievous this time. "You heard the lady, Nathaniel. Help her get my boot off."

"I'll cut your damned boot off," Rothhaven growled. "The sheer, inconceivable hubris, the utter lack of thought, the risk for the sake of a mere—"

Althea put her hand over his mouth. "Boot off now, snorting and pawing later. You race about on your horse at perilous speed in fading light without so much as a groom to get you home should your gelding take a mis-step. This is how all too many men behave. Anybody can slip on a damp patch of grass. Either make yourself useful or go threaten some children with trespassing charges."

At first Althea thought Robbie was in distress. His shoulders heaved, then he took a hitching breath, and then he was laughing as if all the merriment in creation had been visited upon him in a single moment.

Rothhaven ran a hand through his hair. "I apprehend that I am out-numbered and I yield to the superior odds. I'll see what's keeping Treegum."

Althea bent to the task of easing off Robbie's boot, which put an abrupt end to his laughter.

* * *

"What do you mean, our stores are low?" Nathaniel kept his tone civil with effort. The herbal usually fell under the housekeeper's purview, and Treegum should have been able to rely on Mrs. Beaseley to mind the inventory.

"Exactly that, Your Grace. Winter brought its usual share of influenza, colds, and catarrhs, apparently. We have a bit of the comfrey and arnica and plenty of linen, but we're nearly out of the willow bark tea."

"Feverfew?"

"Afraid not, Your Grace."

"Then let us hope lung fever doesn't become an issue." Except that it all too easily could. A long seizure usually left Robbie exhausted and disoriented, in this case apparently so exhausted he'd succumbed to sleep immediately thereafter, right on the cold, damp earth *and half in the river*.

Or perhaps he'd lost consciousness during the seizure itself and never awakened. Nathaniel had no way to tell, and Robbie refused to see physicians competent to treat his ailment—if any there were.

Nathaniel took the basket and a basin of ice water up the steps, pausing on the landing to let old Thatcher shuffle past.

"Morning, Master Nathaniel."

"Good morning, Thatcher."

"Shall I bring up a rack of toast, sir?"

"No thank you. I haven't much appetite this morning."

"Very good sir." He tottered off down the steps, in charity with whatever world he inhabited.

"I see the boot was salvageable," Nathaniel said, setting the basket down beside the estate office's sofa.

"Oh, quite," Lady Althea replied, rummaging in the

basket. "I'll take that basin of ice water, and I daresay Robbie could use a cup of hot tea and perhaps some victuals."

Robbie never ate or drank after a seizure until his mind was clear. He reclined on the chaise, both boots off, feet bare.

"Robbie?"

"A spot of tea wouldn't go amiss, neither would a blanket."

"Take my shawl." Lady Althea passed a wad of blue merino wool to Nathaniel. "It's warmer than it looks."

Nathaniel draped the soft wool about his brother's shoulders, catching a whiff of roses as he did. "Do you need anything else?"

"A pillow and some blankets," Lady Althea said, dragging a hassock closer to the sofa. "Somebody ought to have a go at those boots too, once they've dried."

Robbie was enjoying himself thoroughly, doubtless delighted to see Nathaniel scurrying about like a new under-footman.

Nathaniel was not enjoying himself *at all*. He took up Robbie's damp boots. "You find this amusing," he said, aiming a scowl at his brother. "If you'd fallen another three feet closer to the river, we could be laying out your corpse."

The humor in Robbie's gaze faded. "I knew enough not to get that close to the water."

Lady Althea unrolled a length of white linen and dipped it into the ice water. "Gentlemen, you have both had a fright, but the situation is resolving itself well enough. Anybody can turn an ankle. Rothhaven, the tea if you please, and I wouldn't mind a cup myself."

"Yes, Rothhaven, please do bring a cup for the lady."

Robbie was *twitting him*, as any sibling might poke fun at another. Not five minutes past, Rothhaven had heard Robbie laugh—out loud—for the first time in years. In any other circumstances, this display of humor would have been cause for rejoicing.

But there was Lady Althea Wentworth, giving orders and making herself quite at home in Nathaniel's estate office, while a half-daft footman tottered about with imaginary racks of toast.

"Shall I bring some sustenance with the tea?" Nathaniel asked.

"I could use a bite to eat," Lady Althea said. "And please have the housekeeper brew up a full pot of willow bark tisane too."

"We haven't enough for a full pot," Nathaniel said. "We're out of feverfew as well."

Lady Althea scooted closer to the sofa and took Robbie's foot in her lap. His ankle was properly swollen and already turning various painful colors.

"Then make a tisane of basil, boil a good fistful of the dried leaves in a quart of water for at least five minutes. Then simmer until you've reduced the water by half. Toss in some ginger and a dash of honey, plus a squeeze of lemon juice if you have it. Prepare enough for a serving every few hours. I'll send to Lynley Vale for the willow bark, but the basil will do to ward off fever for now."

She opened a tin and the scent of scythed meadows and blooming mint wafted across the office. Nathaniel stood in the doorway, trying to put a name on the emotions rioting through him.

Gratitude, of course, that Robbie was mostly hale and whole.

Dread, because Nathaniel could never become Robbie's

jailer, but wandering down to the river again had proven unsafe and must not continue.

Resentment, because the whole deception was spinning beyond what was manageable.

And *profound relief*, because somebody competent was taking matters in hand at Rothhaven Hall, solving problems, and dealing with an unforeseen difficulty, and for once—for bloody damned once—that somebody was not Nathaniel.

He closed the door behind himself and went to fetch the tea.

* * *

Who are you?

Althea could not ask her patient that question. Whoever Robbie was, he was clearly dear to Rothhaven, vulnerable in some way, and dependent on the duke. He was too old to be Rothhaven's son, though the resemblance between the men was strong.

She finished wrapping Robbie's foot, an ordeal he bore with stoic passivity. "There," she said, rising and placing a pillow on the hassock. "You should keep that foot up. Another application of salve and a cold wrap before bedtime ought to see the swelling reduced by tomorrow."

"You know what you're about," he said, wiggling his toes. "The bandage is snug but not tight. The salves are helping, and the pain is already subsiding. How does a duke's sister know her way around an injury?"

Althea gathered the medical supplies, taking a seat to roll up a bandage she hadn't used. The salves also reminded her of Stephen, of the years when they'd been too poor to afford even the cheapest balm for his aches.

"I wasn't always a duke's sister. For most of my childhood, I was one of those filthy, pathetic children you see begging all over the streets of York. Physicians are mostly for the rich. The rest of us make do with herb lore and common sense. My brother's injury inspired me to learn what I could, not that I was ever any use to him." Althea had tried, though, and perhaps that counted for something.

"I can't picture you as a feckless urchin."

She stuffed the rolled bandage back into the basket. "While polite society can't see me as anything but."

Robbie regarded his bandaged foot. "Polite society. Was there ever a greater misnomer for a bunch of judgmental hypocrites?"

Who are you? "Probably not, though I am the sister of a duke now and I am grateful for that. But for my brother's good fortune, I'd likely be dead or wishing I were dead."

Robbie sat up a little straighter. "Instead you are free to wander the beauteous Yorkshire countryside where you can make the acquaintance of tall, dark, handsome strangers."

Rothhaven chose that moment to appear bearing the tea tray and a thunderous scowl. "Are you flirting with Lady Althea, Robbie?"

Althea rose, setting the medicinals aside. "I believe the tall, dark, handsome comment referred to *you*, Your Grace." Or it should have. Robbie was good-looking, but Rothhaven was *attractive*. "I will happily pour out if you'll join us."

Her motivation had nothing to do with propriety—propriety be hanged when illness or injury came to call—but rather, with a pathetic yearning to simply spend time with Rothhaven. He looked tired and out of sorts, and when was a hot cup of tea ever a bad idea?

He set the tray on a second hassock and took the chair behind the desk. "Will you be missed at Lynley Vale?"

Althea fixed him a cup with milk and sugar. "Not until supper time. I often hike the property on my own when the weather is fine. Today I thought to visit my sows, and that requires a chat with Mrs. Deever at the home farm. She makes the best bread, and insists I have mine with our own butter and honey. This invariably involves a protracted visit."

Mrs. Deever was lonely—many farmers' wives were lonely—and Althea hadn't the heart to refuse her.

"You should stay for luncheon," Robbie said. "I take my tea with just a drop of honey. A literal drop."

A man of particulars. Why didn't that surprise her? She served herself last and took a slice of buttered cinnamon toast as well. Cinnamon toast was an odd choice for a tea tray, but appealing.

"How is your head, Robbie?" Rothhaven asked, setting his empty cup on the tea tray.

"Aches a bit," Robbie said. "Just a bit. Don't be waving the laudanum at me, Nathaniel."

Perhaps they were brothers, for they bickered like siblings, or maybe Robbie was a by-blow or a cousin raised at the family seat.

"I believe His Grace was expressing concern for your welfare," Althea said. "You made your sentiments regarding laudanum plain enough before we'd left the river."

"I did?"

Rothhaven collected Robbie's cup. "You did. More tea?"

"No thank you. If it wouldn't be unpardonably rude, I believe I'd like to cadge a nap."

"A nap only," Althea said, gathering up the rest of the tea things. "If you smacked your head when you slipped, then we must not let you fall into a coma. His Grace will waken you in an hour or so."

"From footman to nanny," Robbie murmured, closing his eyes. "Who would believe it?"

Rothhaven set the tray on the desk. "Rest. I'll look in on you soon, and we can move you upstairs when you're feeling more the thing."

His Grace was neither footman nor nanny, but he was tired and worried and could use a friend. "Let's sit in the garden," Althea said, taking him by the elbow and leading him into the corridor.

When they'd gone not six feet from the door of the estate office, he surprised Althea by wrapping her in a hug.

"Thank you." He held on to her, his embrace secure and warm. "I was terrified. . . . To lose him again would be . . . I cannot lose him again. Cannot."

Althea stroked Rothhaven's back, very much aware that she held a duke in her arms, also a man who'd suffered a serious upset. She liked them both, the grouchy, taciturn duke, and the man who fretted so for a relative.

"My older brother was sent to prison," she said, the words a surprise even to her. "Charged with manslaughter and marched off to Newgate after a sham of a trial. We had all that money, and I knew him to be innocent, but I was powerless to help. My rage was without limit."

Rothhaven peered down at her. "A *duke* was convicted of manslaughter?"

"Quinn wasn't a duke yet. People in high places resented how he'd bettered himself, though. I know what it means to feel powerless to protect a loved one."

Rothhaven kissed her brow, then slipped his arm around her shoulders. "To the garden. Some time sitting among the flowers and sunbeams is in order."

He walked with her down the corridor until they came to the door that led to the back terrace. Rothhaven Hall was a bit dusty, the carpets needed a good beating, and the footmen should give the sconces a proper polishing, but as stately homes went, the interior of the Hall was aging with dignity. A bouquet of tulips sat before the window of an alcove, a large gray cat curled in the sunny windowsill.

"No headless specters," Althea said, "no shrieking ghouls. A lot of heavy curtains, though."

Rothhaven opened the door to the terrace for her. "Sorry to disappoint. I can explain the heavy curtains."

She stepped through and waited for him on the terrace. "Can you explain Robbie?"

Rothhaven's gaze traveled over a garden awash in blooms and sunshine, then came to rest on Althea. "If I tell you, then you become part of a deception that weighs more and more heavily with time. I am reluctant to burden you with our secrets."

While Althea did not want him to have to carry those secrets alone. "He's family, I can see that much."

"He's more than family," Rothhaven said. "Alaric Gerhardt Robert Rothmere is the rightful Duke of Rothhaven. He was named for my father and grandfather, but my mother—who came to have little regard for either of those men—insisted we call him Robbie."

"I beg your pardon?"

"Robbie is my older brother and the rightful duke." Nathaniel went back to studying the garden.

Did he expect her to laugh? To flee in horror? To summon the magistrate? She took him by the hand. "Let's have a seat. This story will doubtless take some time to properly relate."

He stood unyielding, his hand entwined with hers.
"Althea, you must promise me..."

"Don't be insulting, *Nathaniel*."

She'd made him smile, fleetingly, more a quirk of the
lips than a proper smile, but he walked with her hand
in hand to the nearest bench and came down beside her,
then fell silent as if pondering how in the world to begin
his tale.

Chapter Nine

The situation at Rothhaven Hall was simple enough for Nathaniel to explain—one lie had led to others, some of them well intended, some of them despicable—but before airing the Rothmere family's dirty linen, Nathaniel took a moment to savor the pleasure of Lady Althea's company.

He'd presumed terribly by taking her in his arms, and the feel of her had been wonderful. He had kept an arm around her shoulders as they'd walked to the terrace because her compact, feminine form tucked against his taller frame was a greater pleasure than all the wild rides and pounding gallops in creation.

Holding her hand, such an unprepossessing gesture, made him want to bow down in gratitude. The friendly widows in York did not hold his hand, they did not hug him. They did not speak his name with humor and affection, daring him to take offense at a little teasing.

They did not sit beside him, adding the scent of roses to his walled garden, long before roses could bloom.

Where to start?

"My father was an angry, dutiful man," Nathaniel said. "He married where he was told to, when he was told to, and then treated his wife like a burdensome stranger. He did his duty at court. He was a conscientious steward of the Rothhaven estate, though he had little head for investing, and our holdings did not prosper under his management. He regarded his heir as his compensation for all indignities, as my grandfather had regarded his heir."

Nathaniel rested an arm along the back of the bench, though reciting this tale in this lovely little Eden was a sacrilege.

"Go on," Althea said.

Nathaniel heard no judgment in her tone, no dismay. That would doubtless come later.

"Mama presented His Grace with an heir and spare in quick succession. We were sturdy, lively boys who managed to have happy childhoods despite our father's severe disposition. Mama did what she could, choosing tutors with a sense of humor and governesses who held us in genuine affection. His Grace tolerated that until Robbie was eleven, and then the game changed."

Althea remained right beside him on the bench, as if she listened to the makings of great scandal every day.

"Our father decided that we must embark on the path to manhood, and our first step was to graduate from ponies to horses. We loved our ponies, but were excited at the prospect of full-sized mounts. His Grace would not listen to the stableboys who counseled prudence, and instead he bought us handsome, half-wild youngsters. The duke thought we ought to learn to train our own mounts, a job many a grown man would shrink from. Robbie came off his horse frequently, as did I, but one day, Robbie came off and didn't get up."

The morning Robbie's fate had changed had been like this one—sunny, benign, Yorkshire in her spring glory. Nathaniel had perched on the rail as Robbie had come off his horse yet again. Nathaniel had called encouragement to his brother and cursed the horse as manfully as he was able to at ten years of age. Elf had known something was amiss, though, and had dashed across the arena to wave the colt away from the fallen rider.

"The horse wasn't a bad animal," Nathaniel said. "He was simply young and lacked training. My father had made a bad choice and could not admit it, even when that bad choice put his heir at risk for grievous harm."

"Doubtless," Althea said, "the fault was with the boy for coming off the horse, with the horse for being too fractious, with the very ground for being too hard. The hubris of some men beggars description and seems to be inversely proportional to their human decency."

Nathaniel let his arm rest ever so lightly around her shoulders again. "Just so, my lady. Exactly so. My brother lay unmoving in the dirt, and the duke stood over him, bellowing for Robbie to get up, to stop being a coward, and to climb back on the damned horse. He ordered a bucket of cold water tossed on his own child, and still Robbie did not awaken."

Althea scooted around as if the hard bench were uncomfortable. The result was that she sat infinitesimally closer to Nathaniel.

"My father used to rail at Stephen," she said, "for *limping*. Accused him of faking and shirking, and Stephen could not run away. I think Papa delighted in the fact that he could abuse a boy who had no means of escape."

Nathaniel knew Althea would not have left her brother alone with such a monster, but where was that brother now, when she had been all but hounded from London?

A question for another time. "Robbie did not awaken until that night," Nathaniel went on, "and when he did, he had no memory of coming off his horse. The physicians said that wasn't unusual, so we all breathed a sigh of relief. The physicians also said Robbie ought not to ride again or otherwise risk another injury to his head for at least a month, but the duke would not listen. Three days later, he insisted Robbie resume his riding lessons. Robbie insisted too, said he wanted to show the horse what was what. But then, what could he have said, with the old man threatening him with every punishment known to English boyhood?"

"Somebody should have put your idiot father on that horse."

Exactly what Elf had suggested. "His Grace told Robbie that if he didn't get back in the saddle, I would be made to ride the beast. At the time, I was the smaller brother, and I was not a confident rider. Robbie climbed aboard, and all seemed to go well at first."

The next part was hard to relate and impossible to forget. "The horse walked and trotted to the right well enough. Robbie rode across the middle of the arena to change directions, and then simply... left his body is the only way I can describe it. He stared at a fixed point, the horse became more and more unruly, and Robbie did nothing to correct the animal. We shouted, and he appeared not to hear us. He simply stared and bounced about in the saddle like a marionette on loose strings. When the horse bolted,

Robbie came off again. He has had the falling sickness ever since."

There was more to the tale, much more, most of it bad.

"I'm sorry," Althea said. "I'm sorry you had an arrogant beast for a father, sorry you had to watch your brother all but destroyed for the sake of a grown man's pride."

Destroyed—that was the word Nathaniel had instinctively shied away from, the word that fit the situation exactly.

"His Grace did, eventually, destroy Robbie in fact, or as good as. Robbie began to have seizures as well as staring spells. I woke up one day and was told Robbie had been sent off to school. My mother refused to come out of her rooms for two weeks. My father eventually left for London, though they had been estranged while living under the same roof. I did not see my brother again for years."

Althea slipped her hand into Nathaniel's. "He wasn't at school."

"He was placed with a physician, a Dr. Soames, who claimed to provide humane care for the insane. Robbie wasn't insane when he went there, but he nearly was by the time I brought him home. I don't even know the whole of it—ice baths, restraints, purgings, bleedings, beatings, long confinements indoors, strange diets—but either Soames eventually deduced that Robbie was merely ill, not insane, or Robbie learned how to outwit the lunacy that passed for care there. Then too, Robbie was heir to a dukedom. Abusing a ducal heir is seldom smart."

"I take it your father died and you were able to extricate your brother from this hell?"

Althea's hand in Nathaniel's was warm, a comfort freely offered and dearly appreciated. Not what Nathaniel had expected, but then, this was Althea Wentworth, who knew what it was to have a monster for a father.

"Shortly before I turned twenty-one, my father called me into his study and informed me that my brother—the one perpetually at school, then at university, then traveling to distant capitals—had succumbed to an influenza that had become a lung fever. Robbie was dead, I was the heir, and no more need be said on the matter. The house observed mourning. A coffin eventually arrived and was buried in the family plot. I have since confirmed that all we buried was a large bag of sand."

"Your father told you that your brother was *dead*?"

"Told me, my mother, the vicar, the world. He accepted all the condolences a grieving father was due, and I believe, for my father, Robbie was dead. A Duke of Rothhaven who fell to the ground shaking, who stared off at nothing for minutes at a time, who could not ride to hounds or swim or even miss a night's sleep without risking public humiliation...my father could never countenance such a thing, so Robbie was simply erased. For a duke, erasing the life of a boy is appallingly easy, and in Papa's mind, he was erasing a disastrous family scandal at the same time."

Althea rose and strode off. "He *erased* your brother? Blotted out the life of his own son?"

"Noted Robbie's death in the family Bible, ten years to the day from when my brother was sent away. His Grace was nothing if not thorough. I suspect he gave Robbie ten years to outgrow his illness, which Robbie failed to do."

Althea whirled, her swishing skirts making the tulips bob. "Your father was a thorough devil. I cannot believe...but then, Yorkshire might as well be Cathay as far as most of London society is concerned, and many a family secret has been buried on the moors. How did you learn that your brother yet lived?"

Nathaniel wanted her back by his side, wanted her hand in his, but he also wanted to see her reaction when he told her the last of it.

"I almost didn't find him. Thank the blessed powers for small mercies, my father died less than three years after telling me Robbie was gone. Lung fever, oddly enough. I went through the usual rituals of investiture, took my place in the House of Lords, and prepared to get on with my duties. One of those duties was tending to the family finances."

Althea bent to brush her hand over a greening border of lavender. "Nobody keeps a secret for free, do they? Dr. Soames wanted his thirty pieces of silver."

"My father had paid an annual fee—a staggering sum— and the next installment came due. Either Soames was so backward as to fail to note the passing of a duke or he assumed I would continue my father's scheme. He reported that 'Master Robbie' continued to thrive in his care. Robbie was the rightful duke, a grown man, and Soames wrote about him as if he were a fractious schoolboy."

Althea peered up from the flower bed. "Your rage is without limit?"

"Rage is too tame a word. When I went to retrieve my brother, he was furious too. He'd written to me over and over, and I'd never responded."

"You never received the letters."

"Soames admitted to Robbie that he didn't send them, and that's the only reason Robbie agreed to leave the place. He hadn't been out of doors in years, hadn't so much as sat by an open window. His world was books, an old violin, the other residents. He learned French from one of the guards, he memorized enormous quantities of Shakespeare, he read newspapers from all over the world, and he experimented endlessly regarding the metes and bounds of his illness, but he also grew…"

"Eccentric," Althea said, resuming her place on the bench. "He became peculiar. How could he not when he'd been all but imprisoned, and by his own father's hand?"

"He wasn't simply fearful beyond the walls of his prison, he was terrified. He felt safe only behind a locked door with the windows nailed shut and all the curtains drawn. He could not bear to be touched. He had to bathe in absolute solitude behind more locked doors, a thought that gives me nightmares. He subsisted on meat, cheese, weak tea, and greens. When I first brought him home it was early spring, and he had the beginnings of scurvy. No duke has ever before had scurvy, but my brother…"

Nathaniel fell silent, because Althea did not need to hear the details. Nobody did. The general description was bad enough.

"But I found him by the river, Rothhaven, far from any locked doors. He has apparently made considerable progress."

Althea would focus on that. "Robbie first left the walled garden six months ago, but finding the courage—the very great courage—to take that step required years of effort. He cannot abide the thought that he might someday have to be the duke. I promised him, before he left that vile prison Soames referred to as an asylum, that I would never force him to leave Rothhaven Hall, and that I will play the duke as long as he needs me to fulfill that role. Those are promises I shall never break."

* * *

Stephen Wentworth tottered into Althea's parlor, put his canes in one hand, and bowed to Millicent McCormack as extravagantly as he was able. He had realized years ago that a lame man had to flirt boldly or not at all, lest his overtures be taken as a serious attempt at winning a lady's favor. When he was forward about his teasing and bantering, he was viewed as charming rather than pathetic.

"Mrs. McCormack, at long last I behold the wonder of your smile. How I have missed you."

He *had* missed her. She was the auntie Stephen had never had, the pragmatic, kindly soul who could defuse tensions with a slightly naughty or too-honest remark. She took the Wentworths as she found them, which was more than he could say for most of the world.

"Lord Stephen!" She popped to her feet and gave him a jaunty curtsy. Nobody with any sense hugged a man who was perpetually unsteady on his pins. "What a pleasure— and a surprise—to see you." She kissed his cheek, bringing Stephen the scent of peppermints. "You might have at least allowed Strensall the pleasure of announcing you."

"And spoil the surprise? I think not. Let's do have a seat. I am knackered beyond bearing from too many hours on the North Road."

From crossing muddy inn yards ever so carefully, dealing with narrow stairways with too few landings, and— when it all became too unbearable—spending miles in the saddle on rented hacks with gaits akin to those of a foundered pony.

"Tea, my lord?"

"Bless you, yes." One of the joys of visiting Althea was her chef. Monsieur Henri took every tray and plate as an opportunity to prove the superiority of French cookery and, without fail, he succeeded.

"What brings you north, my lord?"

"You know how prone I am to wandering." Travel had become a habit, though since finishing a Grand Tour with Cousin Duncan, Stephen had questioned whether the habit served any purpose.

"I know you are prone to sticking your lordly nose into any corner or cranny that piques your curiosity. Have you any new patents in train, my lord?"

The tray arrived, though Althea did not. Mrs. McCormack steered the conversation from one flattering question to the next, but she never got 'round to explaining her employer's absence. The tray was nearly empty before Stephen even noticed that odd omission.

"So where is my sister?" he asked, offering Mrs. McCormack the last jam tart.

"Out and about, my lord. Tell me how your nieces go on. If Lady Althea misses anybody in London, it's the children."

"She doesn't miss her siblings? How lowering."

"Of course she misses you as well. Shall we have a bath sent to your room? All that travel must leave you longing for a soak and nap."

Althea alone of Stephen's relations kept a room for him on the ground floor of her house. She had a lift that rose as far as the first floor that Stephen himself had designed and installed, but he never resumed use of a lift until he'd first inspected it.

"A bath and a nap sound lovely, but you must be honest with me, Milly. Where is Althea?"

"Mrs. McCormack to you, sir. I honestly don't know where her ladyship has got off to. She visits the home farm frequently, calls on the vicar to discuss various charitable endeavors, has a cup of tea with this or that tenant.

She's not like some, roosting on a velvet pillow the live-long day."

"If I were to ride over to the home farm, would I find her?" Not that Stephen wanted to sit a horse for at least a week.

"I cannot say, my lord. When Lady Althea is in a certain mood, she isn't to be questioned."

Now they were getting somewhere. "And why would she be in that mood?"

Mrs. McCormack gathered up the tea things. She glanced about the parlor as if looking for a lost book. She twiddled the fringe of the pillow at her elbow.

"It's that wretched Lady Phoebe and her miserable friends. I could not accompany Lady Althea to last night's supper due to a touch of dyspepsia. Lady Althea was apparently treated to less than genuine hospitality. Lady Phoebe tried to spill tea on Lady Althea's gown, then cast aspersion on His Grace of Walden's wealth, and intimated that Lady Althea was hiding from some scandal in London by biding here in Yorkshire."

"Althea *told* you this?"

"She made a few remarks when she got home. I pried the rest out of Vicar earlier today."

"I see." Though truthfully, Stephen was baffled. Althea's transgression was that the Wentworths had come up in the world through a combination of luck and hard work. In London, a veritable herd of young women and their mamas apparently resented Althea's good fortune because it threatened their own prospects, but what motivated such pettiness in rural Yorkshire?

"Althea is off somewhere licking her wounds?" She was like a cat in that regard. When injured or ill in spirit, she sought solitude, a tonic Stephen had found only marginally effective.

"That she owns this property, or as good as, is a comfort to her, my lord. Here, she can order all as she sees fit. Few women have that much authority so early in life, and she does well with it."

Stephen did not enjoy owning property, but understood that no English gentleman would be taken seriously among the peerage without at least a few acres to his name.

"I will have my soak and my nap," he said. "Then I'll have a trot around the estate. Constance mentioned that Althea had some sort of dustup with His Grace of Rothhaven. Did that get sorted out?"

Mrs. McCormack had reached for the last tea cake. She paused, hand hovering over the tray. "Oh, I wouldn't know anything about that, sir. I was visiting my sister in York. Never heard a word about it."

Balderdash. Milly McCormack would have caught up on all the talk with the housekeeper before the teakettle had reached a boil. She would have chatted with Monsieur Henri directly thereafter, and probably exchanged a few words with the wives of the nearest Rothhaven tenants.

Stephen treated himself to a long soak and a short nap, then rose and dressed, determined on one objective: to find out exactly why his sister, who had perfected the art of avoiding social confrontations, had purposely antagonized a duke known for his sour and solitudinous disposition.

* * *

Althea knew a duke when she saw one, and Rothhaven—sitting in the pretty garden, looking tired and resolute—fit the description perfectly in all but name. His honor was unshakable, his word ironclad. His self-discipline knew no limits and his sense of responsibility toward his family and dependents was bottomless.

What a lonely business, being a duke without a duchess. The least Althea could offer Rothhaven was companionship and affection, and that was doubtless the most he'd permit himself to accept.

"You have allowed a good-faith mistake to turn into a fiction perpetrated on the entire world," Althea said. "Why?" *And will you put your arm around my shoulders again?*

"You have not seen one of Robbie's more spectacular fits. He falls to the ground shaking. In the worst cases, he loses control of his bladder. He thrashes and twitches for the longest minutes in creation and is then exhausted and foggy, as you saw him at the river. In that state, he is not mentally fit to care for himself. He tried to hide his seizures from me at first because he feared I would return him to Dr. Soames's care."

"Then he doesn't know you very well."

Rothhaven's lips quirked. He clearly wasn't about to thank her for a compliment though.

"His own father betrayed him, my lady, and I benefited from that betrayal. What sort of brother am I, that I accepted years of excuses about perpetual school terms or one holiday after another spent with friends? What sort of brother am I, that I didn't question years of unanswered letters?"

Oh, that was miles past the outside of too much and proof everlasting that Rothhaven had become the duke in truth.

"What sort of *mother* allows her sons to suffer through such a fiction? Her Grace had to have known where Robbie was, at least in a general sense, and she didn't communicate that truth to you even when you approached your majority. Let's get away from these walls, shall we?"

"The duke did not tell his duchess where he'd stashed her firstborn, only that Robbie was receiving good care. Then Robbie supposedly died before I attained my majority, and he..."

"Is sleeping." Althea rose, because a flowery little haven had abruptly become too confining. "Your orchard has started to bloom. Let's enjoy that fleeting beauty while it lasts."

Rothhaven was silent as they passed through the gate, and Althea marveled that he was sane, much less civil. An older brother *erased*, a father without an ounce of paternal tenderness, a mother kept in ignorance...And all of it landing on the shoulders of a blameless young man with no allies to aid him.

"What did your steward say when you asked him about the funds your father had sent year after year to some obscure asylum on the moors?"

"I haven't asked him. Treegum doubtless concluded my father was making a charitable donation."

Proving that Rothhaven had at least considered the question. A winterbourne crossed the path to the orchard. Althea gathered her skirts to step over and found herself grasped by the elbows.

"On three," Rothhaven said. "One, two..." He lifted her over the water as if she were one of the little sheep dotting the Cheviot Hills—mostly fluff and bleating.

And then, neither of them moved, until Rothhaven slipped his arms around her waist. "I have not put this story into words, ever. You make me reconsider my assumptions, and that is uncomfortable."

His embrace, by contrast, was very comfortable. He

held her as a man holds a woman from whom he has no secrets.

"Your father likely made no charitable donations beyond his tithes," Althea said, "and yet, the steward, who had to know the heir had been banished, never questioned that expense. The adults all around you refused to question why Robbie never wrote to his parents, which every schoolboy is expected to do at least monthly. They never questioned why he spent all of his holidays anywhere but at the only home he knew, with the brother he'd been inseparable from as a lad. The local vicar never challenged this situation. If the adults around you weren't raising those questions, you learned quickly that those questions weren't to be asked."

She let him go, furious with a duke long dead for scheming against his own family. And for the sake of what greater good? Pride? Appearances?

"Why don't you simply have yourself appointed Robbie's guardian?" Althea asked. "If he's truly unsound of mind, you can protect him and his assets by obtaining legal authority."

The orchard lay up a slight hill and the trail Althea traveled was smooth. She wanted either an exhausting climb or a few stones to kick, but the path obliged with neither. The orchard walls were not quite as high as those of the garden, the objective being to keep out hungry deer rather than the whole world.

"I cannot be appointed guardian of Robbie's wealth if I am his heir," Rothhaven said. "I would have a motive to hurt him or mis-manage his assets, to thwart what authority he can exercise. A guardian should be financially disinterested, and I am not. Then too, English law takes a dim view of those aping anybody with a title. Fraud upon the Crown is a short step from treason.

"The irony is," Rothhaven said more quietly, "when I agreed to continue being the duke, I thought I was protecting my brother, but now I have left him more vulnerable than ever."

"Have you considered a quiet word with King George?"

"His Majesty hated my father. I have been introduced to the sovereign exactly once, and he all but cut me in front of every other young man at the levee."

"George all but hated his own father, and the sentiment was apparently mutual." Althea had no more remedies to suggest. As far as she knew, Rothhaven's situation was without precedent. Long-lost heirs usually had seven years to wander home and unseat somebody in line for the inheritance, but in the present case, the heir had no intention of unseating anybody.

Rothhaven had gone to great lengths to hide the truth, and that he'd done so at enormous inconvenience to himself would hardly matter in the court of public opinion or before the law. From a certain perspective, Robbie was still a prisoner, and his own protestations to the contrary might be regarded as the desperate fiction of an unsound mind. Then too, the falling sickness was evidence of tainted blood in the minds of some, and that was scandalous in and of itself.

"This is complicated," Althea said as Rothhaven opened the gate to the orchard.

Althea stepped into a world awash in cherry blossoms. They captured the sunlight, scattering it across pale, fallen petals and blooms yet clinging to the branches. The trees would leaf out over the next few weeks, but for now, they offered only their flowers to the perfect blue sky.

His Grace shut the door, enclosing Althea with him. "I forget how lovely Rothhaven can be," he said. "I want Robbie to be able to see this. We're planning on extending the garden walls to join the orchard walls, though that project will likely take all summer to complete."

The scent here was delicate, barely floral at all. Mostly grass and the green Yorkshire countryside. The pears and plums would blossom next, with the apples providing a final display.

"I wish your ambition was not limited to building yet more walls," Althea said, walking off a little way.

A shower of petals wafted to the ground and Althea realized that Rothhaven had brought her here to say farewell. The orchard had begun her personal dealings with him, and the orchard would see them end.

"My ambitions do not matter," he said. "My duty is to see my brother kept safe and happy, and I take joy in knowing that I have succeeded to a modest extent."

He sounded like Quinn, and not in a good way. "Where does this end, Rothhaven? Do you and Robbie grow old here in your outwardly bleak house, your servants sworn to secrecy, your title eventually going to some tailor in Dorset?"

"That is the best I can hope for, and it's not a bad end, compared to the hell Robbie endured for more than ten years."

It wasn't a good end either. "And your mother allows this?"

He ambled away from the wall, petals drifting onto his shoulders and chest. "She supports Robbie's choices, as do I. We regard him as the rightful duke, even if he's reluctant to take on the outward trappings of that office. Her task is to draw attention away from the family seat, to be the public presence of the Rothmeres where Robbie and I cannot travel. My task is to keep all and sundry from peering over our walls."

Robbie struck Althea as a dog in the manger, accepting all the familial deference due the titleholder while refusing to shoulder any of the responsibility.

But then, she'd never wet herself in public. Never fallen to the floor in a shaking fit. Never awoken to find strangers and friends alike peering down at her, half of them concerned, the other half ghoulishly curious, her mind in a desperate muddle.

She did, though, know the weariness of soul that came from wrestling a problem that had no solutions.

Where to spend a day begging that would not be so far from the bad neighborhoods that simply getting there exhausted Stephen?

How to beg so her pleading came off as humble rather than disgusting?

Where to find the fortitude, once again, to face Jack Wentworth when she had only tuppence to show for a day in the cold?

The mind eventually stopped looking for solutions and resigned itself to enduring on the memory of hope. The body did without rest or sustenance, and the heart shrank until death became a dangerous friend.

"Promise me something, Rothhaven."

He brushed cherry blossoms from her shoulders. "I am not in a position to make many promises, Althea. Where you are concerned, that pains me more than I can say."

"I used to pick violets from the alleys," she said. "I never stole flowers, but weeds grow where they will, and this time of year, the violets spring up everywhere. I would gather them to offer to passersby and pick a few more on my way home. I needed the violets."

She caught his hand when he would have plucked blossoms from her hair. "Promise me you will save a little pleasure for yourself, Your Grace. That's why you careen about the shire at dusk on that great black beast, isn't it? You need to feel alive, to feel free, even if it's only for a few miles as night falls. You deserve that much. As long as you take pleasure from it, don't give it up. Don't give up on a sliver of life lived for yourself."

His grasp was warm, his gaze sad. Althea hadn't cried in years, not even when Quinn had been sent away to prison, not when she'd believed him murdered by the king's excuse for justice. Here amid old trees renewing themselves in the spring sunshine, her throat ached with unshed tears.

"I would take pleasure," Rothhaven said, "from two boons, if you are willing to grant them to me, and then I will bid you farewell."

"Name them."

"First, a kiss."

He drew her by the hand as Althea stepped close. She forced herself to go slowly rather than plunder, running a hand over Rothhaven's chest, then treating her fingertips to the soft texture of his hair.

He closed his eyes, which she took for permission to explore his features one by one. Severe brows that would grow heavier with age. A splendid nose, firm chin, and stubborn jaw. His mien was fierce and determined; later in life his visage would shade closer to that of a raptor in winter.

He smiled as Althea brushed her touch over his mouth.

That smile revealed a sweetness belied by the rest of his countenance.

Althea kissed him gently at first, but as his arms closed around her and her grip on him became desperate, the gentleness was put to flight by frustration. Why must he be so dutiful? Why must society have so many stupid rules? Why did a dead father still have the power to strangle his family's joy?

Those questions were of no use to anybody, so Althea instead pressed herself close and gave Rothhaven every ounce of passion she possessed. She wanted him, she cared for him, and she must leave him. The last thing he needed was to become an object of curiosity, and if Althea was seen frequenting his property, others would be emboldened to violate his peace.

So she would abandon him to his stratagems, as he needed her to do. First, she'd take pleasure with him, even knowing that pleasure once past can turn to bitterness.

When Rothhaven broke the kiss, Althea was bundled against him as if the winter wind had left her desperate for warmth. She wanted to lay him down on the soft green grass and steal greater intimacies before they parted, but didn't make that overture, confident that Rothhaven's self-restraint would require him to reject it.

Bloody masculine honor. "You asked for two boons," Althea said, nose pressed to Rothhaven's chest.

His hands moved on her back, a lovely, soothing touch that nonetheless made Althea want to weep.

"When you leave here, please don't think of me as His Grace of Rothhaven. Think of me as Lord Nathaniel Rothmere, or simply as Nathaniel. I want at least one person to know me for who I truly am."

What a paltry, profound request. "Then I'd be simply

Althea Wentworth to you, not her ladyship, not Lady Althea."

"But you are a lady," he said, stepping back. "You always will be."

And you are a duke by any other name. "I would rather be your friend."

"If you would be my friend, you must leave here and go about your affairs. We are happy in our way at Rothhaven, and I want—more than anything—for you to be happy too." He bowed, no smile, no lingering over her hand, and then he slipped through the door, leaving Althea alone amid the fading blossoms.

Chapter Ten

Nathaniel made himself leave Althea Wentworth in the orchard, made himself walk back down the hill at a pace no servant would remark. With each step his anger grew.

Anger at his father for banishing Robbie and lying to the world about the rightful heir's death.

At the duchess, for submitting to the old duke's schemes, though her husband had intimidated all whom he met, very likely including his wife.

At the army of servants who'd kept questions to themselves rather than warn the younger Nathaniel that something untoward was afoot.

At himself, because even given those warnings, what could he have done? Like his mother, he'd been dependent on the duke, without legal authority, and without powerful allies.

And yes, he was also angry at Robbie. Nathaniel's brother could not help his illness, could not help the damage that had been done to his mind. Could not help that society was at heart cruel, shallow, and stupid. But now Robbie had gone wandering by the river, courting injury, illness, and discovery.

"I know not which is worse." Nathaniel's words were snatched away on a stray breeze, one that bore the scent of the stables. He turned in their direction rather than cross the garden again, and Elf greeted him in the yard.

"Mornin', Yer Grace. Fine day 'tis. Have you come to see the new colt?"

"We've a new colt?"

"Black as your Loki, at least for now. Mare's a gray, so who knows what will happen to his coat as the lad ages. Come take a look."

The baby horses were lads and lasses to Elf, new life to be proud of and cosset into grand good health. To Nathaniel, the colt looked like what it was: another mouth to feed, another vulnerable dependent, though thank heavens the mare was experienced and conscientious.

"He arrived in the night?" Nathaniel asked.

"They usually do. Mares are canny. Wee beast was still wet behind the ears when I came down to start the haying this morning. He was up and about, no help from anybody, and at his dam like Thatcher at the first batch of summer ale."

And the mere sight of the colt, little tail whisking as he curled in the straw beside his mother, made Elf smile.

I will never have a son, and neither will Robbie. "Congratulations on another new arrival," Nathaniel said, shoving away from the stall's half door. "Robbie has begun his day with a turned ankle, so I'm for the house."

Elf walked with him down the barn aisle, though Nathaniel wasn't fit company. "Turned an ankle, did he?"

"Down by the river, where you have doubtless seen him wandering on foggy mornings for the past half year, but about which neither you, Treegum, Thatcher, nor anybody else saw fit to inform me. Now he's injured, he could very well end up ill, and he's forbidden me to send for a doctor."

Nathaniel quickened his pace, which was petty of him when Elf was old and small.

"Will he recover, sir?"

Who knew? If lung fever or an ague set in, seizures could accompany them. "I hope he'll be back on his feet in no time, but Elf, how can I protect a man from harm when my own staff won't be honest with me?" The staff wasn't in fact Nathaniel's, but rather, Robbie's.

Or should have been Robbie's.

Elf came to a halt at the end of the barn aisle. "Robbie asked us not to mention his little jaunts. Seemed no harm in them. We thought you'd be pleased if you learned he was venturing beyond the garden."

So why keep the news a secret? "Pleased? He was found nearly unconscious, all but in the water, disoriented, unable to walk without assistance. The loyal Rothhaven staff hadn't informed me I might have to look for him by the river when he turned up missing, and I wasn't the one who came across him."

Elf's rheumy gaze went to the Hall, which from the stables resembled a monstrous dark boulder hunkered beneath the blue sky.

"I guess you'll have to take that up with your brother, then."

A fair and diplomatic answer for which Nathaniel wanted to plant his loyal stableman a facer. "A fine suggestion. Good day." He stalked off, knowing Elf didn't deserve his rudeness. Treegum met him inside the Hall, and Nathaniel wanted to plant him a facer too.

"Please ensure the medicinal stores are replenished," Nathaniel said, striding past Treegum. "Illness is no respecter of season, and if the housekeeper can't be relied on to manage the herbal, somebody else will be given that responsibility."

Treegum shuffled along beside him. "Did Your Grace have anybody else in mind?"

"You. You're my steward, or the closest thing to it." Thatcher ought to have been next in line for such a task, but Thatcher was growing more hopeless by the day.

"But sir, I have no familiarity with the remedies and tisanes. That is the province of the ladies."

"Then approach the under-cook."

"She cannot read, sir."

Very likely, she was so old she could not see. "Then I will do it myself, Treegum. When the household includes a member in unreliable health, the last inventory we can neglect is the herbal, wouldn't you agree?"

Treegum mumbled something, and like a fool, Nathaniel took the bait. "I beg your pardon?"

"I daresay, sir, anything needed urgently could be borrowed from Lynley Vale. Lady Althea seems quite competent to manage a household."

She was a wildly competent kisser too, a thought that made Nathaniel want to plough his fist into the nearest pier glass.

"Have the housekeeper prepare a list of supplies we're lacking, and pick up what we need in York when you and Elf make the monthly trip next week."

"Very good, sir." Treegum bowed, though something about his tone was less than deferential.

"If Master Robbie had fallen three feet closer to the

river," Nathaniel said, pausing at the bottom of the steps, "he could well be dead. Somebody ought to have told me he was venturing beyond the walls, Treegum."

"Agreed, sir. Perhaps you and Master Robbie will see fit to discuss the matter now."

Treegum glided away, leaving the distinct scent of a scold in the air as Thatcher came doddering up the steps.

"I don't want any damned toast," Nathaniel said.

Thatcher exchanged a look with Treegum, then tapped a bony finger against his temple. "Oh, the Quality. As if I'd be bringing up toast when the day's half gone." He shook his head and retreated down the steps. His knees popped as he reached the landing, and he disappeared into the lower reaches muttering about back-in-the-day and the King Across the Water.

"Can we pension him?" Nathaniel asked, hating himself for posing the question.

Treegum turned, his expression unreadable. "If we pension him, Thatcher will spend his remaining years sitting in the snug at the posting inn, reminiscing about his time in service here at the Hall. Is that what you want, Your Grace?"

Nathaniel wanted to gallop hellbent in broad daylight. He wanted to have a rousing argument with anybody about anything. He wanted—heaven defend him—to get drunk.

"Valid point." Though Thatcher had earned the right to sit with a pint wherever he pleased. "We need to hire somebody else who can manage a footman's duties."

"Right, sir. Any suggestions where I might find such a fellow? The staff now at Rothhaven knew you and Master Robbie when you were in leading strings. Some lad brought in from the village will be loyal to his wages, rather than to the family."

What family? A ducal family ought to consist of more than two grown men, neither of them bound for marriage, and an aging duchess who hadn't been to the family seat in years.

"I'll mention the matter to Vicar," Nathaniel said. "He might have some suggestions."

Another shallow bow, and then Treegum followed Thatcher down to the kitchen. They would likely sit in the servants' hall swilling tea and longing for the good old days, but when had those days been?

Nathaniel took himself to the estate office and found Robbie still asleep on the sofa. A hand to his forehead revealed only normal warmth, which was cause for guarded relief. Fever and ague could take some time to develop, and for Robbie, fevers were to be dreaded.

Nathaniel gently extracted Lady Althea's shawl from among the blankets covering Robbie's sleeping form, and wrapped it around his own shoulders. He took the place at the desk and prepared to deal with ledgers and correspondence until Robbie wakened.

Lady Althea's rosy scent should have soothed Nathaniel's temper, but all it did was force him to admit that what he really *truly* wanted was not to race headlong over the same worn bridle paths, not to sack an old fellow after decades of loyal service, and not even to brace Robbie on the same issues they'd been struggling with for years.

What Nathaniel wanted was to meet Lady Althea in the orchard again, and do much, much more than merely kiss her.

* * *

Althea allowed her temper to rage for the duration of the hike back to Lynley Vale. She was furious on behalf of two men who'd been backed into a corner by their father's arrogance and by a losing ticket in the lottery that determined a boy's health.

She was furious with the Almighty, with whom she usually observed a pact of mutual indifference. Any god that allowed Jack Wentworth to be unsupervised in the presence of children lost all credibility as a benevolent deity. To inflict the falling sickness on Robbie was cruel, to have allowed a boy of sound mental processes to be banished to an asylum by his own father was crueler still, and to inflict the whole bizarre deception resulting from it on Rothhaven...

"But what else can they do?" she muttered, climbing a stile over the wall that separated Rothhaven's holdings from her own.

If guardians were appointed for Robbie, he'd be prohibited from marrying, from ordering the particulars of his own life, from defending his estate against pillaging by those imprisoning him "for his own safety." The falling sickness alone might not merit him such a fate, but the falling sickness, withdrawing from society, asking Nathaniel to perpetrate a fraud, spending years at an asylum for the deranged...

Polite society judged a man harshly for being a bad dancer. What would they do to a duke who was terrified by the sight of a pretty blue sky?

A horseman turned through the gateposts at the foot of the Lynley Vale lane, though the trees obscured Althea's view of him. She did not recognize her visitor, which was to be expected, when her neighbors rarely called. A gig turned up the drive behind the rider, and some hint of familiarity plucked at Althea's memory. She *did* know that horseman, knew that elegant, relaxed seat, but he was ...

"Stephen." If ever a Wentworth had a penchant for charging toward trouble rather than away from it, Stephen was he. So why would he have come north now, when all the best scandal and intrigue was to be found in Town?

Althea picked up her skirts and walked faster, because she also recognized the couple in the gig. William, Viscount Ellenbrook, had brought Miss Sybil Price to call, drat the luck, and Stephen had apparently already made their acquaintance.

Althea met her guests at the foot of Lynley Vale's front steps.

"What a pleasure on such a fine day," she said, preparing to apologize for her damp hems and muddy boots. But then, her guests hadn't thought to send a note, because this wasn't London. In the country, muddy boots were of no moment and casual calls were a fact of life.

"Lord Stephen," she went on, "I gather you've introduced yourself to Miss Price and Lord Ellenbrook?"

Stephen loved to ride. All the mobility he was denied on two feet became his in the saddle, and he cut an excellent figure in breeches and riding jacket.

"I confess I was tempted to abandon all propriety in the face of Miss Price's boundless charms," Stephen replied. "As it happens, Ellenbrook and I are acquainted and introductions were appropriately made. No lapse of decorum has *yet* occurred."

He sent Miss Price a coy smile and tipped his hat to her. She blushed and laughed while Ellenbrook looked amused.

"One cannot help who one's brother is," Althea said.

"Stephen, I will escort my guests to the blue parlor. Join us when you've located your manners, won't you?"

"I'll hand my steed over to the stable lads, and then nothing could keep me from such an abundance of feminine pulchritude."

He trotted off to the stables, because—as Althea well knew—he was loath to dismount in front of strangers. He carried a pair of canes in a scabbard affixed to his saddle, but the business of getting off the horse and safely to the ground was ungainly.

"Let's find a tea tray," Althea said, offering her callers a smile. "I am famished from hiking the lanes, and my cook takes his job very seriously. What a delight to come home to some company."

She meant that, oddly enough. Compared to the intrigues and heartache at Rothhaven Hall, a simple skirmish with Miss Price, an ambush by Stephen, and some small talk with Ellenbrook would be nearly soothing.

"One must wonder," Miss Price said as Althea settled her guests in the semi-formal parlor, "why Lord Stephen would abandon the blandishments of Town in spring. He's a ducal heir, after all. I'm sure he's much missed by the hostesses."

Ellenbrook sent Althea a glance, part long-suffering, part humor. "As best I can recall," he said, "Lord Stephen is an indifferent participant in the London whirl. He accepts a few invitations, but has interests that appeal to him more strongly than do social calls and gossip."

Not quite true. Stephen loved gossip, though he could be as discreet as a fence post when it mattered. "He accepts the invitations that our sister-in-law, Jane, Duchess of Walden, tells him to accept. Stephen holds her in quite high regard, as do we all."

Stephen avoided any entertainment that involved dancing or significant walking. Card parties, musicales, boating parties he endured with cheerful bad humor. Balls, rural breakfasts, assemblies he eschewed.

"I will abandon you for a few moments to see about the tea," Althea said. "This parlor was the last one to be redecorated. Let me know what you think of the appointments."

Miss Price had taken a seat on the end of the sofa, like a broody hen claiming her nesting box. At Althea's invitation, she glanced about as if actually seeing the parlor for the first time.

Althea sent a footman to the kitchen and took five minutes to trade boots for house slippers, change her dress, and tidy her hair. By the time she returned to the parlor, the same footman had arrived with a full tray.

"The tray can go on the low table, Timothy. Thank you."

Monsieur Henri had risen to the occasion, as usual. Cakes, tarts, sandwiches, two teapots, and all the trimmings had been artfully arranged on the tray along with a vase holding three daffodils.

Althea served her guests, finding a blessed sense of normalcy in talk of the weather—lovely—the tea—also lovely—and the benefits of allowing cats abovestairs—not always lovely, but there was Septimus, daring Althea to betray his majesty before callers.

"Where can Lord Stephen be?" Miss Price asked when she'd finished her first cup of gunpowder.

The question was marginally rude, but then, for Miss Price to boast of having met a ducal heir would likely sustain her for days.

"He's a bit horse-mad," Ellenbrook said, "as I recall. If the stable lads asked his opinion on a new foal or wanted him to look at a carriage horse going a bit off, he will be lost to us until Sunday."

"Just so," Althea said. "A bit horse-mad, a bit machine-mad, a bit book-mad. My brother's curiosity is never-ending, and his ability to resist the many questions posed by his imagination almost nonexistent. Would you like some more tea, Miss Price? And you never did tell me what you think of this wallpaper."

Miss Price had not expressed an opinion other than "lovely" for the duration of the visit. She had taken the most predictable seat in the room immediately upon being invited to sit. Her dress was in the first stare of last year's fashions, and she had not a hair out of place nor a speck of mud upon her hems. She was not pretty in the blonde, blue-eyed sense, but her dark hair and green eyes were attractive, and her figure quite feminine. She dressed fashionably, and her aunt was a formidable ally.

So why did Althea feel a reluctant sense of pity for the young woman?

Stephen did join them, his toilet immaculate, only a single cane in his hand. He nonetheless bowed to Miss Price and took the place beside her on the sofa.

"Don't listen to his flattery, Miss Price," Althea said. "You have the good fortune to be seated in proximity to the tray, and his lordship makes the locusts of Egypt look trifling by comparison."

"I'm a man of appetites," Stephen said. "All that fresh air, you know." He sent Miss Price a charming smile, and she rewarded him with a smack on the arm.

Ellenbrook looked out the window.

Althea had the sense the viscount was trying not to yawn—or laugh. When he met her gaze, he winked.

"Ignore my brother, Miss Price," Althea said. "He

thinks he can scandalize sophisticated young women with his flirtation. You encourage him at your peril."

"I need no encouragement," Stephen said, dipping the corner of an apple tart into his tea. "I have the inspiration of Miss Price's fair countenance, which would move any sighted man to raptures. Also, these tarts are quite good. My compliments to Monsieur Henri."

"You have a French chef?" Miss Price asked.

"Monsieur is from Algiers, though he trained mostly in Paris."

The talk wandered from there, pleasantly so. Althea was a proper hostess to Miss Price, who really was on the timid side, and Stephen was outrageous as usual. Ellenbrook, though, created a sense of sharing with Althea the status of adults-in-the-room, the tolerant wiser heads called upon to chaperone a tea dance or some other harmless pastime.

When the time came to see the guests to the door, Stephen surprised Althea by offering Miss Price his arm.

Leaving Althea to escort Ellenbrook.

"I suspected you of having a kind nature when we met," he said. "Despite Lady Phoebe's provocation, you have been all that is gracious."

What an unexpected compliment. "One tries to be hospitable, my lord. The challenge sometimes defeats me."

"Lady Phoebe would have defeated the Armada and Napoleon, given half a chance. She would have snacked on the bones of the Americans too. Heaven defend us all from embittered women."

Stephen was bending close to Miss Price, whispering some inanity.

"Do you speak from experience, my lord? Has an embittered woman visited her ire upon you?" Althea asked.

"My dear mama," he replied, no hint of teasing in his

voice. "I am honestly taking inventory of my northern properties in hopes of finding a situation that might suit her as a dower home. The stew of scandal and gossip in London makes her only more unhappy. That you have no use for the capital delights me."

Good gracious. The man himself was, well, *lovely*. "I will likely return to Town from time to time—I have family there—but the stew of gossip all too often stirred around my latest wrong word, mis-step on the dance floor, or ghastly choice of bonnet trimmings. I did not *take*."

Ellenbrook paused in the foyer and possessed himself of her hand. "London's loss is Yorkshire's gain, then, and I think it more accurate to say London failed to impress you."

"Who is demonstrating a kind nature now, my lord?" A kind nature, sleepy blue eyes, a friendly countenance.

"I merely state facts. Thank you for your hospitality, my lady. You must feel free to call upon us in return."

Miss Price bobbed a hasty curtsy not at her hostess, but at Lord Stephen. "You too, my lord. We would be ever so pleased to receive you."

"Allow me to first recover from my travels," Stephen said, both hands braced on his cane, "and from this initial encounter with your bedazzling presence, Miss Price."

"I think you'd better go," Althea said, motioning for Strensall to get the door. "I am about to be quite severe with my brother, though it will do little good, I'm sure."

This occasioned smiles all around, even from the butler. When the door was closed, and the gig was wheeling down the drive, Stephen slumped against the wall.

"Is that why you've abandoned me in London?" he asked, as Strensall slipped off toward the semi-formal parlor.

"You will have to be more specific," Althea said. "I

have yet to develop the ability to divine your thoughts at sight. Greetings, by the way, and so good of you to send warning that you'd be visiting me."

"I left London in rather a hurry." Stephen set a course down the corridor, the cat trailing after him. "If that damned feline tangles with my feet I won't answer for the consequences."

Truly, Althea had missed her brother. "If you fall on my cat and do him an injury, I won't answer for the consequences."

Stephen paused outside the door of Althea's private sitting room. "Did you tarry here in the arctic north to further your acquaintance with Ellenbrook?"

"I met him less than a week ago." She opened the door and allowed Stephen to precede her through. For him to have to manage both his cane and the door latches was an unnecessary risk. "I do like him, though."

And he likes me. He likes that I abhor London. He thinks I'm kind. All very ... very what? Charming? Althea could muster no more enthusiastic term, not when she longed to take herself back across the fields to lurk in a certain walled garden, not when she would gladly give up all social aspirations forever if it meant Rothhaven could be free of his obligations.

She missed him already, and more significantly, she worried for him.

Stephen took the reading chair by the hearth, though the fire hadn't been lit. He pulled a hassock closer and propped his foot upon it.

"You also made the acquaintance of the resident recluse," Stephen said. "Tell me about him."

Althea took the other wing chair. The cat jumped into Stephen's lap and commenced purring—the traitor.

"There isn't much to say," she replied. "Rothhaven prefers to keep to himself. He's civil, a conscientious head of his household, and a generous landlord, but his privacy matters to him."

Ellenbrook, by contrast, was genial, sociable, and admiring of Althea's character, so why had she been nearly relieved to bid the viscount farewell, and why was she still fretting about a duke who had all but sent her packing?

* * *

"I vow that woman grows more tedious by the year." Wilhelmina, Duchess of Rothhaven, passed her bonnet to the waiting butler. "In Mr. Johnson's lexicon, Lady Partridge ought to be listed under the definition of *silly*."

"Last year you consigned her to the definition of *tiresome*," Sarah replied, handing off her cloak. She paused for a moment by the mirror, touching two fingers to curls gone strawberry-blond with age. Sarah had been a redhead, and like most redheads, she had aged splendidly. Beautiful skin, thick hair going blonde rather than gray, lovely green eyes that in her youth had been the subject of sonnets.

She still had an impish smile, which she aimed at Wilhelmina in the mirror.

"And yet," Wilhelmina said, "you allowed me to accept her invitation once again. Next year, when she invites us to her infernal Venetian breakfast, please spare us both from an eternity of boredom dining in the company of fortune hunters and other insects. Develop a turned ankle or a head cold, if you please, or remind me to."

"I shall make a note in my diary. Are we in the mood for tea?"

"A tot of brandy, I think. The breeze was a bit nippy."

The breeze had been mild, the day sunny. The chill Wilhelmina felt was one of loneliness, though saying that would insult Sarah. Every year, another old friend became too ill to journey to London for the Season, another girl-hood companion celebrated the birth of a fifth or fifteenth grandchild.

Every year, another crop of lovely young women made their come-outs, and Nathaniel remained immured in the north, tending his acres and…what? Playing chess with Vicar Sorenson? While poor Robbie puttered in a walled garden by day and roamed the Hall at night.

"Brandy it is," Sarah said, leading the way to the duchess's private parlor. "Is it Lady Partridge that has you in a brown study or the prospect of Mrs. Abernathy's ball next week?"

"May providence spare us the tedium of that occasion. I swear I will toss myself down the steps rather than listen to her bleating all evening about Lady Hubert this and Lady Hubert that."

"A marquess's spare for a son-in-law was the answer to Mrs. Abernathy's prayers." Sarah lifted the stopper on the decanter on the sideboard. "How chilly are we feeling?"

"Damnably." Though what a pleasure to be able to speak honestly with an old friend and family member. "It might be time I found a dower property, Sarah. Feel free to abandon ship if that plan doesn't suit you, but one of these days, I will say something regrettable to these inane people who can't think beyond the latest scandal or stupid fashion."

Sarah poured two drinks, both modest. "You are a duchess. You are permitted to pronounce difficult truths, and people will call you wise."

"To my face, but behind my back they will conclude I

am growing querulous and unsuited to proper company." Wilhelmina accepted her drink and took a swallow of smooth, soothing fire. "From there, it's a short hop to vagueness and dementia. I could not live with myself if Rothhaven had to deal with such talk about his own mama."

The talk about Robbie had been bad enough. Sympathetic murmurs that hid unkind speculation, and those conjectures had been aimed at a dear, helpless child.

"I think you are homesick," Sarah said, carrying her drink to the window. "Yorkshire in spring is lovely, and your only son bides there. People will think you estranged from Rothhaven if you never visit him. As it is..."

She took a sip of her drink, and the afternoon sunshine caught her at exactly the right angle that for a moment, she could have been her much younger self—quietly pretty, curvaceous, hands gracefully wrapped around delicate crystal.

Where had the years gone? "As it is?" Wilhelmina prompted.

"As it is, Rothhaven himself causes talk, refusing to leave the family seat, a recluse despite being sound in mind and body, as far as anybody knows."

"He is quite sound in mind and body." Painfully sound. The old duke had insisted that his second son become a robust athlete, excelling at everything from horseback riding to archery to rowing. Nathaniel hadn't been allowed to neglect his scholarship either, or to slight the social graces. He had been groomed to become a paragon, and instead...

"Who has cast aspersion upon Rothhaven, Sarah?"

She stalled with another ladylike sip of brandy. "Mrs. Abernathy joked that His Grace must have a squint or a stammer, to be so perennially shy about taking a duchess."

The spirits curdled in Wilhelmina's belly. "When did she say this?"

"I had the great misfortune to run into her and Lady Hubert in the park yesterday. I assured them His Grace was plagued more by a love of his estate than by any failing. I doubt they believed me."

"They do not want to believe you. They would rather invent unkind fictions than accept a boring truth. Nathaniel has seen London, he's still young. He'll take a bride when he pleases to." The lie should not have caused a lump in Wilhelmina's throat after all these years, but it did. Oh, it did.

Sarah's gaze was sympathetic. "I've often wondered if you didn't do me a favor when you accepted the late duke's proposal. He was a difficult man. I can believe he'd be the father of a difficult son. I'd happily go with you, if you chose to journey north. I can admit to homesickness even if you refuse to. The staff at the Hall was always most attentive."

Sarah was being honest rather than unfeeling, but she could not know how her words cut. The late duke had been colder to his wife than any Yorkshire winter, and even worse to his sons.

"Perhaps we'll nip up to Yorkshire next year," Wilhelmina said, setting her drink on the mantel. "We're in London now. We'll plan an entertainment of our own. A musicale, where we can do a spot of matchmaking and inflict some culture on the young people. No more talk of journeying north, and we will most definitely not invite Lady Hubert or her dratted mother to our little gathering."

Sarah carried her drink to the escritoire, took out paper and ink, and flourished a quill pen. "No Mrs. Abernathy. We are agreed. Whom shall we invite?"

Wilhelmina tried to get into the spirit of the undertaking, considering which unmarried lady and which fellow might benefit from an introduction, who might convincingly perform a romantic duet, but her heart wasn't in it.

As Sarah had suspected, Wilhelmina's heart was in the north, where she would most assuredly not be journeying anytime soon. Nathaniel had no hostess at the Hall. He thus had an excuse for never entertaining, and he had the locals believing he was as sour-natured and arrogant as his father had been. Wilhelmina, by contrast, had been raised in Yorkshire and had been lady of the manor for decades.

She had no credible reason for turning away the social overtures of girlhood friends or neighbors. So she bided in London, slowly losing her wits to boredom as she counted the days between one letter from Nathaniel and the next.

Chapter Eleven

Arguing with Robbie had wasted precious hours, and thus when he finally capitulated, Nathaniel simply donned a coat and hat and took off across the moonlit fields. Sending a note would have wasted more time, and besides, what could Nathaniel have said?

Please come. We need you. The truth, but what if a servant read such a missive? What if Lady Althea, whom Nathaniel had sent packing earlier that same day, wasn't in the mood to be summoned?

What if she wasn't at home? Truly was not at home? Normal people traveled into York from time to time. They had dinner with the neighbors. *They socialized.*

Nathaniel faced a choice as he gained the main drive to Lynley Vale: To use the front door or the parlor on the first floor, where a soft glow in the windows suggested her ladyship was spending the evening. Time was of the essence, and if Nathaniel wasn't precisely a duke in truth, he was still the son of a duke.

He marched up to the front steps and rapped the knocker smartly.

An eternity passed before Lady Althea herself opened the door. A young man stood behind her, his hands braced on a cane.

"Your Grace, won't you come in?" Her gaze was wary, which was better than angry.

"Thank you, but I have not the luxury of tarrying. There is…illness in my house. I've been asked to fetch you rather than send for a physician."

The younger man—dark-haired, slim, tall, attired as a gentleman but lacking a coat—watched this exchange with interest. Who the hell was he, to be removing his coat in the presence of a lady after dark?

"Fever?" Lady Althea asked.

"Yes. Cough, aches. The ankle appears to be improving, but lung fever is setting in."

"No, it is not," she countered, stepping back. "Not this soon. A spring cold, influenza, a bit of both, but there hasn't been time for full-blown lung fever to develop."

The younger fellow showed no intention of taking himself off, as any polite guest might have done. His eyes were a vivid blue, a noticing sort of blue that put Nathaniel in mind of Althea.

"Lord Stephen Wentworth, I presume?" Nathaniel asked.

"At your service." He bowed, balancing his weight on his cane. "You are Lynley Vale's nearest neighbor, the duke of curdled milk and colicky infants, I gather?"

"Rothhaven, at your service, and now is not the time for tedious attempts at humor."

His lordship's brows rose—brows very like Lady

Althea's. "Thea, you'd best go with him. His Grace might take to demanding sacrificial maidens or the village's most handsome youths if his whims are not immediately indulged. I, of course, would be compelled by inherent nobility to offer myself as the first casualty in that event. You know how dukes can be."

Althea drew Nathaniel by the arm into the house and closed the door. "I know how brothers can be. The patient turned an ankle and as a result spent several hours half-immersed in my stream. He's an otherwise fit man of about thirty years."

"But he's taken chill," Lord Stephen said, gazing off into the middle distance. "Whiskey with honey and lemon for the cough, willow bark tea for the aches. Avoid laudanum, because he might have taken a knock on the head when he slipped."

A duke's heir would not normally study medicine, but his lordship sounded quite confident of his advice. "Are you a physician?" Nathaniel asked.

"I am an invalid," Lord Stephen replied, gesturing with his cane toward his left leg. "Did you know that invalid and in-valid look the same on paper? They can look the same in life as well, so I learned all that I could pertaining to the preservation of human health. I'm more knowledgeable regarding bones and injuries than I am about illness, but I've picked up a few things."

"What do you suggest for fever?" Lady Althea asked.

"The willow bark tea will help with that, but cool sponge baths—cool, not too cold—will also help. Not ice water, and not surgical spirits, for they will remove too much heat from the body too quickly and propel the patient into the cycle of fever followed by chills. Don't forget to bathe especially the face, neck, feet, and hands. If the congestion gets bad, make a towel sauna over a bowl of boiling water into which you crush a handful of peppermint leaves."

"I'd forgotten the towel saunas," Althea said, reaching for a cloak.

"While I have nightmares about them," his lordship replied airily. "I'll have a bundle of supplies sent over to Rothhaven in the next hour."

"We'll take them with us now," Nathaniel said. "If you please."

"Give me five minutes." Althea strode off in the direction of the steps, pausing before descending. "Don't kill each other."

Nathaniel was thus left in the company of a man new to his acquaintance, a novel and curiously welcome experience. He'd not met a strange gentleman in years, and Lord Stephen was looking at him with an interest that suggested his lordship was equally intrigued.

"I notice your lordship isn't warning me to treat your sister with utmost care."

Lord Stephen propped himself against the sideboard. To appearances he was lounging, but he kept hold of his cane and took weight off his left leg.

"If you need such a warning regarding proper behavior toward a female, Althea will see that you receive it and in a manner that could jeopardize your titular succession. That could be a problem for a man far from the services of a physician and without an extant heir." He smiled, much as a fox likely smiled at a dim-witted hen.

"Warn me anyway," Nathaniel snapped. "She is your sister and I am unknown to you. Assuming that her efforts alone will check my untoward impulses is less than sibling loyalty demands."

His lordship straightened without quite taking his weight

from the sideboard. "Very well." His brows knit as he studied the handle of his walking stick. "Make my sister cry and I will kill you, slowly and painfully. How's that?"

The warning was that of a boy, but the light in his lordship's eyes belonged to a man—a dangerous man.

"Lacks originality but manages to get the point across," Nathaniel said. "Expand a bit on the slow, painful death and you'll be more convincing."

"Said the man whose worst trait is that grannies make up stories about him to entertain children on stormy nights. Do I offer you a brandy now?"

"You do, being a quick study despite appearances to the contrary. I politely decline because I am in something of a hurry."

"Dukes often are," Lord Stephen opined. "Poor sods. That's why they need duchesses, ladies who will stand between the titled idiot and all that distracts him from what matters, or so my brother claims. Althea hasn't had to remind you of your manners yet, has she?"

Lord Stephen's gaze assessed, the same way an art dealer examined a dusty item of statuary, seeing the quality therein, but also the restoration needed after years of neglect. If his lordship was the spare, what on earth must the Duke of Walden be like? But then, spares were often fierce in their own way.

They had to be. "Her ladyship has not objected to my behavior thus far," Nathaniel said. "I trust I will never give her cause to regret her association with me."

She already did, or she should. The lady herself emerged from belowstairs, a covered basket over her arm.

"Did you remember to fetch some ginger?" his lordship asked. "Illness and its treatments can occasion dyspepsia."

"I forgot, drat and damnation."

"Never mind," Lord Stephen said, pushing away from the sideboard. "I'll send some along at first light. Wash your hands frequently when you're tending an illness, Thea. Paracelsus advised cleanliness in the sickroom, and he was a man of considerable judgment. Rothhaven, I really will kill you."

He held out a hand.

Nathaniel shook, finding his lordship's grip firm to the point of painful. "As you should, if I transgress. Lady Althea, shall we be on our way?"

She passed Nathaniel the basket, snatched a straw hat from a peg, and preceded him out the door. Lord Stephen remained in the foyer, looking far too pleased with himself for a man watching his sister disappear into the darkness with a stranger.

"Nighty-night," he said, waving gently. "And don't worry. Althea refused to let me die, though I gave the quest my all on more than one occasion. The patient will be up and about in no time." He blew a kiss not at his sister, who was off down the steps, but at Nathaniel.

"Good night, and my thanks for your reassurances—such as they are."

Nathaniel and Althea kept up a brisk pace along the moonlit paths, but when he ushered her into Robbie's apartment they found the patient's condition was worse than when Nathaniel had left less than an hour past.

Much worse.

* * *

"I did not stop to inquire if you know your way around the actual sickroom," Rothhaven said. "Clearly you do."

Robbie had lapsed into a fitful slumber, though Althea

wasn't fooled. His fever had been building quickly when she'd arrived. He was comfortable for now, but the worst was likely ahead.

"The poor have no physicians to speak of," she said, "and what few medical men open their surgeries to charitable cases crowd every patient—consumptive, fevered, rheumatic, poxed—into the same airless waiting rooms. A visit to the quack is all too often followed by a visit from death itself. We learned to take care of our own."

Rothhaven poked at the fire, though Robbie's bedroom was warm enough. "You truly were wretchedly poor."

Althea could be honest with him, which was both a relief and a little sad. Rothhaven saw her for exactly what she was—a woman on the outside of society longing to be welcomed into it. How ironic, that a man who'd set aside all the entrée and influence in the realm should be her confidant.

"I was so poor that by the time I turned ten years old, my father encouraged me to be friendly to any man who put a copper in my begging bowl. Jack Wentworth was nasty when drunk, but he was cruelty personified when sober, and gin is not free."

Perhaps she'd been a little too forthcoming, but the hour was late, and Althea was already tired. Robbie had grumbled about drinking willow bark tea, grumbled about sipping the whiskey with honey and lemon. He'd refused a sponge bath until Althea had taken his hand and put it in the bowl of tepid water so he could feel its temperature.

He was still, apparently, terrified at the prospect of an ice bath.

He'd muttered about damned women and damned infirmity and damned brothers who worried about every damned thing, but he'd also been far hotter than he should have been when Althea had arrived. Chills might come next or another bout of fever, and the grumbling would be nigh constant until he was well again.

Assuming Althea was still here to tend him.

And assuming he recovered.

"Were you?" Rothhaven asked. "Friendly to the gentlemen?"

With only the firelight to illuminate him, he looked like a dark angel of justice, ready to pronounce sentence upon her—or possibly on Jack Wentworth, may he suffer eternal unrelenting agonies of every description.

The clock ticked quietly on the mantel, the fire crackled in the hearth.

"I let some of them touch me," she said. "Stephen wasn't nimble enough to work, and Papa said a boy who couldn't work had no business being alive. He'd eat in front of Stephen, using a stale crust of bread to torture a small boy. So yes, I let some of those men touch me or look at me—only that—but they paid first and paid handsomely."

Rothhaven rose and paced silently before the fire. He'd taken off his coat an hour ago in deference to the room's warmth. His cuffs were turned back, and his cravat had long since lost its starch.

And yet, his appearance remained imposing, his expression severe.

The quiet took on a density, while Althea waited—for judgment, for disappointment, for awkwardness at the very least. The Wentworth family never spoke openly of the past, not if they could help it, but in Althea's experience the pain and rage only festered more virulently for being consigned to silence.

She faced the memories squarely, of drawing up her tattered skirts while some fiend rubbed his crotch and stared.

She'd not closed her eyes then, she didn't close them now, but her throat hurt as badly as if she'd fallen ill, the ache familiar and bitter. She was on the point of rising to see herself out when Rothhaven spoke.

"Please assure me," he said, "that the gin truly did kill your father. If he yet lives, he won't for long."

The clock ticked a few more times before the meaning of Rothhaven's words came together in Althea's mind. "You'd kill him?"

"With my bare hands, at the first opportunity. The wrath of God should have struck him down before allowing him any progeny, but then you would not be here. For my brother's sake, also for my own, I am very glad you defeated the monster you were compelled to acknowledge as your father."

"He was a monster," Althea said, the words imparting an odd lightness. She hadn't put that name to Jack, not aloud. "He lacked humanity, lacked... basic decency. Something in him was broken, dangerously so, and no-body dared intercede. I'm convinced my mother died from the sheer weariness of spirit that comes from living in proximity to such evil. He's dead, and yes, the gin did him in."

As far as the world knew. The truth was more compli-cated and not Althea's tale to tell.

"I am pleased for the sake of all humanity that he no longer draws breath. A father like that..." Rothhaven's gaze went to the bed, where Robbie slept on. "A father like that should be left to the mercy of the elements on the moors, preferably in January. No walls to shelter him, no light to illuminate his path."

January was the coldest, darkest month of the year—an ice bath—and yet, Rothhaven's sentiment lit a warmth inside Althea. "Just so, with a hole in his boot, a broken compass, and a storm bearing down."

"I do admire a woman with a sense of justice and a vivid imagination," Rothhaven said, his smile tired. "I can stay with Robbie if you'd like to rest. My room is across the corridor. You're welcome to use it."

Althea wanted to tarry in the warmth of Robbie's chambers, wanted to bask in the pleasure of Rothhaven's ire on her behalf—when had a man *ever* expressed lethal indignation for her sake?—but Robbie was far from out of danger, and what lay ahead could be taxing.

"A nap makes sense," she said, rising. "I will rest briefly, then wake you so you can take a turn at napping."

Rothhaven lit a carrying candle and showed Althea across the chilly corridor. Whereas Robbie's rooms were full of books, atlases, treatises, a telescope, orrery, and several stringed instruments, Rothhaven's sitting room was plain and cozy. A blue-and-cream afghan sat in a rumpled heap on a sofa upholstered in gold velvet, writing implements were scattered across a much-stained blotter on the desk.

"The bedroom is through here," he said, pressing on a panel beside the fireplace. "I prefer a cold room for sleeping, but there's warm water on the hearth, and I can put some coals in the—"

She waved him to silence.

"I'll manage. If I don't come wake you in a couple of hours, send out the hounds, for I've gone missing in that great monstrosity where you sleep." The bed's regal dimensions dominated the room, blue velvet hangings sweeping down from the canopy nearly to the carpet.

"You don't want anything?" he asked. "I could pop

down to the kitchen and find bread and butter and a pint of ale."

Althea was too tired to eat, but a difficulty did present itself. "Could you send me a maid?"

"I can manage the warmer," he said, moving toward the hearth, where a warming pan hung from a hook beneath the mantel. "Won't take but a moment."

"I'm not daunted by cold sheets, Your Grace. I had company earlier today, and I changed into one of my fancier...I wasn't expecting Stephen, and he's not one to dress for dinner, which means my hooks..." This was why upsetting a routine was seldom wise. "The hooks on my dress need undoing."

She was blushing, and Rothhaven was smiling. He set aside the warmer. "As it happens, I am competent to undo a lady's hooks, unless fashion has changed enormously in recent years. The alternative is to make you wait eternities while a maid bestirs herself from slumber. Turn around."

He went about the business with brisk dispatch, no wandering hands, no subtle caresses, more's the pity. Perhaps that was for the best. Althea wanted his hands to wander and longed for his caresses, but mere satisfaction of the carnal urges would not do for her in his case.

"Thank you," she said, stepping away.

Rothhaven reached past her, to take down a dressing gown from the bedpost. He draped it around her shoulders, enveloping her in velvet lined with flannel, and in the subtle scent of sandalwood.

"Can't have you taking a chill. Get some rest."

He remained before her, slightly disheveled, tired, and doubtless worried for his brother, and yet, Althea didn't want him to go.

"I don't talk about the past," she said. "Not with anybody."

Rothhaven drew the lapels of the dressing gown to-gether. "Neither do I, but with you..."

They had shared confidences, and now Althea very much wanted to share a bed with him. In a day or two, she'd return to Lynley Vale, resume her quest for a proper place in society, and leave Rothhaven to his secrets and intrigues.

But she'd also leave him with a much-guarded piece of her heart—if not the whole of it—which is why she kissed him on the cheek, and gave him a shove toward the door. Perhaps Rothhaven grasped her dilemma, for he paused at the threshold only long enough to bow, then he left her alone in the cold and darkness of his bedroom.

* * *

"I did not go to the expense of kitting you out, scheduling a half-dozen costly entertainments, hosting houseguests, and denying myself the pleasures of Town during the Season so you could cede the field to a glorified streetwalker."

Lady Phoebe's tone was pleasant, for a lady's tone was always pleasant. The look on Sybil's face was most unpleasant, but then, Sybil's mother had been headstrong to a fault, and a hasty wedding had been the result.

"Lady Althea was perfectly decent to me, Aunt, and whatever else is said about her, nobody has impugned her virtue."

"Hand me that *pipette*." Phoebe bought her wine in barrels, which made the product much harder to adulterate than if she purchased her inventory in corked bottles. Then too, wine by the barrel was cheaper, and Phoebe could monitor the aging herself rather than trust to the indifferent palate of a lowly butler. The barrel on its side before her had been a particularly good bargain.

"Is this a *pipette*?" Sybil passed over a slender tube of hollow glass.

"French for 'little flute.'" Phoebe dipped the glass into the open hole in the side of the barrel.

"I'm chilly," Sybil said. "Why must I lurk in this damp cellar when I could be upstairs waiting for Lord Ellenbrook to come down to breakfast?"

"He had breakfast some time ago. Be quiet and watch." Phoebe slowly dipped the glass into the wine, stopped the top of the tube with her finger, brought the tube to her mouth, and let the wine trickle onto her tongue.

She breathed in, she breathed out, lips slightly parted as she'd been taught. The flavors developing were complicated, as a hearty claret could be. Plenty of fruit, of course, also a hint of spices and a touch of leather all laced up with oak.

She swallowed and considered the fading hues of taste and sensation trailing in the wine's wake.

"It's time," she said. "Mustn't allow too much wood. Wine and women can pass their prime so easily."

"If Ellenbrook has already had breakfast," Sybil said, pacing away, "where is he?"

"Out riding. Men can only do the pretty so long and then they must exert themselves, lest they become cross and difficult. Where did I put the—?"

Sybil passed her a wooden mallet. "If you knew he was going riding, why did you not tell me? I could have gone with him."

Phoebe tapped the cork back into the side of the barrel. "If he sought to spend more time in your company, he would have asked you at supper last night to join him this morning, but because you are allowing him to fall under that Wentworth woman's spell, he's likely off trying to meet her by chance where none are on hand to chaperone."

Sybil clearly did not enjoy time spent in a wine cellar. She stood in the center of the room, where her hems would not touch the barrels, where her sleeve wouldn't inadvertently collect a streak of dust.

Phoebe, by contrast, loved the place. Loved the peace of it, the wealth symbolized by having a store of good vintages, loved that she controlled every aspect of what happened here.

Would that she could control Sybil, or better still, Althea Wentworth.

Sybil took up the pipette and touched it to her mouth. "How can Ellenbrook meet by chance a woman who's likely sipping her morning chocolate as we speak?"

"For God's sake, you don't suck on the pipette like a child with a sweet. The glass is not to touch the barrel or any part of your mouth, ever."

Sybil met Phoebe's glare and licked the end of the pipette. "Lady Althea entertained both me and Ellenbrook graciously, and Lord Stephen took a liking to me. He's a ducal heir. Why should I cultivate Ellenbrook when I can look much higher?"

Just like her mother. Phoebe set the mallet atop the barrel, though she was tempted to strike Sybil a blow to her pretty head.

"Sybil, I could not love my own daughter more than I do you, but you are a commoner. This is evident in your thinking if not in your settlements."

"Nearly all women are commoners."

At least the dear child hadn't accused Phoebe herself

of that failing, though technically, Sybil would have been correct.

"I am the daughter of an earl, while you are..." Not quite beautiful, not quite wealthy, not quite shrewd. Dark-haired instead of a fetching blonde; green-eyed when gentlemen of breeding preferred blue eyes. A challenging combination to marry off, and that was assuming nobody pried too closely into Sybil's antecedents. "A ducal heir is beyond your reach, and women who overreach are vulgar."

"Women who overreach are vulgar, women who marry beneath themselves are pathetic." Sybil started for the door. "Is marriage a sort of nursery rhyme such that only a middle door leads to happiness?"

"Yes," Phoebe said, taking one last look at her wine cellar. She'd oversee the bottling and decanting, but for now, she had other tasks to carry out. "Marriage is exactly like that. You seek a match that is advantageous to both parties without reflecting poorly on either one. If a woman has looks, then the fellow can be wealthy. If she has the money, then he can bring a title to the union."

"But I have only modest assets of any kind. Papa is well-to-do, though—"

Phoebe held up a hand. Sybil's father had earned much of his wealth supporting the British army in its ceaseless quest to conquer the known world. He was the younger son of a baronet, which helped a very little, and he owned several estates, which added a patina of respectability. Nonetheless, he was firmly *in trade*. No amount of silk bonnets or embroidered slippers could obscure that reality.

"You are lovely," Phoebe said, "well dowered, and will make Ellenbrook an excellent wife, but not if Lady Althea snatches him up first."

"She's lovely too, I tell you, and the Wentworths were

obscenely wealthy even before they stumbled into a title. Lord Stephen is witty and not bad looking."

Phoebe took the ring of keys from her pocket and locked the wine cellar, graft among the servants being a fact of life.

"The Wentworths are the last family you should seek to marry into." Phoebe set a brisk pace for the stairs. "The duke was convicted of a heinous crime and juries don't convict a man unless he's guilty as sin." He'd been pardoned *and* supposedly exonerated, but Phoebe trusted an English jury to be more discerning than royal favor or gossip.

"But what about—?"

"The Wentworth fortune? They are bankers, and bankers become paupers overnight. Besides, Lord Stephen is only the heir, and his brother yet enjoys good health. Lord Stephen could be knocked from his expectations by this time next year. Then where would you be?"

Sybil stopped on the landing. "Married into a ducal family? Expecting the next spare? Free from godforsaken Yorkshire, where winters never end and everybody is cousins with everybody else?"

"You sound like me, when I was young and foolish. Apply yourself to wooing Ellenbrook and you will be a viscountess with more annual pin money than most women see in a lifetime."

They gained the upper reaches of the house, morning sunshine showing off all the marble, gilt, and art to good advantage. Phoebe had worked hard to appoint her household in elegant good taste at a time when ostentation was becoming fashionable.

Sybil ran a finger along the frame of Great-Uncle Blanchard's portrait, then rubbed the dust away with her thumb. "Should I call for my horse and attempt to meet Ellenbrook by chance?"

"We will call for the gig and pay a call on Vicar Sorenson. Wear your plain bonnet and everyday cloak."

"Why are we calling on Vicar?"

Phoebe's resolve faltered, because really, Sybil was so far from shrewd that she'd be a tiresome mate to any man with half a wit. But then, men did not generally marry to debate philosophy with their wives.

"Because when Ellenbrook comes in from his ride, you won't be here, will you? You will be tending to social obligations, and leaving his lordship to rattle about without a companion for whist, without anybody to flatter him the livelong day or ask his opinion about the most interesting articles in the newspaper. He's male, so sniffing at Lady Althea's skirts is to be expected, but the domestic peace and ease he needs aren't to be found with a strumpet. Change out of your slippers and we'll be on our way."

Sybil ought to have scampered up to her room, but she instead waited on the stairs, two steps up. "Why do you call Lady Althea a strumpet? That is a low insult, and she strikes me as very careful to tend to the proprieties."

"The best strumpets always do. I have it on good authority that her ladyship wanders her acres unescorted, she takes tea with the farmers' wives, and she is not well regarded in London. Of course she's a strumpet. It only remains for us to expose her as such to Ellenbrook and any other man foolish enough to give her a second look. You, meanwhile, will be a pattern card of ladylike deportment and charitable sentiments."

Sybil looked like she might say more, but the sound of hoofbeats on the drive intruded.

"Away with you," Phoebe said, motioning with her

hand. "Ellenbrook mustn't find you panting for him on the front steps, my girl. Mustn't find you panting for him anywhere."

No good came from panting after a man. Given Sybil's antecedents, she should have been made to grasp that truth from the cradle onward.

"About Lady Althea," Sybil said.

"Never fear. We'll see her ruined once and for all, and every hostess in London will thank us." Phoebe donned her best gracious, carefree smile and prepared to invite Ellenbrook to join them on their call at the vicarage. He was already dressed to go out and had no polite means of refusing to accompany them.

But then, why should he? Given a choice between a woman of lowly antecedents who only looked like a lady and a decent female minding her social obligations conscientiously, Ellenbrook's decision should be easy to make.

Chapter Twelve

Nathaniel had passed into the phase of exhaustion where waking, interrupted slumber, and reality all merged into a philosophical peace that observed life with benevolent detachment. Soldiers and the mothers of young children doubtless reached this state frequently, while Nathaniel, whose household thrived on order and predictability, was pleasantly disoriented by the muting of chronic anxieties.

Robbie was on the mend, according to Althea. Sometime after midnight, she'd thrown a wet flannel at Nathaniel for referring to her as *your ladyship*. He'd barked at her that as long as she addressed him as *Your Grace*, he'd observe similar proprieties and she'd responded with a purely amused laugh.

Robbie had regarded them both with a wary smile, then gone back to complaining.

"He should not be allowed to sleep the day away," Nathaniel said, passing Althea the toast rack. They were eating on trays in his sitting room, the doors between Robbie's rooms across the corridor and Nathaniel's apartment open in case the patient should summon them. "Robbie believes firmly that a schedule is integral to his good health."

"He should be allowed to sleep some," Althea retorted. "We're barely keeping our eyes open and he got little more rest than we did."

Her bun was a frizzy mess, her dress wrinkled. She had long since turned back her cuffs, and one sleeve bore evidence of spilled willow bark tea. She was slathering extra butter on toast that had been liberally buttered in the kitchen, and she ate with unapologetic appetite.

This is the woman I was meant for. That truth clobbered Nathaniel as Althea passed him the toast rack and set the butter on his tray. He had learned as a very young man to manage lust. In recent years, he'd learned to all but ignore it, but the longing he felt for Althea was more complicated than physical desire.

"I will eat every morsel you put in front of me," she said, licking butter from her fingertips. "You must not stand on ceremony now that we've spent the night together."

Her smile was devilish and tired. She'd inflicted endless good cheer on Robbie too, sparing his modesty by flaying him with teasing. *Roll over, Sir Slugabed, or the wrath of Rothhaven will befall you.* She'd found excuses to leave the sickroom periodically, which allowed Robbie to tend to more personal needs without a female audience.

She had read *Tom Jones* by the hour, playing all the voices with uncanny skill.

Althea was a good woman, simply good. Kind to others, patient in the face of human foibles, *loving* in her brisk, practical way. Given her wealth and station, she could have destroyed Nathaniel, Robbie, and the whole tissue of lies holding the Rothhaven dukedom together.

Instead, she was yawning over her morning tea and covetously inspecting a plate of cinnamon buns.

"I'll let you have first crack at the bed this morning," Nathaniel said. "You've earned your rest."

"We all have," she said, stirring honey into her tea. "I would eat sweets all day, left to my own devices. We never had them as a child. Stephen once stole a currant bun. He dreamed about that currant bun, described it to me the way some boys would have described a sighting of Wellington on horseback. When a neighbor gave Stephen some jam and bread, he vowed to apprentice himself to a baker."

This recollection had dimmed her smile.

"But what baker wants an apprentice who limps?" Nathaniel asked. What peerage wanted a duke who fell to the floor, twitching and shaking, then rose from his fit—assuming he survived it—as unsound of mind as the village sot?

Althea put the wooden spoon back into the honey pot. "You understand about brothers who are infirm in one regard and hale in others. Their lives are a difficult balance of ferocious independence and blatant need. Stephen was four when he was injured, old enough that he recalls what running and jumping and normal balance feel like."

Nathaniel took her hand. "And nothing you can do, nothing you can ever do, will make your brother sound again."

She leaned into him, the moment perfectly sweet and crushingly sad. "I will take you up on that offer of a nap, sir. Robbie will think himself in the pink by noon, but tonight he could well see a recurrence of the fevers, if not before."

Right. Mustn't forget dear old Robbie. Ever. "If you'd like to return to Lynley Vale, we can probably manage from here."

"For me to leave now would not be wise," Althea said, rising. She wrapped a cinnamon bun in a table napkin and stuffed it into a pocket. "Robbie argues with you, while he merely grouses at me. If I tell him to endure a sponge bath, he puts up with it. You ask him, and he refuses, and that's an end to it. Now, when he thinks full recovery assured, he'd win all the arguments."

Nathaniel stood as well, mentally reviewing the previous night's activities, to the extent his recollection functioned at all.

"I am in the habit of respecting my brother's wishes."

"Respect your brother," Althea said, preceding him into the bedroom. "Take issue with his wishes when they're patently foolish. Ye saints, I haven't been this tired since the Crown tried to execute Quinn."

The maids had managed to remake Nathaniel's bed and tidy the room. The bed abruptly loomed like a promised land of bliss, and that was irrespective of any cavorting Nathaniel might envision with a woman who casually mentioned her brother's attempted execution.

"Get some rest," he said. "I'll keep Robbie in line as best I can. He's stubborn."

"For which God be thanked or he'd be long dead. Would you undo my hooks?"

Nathaniel had undone them late last night, he'd done them up again a few hours later. Althea wasn't blushing, but rather, standing with her back to him, her hair swept off her nape. Fatigue must have made his hands clumsy because the dress abruptly sported ten thousand hooks, each one smaller than the last.

"Thank you," she said, moving away long moments later. "I don't dare leave my hair in this state, or bachelor hedgehogs will send me flirtatious glances. You must not allow me to sleep more than a few hours. If Robbie worsens, you will awaken me regardless of the time of day. You should sleep as well. The second night of an illness can be the worst even if the day goes well."

She disappeared behind the privacy screen, and Nathaniel sat on the bed rather than gawk at the triangle of bare flesh exposed below her nape.

He pulled off his boots, intending to find some house slippers, but that would require traversing the length of his bedroom, rummaging in his dressing closet, and trekking back to...where? Where was he supposed to be? From behind the screen came the sound of teeth being brushed, then quiet humming.

Do not fall asleep. Have some damned dignity. Althea slept less than you did.

Closing one's eyes was not falling asleep, and Nathaniel's eyes stung with fatigue. He did not decide to lie back on the bed so much as he bowed to the inevitable conclusion reached by his body when his eyelids shuttered and his bum encountered a soft mattress.

The bed was bliss, the pillow his most cherished friend. His aching body relaxed, his mind gave up. He had never been this tired ever, in body, mind, or spirit.

"How are the mighty fallen in the midst of battle," some female murmured, just before a weight dipped the mattress.

Fallen indeed. Nathaniel's last thought was that he really ought to get up and do something, be somewhere, accomplish a task....He most assuredly should not tarry here, where...

The scent of roses came to him, and his thoughts wafted away into dreams.

* * *

Althea woke to the disorienting awareness that somebody was sopping a cloth in a basin of water. When an entire family lived in a single room, no sound, regardless of how private, remained unheard by others.

Constance, whimpering through another nightmare.

Stephen's restless shifting in a doomed quest for a comfortable position.

Jack, stepping an entire two yards up the alley before relieving himself against a wall.

Scents and sensations came to her rescue, reassuring her that she was not dreaming, but rather, waking to an unfamiliar reality. The sheets she lay upon smelled faintly of sandalwood and lavender. The covers were ample and soft. She had the bed to herself, no sibling elbow or knee impeded her stretching.

Althea was in Rothhaven's enormous bed, where she had enjoyed a good long nap, her sleep more rejuvenating than the snatches of rest stolen from her duties in the sickroom. She was stiff, as she expected to be when great fatigue was followed by real repose.

"You are awake." Rothhaven emerged from behind the privacy screen. "I had hoped not to disturb you." Beneath an open dressing gown he wore a shirt tucked into breeches. The buttons at his throat were undone, no cravat in sight. He scrubbed at his face with a linen cloth, his cheeks newly shaved.

"I am barely awake," Althea said, struggling to sit up amid a sea of pillows. "What time is it?" Her voice was rusty, and she must look a fright, but self-consciousness could not push aside her fascination with that patch of bare male chest on view several feet away.

"Time for luncheon," Rothhaven said, "and I, for one, am famished. Robbie slept for most of the morning, took some porridge and tea, then asked for the London news-papers."

Althea pushed a lock of hair behind her ear. "London newspapers? Is he trying to bring on dyspepsia?"

Rothhaven took off his dressing gown and draped it over her shoulders. "He reads the financial pages from many newspapers with more focus than a fortune-teller at her tea leaves. Thanks to his interest in the estate's investments, our fortunes prosper, I'm pleased to say. If anything ever happens to me, he'll be able to afford good staff, assuming he remains in control of his affairs."

Althea patted the mattress on the empty side of the bed. "You have rested enough to resume your worries."

Rothhaven settled beside her. She hadn't shared a bed with a man previously. With him, she liked the companion-ability. He helped her get the sleeves of the dressing gown sorted out and passed her a glass of water.

"What does it say about me, Althea, that I *enjoyed* being exhausted to the point of witlessness? I grasped this morning what it means to have a mind truly numbed by fatigue. The peace of it was seductive, like strong spirits but without the bodily reproach for over-indulging."

The water revived her, though she stopped at half a glass and passed it back to Rothhaven. He took a sip and set the drink aside. He was so casual about intimacies that drew her the way blooming honeysuckle called her to the out-of-doors on a beautiful day.

Sharing a dressing gown that yet held Rothhaven's body heat and the scent of his shaving soap.

Sharing a glass of water.

Sharing a bed.

"What does it say about me," she asked, "that I'm supposed to be at Rothhaven Hall to lighten the burdens in the sickroom, but all I can think about right now is spending more time with you in this bed? And I do not refer to another nap."

Rothhaven's smile was wry and a little sad. He took her hand and kissed her knuckles. "It means we are both human, for I'd delight in disporting with you as well. Naughty of me, but with you, only honesty will do."

"So why don't we disport?" Althea knew why: because she cared for this man and respected him, and what might have been a casual, giggling romp for a girl raised in the slums would be a different undertaking altogether with him.

Different and wonderful, but so very ill-advised.

He brushed his thumb slowly back and forth over her fingers. "I can offer you nothing, Althea. Not tomorrow, not marriage, not a discreet liaison. You deserve devotion and propriety, a public union with all the trappings, a courtship for the ages—all the dignities and graces I cannot provide—and you well know that is your due, my lady."

She was coming to hope that was her due. "Robbie will never recover?"

"Apparently not, and the fits aren't the worst of his problems. You saw how he was at the mere mention of an ice bath. He still keeps the drapes closed in his sitting room because even the sight of the moors unnerves him on his bad days. He won't eat many foods because he was forced to subsist on them for years. Others he shuns because he thinks they aggravate his condition. He's in no fit state to take on the world and probably never will be."

Once upon a time, Althea had thought her life would *never* change. She'd been doomed to suffer Jack Wentworth's violence and evil, to suffer poverty and desperation. Quinn's determination, shrewdness, and good luck had proved that *never* could turn into *someday*.

She was determined that society's decision to never accept her also turn into a someday.

But this *never* besieging the Rothmere family was beyond her control.

"I understand that you must heed your duty to your brother, Nathaniel, and I will not beg for what you cannot promise, but I can offer you myself, here and now. Will you refuse that too in the name of duty, or will you share with me a comparable gift?"

He dropped her hand. "I am no gift, Althea."

"You are wrong." Rothhaven had instructed her brilliantly on how to improve her standing in society—a task nobody else had been able to do. He'd paid her the very great compliment of seeking her aid when Robbie had fallen ill. He'd laughed with her over a few hands of cards, and he was in this bed with her now, inspiring feelings so precious and rare Althea had no names for them.

He scrubbed a hand over his face and slanted a look at her. "Shall we argue over my various attributes, or shall I kiss you?"

"Neither." She won free of the covers, straddled his lap, and planted a smacker on his mouth. "We'll start with me kissing you, and then you may comment on what our destination should be, assuming your powers of speech have not deserted you."

She wrapped her arms around his neck and snuggled

close enough to learn that despite his gentlemanly misgivings, Rothhaven was already impressively aroused.

He untied the bow of her chemise and planted a slow, sweet kiss on her shoulder. "So be it. Here and now, so be it."

Althea barely gave him time to get the words out before she pulled his shirt over his head and recommenced kissing him.

* * *

Nathaniel's first impression of Althea's lovemaking was that she had the wisdom to demand a leisurely exploration when he would have galloped past the preliminaries.

He wasn't ashamed of himself for calling on the widows in York, but something about that whole business had annoyed him, even as it had eased his appetites. The result was an exchange of frustrations. Erotic satisfaction on the one hand, but on the other, an acknowledgment that sexual gratification alone wasn't all he craved.

Althea, with no expectation of a costly gift or anything beyond the moment, offered him so much more of what he sought. Her hands slid around his neck while she gently pressed his forehead to her throat. This close, she smelled of roses and the lavender sheets. She was wonderfully warm, and her slow, sweet touch unraveled a tension Nathaniel had carried for years.

"I could *devour* you," she whispered, biting his ear gently. "Gobble you up over and over."

She kissed him, sparing him the effort of replying with words. Her kisses were tender, a promenade of mouth upon mouth that invited a mutual tasting.

"I could kiss you endlessly," she murmured, stroking

her fingers through his hair. "But I want you out of these damned breeches."

Nathaniel was so absorbed with kissing her back and with shaping the contour of her ribs, waist, and hips that her meaning took a moment to sink in.

"And I want out of my damned breeches."

Althea sat up, he scooted, she helped, and soon he was naked. "The dressing gown," he said. "Please."

She shrugged out of it, sniffing at the flannel lining. "I like wearing your scent."

"The things you say…" Honest, erotic, un-self-conscious. "I like wearing *you*."

She kept her chemise on even as she resumed her place straddling his lap, likely the better to tease him with full breasts straining against delicate linen. He glossed his thumbs over her nipples and she arched like a happy cat.

"Good hands," she said. "I love that you have good, knowledgeable hands." She brushed her sex over his arousal in a maddeningly slow, hot caress.

Even as desire spiraled upward, Nathaniel was aware of a discontent separate from bodily yearning. The pleasure was most exquisite and soon to surpass even that superlative, but Althea would be intimate with him only this once, only here and now.

That was wrong. Unfair to them both, and no amount of racing on horseback over the darkening moors would ease that sorrow.

So here and now must be worth a lifetime of recollection. Nathaniel eased Althea's chemise up and over her shoulders, leaving her wonderfully bare and rosy.

"You are…magnificent." In appearance she might not be remarkable from an artistic perspective—she was beautiful to him—but her direct gaze, the lovely *listening* quality of her touch, the intensity of her lovemaking made him ache.

Her smile became devilish as she took him in her hand and slowly, slowly slid her body down over his arousal.

"If I am magnificent, what is this?" she asked, when she'd hilted him inside her. She *did something*, a little feminine caress from within, and Nathaniel nearly came undone.

"*That* is almost more delight than I can bear. Take your pleasure swiftly, Althea, for I won't last worth a damn."

"Neither will I," she said, cuddling down to his chest. She moved at a deliberate tempo, and Nathaniel tried to hold the sparkling heat loosely as it built, but his restraint was barely equal to the challenge.

Fortunately, Althea wasn't interested in a contest of delayed gratification. She let go with a soft laugh against Nathaniel's shoulder, yielding to pleasure vigorously. He held her until he was certain she'd wrung the last ripple of satisfaction from him, then lifted her up far enough to withdraw.

She must have known what he was about because she immediately tucked close again, giving him weight, heat, and her body to finish against. Very soon he would doubtless find the mental resources to resent withdrawing, but as satisfaction overcame him, all he could be was grateful.

Very, very grateful, and at peace.

He held her as their bodies cooled, his hand finding the discarded dressing gown and using it as a blanket over them both. Althea quieted, and Nathaniel, with no conscious thought, matched his breathing to hers.

The moment was perfect. He was replete in ways he hadn't been, ever. To hold Althea thus, skin to skin, no pretenses or secrets between them, was more intimate even than what had gone before, and Nathaniel was certain he would miss both equally—the passion and the sweet contentment that followed it.

He'd not known either previously, and that had been a backhanded mercy. What a man did not know, he could not long for—or beg for—but throughout the rest of his days, Nathaniel would long for Althea Wentworth and the joy of intimate union with her.

* * *

"What do you think you're doing?" Milly asked.

Stephen could barely recall his mother, but he'd heard Jane take that tone with his little nieces. He set the wicker panniers on the sideboard in Lynley Vale's foyer, ceramic jars clanking gently.

"I'm on my way to aid a neighbor beset by illness. Althea didn't have time to pack ginger when she decamped on the same mission, and if she intends to bide at Rothhaven any longer, she needs a change of clothes."

Milly folded her arms. "Then Rothhaven should send for those items."

"I promised them I'd bring the ginger. I keep my word."

"You are meddling."

"Then what are you doing, darling Milly?" He'd passed the open door of Althea's private sitting room and seen Milly at the desk, scratching away at some list or other.

Her response was to look away and drop her arms. "I am planning a ball."

Not a reply Stephen could have anticipated. "I beg your pardon?" He propped himself against the sideboard—God bless all homes liberally stuffed with sturdy furniture—and prepared to hear a confession.

"I've been thinking," Milly said. "Her ladyship is the ranking female title biding in the shire. Now you are here to be the host if she would like to entertain. She has one of the most elegant ballrooms in all of Yorkshire, and anybody who hasn't gone south for the Season would eagerly make the effort to attend an affair at Lynley Vale."

"I hate balls." Hated watching all those graceful, athletic glissades and chassés, hated sitting among the wallflowers and pretending he wasn't more envious of the dancers than were the chaperones and spinsters.

Milly fixed him with a hard stare. "Well, that settles it. Lord Stephen Wentworth has spoken. We must outlaw the waltz and all its kin. Put them to the horn. Never let it be said that the wishes of one as selfless and wise as he were held in anything but highest regard. Let me fetch my stone tablets, for such a proclamation merits no less dignity than to be graven eternally beside the Commandments themselves."

"You are a terror." Stephen set his hat on his head and adjusted the angle. "Did you know that?"

"While you are a brat. That you are bright and reasonably good-looking only renders the offense more disappointing."

"You should marry me," Stephen said, taking up the panniers. "Take me in hand, give me what for. Spank me when I'm naughty."

The teasing had the desired effect, making Milly smile. "My hand would tire before the punishment had any effect. I'd rather focus on her ladyship's dilemma. Althea has done as any infantry unit knows to do when facing larger and better armed forces. She's fallen back to regroup here in Yorkshire, but that doesn't mean she should surrender. We have bachelors here of suitable station. Even Vicar

Sorenson has a baronet or two somewhere on his family tree."

"A duke's sister does not marry a baronet's less-than-wealthy great-nephew." And yet, Milly had a point. Althea wanted what any reasonable adult wanted: a friend to go through life with, some babies to cluck and fuss over. Not too much to ask, regardless of a woman's station—or a man's. She wouldn't find that fellow if all she did was sit in the garden and wait for him to trot up on his white charger.

"Althea won't allow any balls, Milly. The idea has merit, the premises could easily accommodate such an entertainment, and I've no doubt the gawkers would love to come swill her punch and hop about on the dance floor, but she won't put herself forward that way."

"She will if you ask her to. You are the heir to a dukedom, and the succession, last I heard, rests on your broad and handsome shoulders. You are of an age to take a bride."

The panniers were becoming heavy, though Stephen refused to put them down. His leg could not be helped, but he kept the rest of himself inordinately fit.

"I was not-bad-looking two minutes ago, and now I'm handsome?"

"Don't try to distract me." Milly fluffed his cravat. "You need a wife. Althea needs a husband. These conundrums are often solved by socializing with the opposite gender. Althea should hold a ball, and you should summon Walden and his duchess up here to lend their cachet to the occasion."

"If Quinn and Jane come all this way, they can and should host the blasted ball. They are the duke and duchess and this property only came into family hands through the title."

"An excellent idea, my lord. So glad you thought of it. Will you send Their Graces an express?"

Stephen had been maneuvered, not quite manipulated. He admired Milly's shrewdness, even as he did not care for the view from a tight corner.

"I will discuss this with Althea, whose household this is. We thwart her wishes at our peril."

"Oh, right. Happy spying, my lord." Milly waggled her fingers at him and bustled back to her lair, from which she could no doubt order the affairs of the whole shire, should she choose to do so.

"I hate balls," Stephen muttered, as a groom fixed the panniers to the saddle of a raw-boned gray gelding.

"Beg pardon, my lord?"

"Nothing of any note, apparently." The next bit was delicate, and Stephen usually preferred to climb aboard his horse in the relative privacy of the stable yard. He hadn't wanted to lug the panniers that far, though, so needs must.

The groom stood at the gelding's head, gaze on nothing in particular as Stephen stashed one cane into a scabbard affixed to the saddle. The gray gelding, a stalwart soul traveling under the *nom d'écurie* of Revanche, knew to stand until Kingdom Come when Stephen was mounting.

"Good lad," Stephen said, swinging aboard, sliding the second cane into the scabbard, and patting the horse. "Away with us to Rothhaven Hall."

The groom stepped back. "You're for *Rothhaven*, my lord?"

The stable lads would not know where Lady Althea had got off to or why. Best keep it that way. "I am. One pays calls when biding in the country, as best I recollect."

"One might pay calls, sir, but Rothhaven Hall never

receives visitors." The groom was an older fellow, gray-haired and lean, with the Viking-blue eyes common in the district. "Our duke is a man of particulars and likes his privacy."

"Then I won't be gone long, will I?" Stephen said, kneeing Revanche away from the mounting block. He kept the horse to the walk, in deference to the panniers behind the saddle, also to give himself time to think.

Stephen detested balls with the unrelenting passion the musically disinclined reserved for bad opera. Hated watching the couples flirt and twirl, hated that the long evening forced him to roost in his Bath chair like a dropsical dowager too stout to properly socialize. Hated the awkward conversations that resulted when one person remained seated and most around him stood. Hated the difficulty of maneuvering a Bath chair through a crush, particularly with a drink to hold as well.

But he loved his sister, and a ball was a logical next step in her campaign to secure the honors of social acceptance, and thereafter, wifehood.

He kicked the horse into a canter and prepared to do some spying.

* * *

Althea did not want to leave Rothhaven's bed. Part of her reluctance was fatigue—the bed was so comfy with him in it to cuddle up to—and part of her reluctance was because she had no experience with what came after lovemaking.

She knew what followed a tupping—smiles, a little affection, a mutual need for distance lest anybody read too much into the encounter.

But she and Rothhaven had not engaged in a tupping.

His hands had been nearly reverent, his caresses lighter than wishes and more sincere than prayers. Nobody had ever touched her that way before, such that physical sensations conjured an emotional certainty of caring, desire, and respect.

Dear God, his touch had been lovely and *loving*. What did one say after such a joining?

"Are you awake?" Rothhaven murmured. "I can hear your mind whirling, while I cannot catch a coherent thought."

He was spooned around her, and she could feel the words rumbling from him. "I am awake," she replied. "I feel as if I ought to offer a witty remark, something charming and sophisticated, but I know not what. I want to cry but I am certain that is not the done thing, and why should I cry when I'm so...when that was...Rothhaven, for pity's sake, say something."

He moved away, and Althea nearly did start crying, but then he shifted her to her back and draped himself over her.

"Please don't cry. If you cry, I will go mad. You never cry and neither do I, are we agreed?" He was smiling, but his gaze begged her for understanding.

She brushed his hair off his brow. "We are agreed. No tears, though I am moved far beyond joy, Rothhaven. I am utterly lost on the moors."

"Let's find each other again, shall we?"

He was fully aroused, and Althea had neither the will nor the desire to deny herself a second joining. Allowing Rothhaven to keep her on her back, though, was most unwise. He had more control over the dimensions of their passion this way, and he used that advantage to drive her mad.

When she would have hastened toward pleasure, he held back, then held back more. She retaliated by learning every muscle and bone of his back, shoulders, and buttocks; by using her tongue in the same rhythm he set with his hips.

They became a seamless oneness, suspended on the edge of yearning and yielding, until Althea could hold the balance no longer. She cast off into pleasure, becoming mindless—without a mind—simply a body and a heart, and both were entirely entrusted to Rothhaven's care.

He waited until she was a panting heap, barely capable of languid caresses to his biceps, before he slowly withdrew. He braced one arm beside the pillow and wrapped his free hand under her backside, then began to move again.

She held him with all the fierceness she had to give, until he too was winded and replete. Then she held him some more, knowing that when she let him go, she'd be letting him go forever.

Rothhaven allowed her a few more minutes of intimacy, then made a brisk business of tidying up. He sat back, naked, his hair tousled, his gaze mirroring everything Althea felt—wonder, tenderness, despair, but some joy too. Taking a lover should always occasion at least a little joy.

"I have been greedy," he said. "I like the look of you, loved witless in my bed."

"Not greedy," Althea said, struggling to sit up. "More generous than you can possibly imagine."

His smile faltered. "You have been generous, Althea, but now we must be..."

"Sensible," Althea rejoined, tossing a bolster at him. "You and I are always sensible, Rothhaven. I find the fit between me and sensibility much poorer than usual at the moment. Duty and I will barely be on speaking terms for weeks. I would like to become better acquainted with—"

He touched his fingers to her lips. "I know. Better acquainted with joy, spontaneity, laughter, indulgence."

He stopped short of speaking the word *love*, but Althea was thinking it. Worse, she was feeling it. Love for the man who could be so devoted to an ailing brother that his own wishes and wants all but disappeared from his view. Love for a man with whom physical intimacy meant emotional closeness as well.

What a novel and daunting concept.

"Better acquainted with you." She held up a hand. "I know, Rothhaven, here and now, you said, but your version of here and now rather leaves me...at a loss."

He crawled to the edge of the mattress and sat on the side of the bed, half-facing her. "I am at a loss as well. I suspect I will be for quite some time."

"You are gallant even in this, you varlet." And he needed her help if they were to make it out of this bed without one of them collapsing into strong hysterics. Althea mentally rummaged for something a sensible woman would say in the circumstances. "I suppose we should get dressed lest the patient summon us."

She did not want to put on her clothes, did not want to adopt the grumpy-cheerful tone of the soldier on a forced march, commiserating with his mates and urging them onward to the next battlefield. Why was life a progression of battlefields and defeats, anyway?

Rothhaven did his best to fall in with her tactics, helping her with buttons and hooks, passing her the boot that was half-hidden by the bed skirt. He allowed her to tie his cravat and manage his sleeve buttons, but these domestic gestures only dealt Althea's heart so many more blows.

She wanted even this un-romantic time with him, even the sight of him dragging a brush through his hair, tilting his head this way and that as men did when assessing their own appearance.

She wanted the knowledge of how he shrugged into his coat, left sleeve followed by the right, a roll of his shoulders, then adjusting his shirtsleeves before doing up the buttons.

She wanted every boring, mundane detail about him. Althea was assailed by the realization that she'd wasted years courting society's favor, when she'd gladly toss aside acceptance in Mayfair for an obscure life with Rothhaven on the Yorkshire moors. Should she be relieved that such a choice would never be put before her? If so, the relief was slow to manifest.

"You are troubled," Rothhaven said, putting down the hairbrush. "Come here." He held out his arms and Althea buried herself in his embrace.

"I cannot offer you what you deserve," he said, stroking her back slowly. "I cannot offer you anything. I regretted that an hour ago. The limitations of my station where you are concerned have now become my defining sorrow. I am sorry, Althea, if you regret what we've shared, but my regret is that we cannot share more."

A ducal expression of sentiment that fell short of a true apology. Careful, sincere, complete. No room for negotiation, no convenient gate left unlocked in the garden wall.

"I will comfort myself," Althea replied, stroking his chest, "that a mile of countryside and a vast moor of regret lie between us. I am not sorry for what we've shared, and I never will be." She offered that half-truth in good faith, hoping it brought him some comfort. Rothhaven was afflicted with an abundance of honor, and left to his own devices, he'd doubtless locate some manly guilt.

Not enough manly guilt to change his mind, of course, but enough to add to his burdens.

He held her for the space of one more breath, a slow rise and fall of his chest, a few beats of her heart, then he stepped back.

"I'll leave you here to finish your toilette," he said, "and I will check on the patient."

Considerate of him, to give her a bit of solitude, but then, her appearance was far from composed, and even a woman who never cried sometimes needed to stare out at the moors and wonder how the hell she was supposed to carry on.

Rothhaven not only bowed over her hand, he kissed her knuckles, a sweet, courtly gesture of farewell. Then he left, closing the door with a decisive snick of the latch.

Chapter Thirteen

"And who might you be?" The old fellow stood in the Rothhaven Hall front doorway, the coat of his dark livery mis-buttoned.

Never had Stephen been greeted thus in a titled household. "Lord Stephen Wentworth, calling upon His Grace of Rothhaven. I believe my sister, Lady Althea, is biding here."

"I wouldn't know anything about that." The footman remained in the doorway, one veined hand braced on the jamb. "It's 'Thatcher, fetch me some toast' and 'Thatcher, polish that sconce' until I'm run off me tired feet. We don't have callers at t' Hall, but here you are, Lord Somebody, looking like you expect a dish of tea and a plate of crumpets."

"Thatcher, might you let me in? I've brought a few things for Lady Althea."

"We don't have callers here." He stepped back nonetheless. "Except lately, apparently."

"I'm not a caller," Stephen said, crossing the threshold. "I'm simply a neighbor delivering some supplies."

"We don't take no deliveries, but then we're supposed to get a jolly lot of building stone from t' quarry so we can connect t' orchard and t' walled garden. T' Quality, you know. Daft as curates at t' communion wine."

Stephen took off his hat and hung it on a peg. "How is the patient?"

"I'm always patient, thank you very much. Have to be. Served this hall, boy and man, didn't I? Suppose I'd best put you in the estate office if you're here to dicker about t' building stone."

"I'm not—"

The old fellow tottered off down the corridor, muttering about marmalade and Master Robbie. Stephen tottered along behind him, taking his time so a neighbor on an errand of mercy could do some reconnoitering.

Whatever Stephen had been expecting—splendor in decline, dusty neglect, strange moans welling from unseen dungeons—Rothhaven Hall appeared to be yet another large, reasonably maintained stately home. The mirrors needed some polish, though they weren't tarnished; the carpets could use a beating but were far from moth-eaten. The dust and cobwebs were of the everyday sort.

"Who is Master Robbie?" Stephen asked as the footman showed him into a comfortably appointed, if somewhat large, estate office.

"We're not supposed to say," the footman replied. "That's 'im." He gestured with his chin at a portrait over the mantel. The portrait featured a woman seated between two dark-haired little boys, both of whom looked about two seconds away from fidgeting right out of the frame. The woman was dark-haired as well and young matron–ish. While she was pretty, her gaze lacked the serenity of the average aristocratic female enduring a commissioned sitting.

She looked like she was ready to fidget too.

"Who's the other fellow?" Stephen asked, setting his panniers down at long last.

"Master Nathaniel, but we call him Rothhaven." The footman gave an exaggerated wink. "Mum's the word, aye? I don't suppose you'd like some toast, Mr. Quarry?"

"Toast would be lovely, and please do let Lady Althea know she has a caller."

The footman stopped at the door. "Is she here? Woman knows how to raise swine. Damned pigs could have sacked London. Treegum said she'd be trouble, but then, females is always trouble, bless 'em."

"Thatcher, you speak in eternal verities." Also in riddles.

Thatcher went mumbling on his way, leaving Stephen alone in the ducal estate office. He was having a much-needed lean against a massive desk, and debating whether to engage in a bit of casual snooping, when the door opened, and a man in a dressing gown and slippers stepped into the room.

An interesting pause ensued, during which Stephen did his best to look harmless and unassuming. The other fellow swept him with an imperious inspection.

"What are you doing in my house and who the hell are you?"

My house?

"Lord Stephen Wentworth, at your service." He pushed away from the desk enough to sketch a bow. "I've brought some clothing for my sister Lady Althea, also some ginger for the patient, in case Althea's remedies occasion dyspepsia."

Stephen could not have named the emotions crossing the

man's countenance. Dismay and consternation flickered in his green eyes, followed by fear or possibly anger. He bore a close resemblance to Rothhaven, both in his features and in the way he held himself, though his complexion was very fair and his eyes a lighter shade of green. He wasn't quite as tall as Rothhaven nor as robust, but he was still a substantial specimen.

"You should never have been allowed into the Hall. This is Thatcher's doing, I take it?"

"He went off in search of toast or the Holy Grail, I'm not sure which. He believes I'm here to discuss quarry stone."

"He believes German George still sits on the throne. You are brother to Lady Althea?"

Stephen took a step forward, thinking to heft the panniers from the floor to the desk, and the man in the dressing gown stepped back. The movement was reflexive, as a groom turning out a horse in a pasture will step away if the horse has been too long confined in a stall.

For in distance lay safety.

"I am her ladyship's younger brother. Are you Master Robbie?" Stephen's host was at least twice as old as any Master Anybody of Stephen's acquaintance.

More complicated emotions went flitting past. "You may call me that, but it's best if you say nothing of this encounter. I'll show you to the library, which is more commodious than this office."

Who was the patient, where was Althea, and what the hell was going on in this household?

Master Robbie led Stephen down another paneled corridor, this one tastefully appointed with flowery landscapes, an interesting collection of scrimshaw carvings, and an occasional porcelain bowl of venerable pedigree.

"Who's this?" Stephen asked, pausing before a portrait

of an old gent in a splendidly embroidered coat and powdered wig. Nothing about the man suggested humor, warmth, or even human frailty. His eyes could have been chips of green ice.

"The old duke. He was hanging in the estate office, but—"

"Treegum! Treegum, where the devil have you got off to!" That sounded like Rothhaven, coming down the main stairs at a good clip. "The patient has eloped, and I refuse to lose my brother twice in two days."

"I'm here," Master Robbie called, which solved one mystery.

A rather large one, while it raised more riddles.

Rothhaven strode up the corridor, then came to an abrupt halt and scowled mightily at Stephen. "What in damnation are *you* doing underfoot?"

The footman, Thatcher, emerged from the kitchen steps at a stately pace, a silver tray in his hands. "And isn't this just the way?" he groused. "I have Cookie put together this lovely tray for the gentleman in the estate office and now you're making off with him. First proper guest we get in donkey's years, and you lot can't leave him be long enough to enjoy a plate of toast. I ought to give my notice, I really ought."

"Now, Thatcher," Rothhaven said quietly, "you know we'd be lost without you."

"I'll just retrieve a book and return to my room," Master Robbie said. "Lord Stephen, a pleasure." He bowed with more dignity than a man in slippers and a dressing gown ought to be able to muster, then departed in the direction of the estate office.

"Into the library," Rothhaven said, holding a paneled door open. "Please."

Stephen limped forward, more entertained than he had been in ages.

"And what am I to do with this tray, I ask you?" Thatcher muttered, following in Stephen's wake. "I'm not getting any younger, and I have better things to do than watch you lot waste good food."

Rothhaven held the door for the footman. "On the reading table, please, Thatcher. I believe it's time for your morning tea break too."

Thatcher set the tray on the table and fairly sprinted for the door. "I do fancy a spot of tea from time to time. Mind you finish every bite, Master Nathaniel."

He closed the door behind him, still muttering, as Stephen took a seat at the reading table.

"So your brother is alive?" Stephen poured two cups of tea and selected a slice of golden toast soaked with butter. "Bit of a pickle, that."

Rothhaven—or Lord Nathaniel?—took the seat at Stephen's elbow. "It's a bloody damned mess and has been for years. You are sworn to secrecy. Pass the jam."

"I don't care for secrets, especially when my sister is entangled in them."

"That is precisely why you will keep your mouth shut. You didn't put any sugar in my tea."

Stephen passed him the sugar bowl. "Sugar it yourself, and tell me what in seven sulfurous hells is going on here."

Rothhaven dropped a lump of sugar into his tea. "It's truly better if you don't know."

"I'll be the judge of that." The toast was wonderful. Cut thicker than bread was usually sliced, done to a turn, still warm, and dripping butter. Nursery food, but then, nurseries were supposed to be happy, healthy places.

Rothhaven stirred his tea and sat back, an odd smile lurking in his eyes. "You really are Althea's brother. I suppose you should hear the tale from me, but you are not to badger Althea for more details. She doesn't have them, and that's for the best too."

"Your front door is manned by Methuselah's great-uncle, you are impersonating a peer of the realm who is very much alive, and exasperated mothers invoke your name as a curse. Who are you to be telling me anything where my sister is concerned?"

Rothhaven's lashes swept down, his head remained bowed for a moment, and in his silence Stephen lit upon the answer to his own question: Rothhaven was the man who'd fallen in love with Lady Althea Wentworth, a woman determined to take her place in society, a woman connected to one of the most prominent—some would say notorious—families in the realm.

While Rothhaven was determined on a life of secrecy and obscurity.

His Pseudo-Grace took a sip of tea—no hurrying this fellow—and set down the cup and saucer. "Who am I? I am the man who will see you ruined if you take the smallest risk with your sister's happiness. You will say nothing of her presence here and nothing of what you've seen. Do have some more toast. It's about the only thing Cook prepares well."

"A fine speech, but a bit of work on the particulars of your threat will make it more convincing." Stephen helped himself to more toast. "Now why have you spent years lying to all of society, pretending to be somebody you are not, and very possibly breaking the law?"

* * *

The seizure came without warning in the darkest hours.

Robbie had dozed off shortly before midnight, his temperature warm but not alarmingly so. Althea remained awake in the chair beside his bed while Rothhaven was across the hall napping. He'd told her that if Robbie had a seizure, there was nothing to do but roll him onto his side and safeguard him from anything that might fall upon him. The bedroom had a double thickness of carpet both because that helped keep Robbie's chambers quiet and because he was less likely to injure himself if he fell to the floor.

When Robbie had awakened, she'd bathed his brow and hands with cool water, something he seemed to enjoy now. If he had any fever it was mild, and his cough was subsiding with regular applications of a honey, lemon, whiskey, and ginger tisane.

He had seemed in every way to be regaining his health.

Althea had been reading aloud to him from *Tom Jones* when she became aware that the bed had begun to tremble. Robbie's expression went from a fixed stare to a faint, and then his limbs commenced to shake. She rolled him to his side—not easy when a large man was thrashing and twitching—and waited a small eternity for the convulsions to cease.

She didn't want to watch, and yet she could not look away. Years ago, on the streets of a bad neighborhood in York, she'd seen an older woman overcome with a seizure right on the walkway. Passersby had stopped and stared, though nobody had offered a word of derision. The woman's daughter had been with her, and when the shaking had stopped, she'd helped her mother to her feet and onto the nearest bench.

This seizure was worse for befalling Robbie in his very

home. The one place where he ought to be able to bar his door against all evils, Robbie was not safe.

He quieted, seeming to fall into a doze while Althea straightened the bedclothes. On Nathaniel's orders, she was not to offer Robbie even water until he was awake and somewhat clear-headed.

"I did not wet myself." He spoke slowly, like an inebriate. "I ought not to say that. Lady present." He was still lying on his side, as if truly felled by strong spirits.

"Would you like to sit up?"

He pushed himself to his back with a great sigh. "I would like to die."

Stephen had said the same thing on many occasions. He'd even made plans to end his life when adolescence had begun changing the body he'd barely learned how to manage as a boy.

"Are you in pain?"

Robbie turned his head on the pillow to regard her. "Not of the physical variety, but for a slight headache."

"Ah, then you are simply feeling sorry for yourself. Shall I fetch your brother so he can feel sorry for you too? Perhaps you'd like the staff to stand about your bed with long faces, muttering prayers for the dying and composing your eulogy."

His smile was like Nathaniel's, but more bitter. "Let my brother sleep. It's the least he deserves, and Nathaniel's pity is unbearable. Tell me about Lord Stephen. How did he acquire that limp?"

The question was intended to shift the focus from Robbie's seizure to something else—anything else. Althea allowed the change in topic because Stephen's situation was relevant.

"Our father broke Stephen's leg when Stephen was four

years old. Stephen was hungry—he was always hungry—
and Papa had filched a loaf of bread from somebody's
windowsill. He enjoyed tormenting his children by eating
in front of them, bite by bite, knowing they longed for
even a stale crust. Sometimes he'd toss a bit of food to the
floor for them to fall upon like stray dogs, sometimes he'd
eat the lot and laugh at the children's silent misery."

She had Robbie's attention. In fact, he looked like he
wished she'd say no more, but Althea denied him that
indulgence.

"On one occasion," she went on, "Stephen refused
to remain silent. A four-year-old boy can hold a lot of
rage, especially when his own father taunts him for being
hungry. He railed at Papa, and Papa—who was perennially
drunk—either tripped over him or purposely stomped on
his leg. In either case, the result was a child better suited
to begging effectively, and Jack Wentworth saw that as an
advantage."

Robbie closed his eyes, which was wise of him. If he
renewed his lamentations regarding a condition that had
befallen many a hapless soul, one to which no shame or
disfigurement ought to attach, Althea would...

She'd do nothing. "I'm sorry," she said. "I know your
situation is not purely a case of the falling sickness, and
you have suffered much." *As has your brother.*

Robbie remained quiet for so long she thought he'd
gone back to sleep. Seizures apparently left him tired as
well as foggy, while Althea was wide awake.

"You refer to your father's children in the third person,"
Robbie said, eyes still closed. "'*They* longed for even a
stale crust.' I cannot set my disability at the same distance,
my lady. At any moment, I can collapse, shaking on
the ground like some helpless, pathetic...Old people still

think the falling sickness is the work of demons, while I regard it as a curse."

Robbie was bedeviled, of a certainty, but the seizures alone were not the problem. "Would you like a drink of water?"

He sat forward. "You do not feel sorry for me."

"I hope I have a normal complement of compassion for anybody afflicted with difficulties." Knowing she would leave in the morning, knowing Robbie's troubles afflicted his brother, their servants, and others outside Rothhaven Hall, Althea's sympathy for Robbie was tempered with frustration. He could have been a duke, could have had his pick of duchesses, taken his place in the Lords, and made a life outside the Hall, or simply lived in quiet obscurity without creating a whirlpool of intrigue and deception.

Her judgment assumed, though, that the man who'd chosen to remain a stranger to the world years ago had also been the same articulate, intelligent, reasonably fit specimen Althea beheld now.

"My choices seem to be self-pity or self-disgust," he said. "When I have good days, I exhort myself to do more and *be* more, and when the good days come along in succession, I start to hope. Hope is a wretched torment. Then another bad day comes, and I'm reduced to . . . well, you've seen the result. I cannot remain upright, I cannot form a complete sentence, and I cannot see past the complicated situation here at the Hall."

"Are you apologizing, Your Grace? If so, then I think the party deserving of your words is asleep across the corridor."

His brows rose.

The form of address had been unintentional, though Althea did not regret it. "My brother Quinn wanted no parts of a title. He was willing to die—horribly—to avoid it, but he'd married his Jane, and he had me, Stephen, and Constance to consider. Quinn is defined by the need to not be what Jack Wentworth was. Petty, selfish, ugly inside and out, a creature without morals. Quinn is a competent duke, but only because he's a spectacularly determined and honorable man. I wish you could meet him."

Althea missed Quinn, which came as something of a shock. He was significantly older than his half siblings, and in Althea's childhood, Quinn had always been off trying to earn coin. And yet, he and Althea had had an alliance, she being the oldest of the children forced to remain in Jack's care. Quinn would slip her the bulk of his pay or leave it in a hiding place she kept secret from Jack.

Quinn had relied on her to shield Stephen and Constance from the worst of Jack's temper, and he'd always let her know how to reach him. He'd shown her how to protect herself from men bent on mischief and told her quite plainly to protect herself from Jack in the same manner if the need arose.

"Having had the pleasure of meeting Lord Stephen," Robbie said, "I can only imagine what the Wentworth patriarch must be like. I do fancy a sip of water, if it wouldn't be too much trouble."

Althea passed him the glass as the clock struck three.

"I see the patient is awake." Nathaniel closed the bedroom door. He wore no coat, only shirtsleeves and waistcoat, but he looked rested and tidy.

"Not much of a patient," Althea said. "I believe the fever has all but departed, leaving only the restlessness of a man on the mend."

Robbie handed her back the glass. "We were enjoying the adventures of young Tom Jones. Perhaps you'd like to pick up where her ladyship left off?" His tone was casual, and apparently the seizure was not to be mentioned.

Althea had kept much from Quinn's notice, unwilling to burden him regarding problems he could not solve. Robbie was clearly intent on the same courtesy where Nathaniel was involved.

"I'll catch a nap," she said, "and plan on leaving in the morning."

"We'll miss you," Robbie replied, while Nathaniel said nothing as he took up the book and assumed the seat Althea had vacated.

* * *

"Trying to sneak away?" Nathaniel asked.

Althea had her basket over her arm, though now the basket was empty. She opened the door to the walled garden and let a gust of damp, dewy air into the house.

"I thought to get home before anybody is abroad. Robbie is all but recovered, and…"

And there's nothing for you here. "And you would never impose," Nathaniel said, "even to ask for an escort onto your own land. Robbie has been snoring peacefully for the past two hours. Let me fetch my cloak." He waited for her to nod before he left her by the side door.

Althea's departure should be a relief. She and her rubbishing nosy brother were a disruption, a disturbance in a routine of privacy that had been established for very good reasons. As Robbie lay dozing the night away, Nathaniel had reviewed those reasons and still found them compelling.

Robbie was not well in body or mind, at least some of the time.

Enlightened thinkers attached no stigma to the falling sickness, but much of society remained downright backward about any illness, muttering about tainted blood, curses, and worse. If Althea could be ridiculed for years simply because she had humble origins or held her fan incorrectly, Robbie would face even worse judgment.

And for Nathaniel himself?

He snatched his cloak from a peg in the foyer, grabbed Althea's straw hat, and trotted back to her side rather than ponder his deserts. What became of him did not matter in the slightest, except that Robbie needed and deserved an ally. The staff needed and deserved guidance.

"You waited," he said, passing Althea her straw hat.

"The morning has obliged us with a mist. I will not be seen crossing the fields."

A mist, less than a true fog. "We'd best be going, then." He did not offer his arm, he did not take her hand. The morning air was brisk, but did nothing to clear his head.

"Robbie had a seizure last night, didn't he?" Nathaniel said as they crossed the garden.

"Why do you ask?"

Althea was back to being the cool, self-possessed lady he'd met at Lynley Vale, and that was for the best.

"Robbie always sleeps without moving after a fit, and he was too cheerful about Tom Jones's tiresome behavior."

They reached the garden gate. Althea opened the door with no assistance from Nathaniel and marched right on through it.

"Was Tom's behavior tiresome, or was he born into a tiresome society?" Althea rejoined. "When a wealthy squire doesn't know who his own nephew is, when lawlessness and licentiousness are held up as amusing, when a hanging is supposed to be hilarious...I believe Mr. Fielding must have been a savagely angry man, and rightly so."

Althea was savagely angry, and rightly so, while Nathaniel was...annoyed, but resigned. He'd been annoyed but resigned for so long the habit fit him like old boots.

"Things have changed some since Fielding's day," Nathaniel said. Outside the garden, the mist was thinning. Althea's decision to depart early had been wise and considerate, though some small, selfish part of Nathaniel wanted to carry her back into the Hall and beg her to bide there just a little bit longer.

Never, ever beg. What fool had said that? "What will you do with yourself today, Althea?"

She slanted a glance at him, half-amused, half-exasperated. "I will be interrogated by Stephen and Milly, and refuse them any information relating to you, Robbie, or the Hall. How much did you tell Stephen?"

"The basics. Robbie was and is in no fit state to be the duke, his death was believed genuine because my father made it seem so, the situation is in hand provided..."

Provided nothing ever changed. Annoyance acquired an edge of despair.

"I will probably spend the day going over my books," Althea said. "I will hear the latest family news from Stephen, and I will take a nap."

How Nathaniel wished he'd seen her bedroom, the better to picture her cuddled beneath her own covers.

"What else will you do with your day?" Nathaniel's question was selfish. He wanted to envision Althea resuming her normal life, chatting with her tenants, beating her companion at cribbage. He *needed* to see her thus in his mind's eye.

"I've lately had callers," she said. "Viscount Ellenbrook

and Miss Price. I believe Miss Price is supposed to be tossing her cap at Ellenbrook, but she's noticed Stephen. Her aunt seems particularly desperate to get her fired off."

"Do you underestimate your brother's charms?"

"Not in the least, but Stephen well knows the difference between flirtation and courtship. He excels at the former, while the latter frightens him witless."

They passed the orchard on its hill, dark limbs stark against the thinning mist.

"Lord Stephen strikes me as excessively courageous, to the point of recklessness. Why would courtship frighten him?"

Althea picked up her pace. "Because courtship ought to frighten anybody who can admit to human frailties. We are none of us lovable all the time, and Stephen can be exceedingly difficult. What ails Miss Price that Lady Phoebe should be so ruthless about making a match for her? Miss Price is pretty, agreeable, and quite young, but I gather Lady Phoebe is my enemy because I might steal one of her niece's prospects."

Perhaps Althea was punishing Nathaniel with this topic, perhaps she was simply airing any subject to keep the conversation from wandering off into impossible declarations.

"Miss Price's parents had been married only six months at the time of her birth," Nathaniel said. "My mother's companion remarked that matter more than once."

"Such a situation is far from unusual."

"True, but Mr. Price had been abroad until three weeks before the wedding, and the ceremony happened by special license."

"Oh, dear. Have you any idea who her father might be?"

Althea already knew the worst of the Rothmere family

secrets, and she needed to know as much as possible about the sources of Lady Phoebe's spite.

"Miss Price is my half sister. Papa was indiscreet. Lady Phoebe is doubtless concerned that even ducal anteced-ents, when irregular, will limit Sybil's chances should they become widely known."

Althea came to an abrupt halt. "A *duke* had an irregular liaison with a proper young woman?"

"A duke's brother has had a liaison with you, Althea, and you are of higher station than an earl's wayward daughter."

She patted his lapel. "If I am with child, don't expect me to marry the baronet of your choosing, Nathaniel. Though as to that, I will swill pennyroyal tea three times a day until conception is ruled out."

"Sensible of you." Just as *coitus interruptus* had been sensible of him, but when had behaving with unrelenting good sense become a cardinal virtue?

The day he'd learned Robbie was alive and immured in that detestable madhouse, that's when.

The mist thinned more as Nathaniel and Althea topped the rise, the wisps of white remaining mostly by the river and in the folds of the rolling fields.

"You should leave me here," she said. "I know the way."

"I'll walk you to your own property, if it's all the same to you."

By now, Nathaniel should be inured to the toll common sense took on his spirit. He'd learned to ignore loneli-ness, the fearful glances of small children, the gossip and speculation of his neighbors, the sheer boredom of seldom leaving his own land, the tedium of dealing with aging retainers. The never-ending frustration of Robbie's limitations.

He had the litany memorized: *You are in good health. You want for nothing. You can do any one of a thousand things, and yet you pine for the seventeen things you must not do. Your only brother has been returned to you from the dead and he is making progress. Stop whining.*

But the lecture refused to subdue his aching heart. Another litany was taking its place: *I want to walk through the market with Althea, holding hands and inspiring a different kind of gossip. I want to ride with her over the moors. I want to lie down beside her at night and feel her snuggle up out of habit. I want to raise children with her.*

"I will miss you, Nathaniel."

"I will miss you as well."

She kept on walking, until the stone wall separating the properties came into view. "This is hard. I am good at the hard things. I can smile at the people who insult me Season after Season. I can sit calmly while my older brother is accused of taking the life of a man he only tried to help. All I ever wanted as a girl was for somebody to pick me a few violets, and I contrived well enough without such a bouquet. I can go three days without eating and barely feel it. I can watch Stephen lurching and raging through life and be the sister he needs me to be. But this…"

"I'm sorry, Althea." More than his own heartache, Nathaniel regretted causing her this pain.

"Don't be," she said. "Don't ever, ever be sorry that for a few hours, you had what you wanted and needed. Heartaches fade, I'm told, but that memory—of being with somebody who valued me for my true self, not for how well I waltz, flirt, and wear jewels—will sustain me through much. I am not sorry. I thank you for it."

They came to the stile, and Althea climbed the steps. Nathaniel caught her hand, unconvinced by her speech, though it offered some comfort. She was putting a brave face on matters, and at some point, she would recover her balance and renew her search for a match that was all she deserved.

"Ellenbrook is accounted a decent fellow, Althea."

The mist had cleared away here, leaving a soft, golden dawn. A lone robin sang from the tree line, while a cowbell tinkled in the distance. Spring had arrived, which only made the moment of parting more difficult.

"*You* are a decent fellow," Althea said, peering down at him and slipping her arms around his neck. "Beyond decent."

All the unease inside Nathaniel went still while he savored one more moment of what he needed and wanted. He held Althea close, recalling tenderness, warmth, humor, all the good, dear wonders they'd shared so briefly.

He brushed a kiss to her cheek, only that.

"Farewell, Lord Nathaniel Rothmere." Althea had recalled his wish, and she was smiling at him as she held him loosely. "Be as happy as you can and know that I will remember you with joy."

He must be the gentleman, must be the one to step back, but Althea was too quick for him. She scampered down the steps on the far side of the wall and marched off across her own pasture without looking back.

Such strength she had. Such decency and determination. "Farewell, Althea," he said to her retreating form. "Farewell, my love."

Chapter Fourteen

Lady Phoebe awoke as the coach rattled over the rise that led down to the village. Yesterday had been long, dealing with the endless preparations necessary before making the trek into York with Sybil.

The effort had been worth the bother. Ellenbrook had paid Sybil just the right amount of attention, enough that the other guests at the ball had noticed, not enough to cause talk. Sybil had been resplendent in a gown fashioned for her in London last year, one that still passed for *à la mode* here in the north.

Best of all, Lady Althea had not been among the attendees.

The dancing had gone on until three in the morning, the final buffet had been lavish, and Phoebe could count the excursion a victory. Ellenbrook was making the journey on horseback, which meant Phoebe and Sybil had the coach to themselves.

"You're awake," Sybil said, from the opposite bench. "How you can sleep in a moving coach is beyond me."

"You took a nap yesterday afternoon, while I did not. Did you enjoy the ball, Sybil?"

The required answer was yes. *Yes, Aunt. I had a wonderful time, thanks to you.* Sybil was at a dangerous age, when youthful confidence had yet to be tempered by bitter experience. She did not see the near disaster of her mother's indiscretion for the liability it was because the man Sybil called Father loved her and doted on her.

Less doting and larger settlements would have served the girl better.

"I enjoyed standing up with Ellenbrook," she said. "He's a fine dancer. Mr. Petersham is droll and has a merry smile. Why do you suppose Lord Stephen and Lady Althea were not among the guests? Lady Stebbins considers herself quite the hostess, and she's sure to have sent them an invitation."

"Mr. Petersham hasn't a feather to fly with. As for Lady Althea and her brother, nobody knew her brother was due to pay a visit, and Lady Althea is simply *not good ton*."

Sybil left off admiring the countryside. "She is the sister of a duke. How can Lady Stebbins be good *ton* if she's snubbing a ducal family with its seat right here in Yorkshire?"

"Don't be impertinent. Just because I have been willing to overlook Lady Althea's reputation doesn't mean she can expect that kindness from everybody else."

The morning sun had broken the horizon, revealing the same dreary cows, sheep, and rolling green fields it had been revealing for every day of Phoebe's life. She was abruptly impatient with Sybil, and with the conversation.

"Recall what I told the vicar, Sybil. A young woman

dwelling without the protection of her family must have a particular care for her standing. Raising ill-behaved swine, marching about unescorted, wearing bright colors, and thwarting the rules of decorum are not the done thing. I hope Vicar can have a quiet word with her ladyship, or with Lord Stephen, and see her returned to her family's loving care."

Far, far away from Yorkshire.

"Aunt, you tried your hardest to spill tea on Lady Althea so she'd have to leave your dinner party early, and you're criticizing *her* for bad behavior? She never leaves her property unescorted that I know of, she has a companion in residence, she's biding at a family estate, and she looks good in bright colors. What do you have against her?"

Phoebe itched to slap Sybil's face, but that would only inspire more of this lamentable contrariness.

"I have nothing against her. I wish her well, in fact, but she must learn to keep to her place. That place is not flirting with young men who ought to be currying your favor or seeking the attentions of *properly* reared young women."

To emphasize the point, Phoebe reached over and pulled down the shade on Sybil's side of the coach. The sun was no friend to an Englishwoman's complexion, nor did it treat coach upholstery kindly.

As Phoebe sat back, a pair of figures across the pasture caught her eye. She hooked the shade closed on Sybil's side of the coach while leaving her own shade up.

A man and a woman stood at a stile perhaps seventy yards from the road, the lady on the steps, the man standing quite close and holding her hand. While Phoebe watched, an embrace ensued, shocking not for its carnal nature— kissing on the cheek was merely kissing on the cheek—

but for the intimacy conveyed. These two were lovers, or all but, and they were parting at dawn.

The woman strode away, across Lady Althea Wentworth's fields. Phoebe knew that proud posture, knew that bold stride. The gentleman was something of a mystery. Tall, broad-shouldered, bare-headed, attired in black despite the early hour. He remained for a moment watching the woman's retreat, and then he turned his steps in the direction of Rothhaven Hall.

"That cannot be," Phoebe murmured.

"I beg your pardon, Aunt?"

"Nothing. Try to rest, dear. A lady must always look her finest, and the late-night entertainments can take a toll."

Was His Grace of Rothhaven trifling with a young woman from a family of means? Lady Althea was not exactly from a *good* family, but she wasn't of the lower orders, either.

Not now.

Like father, like son? Lady Phoebe sat back, mind awhirl with possibilities. Driving Althea Wentworth from the shire—from ever showing her face in polite society again— had just become child's play. At the very least, a note to the Duchess of Rothhaven was in order. A mother ought to be kept informed regarding her son's poor judgment, and perhaps the Duchess of Walden would appreciate a discreet note regarding Lady Althea's rash behavior as well.

* * *

The Hall seemed a hundred miles distant as Nathaniel wandered home under the rising sun. He tarried in the orchard, recalling a blossom-scented kiss. He tarried in the garden, where he'd first taken tea with Althea.

He did not want to go inside the Hall, did not want to deal with Thatcher's endless offers of toast, and—God forgive him—he did not want to deal with his beloved brother.

He sank onto the bench where he and Althea had shared a pot of tea, the morning sun gilding a riot of spring flowers. Reclaiming the garden had begun as the duchess's project, her rebellion against a cheerless and lonely marriage. She'd recruited her small sons to assist her, kidnapping them from their studies and daring the old duke to deny his family a few hours of fresh air and frolic.

Robbie had learned the rudiments of painting out here, at a time when Nathaniel had been considered too young to attempt artistic graces. How he'd envied his older brother those hours of instruction.

"There you are." Robbie, fully clothed, freshly shaved, and looking entirely well, stood on the terrace with a steaming mug in his hand. "Enjoying the sunrise?"

Not in the least. "I saw Lady Althea onto her own land before the rest of the world could remark her comings and goings. How are you?"

Robbie descended the steps and joined Nathaniel on the bench, though all Nathaniel wanted in that moment was solitude—and Althea Wentworth.

"I am...restless, I suppose. How soon can we extend this garden to the orchard?"

"That project, with available resources, will take the summer at least. Old men do not wrestle stone so easily. I could hire more laborers from the village, but that would mean strangers working close to the Hall. In the alternative, the quarry could deliver the stone here instead of to the home farm, but again, that brings strangers into proximity with the Hall."

Robbie took a sip of his tea. "You are angry."

"Frustrated. You encountered a stranger by the river, Robbie, and thank God you did. You are the better for having met Lady Althea, admit it."

"I would have recovered with or without her—"

"We had *no supplies*," Nathaniel shot back. "We had no willow bark tea, no ginger, and precious little feverfew because our housekeeper has grown lax with age. The staff cannot be trusted to remain awake in a sickroom over-night. Thatcher has become a problem, but he cannot be pensioned, and I am only one person."

Something has to change. Nathaniel stopped short of that difficult truth because Robbie was gazing intently across the garden. He took another sip of his tea, which put to rout the notion that he was having a staring spell.

"I would set up a household on the Continent," he said, "but how does one hire trustworthy staff in a foreign country?"

That was as close as Robbie would come to admitting a dependence on Nathaniel, and yet, that dependence shaped both of their lives.

"I want to question Soames, and I'd like you to be present," Nathaniel said.

"Because of the notes."

"Somebody knows how we're going on here, and they will not keep the information to themselves. I expect a blackmail demand any day." Another reason that Althea had to return to her own life, where her greatest challenge was dodging Phoebe Philpot's sniping.

"We're rich," Robbie said, setting his mug on the walk-way. "We can spare a few pounds to keep somebody's mouth shut."

The words sounded arrogant and selfish, but Nathaniel could hear the worry beneath them. "We aren't rich enough to endure a lifetime of such demands, particularly when we don't know from whom they could be coming. Can you make a list of any staff you recall from your time in Soames's care?"

Robbie appeared to consider a bed of irises not yet in bloom. "I remember them all. In the entirety of my time away, I had no more than a dozen staff assigned to me, but what's to say the housekeeper or groundskeeper at the madhouse didn't get to gossiping with my attendants? Mrs. Soames had the actual running of the place and she had family in the area."

"What of the other patients?" Nathaniel asked. "Did any of them know your situation?"

"I doubt it. *I* didn't know the particulars of my own situation, after all." Robbie crossed his legs, the posture elegant and relaxed. "If they did become aware of matters here at the Hall, they would never betray me, nor I them.

"They aren't imprisoned anymore, you know," he went on more softly. "I correspond with several of them each year at Yuletide, though they know me only as Mr. Robbie Roth, which was how Soames referred to me when last names were unavoidable. I am most familiar with Alexander Morton, and he keeps me informed regarding the rest. He was the other epileptic, and Soames studied the degree to which our seizures coincided."

"Did they?"

"Only rarely, and never exactly. I fail to see how anybody at the asylum other than Soames or his wife could know I was pronounced dead. Somebody apparently signed a death certificate, true, but nothing in my routine changed. *Nobody* became aware I had been declared dead."

"You're suggesting the malefactor is at or near the Hall. Somebody knew exactly why His Grace was sending money to Soames and knew the money did not stop with your *tragic demise*. They knew His Grace was too tight-fisted to make ongoing charitable donations, and they don't care how revealing the truth affects either us or the staff."

Strong drink early in the day was never well advised, but Nathaniel was tempted. Sorely tempted.

"How well do you trust Sorenson?" Robbie asked.

"A fair question." With no reliable answer. "If he's intent on betraying us, why now? You had last rites more than three years ago." After a particularly bad seizure, which had rendered Robbie insensate for hours. The housekeeper had sent for the vicar because Nathaniel had been on a rare journey into York with Treegum.

He and Treegum hadn't both been away from the Hall at the same time since.

"Perhaps the vicar has marital aspirations," Robbie said. "A spot of the ready would improve his options."

"He's quite comfortably well-off." Which should have been a relief, but then, the vicar was also quite single and a perfectly charming man, damn the luck.

Robbie smacked Nathaniel on the arm. "Vicars don't offer for the sisters of dukes."

"Vicars are considered gentlemen, and our vicar has well-placed connections in Denmark." Very well placed. "What shall we do about questioning Soames?"

"He was in failing health, last I heard, and his missus has already gone to her reward—or her punishment. The last patient left the estate years ago."

Robbie was withholding details, but that he had kept an eye on his former jailer should not have surprised Nathaniel.

"How do you know this?"

"The old duke was forever prying and spying, Nathaniel." Robbie took up his tea. "You were the son spared the weight of the titleholder's worst stratagems. Papa believed that knowledge was power, and he acquired knowledge about the neighbors, his parliamentary foes, and his employees while appearing to keep himself aloof from one and all. I have had the leisure to read his diaries, and you would be appalled at the extent of his intelligence gathering."

"You need not elaborate. A man who will have his own son declared dead is an affront to decency. Will you accompany me to call on Soames?"

The question was mostly rhetorical, and something of a courtesy. Robbie was the damned duke, whether the world knew him as such or not, and he was also best positioned to question a doctor who'd grown rich off polite society's secrets.

"Nathaniel..." Robbie rose and strolled the walk, hands in his pockets. "I want to go with you. I want to ride about the moors as you do, I want to attend the assemblies if only to stand around swilling bad punch and speaking too loudly to the dowagers. I want..."

He wanted a normal life, as did Nathaniel. "You are making progress, Robbie. You walked down to the river for six months without a mishap."

Robbie slanted a glance at Nathaniel over his shoulder. "Then I had a spectacular mishap, one might even say a near disaster. If Lady Althea hadn't happened along..."

"The staff would have eventually said something." Nathaniel hoped they would. He'd been ready to sack the lot of them for their torn loyalties, though.

"Eventually? Just as you eventually found me among Soames's collection of cast-off heirs and genteel oddities?

What if you'd shrugged at the stray invoice from a remote establishment out on the moors, Nathaniel? What if, like Treegum, you had assumed Papa simply supported a charity and you decided you'd keep up the tradition?"

"What if you'd never fallen from your horse?" Nathaniel hadn't posed the question aloud before, but both he and Robbie had doubtless wondered the same thing.

"I'm quits with the jaunts to the river," Robbie said, resuming his place on the bench. "Interesting experiment, but it did not end well."

A month ago, even a few days ago, Nathaniel would have agreed. He'd seen Althea Wentworth march away, though, never to return, and something or somebody at Rothhaven Hall needed to change.

"You appear to be hale and whole. While I grant you that wandering alone near water was a risk, anybody can turn an ankle when enjoying the countryside. Next time take a cane and don't go so close to the water. Lady Althea owns the land, and she will see to it that you can wander in solitude."

Robbie dumped the remainder of his tea into the crushed shells of the walkway. "I think not. I've begun reading the correspondence, Nathaniel. You go through it, make notes for Treegum, then set it aside. I can't step into your shoes, but I can try to lighten your load or at least remain informed. I'm not spying on you."

"We live in each other's pockets, Robbie. If you'd like to take over the correspondence, please do. I bloody hate it." Most of all, Nathaniel hated the regular reports to their mother, though another report was in order.

"You've been pre-occupied these past two days, so while you were seeing Lady Althea home, I went through the mail on your desk."

Nathaniel's pleasure at Robbie's initiative was tempered by experience. Robbie was bored, and correspondence would soon lose its novelty. Three months from now, this interest in estate business might well fade or be supplemented by some other "experiment."

"Did you find anything requiring a ducal signature?"

"I can match your signature easily, but no. I did, though, find another threatening note."

"Splendid." How could such a pretty morning hold so much disappointment and botheration? "Immediately after breakfast, I'm off to interview Soames." *Come with me.* Nathaniel had already asked, he would not ask again.

"Let me know what you find." Robbie shook the last drops from his empty mug and headed back to the terrace. He paused on the steps. "I know you deserve more from me, Nathaniel. I don't know if I'm capable of more."

He continued into the house without giving Nathaniel a chance to reply.

* * *

"I have had the most extraordinary week." Phoebe made that announcement before Elspeth Weatherby could launch into a recounting of the same gossip Elspeth had shared last week.

And the week before.

Elspeth was not the brightest soul, nor was she welcome in exalted circles—her father had been a mere baron—but she did like to chatter, bless her, and Phoebe had known Elspeth would be making her weekly visit to the village subscription library on Wednesday afternoon.

"Extraordinary, my lady? I heard that your Sybil took Lord Ellenbrook to pay a call on Lady Althea Wentworth.

Very gracious of your dear niece, when Lady Althea is such an unknown quantity."

"Not unknown, my friend." Phoebe leaned closer, though other than Elspeth, only deaf old Mrs. Peabody occupied the library. "Lady Althea is *unaccepted*."

"But Lady Althea goes to Town every spring, and I have it on very good authority that she's invited everywhere. I have been meaning to call on her, truly I have, especially now that her brother is biding with her."

Elspeth had two daughters of marriageable age. Of course she'd be inspired to call on Lord Stephen Wentworth when she'd never bothered to more than greet Lady Althea in the churchyard.

"Let's take a turn on the green, Elspeth."

Elspeth tossed her book into the returns box. "Such lovely weather today, it would be a shame not to take the air."

True enough. The village was finally donning spring finery, to the best of its hopelessly rural ability. The window boxes overflowed with heartsease and the walkways were lined with tulips. The row of four giant oaks down the middle of the green was leafing out from the pinkish stage into the luminous hue of new apples.

"Such a pretty time of year," Elspeth said, linking arms with Phoebe. "And I hope your week was extraordinary in a good way, my lady."

"Sybil is getting on very well with Lord Ellenbrook. I would not say they are smitten, you understand, but then, young people today are so serious."

"Lord Ellenbrook seems a most agreeable gentleman."

"You should invite him and Sybil to dine, Elspeth." The more a young man was treated as half of a couple, the more he imagined himself as such. "Your girls would find him delightful and Sybil needs the company of other wellborn young ladies."

"Was that why she called on Lady Althea? She's growing lonely? Yorkshire is lovely, but it's not London."

Elspeth had had a London Season, though her girls had not as yet. Mr. Solomon Weatherby was a wealthy, much-respected solicitor who had the ear of many an influential family, but his choice of profession meant neither he nor his offspring could be presented at court.

Such a pity. Phoebe's own husband was a solicitor as well, which situation had its consolations, meager though such consolations were.

"Your comment," Phoebe said, as they rounded the end of the green across from the church, "raises the question of why Lady Althea did not fly south to London as she usually does. I have made inquiries."

"Inquiries? Do tell."

The curate waved to them from the church steps. He was a frightfully friendly young man, much in need of the civilizing influence of a wife. As with most curates, he could not afford a wife, alas.

"Like you," Phoebe said, "I found it curious that the sister of a duke would choose to bide here in dreary old Yorkshire when she's welcome in Mayfair, but Elspeth, I am shocked to report to you that Lady Althea *did not take*. Rather spectacularly."

Phoebe managed to inject a note of dismay into her tone, as if London had no business turning up its nose at Yorkshire aristocracy.

"Society can be so unfair," Elspeth replied, "though sometimes, society's censure is warranted." A touch of hope colored that last observation.

"I am told Lady Althea's behavior in London has been

above reproach, but the poor woman is simply not suited to genteel entertainments. She's clumsy, she laughs too loudly, she has no grace with the fan, glove, or parasol, and her dancing has an unnatural quality of enthusiasm."

Phoebe had made up that last part, though what was clumsiness, besides ungainly enthusiasm? Apparently Phoebe wasn't the only hostess to consider a judiciously spilled beverage appropriate in Lady Althea's case.

"We cannot all be paragons," Elspeth observed as they passed the blacksmith's shop. The acrid stink of the forge was unavoidable, but must every idle male in the shire stand about chattering and smoking the afternoon away? Several of them touched their hat brims as Phoebe and Elspeth passed, and Elspeth nodded at them in response.

We cannot all be paragons, indeed. "I am inclined to believe that Lady Althea simply met with the natural reception society reserves for the less genteelly reared. She might be a duke's sister now, but her upbringing was most unfortunate."

"So I've heard," Elspeth said, "and yet, you won't see *me* snubbing a ducal family. Mr. Weatherby would say they have a way of snubbing you back at the worst moments."

"Elspeth, I applaud your pragmatism and know you to be the most charitable of women besides. An awkward fit with London society alone should not see a woman judged harshly here in the shires, but then I happened to glimpse Lady Althea on my way home from York the other morning."

"Was she out riding with Lord Stephen? I've heard he manages quite well in the saddle despite his infirmity."

"She was on foot, walking along the wall where her land marches with Rothhaven's." Phoebe waited until they were well past the smithy. "She was not alone, Elspeth, and the sun was barely up."

"She has a companion, a perfectly agreeable woman. I've traded recipes with her. Millicent—"

"Lady Althea *was with a man*, and they exchanged *a most shocking embrace*."

Elspeth came to a dead stop. "A man? There aren't any men on that side of the village. There's Rothhaven Hall and then the moors. I suppose Vicar's hikes can take him out that direction, but he's getting past the shocking-embrace years."

"Does it matter who the fellow was? Lady Althea is an unmarried woman old enough to know better. She's attempting to gain acceptance in local society, and she acts *like that*, in full view of the road. I can only imagine that such untoward behavior is why London society did not warm to her."

"You didn't get any sort of look at the fellow?"

"He was tall, attired all in black, and he strode away in the direction of Rothhaven Hall." Phoebe gazed off across the green, doing her best to look puzzled beyond all vexation. "I haven't any idea who he might be."

Elspeth patted her arm. "Then you are a hopeless gudgeon, my friend. I know of one man who exclusively wears black, who's abroad only at dawn and dusk, and who would dare cross Rothhaven land, and that is the duke himself."

Dear Elspeth. Dear, reliable Elspeth. "Elspeth Weatherby, that is simply not possible."

"Rothhaven threatens to bring trespassing charges against anybody who sets foot on his property, and he's tall. He wears black, and you of all people know how little regard a randy duke has for propriety, particularly a randy Duke of Rothhaven. Like father, like son, don't they say?"

Phoebe resumed walking, her pique genuine. "Mind your tongue, Elspeth."

"I don't mean to be unkind," Elspeth said, falling in step beside her. "I'm simply presenting the relevant evidence. You saw His Grace of Rothhaven in a shocking embrace with Lady Althea Wentworth, and at a scandalously early hour. You must say nothing about this, of course, except perhaps to seek Vicar's guidance on the matter after you've searched your conscience thoroughly. A young woman's reputation hangs in the balance and her older brother isn't on hand to curb her reckless impulses."

What Elspeth meant was, Phoebe should keep this vignette to herself so Elspeth could spread the tale first.

"I hadn't thought to bring the matter to Vicar's attention."

"I believe you must. Lady Althea has no one to counsel her, and she's likely unaware of the example the late duke set for his son. Vicar can have a word with Lord Stephen if he's not inclined to confront her ladyship directly."

Their circuit of the green was nearly complete, and Phoebe's objective all but accomplished. "You are so sensible, Elspeth, and I am so glad we ran into each other. You will invite Ellenbrook to dine, won't you?"

"Of course. Friday suits. I'll send over an invitation."

"And do include Sybil. She would love to see your girls."

"Yes, Sybil too. I must be off. No rest for the weary! Please give my regards to Vicar."

"Certainly, my dear. Certainly."

Elspeth bustled away to her pony cart, while Phoebe considered the relative merits of consulting with Vicar Sorenson sooner rather than later. If she didn't apprise the vicar of what she'd seen, Elspeth would eventually mention it, and then Vicar's reaction to the situation would be harder to gauge.

"No time like the present," Phoebe muttered, turning her steps once again toward the church.

* * *

"You plan to eradicate poverty from Yorkshire with an army of piglets," Vicar Sorenson said. "Now you make a foe of illiteracy as well. Might I have another cup?"

He'd asked Althea to pour out, though she suspected he was trying to distract her from the purpose for her call. Pietr Sorenson had a friendly gaze and quietly charming ways, but he was nonetheless shrewd. She obliged and topped up her own cup.

"Illiteracy is a formidable enemy, Vicar. I've seen its ravages firsthand."

He accepted his tea, his fingers brushing hers, though he appeared not to notice. "Did you come late to your letters?"

"I was eight years old before an elderly woman who lived in our alley took it upon herself to teach me the rudiments. I picked up the rest myself and passed along what I knew to my younger siblings. A child who can read is..."

Vicar sipped his tea, apparently content to let the silence expand to the proportions of the Yorkshire sky over the moors.

"A child who can read has a skill others will pay her for," Althea said. "She can learn to linger at the door of the posting inn when the mail arrives and offer to read letters for those whose eyesight is dim or who haven't the ability to read. She need not beg for spare pennies."

"I see."

Althea rose because she need not sit like a penitent at confession either. Nathaniel had taught her that.

"You do not see. The present Duke of Walden came late to his letters, as you put it. A cousin who was a teacher eventually instructed him, though by then my brother was in domestic service. His Grace learned to read and write with the same ferocious tenacity he brings to everything, but his lack of education has always bedeviled him. Walden escaped a life in livery only because he'd become literate, and because even a boy who can't read can become highly proficient with numbers."

Quinn also had a gargantuan memory, which Cousin Duncan, who had taught him to read, said was typical of the illiterate. Unable to record any part of life in written form, they carried it in their heads instead.

"So you want to open circulating schools," Vicar said, sipping his tea with all the complacence of a dowager at her tatting.

"If half of Wales can learn to read because of the tenacity of one preacher, certainly I can take on a few of York's worst alleys." This compulsion to *do something*, to engage the world constructively, had grown since Althea had turned her back on Nathaniel nearly a week ago. She'd forbidden herself to walk by the river at any hour, and she'd closed all the curtains on the windows that looked out on Rothhaven land.

She'd even let Milly and Stephen talk her into planning a ball, of all the demented notions, but her interest in entertaining, in anything social whatsoever, had sunk to a new nadir. Her energies were absorbed in grieving a future with Nathaniel that could never be. Finding a distraction from that sorrow had grown imperative.

"I will speak to my colleagues in York," Vicar said. "Give me a fortnight. How do you fare otherwise, my lady?"

What was he asking?

"You look surprised at the question," he said, setting his teacup aside. "I am more than just a brilliant biblical orator, you know, more than the agreeable fellow to make up the numbers at Squire Annen's dinners." His tone was humorous rather than bitter. "I am your neighbor, and I know that you've chosen to bide at Lynley Vale rather than join your family in London this spring. I suspect that's why Lord Stephen has troubled himself to visit. He's worried about you, as others might be."

Others, *meaning Pietr Sorenson*?

"I am well." *Except for a severe case of heartache.* "Stephen's company enlivens life at Lynley Vale, though he's a younger brother." Or he used to be. Now he was a gentleman of independent means and a very independent nature. Althea could no longer guess his thoughts, just as she could no longer carry him piggyback through the backstreets of York.

Another peculiar sorrow.

"Would you tell me if you were lonely?" Vicar asked, leaning forward in his chair. "Most widowers are well acquainted with the condition. We know the temptation of the brandy decanter, of ill-advised company, of self-pity. One needn't lose a loved one to fall prey to the same dismal comforts."

He bore the scent of lavender, a pleasant, brisk fragrance that suited him. Althea hoped she could avail herself of Pietr Sorenson's embrace and find a purely platonic hug, though he'd mentioned loneliness, and lonely people did not make the soundest of decisions.

She turned to gaze out the window, and what should she see but the Rothhaven walled orchard on the top of the hill beyond the common.

"I appreciate your concern," she said, "but you will be pleased to know that my brother and my companion have talked me into hosting an entertainment later in the month. We are all awhirl at the Vale, planning this great event, and you will soon receive your invitation."

He rose as any good host would. "I will be pleased to accept. Won't you finish your tea?"

"No, thank you. I must be off to the lending library. Mrs. Peabody says the inventory could use some refreshing, and I have the means to address that situation." Althea wanted out of Vicar's pleasant little parlor, away from the sense of unrelenting gentility his household wore like a favorite shawl.

The housekeeper appeared in the parlor's open doorway. Her usually cheerful countenance looked worried.

"I am sorry to interrupt, Vicar, but a situation has arisen requiring your attention."

"A busy day," he said, his smile back in evidence. "Lady Phoebe did me the great honor of calling upon me earlier, and now somebody has doubtless had a spat with a sweetheart. A vicar's work is never done."

"You like it that way," Althea said as he walked her to the front door. "You like being constantly faced with challenges, like making a contribution that's seldom acknowledged."

"And you," he said, holding up her cloak, "learned to read far more than mere books. I admire you tremendously, you know." He went about fastening the frogs of her cloak, as if Althea permitted anybody *ever* to assume that familiarity. "You don't simply sing the hymns, you exemplify the teachings."

One could not bat at a vicar's hands as if he were a presuming brother, so Althea tolerated his assistance.

"Literacy matters, Vicar. It can matter a very great deal."

He stepped back, his gaze conveying that he knew exactly what point she made. "A system of circulating schools in an urban situation will take some thought."

"I know. Because the impact could be faster and far greater than what was accomplished over decades in the Welsh countryside. All the more reason to be about it." She dipped a curtsy and bid him good day, uncertain what, exactly, to make of the encounter.

Sorenson was a good man, mature, intelligent, handsome in a severe Nordic way, and possessed of a sense of humor. Althea was almost certain he'd been flirting with her, but then again, her inability to gauge flirtation accurately was yet another of her many social shortcomings.

She spent nearly an hour with Mrs. Peabody going over the lending library's inventory and hearing stories of Mrs. P's girlhood. That courtesy meant Althea stayed a good thirty minutes longer in the village than she'd planned to. For that reason, and that reason only, Althea chose for her homeward trek the trail that crossed a corner of Rothhaven land, rather than return to Lynley Vale by the lanes.

She was passing through a copse of slender, greening birches when she became aware that she was not alone on the path.

Chapter Fifteen

Wilhelmina had read the letter twice and knew she would read it many more times.

"Bad news, Your Grace?" Sarah asked, her needle moving in a steady rhythm.

"I hardly know what to make of it." Wilhelmina removed the spectacles she'd begun wearing for close work more than a year ago.

"Is His Grace in good health?"

"If Nathaniel were suffering an ague, food poisoning, and a festering bullet wound, he would admit to being slightly under the weather, no more." In that, he was like his father. All quiet frustration and determination, though Nathaniel—thus far—hadn't his father's arrogance or temper.

Robbie had had a seizure by the river. Nathaniel's description had been oblique, mentioning only a *valued member of the household*, but his code was easy for a mother to decipher. Robbie had apparently made a regular habit of leaving Rothhaven's walls. He'd not told his brother of his adventures, and he'd nearly come to grief as a result.

"What do we know of a Lady Althea Wentworth?" Wilhelmina asked.

Sarah put down her embroidery hoop. "Little, besides what every common gossip knows. The Wentworths rose to prominence more than five years ago, when the oldest brother inherited the Walden ducal title. He already had significant wealth as a result of successful banking activities, but there was that business with Newgate too."

"Lady Althea is from *that* Wentworth family?" The ducal heir had been imprisoned—wrongly, or so the story went—and nearly executed. The College of Arms had named him the successor to the Walden title, and society had been faced with the conundrum of what to do with a ducal family of exceedingly humble and colorful origins.

"The very one. The duke has a younger brother and a male cousin, but no heir of the body as yet."

"The family is from York, are they not?" Wilhelmina had known the previous Duke of Walden, a spry old gent who'd smelled of camphor and put little store in decorum for its own sake. Her husband had avoided him—His Grace of Rothhaven had had no real friends, only toadies and sycophants—though His Grace of Walden had held an estate adjoining the Rothhaven family seat.

"*Those* Wentworths were from the wrong part of York," Sarah said. "The present Duke of Walden's inheritance of the title was quite the scandal, and he chose some preacher's widowed daughter for his duchess. She's managing quite well, from what I've heard."

"The Duchess of Walden who sits on the Committee

for the Betterment of Unfortunates Formerly in Service is a preacher's daughter?" That made sense, given what Wilhelmina knew of Her Grace. Jane, Duchess of Walden, was gracious, dignified, and put a bulldog to shame when it came to her causes.

Exactly as a duchess should be.

"What's the news from home?" Sarah asked, rising and stretching, her hands braced on the small of her back. "Please say we can make a visit. My patience with polite society is exhausted and the Season has barely begun. If I must listen to one more fortune hunter lament his unjust fate or one more dowager discuss her dog's flatulence, I will go mad."

Robbie had recovered from his mishap, but Nathaniel's letter had hinted at other problems. Thatcher required minding, the housekeeper was having trouble with her knees, Mr. Elgin wanted more help in the stable now that two of the oldest lads had been pensioned. Treegum was having a quiet, prolonged tantrum over the notion of extending the walled garden to the orchard.

A plan concocted years ago with the best of intentions was unraveling, and Lady Althea Wentworth had breached the citadel of Rothhaven Hall's secrecy at the worst possible time.

"If I go north," Wilhelmina said, "you need not accompany me. You can jaunt off to Paris, take the waters, or visit the seaside. You are due for a holiday."

Sarah speared her with an uncharacteristic scowl. "What makes you think I'd prefer Paris or Bath to my own home shire? I haven't been back to Rothhaven for ages, and with you, when the topic of going home arises, it's always next year, next summer, perhaps, and maybe. *I am homesick,* Mina. I miss the wide-open sky, the green of the dales, the fresh air and soft accents. I miss our people and your Nathaniel."

Sarah, who never paced, who never raised her voice, was nearly ranting. "How you've racketed about all these years," she went on, "never laying eyes on your own only surviving son...I can only conclude that the late duke was a horror, and you avoid Rothhaven Hall because memories of your marriage are more miserable than even the pain of being separated from your offspring. I'm sorry for that, but I miss Nathaniel and can think of no reason why he'd not like to see your old cousin."

Wilhelmina could think of a reason. He stood two inches over six feet, grew fearful at the sight of the moors, and refused to drink coffee or ride in an open coach.

"I hadn't realized how you felt," she said slowly. "I appreciate your honesty and I do miss Nathaniel terribly, though you are right about the late duke. I at first thought him dignified or shy, but when we took up residence at the Hall, he forbade me to venture into his wing of the house for anything less than a sighting of the French fleet. I assure you, I would have greeted the fleet rather than trespass on my husband's infernal privacy."

For all his coldness as a husband, Rothhaven had been free with his favors outside of matrimony. Wilhelmina had wished his paramours the joy of his company too.

Sarah flopped onto the sofa beside Wilhelmina. "Then why shouldn't we return to the Hall? Your dower house is less than half a mile from the manor. If we send word ahead, Rothhaven can see that the dower apartments are aired and put to rights before we arrive. He will have his privacy and we can be *home*."

Oh, dear. Oh, ballocks and Bedlam. This could not end well, and yet, Wilhelmina did very much miss her sons. Every hour she missed them, worried for them, and wished she could do more than keep a discreet distance and pretend a contentment she did not feel.

Then too, this Althea Wentworth person was an alarming development, inviting herself and her sows onto Rothhaven land, befriending a man whom she doubtless believed to be a duke...But perhaps not. Althea had been an "aid in the sickroom" when Nathaniel's valued member of the household had fallen ill.

What sort of woman could scale the ramparts Nathaniel and Robbie had defended for years? Why bother, when Nathaniel had, like his father before him, cultivated a reputation for overweening arrogance?

"I'm not saying yes," Wilhelmina said. "I will consider the idea, and let Nathaniel know we might pay a visit. Planning such an excursion will take time."

"Nonsense. If anybody knows how to get from one place to another on the king's highway, it's you. I'll need a day to pack and send a few regrets on your behalf, the staff here will require some instructions, and we can be on our way by Saturday at the latest. I do wonder if Everett Treegum will ever find himself a wife. He had a delightful sense of humor."

Sarah looked more animated about hundreds of miles in a lumbering coach than she had about anything for the past five years. Wilhelmina *felt* more animated than she had in at least that long, but she was also more worried for her children, which was saying a great deal.

"Sarah, I have a few calls to pay too," Wilhelmina said, donning the determination of a stubborn duchess. "And before we set out, I must be sure Nathaniel is prepared to receive us. I will not sleep on damp sheets under musty bed hangings in my own dower house."

"Then we shall leave on Monday. I cannot wait to quit London, and I honestly don't know if you'll ever get me back here."

That makes two of us. "Where are you going?"

"To start packing."

"Sarah, I haven't even sent Nathaniel word of what we're thinking!"

"Then send him an express." She fairly scampered out the door, while Wilhelmina remained on the sofa, torn between anticipation and worry. She would send Nathaniel an express, though, and she would wait until Monday to depart from London. Nathaniel deserved some warning that Rothhaven was about to be invaded.

And Wilhelmina needed time to pay a call on the Duchess of Walden.

* * *

Althea stood a cautious two yards from Nathaniel, the birches shielding both Nathaniel and the object of his frustrated dreams. The temptation to take her hand had him linking his own hands behind his back.

"You are abroad, on foot, in the middle of the afternoon," she said. "Is all well at the Hall?"

"If I had any sense, I'd tell you we're getting on quite well and wish you good day."

Still she came no closer. "You are awash in sense, nearly drowning in it, from what I can see. What's amiss?"

"Robbie is in good health, if that's your concern."

She marched up to him. "*You* are my concern. Robbie has the entire Hall fluffing his pillows and bringing him toast because every few weeks or so, he has a bad moment. God forbid such a delicate creature ever has to deal with menses, megrims, or impending motherhood." She stared at Nathaniel's cravat. "I am having a bad moment."

Althea looked tired and angry, also impossibly dear. "Why, my lady?"

"Because I want to wrap my arms around you and never let you go. Because I should not have left you alone to deal with the mess life at the Hall has become. *Because I miss you.*"

"I miss you as well, but we have agreed that such sentiments can bear no fruit." No happy fruit, but all manner of sleepless nights and doomed hopes. Nathaniel made himself say the next part. "We were seen, Althea."

She smoothed a hand over his lapel. "By whom? Your staff knows I was at the Hall. My staff heard that I was off visiting a sickroom, but for all they know I was tending one of my sister Constance's employees."

He took her by the hand and led her to a gray, lichen-encrusted boulder amid the trees, for he knew better than Althea how hard a secret was to guard.

"Your staff will cross paths with your sister's employees at market, or see them at the pub, and they will soon eliminate that possibility. We were seen by a member of the local congregation as she came home from an entertainment in York. Her coach passed by as we parted the other morning."

Parted, meaning kissed each other farewell like the doomed lovers they were.

Althea settled onto the boulder. "Lady Phoebe has been busy."

"How do you know it was Lady Phoebe?"

"Because she made certain I was aware she'd be attending the Stebbinses' ball in York, a gathering to which I was not invited. I can think of nobody else in the neighborhood who would have been in York at an event that lasted half the night, such that they'd be returning at dawn. The road doesn't pass within fifty yards of that stile and yet she will report the identities of the couple in question far and wide."

"Exactly what Vicar told Lady Phoebe, if indeed she saw us. He reminded her that the eyes at that distance are not reliable. That Rothhaven Hall could easily have been hosting a guest, that many women wear brown cloaks and straw hats. He further admonished her to keep her damned mouth shut, but that is the last thing she'll do."

"She was at the vicarage earlier today," Althea said, taking off that same straw hat. "She was driving away as I crossed the green. Given what you are telling me now, I think Vicar invited me to confide our situation to him. He brought up the topic of loneliness and foolish choices."

Did he really? "And did you confide in him?"

"Of course not." She jabbed her hatpin into the crown of her millinery. "You have placed your trust in me."

For Althea, a confidence shared was that simple. For Nathaniel... He again possessed himself of her hand, slid off her glove, and linked his fingers with hers.

"Somebody is threatening to reveal that Robbie dwells at the Hall. I put that matter to Sorenson today, because he is the only person beyond the staff who grasps the situation."

Althea scooted a few inches closer. "The only person besides me and Stephen, you mean. How did he learn of it?"

"Robbie got in a bad way a few years ago. I was in York with Treegum. Thatcher and the housekeeper over-reacted and had Sorenson administer last rites."

"Thatcher with the toast rack?"

"He was a more formidable fellow five years ago." *We all were more formidable fellows, except for Robbie.*

"How has the threat to expose your situation been conveyed, Nathaniel?"

Sorenson hadn't asked that. Hadn't asked many questions at all, now that Nathaniel thought about their conversation.

"Notes delivered with the post."

"Did you see anything unique about the penmanship?"

Another useful inquiry. "An educated hand. The script is neat and regular, not a schoolboy's labored scrawl or a shopkeeper's functional letters. I don't recognize the handwriting, but I might have seen it previously."

"As if a familiar hand was purposely disguised?"

"Perhaps." *Perhaps yes.*

"What of the paper it was written on?"

Nathaniel recollected the feel of the note in his hand. "Not foolscap, now that you mention it. Half sheets of good quality, folded and sealed with red wax."

"As if somebody tore off a watermark or crest on personal stationery?"

Neither he nor Robbie had made that connection. "Yes, exactly like that."

Althea sat forward, staring hard at the packed earth of the path before them. "And was the paper clean, or did it look as if it had traveled a great distance?"

"Pristine. It could have been a hand-delivered invitation brought no farther than from the village itself."

She turned her head to peer at him. "So the threat is likely local."

"Bloody hell."

Althea's smile was impish.

"Excuse my language, my lady."

"I've heard much worse, and if Lady Phoebe is attempting blackmail, that is worth very foul oaths indeed."

"Why do you suspect Lady Phoebe is attempting mischief at the Hall?" And why hadn't Nathaniel and Robbie, or Sorenson, been able to make the deductions Althea reached so swiftly? "I had thought Dr. Obediah Soames, the author of so much of Robbie's misfortune, might be seeking to extort funds from his former patient, but Soames has become a shuffling, mumbling half-wit, of all the ironies. I doubt he is long for this world."

How Nathaniel wished Robbie had been able to see his former tormenter reduced to a dependent status, unable to so much as stir milk into his own tea or recall the day of the week. Soames had barely been able to make his mark on a piece of paper when the pen had been placed in his hand.

"I suspect Lady Phoebe," Althea said, "because her sister was once quite close to your father, and her ladyship might well carry a grudge. If she means to launch Miss Price in London, a large sum would facilitate that aim nicely."

Not a motive Nathaniel would have deduced, but it had the ring of credibility. "My father arranged a significant contribution to the settlements for Miss Price's mother as part of the marriage negotiations. Very significant."

Althea rose and Nathaniel let her go. "That makes it worse. Miss Price's mother gave him everything, bore him a child, consigned herself to a lifelong commitment to a man she did not love. Twenty years ago, your father had his pleasure and wrote a bank draft."

"He was not a man afflicted by sentimental attachments."

She crossed her arms. "I am a woman afflicted by sentimental attachments. Lady Phoebe has no business cutting up your peace. You and Robbie seek simply to dwell amid calm and privacy. Who is she to meddle with that?"

More than kissing Althea in parting, more even than making love with her, this conversation put to flight any notion that Nathaniel could ever regard her as a passing fancy. He was not like his father, at least in that regard, and Althea was like no other woman on earth.

"You are protective of us."

"Somebody ought to be. Your staff grows too old, Robbie is restless, your own mother can't be bothered to lend her assistance, and nobody is taking up for *you*."

Nathaniel rose, the better to remain near to her. "And you must not be that person, Althea. If Lady Phoebe has decided to avenge old wrongs now, that is more than enough reason to keep your distance from me. She saw us kissing, she will not be silenced, and now she's somehow figured out what's afoot at the Hall. Your best option is to pretend you cannot abide a man of my arrogance and conceit."

"You are advising me *to lie*?"

Althea's question was endearingly indignant. "My entire life is a lie, my lady. Falsehood has served well to protect my brother. His welfare matters more than the theoretical preferences of honor."

"Fine for him, Nathaniel, but what of your welfare?"

He hadn't an answer for her. Lying was wrong. He knew that. Putting Robbie at risk to be incarcerated, ridiculed, experimented upon, and tormented for the rest of his life was more wrong still. Even the most humane legal option—the appointment of guardians for Robbie's person and property—meant he'd not be able to manage his own investments or even take a wife.

"You have always given me such good advice," Althea

said, stalking past him. "For your own situation, you have
no wisdom to apply."

"Sorenson said you're planning to host a ball."

She came to a halt and turned like a guard before some
general's tomb. "And?"

"Don't do it, Althea. Not now. Lady Phoebe has taken
you into dislike, she has taken me into dislike, and she
has seen us in a compromising situation. She has significant social influence and can blight your aspirations for
all time."

Blue eyes blazed with indignation. "Do you think I care
what she can do to my aspirations compared to what she
can do to you and Robbie?"

"If you care for us, you will not call attention to yourself just now. You will bide your time, let tempers cool,
and choose another moment to put yourself forth as a
hostess. Wait until Miss Price has made a match, wait until
I have flushed Lady Phoebe from her covert. Blackmail
is a crime."

"And caring about you is gross stupidity," Althea said,
"and yet I most assuredly do. I am not canceling my ball.
That is exactly what she would want me to do, and I refuse
to allow her to shut me up at Lynley Vale the way Robbie
was jailed in an asylum."

She kissed Nathaniel soundly on the mouth. Then, before
he could react, she marched away, spine straight, skirts
whipping. Nathaniel wanted to call her back—wanted to
kiss her and do more than kiss her—but he let her go.

She *most assuredly* cared about him. Fool that he
was, her declaration had him smiling all the way back to
the Hall.

* * *

"Today is a day for unusual epistles," Jane, Duchess of Walden, said as she took the place beside her husband on the sofa.

Quinn tucked his arm around her shoulders, his casual affection as precious to Jane as it was familiar. "You noticed that Stephen has deigned to pen me a note. Such an occasion begs for an announcement from a royal herald. Who has been writing to you?"

Jane insisted on having this hour of the late afternoon in private with Quinn as a defense against the obligations of their station, and against Quinn's sense of duty. He was a duke who actually attended many sessions at the Lords. He was also the owner of a burgeoning financial empire and father to three rambunctious little females.

His wealth and position earned more attention from the sovereign than he liked; his decency and honor made him the love of Jane's life.

"I have a letter from a Lady Phoebe Philpot," Jane said. "She's a neighbor of Althea's, or so she claims."

"The gossip has started already. Is she complaining about Stephen?"

"She's expressing her concern about Althea."

Quinn nuzzled Jane's temple, a thoughtful sort of nuzzle rather than a playful or amorous overture. "She's spreading tales, then, under the guise of a charitable impulse."

"Precisely. She couches her accusation in reluctance and uncertainty, but she claims to have seen Althea enjoying a romantic interlude nearly in the middle of the high street, and with a man of dubious reputation. Lady Phoebe dares—her word—to suggest we send a regiment of chaperones to bring Althea back to the family fold."

"Those chaperones would need pistols, swords, and chains if Althea is disinclined to come south."

Jane would have wagered on Althea's stubbornness being equal to even those challenges.

From boyhood on, Quinn had been able to escape Jack Wentworth's household to search for work. Althea, as a female, and one fiercely protective of her younger siblings, had remained under her father's thumb. Having been burdened with an eccentric and self-absorbed father herself, Jane well knew the demands fortitude could make on a daughter.

"Althea has come south often enough to know what awaits her here," Jane said. "She has not had an easy time of it. I did what I could, but had I taken more of a hand in her situation, she'd have been accused of hiding behind my skirts. That would very likely have made her situation worse. Now she's in Yorkshire where I have no connections, and where the challenge is one of managing rural mores, about which I am entirely ignorant."

Quinn scooped Jane up and settled her in his lap. He was approaching midlife, though he grew only more handsome and formidable with the passing years. In private, his humor was more apparent, and his already affectionate nature frequently turned doting.

"What *situation* did my duchess ever decline to take in hand?" He stroked Jane's hair, gently urging her to snuggle against his shoulder.

"I suspect Althea is frequently bullied."

His hand went still. "*I beg your pardon?*"

"I cannot believe she's prone to spilling punch on half of her ballgowns or stepping on her own hems every other outing. I found her practicing with her fan once, but soon realized whoever had instructed her had given her incorrect meanings for the signals. She'd been told that 'I value you as a friend' meant 'I miss your kisses' and so forth."

"That is cruel. Why wasn't I told?"

Jane brushed his hair back. He needed a trim, but she preferred his hair long and a bit rakish. "Think, Quinn."

"Because Althea is stubborn and proud, and never asked for quarter from anybody. Of all the reasons to wish Jack Wentworth were alive so I could put out his lights, the damage done to my siblings sits at the top of a long list."

The damage to Quinn sat at the top of Jane's list. Althea, Constance, and Stephen had had Quinn to occasionally take up for them and fend off starvation. Quinn had had nobody.

And now, Althea had nobody. "I cannot leave her to deal with this situation on her own, Quinn. She will soon be considered on the shelf, and the fellow taking liberties with her person is well placed."

"Is he courting her?" Quinn asked, drawing a pin from Jane's hair. "Courting couples delight in taking liberties with one another. So do married couples, I'm told."

Three more pins went into Quinn's pocket, and Jane's braided coronet drifted down over her shoulder.

"He is not well liked in the neighborhood, according to Lady Phoebe. He's an arrogant titled bounder from a family of arrogant, titled bounders."

Quinn paused, two more pins in his hand. "She put that in writing?"

"She claims she has reason to know the family history, and it does not recommend the man involved. The Rothmeres have more wealth than decency, in her words."

"So Althea has made the acquaintance of the neighborhood duke, though by reputation, I'd say Rothhaven is retiring rather than randy." Quinn untied the ribbon at the bottom of Jane's braid and trailed the scrap of silk across her décolletage. "People say I lack decency. They delight in saying it, always behind my back, of course."

And it wasn't true. Quinn was enormously wealthy, but he was endlessly decent. "I am concerned for Althea."

"Meddling won't help, will it?"

Jane got off his lap after he'd first stolen a lovely kiss. "I've tried keeping a distance, Quinn. I've tried to allow Althea to manage on her own, and when she decided to miss the Season, I understood. I did not agree with blowing retreat, but a woman grows weary."

"Tell me who I need to ruin, Jane. I haven't ruined anybody yet for the sheer pleasure of it, but what good is owning two banks if I don't occasionally remind the sots and schemers running this country that their power has limits?"

"I suspect you'd have to ruin half the peerage, Quinn. The matchmakers and hostesses took Althea into dislike because they could. Stephen is your heir, Constance has a retiring nature, and your title and influence protect me. That left Althea."

"But she's not alone, is she?" Quinn said, rising. "She's attracted the notice of a peer who also apparently cares naught for the busybodies and gossips of Greater Dingle-berry. That is a very pretty frock, Your Grace. One would hate to see it torn."

"You haven't torn one of my dresses on purpose for three years."

He prowled across the room to take her hand. "Maybe it's time I gave the seamstress some work."

Quinn in a loving mood was a force of nature, but then, Jane had never seen a reason to ignore her own loving moods.

"We should go north, Quinn. I know you are

conscientious about voting your seat, but the man accosting Althea in broad daylight is a duke. By merest coincidence, that duke's mama paid a call on me yesterday. I could not fathom her agenda, though she told me she is shortly to make the journey to Yorkshire."

Perhaps to lend her consequence to Lady Phoebe's gossip campaign?

"Rothhaven is a duke. He's a match for Althea, or nearly so." Quinn embarked on a serious kiss, and when Jane could breathe again, somebody had unhooked her dress most of the way down her back.

"Or Althea's amorous duke is in a position to ruin her permanently," she said. "Lady Phoebe claims the Dukes of Rothhaven hark back to Viking habits. They take what they want and recognize no authority save—"

Another kiss, hotter and more carnal than the last.

"Please recall that I've had a letter from Stephen," Quinn said, turning Jane by the shoulders.

"Your brother does know how to use paper and pen." And Quinn knew how to get a wife unlaced in thirty seconds flat.

"Stephen's fraternal sentiments aren't often in evidence, but I suspect he's worried for Althea. The letter was succinct."

Quinn passed Jane a folded, embossed sheet of vellum. She knew Stephen's exquisite penmanship—he was a brilliant draftsman—but the words surprised her.

Althea headed for more trouble than even I can handle. Millicent abetting the nonsense. Get your ducal arse up here. Love to Jane and girls.

Stephen.

Jane set the letter on the mantel as Quinn looped his arms around her from behind. "So are we going north, Quinn?"

He kissed her nape, the warmth of his lips causing a delicious shiver. "I do believe we are, but first, Your Grace, I suggest we go to bed."

"A fine idea, sir. One of your finest." Jane took him by the hand, led him into the bedroom, and locked the door.

* * *

Althea waved Jane's letter under Stephen's nose, regretting—not for the first time—that smacking a man in a Bath chair would be unsporting. "You summoned the watch on me?"

"I did not summon the watch, I merely…"

He wheeled away to the music room's pianoforte and heaved to his feet. Using the piano, a cane, and the arm of the chair for balance, he levered himself onto the piano bench.

"You merely…?" Althea prompted, stalking after him. "Merely let all of society know my own family doesn't consider me capable of even socializing in the shires without supervision? You merely sabotaged my first humble effort to present myself as an adult female of independent means? You merely went behind my back to tattle to Quinn and Jane when all I'm doing is being neighborly in godforsaken Yorkshire?"

Was there any exasperation greater than a meddling sibling? Jane, at least, had had the decency to warn Althea of Stephen's perfidy, but Jane had also packed up her duke and her household and begun the march north.

"You might be in godforsaken Yorkshire," Stephen

said, folding back the cover over the piano keyboard, "but that only means your consequence makes you a bigger target. I did inform our family of your situation, but you should also know Quinn sent me a note in return. It seems Lady Phoebe Philpot wrote to Jane, suggesting you are in need of your family's loving guidance, and you should be summoned to London posthaste. How many people are you inviting?"

"Don't you dare try to distract me, you skulking rodent." And of course Lady Phoebe would write to Jane. Althea was surprised her ladyship hadn't taken out an advertisement in the *Times* notifying the whole world that Althea Wentworth was prone to dancing naked on the village green.

But that Stephen would break sibling ranks now, that he'd tattle to Jane... Althea was as bewildered as she was angry, and she was very angry.

"The invitations haven't gone out yet," Stephen observed, starting on a stately Beethoven slow movement. "You could put this little gathering for a hundred of the county's biggest gossips off until autumn."

The guest list exceeded a hundred. "Millicent wants the ballroom full, and that means she keeps adding to the tally in the name of balancing the numbers."

Then too, Althea's little corner of Yorkshire was close enough to York itself that mustering a few score families with daughters to fire off, bachelor sons, widowed aunties, and well-heeled uncles was no challenge for Millicent at all.

"Millicent has gone daft," Stephen said, launching into a lyrical melody that involved crossing his hands to add the descant. "This happens in the older female from time to time. Her humors get out of balance and—"

"Millicent is *loyal*," Althea said, setting Jane's letter on the mantel. "Millicent supports me and understands that for me to take this small step, amid a rural society starved for entertainments, with you on hand to be the host, is a prudent means of putting myself above gossip and speculation."

"Is not." He played on, sweet, placid notes filling the music room.

"If you think to soothe me with confectionery tunes, Stephen, think again. I am nearing thirty—"

He snorted.

"—and must set aside the fiction that a gaggle of Mayfair matchmakers can define my fate. Viscount Ellenbrook is not the only eligible male in the north, and—"

"And you think to bring Rothhaven up to scratch," Stephen said, "by luring those other eligibles from their card parties and country dances. You'll be the gracious aristocrat deigning to open her home to the bumpkins and cits, and your hopeless Duke of Deception will come to his senses and offer for you."

Stephen spoke calmly, like the music rippling gently from the keyboard, and that made his accusation all the worse.

All the more credible.

"When did you grow so hateful, Stephen?"

"When Jack Wentworth broke parts of me that I had plans for. Did it never occur to you that relying on *me* to play the part of host is absurd? A man who can barely stand is no asset to a gathering that features hours of dancing. I can hardly manage to wheel myself a short distance without spilling my punch, and I will not sit in my Bath chair while the receiving line files past me. You and Milly simply assumed I could be press-ganged into putting a veneer of familial approval on your mad scheme."

Althea poured herself a brandy and poured one for Stephen too. The day, though sunny, looked warmer than it was, a common trick of Yorkshire weather. A brandy to settle the nerves or ward off a chill was permitted to even a lady on occasion.

"The scheme started out as Milly's," Althea said, "and where's the harm in it? I have a ballroom that's never used. I can afford to feed my guests well and people like to dance."

"But people do not like you," he said, launching into a pianissimo reprise, "and now they can all take you into dislike together while eating your food and criticizing your string quartet. More significantly, you are besotted with a man you can never have, and the whole point of these inane balls is to pair up the willing female and the adoring male. If you are not willing, what's the point of assembling two dozen eligibles?"

The brandy was first quality, but it failed to soothe Althea's temper.

"I want to tell the lot of them to go to hell," Althea said quietly. "They might tear my hems, spill punch on my bodice, and make faces behind my back, but they will not refuse my invitations. When they admit that I have the power to summon and dismiss them, the torn hems and spilled punch will stop."

Stephen brought the music to a soft, sweet cadence. "You are declaring war on Lady Phoebe. Is that what this is about?" He accepted the brandy from Althea, half turning on the piano bench.

"Lady Phoebe has declared war on me," Althea said, "and that was to be expected. Miss Price needs a husband,

and I am arguably an impediment on that path. But Lady Phoebe is maligning Rothhaven now, telling all and sundry that she saw His Grace and me in a torrid embrace at daybreak."

Stephen swirled his drink and held the glass beneath his nose. "Were you in a torrid embrace?"

"We were in a farewell embrace. If kissing me in passing on the cheek qualifies as torrid, England has become a very dull place indeed. Rothhaven's situation is difficult. He can make me no promises."

"Thea, he's promised you his regard can go nowhere. If he'd done otherwise, I'd have to call him out, and lest you think my leg impairs my aim, I've proven that assumption incorrect on two occasions."

"You've fought duels?"

"A gentleman doesn't shoot and tell. Cancel this ball, Thea. It can wait until Lady Phoebe has other quarry in her sights, until Miss Price has wrangled a proposal from Ellenbrook—unless you are setting your cap for Ellenbrook?"

Unthinkable, though Althea should be doing exactly that.

"I am preparing to host a fine entertainment for my neighbors, and to let Lady Phoebe and all of her ilk know that they no longer have anything I need or desire."

This was true, which should have been a relief, though Althea mostly felt…empty. The indifference she'd strived to affect toward polite society was finally within her grasp, and it hardly mattered compared to the nasty threats Lady Phoebe had launched at Rothhaven Hall.

Stephen took a sip of his brandy. Of all the Wentworths, he alone had the natural ease of the aristocrat, the elegance and self-possession of a man born to privilege.

"This is Rothhaven's fault," Stephen said, wrinkling his

nose. "He's roused your protective instincts. Not well done of him, but then, you've roused his. He'd not be wishing you farewell, torridly or otherwise, if you were a mere passing fancy to him. I respect your objective, Althea, and I understand how tedious it is to be found wanting when you've committed no wrong, but I implore you—note the verb and the man using it—to take this step with the backing of your family, not in some furtive rearguard action that could easily go awry.

"Lady Phoebe is begging for a setdown," he went on, "and I would love to be the daring adventurer who spills punch on her bodice, but I want Quinn and Jane on hand when that unhappy accident transpires. For you to ignore them as allies only proves that you are not in fact ready to assume an independent role at all. You have a duke and duchess at your beck and call. So beckon and call to them."

Stephen typically fired flaming arrows of insight and then affected surprise when they struck their targets. He wasn't given to speeches or discourses on strategy.

"You are cozening me. You should have been a barrister."

"Right, a barrister who cannot pace about like Mr. Garrow before the jury box." He took another swallow of brandy and maneuvered himself back into his chair. "A barrister who can barely rise when the judge takes the bench. Some barrister I would be. Instead I am a lowly brother, offering what wisdom I can to a sister whose resolve makes the cliffs of Dover look like so many piles of fairy dust. You can charge the citadel of polite society only once, Thea. If you do not rout the enemy with the first engagement, she will regroup and counterattack. Best deploy all the artillery you can command."

He set his half-empty glass on the piano and wheeled himself through the door.

The longer Althea sat alone in the music room, sipping brandy and watching a relentless wind batter the tulips in her garden, the more she appreciated Stephen's strategy. Jane and Quinn were coming—they were already on their way—and Althea could turn that to her advantage.

Septimus strutted into the room, almost as if Stephen had sent the cat to keep an eye on an unpredictable and unhappy sister.

"I didn't want to bother Quinn and Jane, didn't want to impose."

The cat leapt onto the piano bench and regarded her as if she was supposed to offer to turn pages for him.

"But a slight to me has always been, in a way, a slight to them." Also a slight to every young lady who didn't take, who wasn't born with the grace of a sylph, whose settlements were merely modest. A slight to every young man whose compliments were less than smooth, whose dancing was too enthusiastic.

"And that is rude," Althea said, rising and gathering up the cat. "We have one more invitation to write, my friend, and then we will consult Monsieur Henri regarding the desserts."

The cat began to purr, while Althea's reasons for hosting a ball underwent slight but significant revisions.

Chapter Sixteen

"She's coming! She's coming home at last!" Treegum fairly quivered with the joy of his announcement, while Thatcher went on polishing the good silver, not that anybody would ever use it. "I knew if we were patient and persistent, if we kept to our course, our efforts would be rewarded."

"Her Grace is coming north?" Thatcher asked, peering at his reflection in the bottom of a soup tureen. When had he grown so old? "The duchess leaves her sons to muddle on for years with no help, and now, when we already have a meddling female on the very next property, the duchess is putting her team in the traces?"

Treegum accepted a tankard of ale from Elf, who had come in from the stables for his nooning, or for his mid-afternoon cup of tea, or one of his increasingly frequent restorative pints. Cook often joined them as they sat about in the kitchen, while Thatcher still had to bounce up and down the steps like a lad of seventeen.

"Yes, the duchess is coming, but that's not who I meant." Treegum slid onto the bench at the worktable, sighing an old man's sigh of pleasure simply to sit his arse on a familiar plank. "Miss Sarah is coming home with her. After all these years, Miss Sarah will be home too. They are to bide at the dower house, and I will make it my business to see that they dwell there in comfort."

Elf pulled his pipe from his mouth. "You're the head chambermaid now?"

The head maid was a bouncy little lass of fifty-odd years who went by the name of Penny Piebend. She did not suffer fools, and she and the housekeeper were in a competition to see whose knees gave out first.

Thatcher had them beat, not that he would admit as much to anybody when the family still had need of him.

"You'll have to hire from the village," Thatcher said. "Strict orders never to presume to set foot at the Hall itself, all of that keep-to-your-place nonsense upon pain of excommunication from the holy ranks of ducal servants."

"Any new maids will be so busy putting the dower house to rights they won't have time to wonder about the Hall," Elf said. "Her Grace coming home is a good sign."

"Is she coming home to stay?" Thatcher asked, taking up a particularly tarnished gravy boat.

Treegum peered into his ale. "Only for a visit, but when she sees how badly she's needed here, and when I can explain to Miss Sarah exactly what's afoot, then I'm sure Her Grace will change her plans. What can London offer that's more pressing than the situation at the Hall?"

Elf stumped over to the hearth and used a taper to relight his pipe. "You will not be telling Miss Sarah anything, Everett Treegum. That's for the duchess to do, if the duchess chooses to do it. We agreed that we don't violate His Grace's confidences."

Thatcher dipped his rag into the polish, though his knuckles ached and his fingers hurt. "When Master Robbie first came home, we were all happy to give him some time to adjust. Now he says he's done with strolling by the river, and that is a very discouraging sign indeed."

Treegum took up a second rag and dipped it into the polish. "York wasn't built in a day, Billy Thatcher. So there's been a little setback. We've weathered other setbacks. You never used to be such a pessimist." He went to work on a platter that by rights ought to be trotted out for company dinners at least monthly.

"Not a pessimist," Thatcher replied. "A planner. I've planned for my dotage, for example, putting aside a bit from my wages year after year. I've planned to stay spry and sharp so I can tell the next generation of Rothmere boys all the mischief their papas got up to. Now I'm apparently not to have a dotage, no matter how often I trot 'round waving toast racks at all and sundry and pretending to have misplaced my wits. I'm happy to do an honest day's work, but I did look forward to tellin' those tales."

Elf returned to the table, the pleasant scent of tobacco lightly fragranced with vanilla accompanying him. "You have us to tell your tales to, God knows."

A fine sentiment, though growing tattered about the elbows and knees. "We're all getting on, and Master Robbie has improved a great deal. Something has to change."

"The duchess is coming," Treegum said. "That's a significant change."

"For a visit," Thatcher retorted. "And she won't stay in the Hall. When a woman can't even bide with her own boys..." Except Nathaniel and Robbie weren't boys.

Hadn't been boys for years and years. "Everything has to change."

Elf cradled his pipe in hands gnarled by years in the stable. "I had hoped Lady Althea might inspire some change."

"Not meant to be," Treegum said, his comment on nearly every injustice, frustration, and confoundment in life. "Not at this time, anyway. She's giving a ball, you know. The whole shire will turn out in all their finery."

"And we won't see any of it," Thatcher said, setting down the gravy boat. "Rothhaven Hall should be hosting balls. His Grace of Rothhaven should be opening the dancing, and somebody in this damned house should be finding a wife, or what in the bleedin' hell is all our sneaking about for?"

"For our Master Robbie," Elf said, tiredly. "Drink your ale and mind your silver, Billy Thatcher. We're all doing the best we can."

"I am no longer so sure of that," Thatcher retorted, pushing to his feet. His left hip objected, but then, his left hip also objected to biding on a hard bench for any length of time. "I'm going to make some toast. You lot can finish with this silver, though why we polish cutlery nobody uses, I do not know."

He made as dignified an exit as old joints and tired bones could, knowing that a tantrum would also not change anything. The Duke of Rothhaven had set his course, and nothing, not common sense, royal decrees, comely visitors, or wandering hogs, had swayed His Grace from his chosen path.

So far.

* * *

Learning to ride had been one of the last obstacles Althea had tackled on her campaign to conquer a lady's education, and it had proved to be no obstacle at all. She approached horses with the assumption that domesticity was a compromise they made in the name of ease and safety, but a compromise subject to renegotiation at the equine's whim.

A good system, for those with the muscle to carry it off. Her mounts had always seemed to sense her respect and return the courtesy.

As the sun neared the western horizon, she trotted her mare along the lane to the home farm, then cantered past the beekeeper's cottage and the dairy. The horse was eager to stretch her legs, and when Althea sent her over the pasture that marched with Rothhaven land, the mare lifted into a pounding gallop.

Ye gods, the speed felt marvelous, the freedom even better. The horse cleared the stile in a foot-perfect leap and continued on until Althea's objective came into view.

Not Rothhaven Hall, which sat in the evening sun like a shipwreck beached on a lonely shore, but rather, the smaller version of the Hall that lay behind the rise of the orchard. No carts were parked before the Rothhaven dower house, no groundskeepers pushed barrows along the drive, but a lone black horse stood tethered to the hitching post.

The gelding whinnied to Althea's mare, who trumpeted an answer.

"So much for a surprise attack," Althea muttered, climbing from the saddle. She loosened the girth, knotted the reins, and tied the mare to the lady's mounting block, low enough to permit the horse to lip at the overly long grass.

She spared a pat for the black gelding, who had about

as much dignity as a puppy, then strode across the front
terrace. As she raised her fist to knock, the door opened,
revealing a glowering Nathaniel in his signature black
riding attire.

"My lady, you should not have come here."

She swept past him. "*My lord*, you should not keep a
guest waiting on the steps."

He closed the door behind her, the sound echoing in
the otherwise empty foyer. Maids had clearly been busy,
for Althea saw neither dust nor cobwebs, and the scent of
beeswax and lemon oil was strong.

"You sent out invitations to a ball," Nathaniel said,
folding his arms. "Was that wise, Althea?"

No hug, no kiss, but then, what had she expected?

She pulled off her riding gloves and stuffed them into
the pocket of her habit. "If you know the invitations have
gone out, then you know that the nominal hosts are Their
Graces of Walden, and that my role in the affair, along
with Stephen's, is secondary."

And what a pile of work that had been, to reword dozens
of invitations. Stephen had at least not gloated overmuch
when Althea had conceded to his strategy.

Nathaniel glanced around the foyer, which boasted not
a single tulip or dried rose, nor so much as a sketch on
the walls.

"Are you to be invaded by family too?" Nathaniel asked.

"Show me the dower house," Althea replied, unpin-
ning the collection of feathers that passed for her hat.
"And no, I am not being invaded, scolded, brought to
heel, or otherwise chastised. Stephen and Jane assure
me that when my family shows up to preside at my
first venture as a rural neighbor, they are merely being
supportive."

One corner of Nathaniel's mouth lifted. "I tell Robbie the same thing, frequently. Althea..."

He set her hat on a hook near the door, and such was the depth of Althea's foolishness that she relished even the sight of Nathaniel's back filling out the exquisite tailoring of his riding jacket.

"You need flowers in this foyer, Nathaniel. Bright colors, nothing formal. Set your gardeners to scything the verge to the drive and get a few pots of salvia onto the terrace. First impressions matter, and I hope your mother matters to you as well."

He set off down a corridor that led to the left off the foyer. "How did you know Her Grace was visiting?"

"Your mother called on my sister-in-law." The emptiness of the house was sadder even than the neglect Rothhaven Hall's exterior suffered. No pretty little vases, no gleaming pier glasses, no domestic touches in a dwelling that was meant to be the comfort of a woman's old age.

"When duchesses are conferring with one another, the realm is in peril," Nathaniel said. "Nobody has lived here for two generations. My father used this manor only as a guesthouse for his rare shooting parties. Its best feature is that it has no view of the Hall."

The library was small, more of a study, but then, books were expensive and fragile. If nobody lived in the house, storing unread tomes here would have been an invitation for mice to take up residence.

And yet, despite empty shelves and bare walls, the library was pleasant in a way more imposing chambers could not be. The hearth was large enough to generate significant heat, the French doors looked out over an old-fashioned formal garden that somebody had kept in trim.

"Move some of the tulips from your walled garden to

that bed," Althea said, gesturing to bare dirt surrounding a dry fountain. "Fill the fountain, and you will attract birds even if the water merely sits there. The flowers might attract butterflies, and the color will be cheering."

Nathaniel remained across the room, where Holland covers had been folded and neatly stacked in a reading chair.

"Why have you come, Althea?"

Because I missed you. Because I am worried for you. Because you didn't respond to my invitation. "Because you are making a mistake."

"That's what we Rothmeres do, apparently. We make mistakes. My father was terribly mistaken to put his son on a half-trained colt. He was even more mistaken when that son became injured and His Grace insisted the boy climb back into the saddle almost immediately. That's how mistakes are. They have progeny."

He crossed the room, his boots thumping on the wooden parquet floor. "Now you have joined in the mistaking, coming here when you know we've already been caught in one indiscretion."

He glowered down at Althea, once again the Dread Duke, not an ounce of humor or warmth in his bearing.

Althea fluffed his cravat. "The mistake you make now is in trying to present your mother with a house so lacking in comfort that she'll hare away to the south, never again inconveniencing you with her presence."

Still, no yielding, no humanity in those cool green eyes. "She won't stay long."

"She will take one look at this place and permanently dismiss her coachman. *She is your mother*. If she truly did not care for her sons, would she demand to know how you go on? Would she make this journey when all of society has gathered in London? Would she have called on my sister-in-law?"

He paced away again, this time opening the French doors. "The hour grows late, and this is none of your affair."

Idiot man. "I am making it my affair. If you truly want your mother's visit to be short, then you will fit this place out with every comfort. You will bring Rothhaven Hall to a high shine, at least from within. You will have the vicar to dinner here—God forbid he should cross Rothhaven Hall's threshold for anything less than impending death—and you will escort your mama to Sunday services."

Nathaniel stared out across an empty garden to the moors beyond. In the westering sun, the land appeared to undulate into an endless distance, as vast and unforgiving as the sea.

"And exactly why, my lady, would I work so hard to destroy the walls of privacy I've spent years fortifying?"

"Because your mother's visit is an opportunity to make changes that are long overdue, in the first place, and because people who love us need to know that we're faring well, in the second. Conduct your affairs as usual, present a bleak and cheerless picture of life at Rothhaven Hall, and your mother will banish herself here with her sons."

Dark brows drew down. "I don't want that. I remain at Rothhaven so that she need not. She was party to an unhappy marriage for nearly twenty-five years. She deserves her freedom, and besides, she cannot bide here. Her old friends and London acquaintances would flock to her doorstep, and she knows that will not serve."

No true duke had ever been more stubborn. "What will not serve is for you and your brother to live in perpetual fear of discovery. Robbie is sane enough, you will never abandon him in any case, and you have all paid dearly for the mistakes of a man long dead."

Nathaniel faced her, the sun casting half of his profile in shadow, the other half in the golden light of dusk.

"Robbie's sanity will matter little. The first time he has a staring spell at a social gathering, the rumors will start, and Lady Phoebe and her ilk will soon paint him to be a raving lunatic. I won't even be allowed to preserve the estate for his progeny, and a madman isn't permitted to marry. Robbie will become a prisoner again, and the staff who has been so loyal to us will be scattered to the charity of their families. Mama will die of shame, and that will be a mercy."

Nathaniel's logic, so relentless, so convincingly grounded in both law and experience, had a flaw. What he said was true, but it was not the whole truth or even the most important part of the truth.

"You are all prisoners now," Althea said, the truest thing she knew. "You admit this yourself. Your life is a falsehood. Robbie is doing his best to remain erased, your mother has gone for years without laying eyes on the only people who mean anything to her. Neither you nor Robbie can marry under the present arrangement, and the staff cannot be easily replaced. Is that really an existence worth defending?"

Nathaniel either could not or would not look at her. "It's all we have, and it's a damned sight better than the life Robbie endured for more than ten years. I think you should go."

Althea slipped an arm around his waist, which was like hugging a four-hundred-year-old oak. "I think you should come to my ball. Bring your mother, cast the cut direct at anybody who looks askance at you. You've had plenty of practice. It's time, Nathaniel."

"*Somebody knows,* Althea." Said quietly, wearily. "You are forgetting that somebody knows Robbie bides at the Hall, and that same somebody has threatened repeatedly to reveal the truth. Robbie has considered setting up a household on the Continent, but he doesn't want to go, and I cannot...He would not fare well. His French is limited. He'd need servants he could trust, and those are in short supply even in England."

"You cannot imagine banishing him," Althea retorted, "so you and he both remain at the Hall, prisoners to a past not of your making. You remind me of myself, accepting any social slight, tolerating any cruelty, in hopes that someday I can make even a smidgen of peace with the people who should show me every courtesy." Telling Nathaniel that was probably unkind, but kindness without honesty was for aged invalids and frightened children.

"Althea, don't say that. You will have what you deserve, provided we give Lady Phoebe no more fodder for slander." Nathaniel's arms stole around her, as if he'd physically shelter her from the prying eyes of the world.

"Lady Phoebe doesn't know exactly who or what she saw," Althea said, snuggling close, "and I for one no longer care for her good opinion."

"You must care. The life you deserve, of contentment and tranquility with children to love, cannot be yours unless you do care."

Not a single sconce had been lit in the house, and thus as the sun set, the shadows in the library lengthened and deepened.

"I thought I wanted that, Nathaniel, an obscure little slice of peace and joy. I was raised to want that, to crave it and long for it, but safety and domesticity are not enough. You and Robbie have both, and both of you are unhappy. Striving for happiness takes courage. If I'm to be brave— and I am brave—I will no longer waste my time dodging Lady Phoebe's poison darts. I have better uses for my determination and valor."

Valor was not a word women typically used, but why not? Why not refer to childbed as a place of valor when a woman was as likely to die there as a soldier in Wellington's army was likely to die in battle? Why not refer to taking marriage vows, which robbed a woman of her legal personhood, as an act of valor?

"Althea…" Nathaniel stepped back. "You must be careful. Promise me."

"I have been careful. I have been careful, and wary, and timid. What has it earned me but ruined dresses, torn hems, gossip, and loneliness?"

Nathaniel took her hand, enfolding it in both of his. "I know how tempting it is to gallop headlong across the moors, Althea, but even I, on my worst days, know to ride the beaten paths. The bogs are treacherous and they have claimed many a precious life. Promise me you will observe at least that much caution."

"Come to my ball, Nathaniel. I want to waltz with you before all the goggling squires and gossiping tabbies. I want to introduce you to my older brother and his duchess. I want to meet your mother and watch as Stephen and Robbie befriend each other."

A low blow to point out that Robbie had no friends, also an obvious truth.

"Don't do this," Nathaniel said. "Please, please, don't be rash and foolish and make a mistake from which there is no recovering. The rest of your life—"

Althea kissed him, which was neither rash nor foolish, though neither was it wise.

"Don't beg, Nathaniel—never beg, you said—for my mind is made up. Come to the ball. Come by yourself or bring your mother, but know that I will save my supper waltz for you and you alone."

She eased away from him and strode out through the front door, not even pausing to collect her hat.

* * *

"How comes the dower house?" Robbie asked, sprinkling salt on his roast beef.

"The maids have waged war on the dust," Nathaniel said, sawing away at his steak. "The footmen have aired every room and beaten every carpet. It's clean enough." But not welcoming, not cozy. Althea had seen that in the first instant, recognized it for a strategy, and known what to do about it.

"You are worried about Mama's visit."

Nathaniel gave up on the overcooked insult to cuisine lying on his plate and put down his fork and knife. "Change should worry us both."

"The staff will be discreet." Robbie never drank more than the single glass of claret necessary to wash down Cook's roasts, but his wine was nearly gone while his plate remained full.

Robbie was worried too.

Nathaniel filled his brother's glass halfway. "The staff at the dower house has been augmented by a pair of village women suggested by Vicar Sorenson. That in itself is a risk. Cousin Sarah might not be content to bide over the rise. She'll want to see the Hall, and God help us if

Thatcher should cross paths with her or the new maids. If Mama goes to services, that will cause talk, and if she does not go to services, that will cause more talk."

Robbie sat back, clearly defeated by the steak. "You are brooding about Lady Althea, aren't you? That's what this mood is about."

Everything was about Lady Althea. The sunset, the scent of cherry blossoms, the aching loneliness that welled from places inside Nathaniel he'd sealed up years ago. She'd stirred in him a longing for the impossible: babies, contented evenings reading with his wife by the fire, calls upon the neighbors, and an occasional pint at the posting inn with a local squire or two.

Althea could still have the feminine version of that domestic bliss, but she threatened to toss it all aside—and for what? A petty war with an even pettier society.

"Lady Althea and I have bid each other farewell."

"Do you suppose she's the one who's been sending us threatening notes?"

Robbie had an ability to think on a problem until it lay in tiny pieces at his figurative feet. Of course he would fixate on the notes.

"My candidate is Lady Phoebe. She has a family connection to us and thus might have spies among the staff. The notes were sent locally and were written by an educated hand. Lady Phoebe meets both criteria and has a motive for bringing shame on this house."

Robbie took another bite of his mashed potatoes, which even Cook could not render inedible. "But we can similarly bring shame upon her. A word here or there about Miss Price's antecedents, and old gossip finds new life."

"We are gentlemen. We would never speak ill of a lady,

much less of our half sister." Another half sister had been born to the wife of a viscount down in Leeds.

Robbie considered a forkful of potatoes. "What could Papa have been thinking?"

"Perhaps he was lonely."

Robbie looked up from his plate. "You are lonely. I suspect I am too, but the condition has become my natural state. I have been wondering, Nathaniel, if it might be time for me to die again."

Nathaniel's wine went sour in his belly. "Don't talk nonsense. You have made enormous progress lately and if you were anybody but a duke, you'd simply become like the relation who went off to war and came back somewhat the worse for the experience. None of this skulking about, secrecy, and threatening the village children would have been necessary."

"What a flattering analogy," Robbie replied, "though the only war I fought was to maintain my sanity. Mind you, I am not proposing to take my own life, but I was pronounced dead once. Why not simply pronounce me dead again, in a manner that convinces the staff I am well and truly expired, and then you can set aside all the whatnot and marry Lady Althea."

The idea was preposterous and demanded sacrifices of Robbie that Nathaniel could never ask. "Assuming the invalidity of a marriage undertaken under a false identity is never raised—though eventually, it would be—what becomes of you?"

"I go back out on the moors," Robbie said, casually voicing his worst fear. "I suspect that's why I've dreaded them so. I always knew they would reclaim me. This time I can be Mr. Smith, an eccentric gentleman who made his fortune in trade. Perhaps Scotland should be my home."

Robbie *had* made a fortune in trade, indirectly. Several fortunes that would likely end up reverting to the Crown, of all the damned injustices.

"Have you located a property already? Contacted a hiring agency? Determined how you will explain this scheme to the mother who has waited years to see you again?"

Robbie stopped playing with his potatoes. "We have had five good years, Nathaniel, and I thank you for them, but you must marry, or what have those years been for? Lady Althea is up to your weight socially, she's smitten, and so are you. For God's sake, you cannot turn your back on an opportunity like that simply to keep me puttering in Yorkshire's largest walled garden. We will both go mad in truth."

For the past several years, Nathaniel had comforted himself with the belief that as long as he worried for his sanity, he was likely of sound mind. The notion no longer quelled his anxieties.

"You saw her ladyship's invitation," he said. Robbie was conscientiously handling the correspondence, as he'd said he would. Nathaniel should have been relieved to be free of the tedium, but instead he worried that his brother had taken on an unnecessary burden.

"Thatcher put the invitation on the top of the stack. Of course I saw it."

"And you think I should attend her ball? I have so far not publicly held myself out as His Grace of Rothhaven, not since discovering you lived. I ride around on Loki, I sign correspondence with a signature that's identical to yours, but I never claim to *be* Rothhaven." Which was likely of no legal significance when Nathaniel tacitly encouraged everybody to assume he was still the duke. "If I attend that ball, there is no turning back, Robbie. No pretending I was unaware my own brother was declared dead in error."

Robbie rose, the flickering sconces bringing out his resemblance to their late father. "If you refuse to go, if you refuse to let me wander away to a life of quiet obscurity on the moors, then you will have become worse than our father. You will have incarcerated both of us, rather than only me. I can adjust to the notion of being Mr. Smith. I'll hire a pretty, friendly housekeeper, and content myself with reading, music, and tending a walled garden. You and I will correspond as you and Mama do, and you will marry Lady Althea. Compared to what I endured previously, that is a lovely little existence."

A thousand retorts sprang to Nathaniel's mind: At the first seizure, Robbie's staff would flee. They'd steal him blind in the hours when he was groggy and muddled after a fit. They'd gossip about him and start talk that he was deranged. They'd determine who he truly was and do worse than send threatening notes.

"A plain Mr. Smith who doesn't get out much," Robbie said, "can suffer the falling sickness with much less drama than can a duke who's afraid of the open moors, Nathaniel. It's time to move on to the next phase of the deception."

Nathaniel remained seated, weary in body and spirit. "I cannot protect you if you attempt this new charade, and I will never be the duke in truth."

"She loves you, Nathaniel, and I love you. I've lived in obscurity for most of my life. I'm used to it. Plase say you will consider my suggestion."

This wasn't a suggestion. Robbie's proposal was an abdication of hope.

"At least, Robbie, while you've been here at the Hall, you have been who you know yourself to be. The staff and

I recognize you for the firstborn Rothmere son, and you need never pretend otherwise. Leave here, and you must perpetrate a fiction that grows heavier and more complicated with time. I know of what I speak, and I advise you to reconsider."

"My thanks for your opinion." Spoken with all the gracious forbearance of a very patient and determined duke.

Robbie finished his wine and left, and Nathaniel had never—never in all the years of managing a vast falsehood, never even when he'd believed Robbie dead—felt so alone or so angry.

* * *

"Perhaps we ought to send Lady Althea our regrets," Elspeth said, emptying the basket before her and rearranging the sacking in the bottom so it didn't show above the wicker sides. "If we pretend we don't know of Lady Althea's wanton acts, we are tacitly approving of them. Why are we giving the poor perfectly good sacks?"

The sacking, as Phoebe well knew, was intended to make the baskets look fuller without adding strain to a donor's generosity.

"Everybody needs a sack on market day." Phoebe tied a short length of twine around a small bundle of dried lavender. The string wasn't quite long enough to fashion a bow, but then, the poor did not need bows. Being poor and without much coin, they probably didn't need sacks on market day either.

Thank heavens one could pray that the poor developed the fortitude their unfortunate circumstances so often required.

"I am glad you have given the matter of Lady Althea's

ball some thought, Elspeth, for I confess the very question you raise has vexed me exceedingly. You need lavender for your basket."

"Why do the poor need a lavender sachet?" Elspeth asked.

Not even a sachet, for sachets required cloth or lace. "To keep bugs away from their hovels, I suppose." Then too, every proper squire's garden had a lavender border, so the pile of dried flowers had been free. "I fear if we decline Lady Althea's invitation, Their Graces of Walden will learn of it."

Elspeth put together a spray of lavender from the bundle in the center of the table. The church assembly room was the best place for the charitable task of putting together poor baskets—dried lavender could make quite a mess— though the chairs were exceedingly hard.

"Their Graces of Walden are only the nominal host and hostess," Elspeth said. "I can't believe they will trek all the way up to Yorkshire to watch a bunch of yokels hop about in evening clothes and swill punch until the moon sets. Pass me the twine."

Phoebe obliged and paged through the improving tract that was also being gifted to the unfortunates of the parish. *In lowliness of mind, let each esteem others better than themselves... With all lowliness and meekness, with long-suffering, forbearing one another in love....* Holy Scripture offered such comforting words.

"Their Graces of Walden have left London," Phoebe said, "and the talk is, they are journeying north, not that our decision should rest on whether your daughters or my niece have an opportunity to stand up with a duke. We must be guided by conscience. Not so much lavender, Elspeth. We have eight baskets to fill."

And any left over would go home with Phoebe for use in her linen closets.

"Conscience says we decline the invitation of a woman with loose morals," Elspeth replied. "My girls will be disappointed if we don't go, but they understand the need to safeguard their reputations. Is this too much lavender?"

"A bit less." Phoebe stashed the tract into the nearest basket. "I believe duty compels us to attend Lady Althea's ball, much as the prospect troubles me. These are rather large jars of marmalade."

Pandora Biddle was as generous with her marmalade as she was sparing with the sugar her recipe called for. The stuff was downright bitter, which might be why nearly every manor in the shire had donated a jar, minus Pandora's Christmas label.

"The poor have too many children," Elspeth said. "They need large jars or there won't be enough marmalade to go around. I would like to see the ballroom at Lynley Vale, and that nice Lord Stephen was ever so gracious to my girls in the churchyard. He barely limps at all, though I doubt he dances. It's not his fault his sister is a strumpet."

Seeing Althea Wentworth labeled a strumpet by the neighborhood gossips had required all of Phoebe's patience, endless cups of tea, and much genteel fretting over the morals of today's young women. Phoebe had been determined, and knew how well rural neighbors valued propriety—and good gossip.

"You raise a very significant consideration, Elspeth." Phoebe arranged a cast-off tea canister beside the pamphlet in her basket. The canister was empty, but pretty in a cheap, slightly dented way. "The Wentworth family as a whole cannot be criticized for the actions of one wayward sister, but that is not why I suggest we make the sacrifice of attending her ladyship's ball."

"You are thinking of Sybil," Elspeth said, tucking her few sprigs of lavender into the side of a basket. "Ought we to put some food in these baskets? The poor are legendarily hungry. A potato or two?"

"Food attracts mice, and the poor have enough problems without battling rodents. I am thinking of Sybil and of the fine impression she seems to be making on Lord Ellenbrook, but I am also thinking of our neighbors. They will take their direction from our example. If we attend but make our censure of Lady Althea known, we can appease the dictates of good manners toward a family of significant standing while holding Lady Althea to account."

Elspeth removed a worn little one-eyed cloth bear from Phoebe's basket. "Some child loved this once."

"A different child can love it now."

"We could sew another button on it."

"And then the eyes wouldn't match, Elspeth. Children like things to match."

Elspeth replaced the bear among the other gifts in the basket. "How do we make our censure of Lady Althea apparent while dancing under her very roof?"

"That part is simple, and only requires that we share the truth of her behavior with any neighbors on her guest list. When they learn how she has comported herself, they will understand why duty compels us to emphatically express our disappointment in her."

Elspeth regarded the baskets, which held the generous goodwill of the parish's better families. "Have you discussed this with Vicar?"

"Indeed I have, and he too regarded Lady Althea's behavior as most unwise. He cautioned me to be accurate about my recollections of that dreadful scene and commended me for the concern I feel regarding Lady Althea's immortal soul. She cannot continue on the path of sin without incurring higher costs than she already has, Elspeth. We have a duty to speak the truth before she errs even further."

Vicar's counsel had weighed very heavily on the side of accuracy and discretion, but even he had been subtly dismayed at the notion of a couple passionately embracing on the very roadside.

"So we accept Lady Althea's invitation?" Elspeth said, sitting back.

"We do, as much as it pains us to give her the satisfaction of a full ballroom."

"Have you told Ellenbrook what you saw?"

A delicate question. "Not as of yet. He might decline his invitation if he knew, and then who would Sybil stand up with for the supper waltz?"

"You have given this a great deal of thought," Elspeth said, rising. "While I have dithered and fretted and pondered. What would I do without your example, my lady?"

Elspeth would waste her time sewing button eyes onto worn little bears destined for the ash heap. "You are a comfort to me too, Elspeth. Heaven knows a rural life would be tedious but for good friends and worthy projects."

They arranged the baskets in a row, the better to display the neighborhood's generosity, and left the church arm in arm.

Chapter Seventeen

Althea allowed herself a cautious sense of relief, though the ball wasn't until tomorrow. All but one of the invitations had been accepted, Quinn and Jane were planning to stand with her in the receiving line, and Monsieur Henri was in transports to be cooking for an event worthy of his talents.

Now, to put the finishing touches on her ensemble.

"That is an unusual choice," Jane said, running her fingers down the sleeve of a bronze silk evening gown. "Neither a debutante's pastels nor the bold impression a brighter hue would make. Gold will go well with this shade, and perhaps rubies? Emeralds would work too."

"Amber," Althea said. "I have a necklace and earbobs of amber in gold settings."

Jane gave the dress a final caress and closed the door to Althea's wardrobe. "Quinn insisted on bringing my sapphires north, in case we encountered any formal occasions. I would be happy to lend you the entire set."

Jane had thus far been content to be a guest at Lynley Vale. She hadn't asked to see tomorrow's menu, hadn't countermanded Althea's decision to decorate with spring flowers rather than the more expensive—and cloying— hothouse lilies. She had, in fact, seemed content to rest from the journey and enjoy the company of her husband and children.

"No precious jewels," Althea said. "They will outshine the finery of my guests, and that would be ungracious."

Jane leaned back against the wardrobe and aimed a considering gaze at Althea. The duchess was tall and sturdy, and when she chose to wear her consequence, the effect was majestic. She was also a mother to three little girls and inconveniently perceptive.

"Outshining your neighbors would be a tactical blunder, you mean. When did you grow so shrewd, Althea? That's why you're decorating with garden flowers instead of a fortune in lilies, why you forbid Monsieur his more exotic flights."

Althea opened the wardrobe on the other side of her dressing closet. "Those choices are also less expensive and more colorful. I'll wear this shawl and my gold slippers." She held out a length of shimmery copper silk patterned with subtle rose and jade hues. Her slippers were embroidered in the same colors.

"An excellent, understated, and unexpected ensemble," Jane said, exiting the dressing closet, "in which you will outshine them all with your good taste. What of your corsage?"

"A wrist corsage of gardenias."

Jane continued on through the bedroom and into the

corridor, pausing at the top of the main staircase. "In that silk dress, with touches of gold and amber catching the candlelight, and the scent of gardenias wafting about your person, you will have three proposals before the supper waltz."

Jane was trying to fortify Althea's confidence, which was both pointless and dear. "I sent an invitation to Rothhaven. He has not accepted. Every bachelor in the shire could propose and I'd turn them down for one waltz with the duke."

Who wasn't a duke, not truly. Nathaniel was something more precious than a mere title, and Althea's heart ached for him.

"So that's it." Jane proceeded down the steps, Althea's admission apparently solving some mystery. "Then Quinn needn't do anything but smile pleasantly and stand up with the wallflowers."

"He will open the dancing with the ranking lady in the shire." Lady Phoebe, very likely, which would leave Jane dancing with Lord Ellenbrook.

Assuming Nathaniel didn't show up at the last minute. He hadn't sent regrets, hadn't even replied to Althea's invitation, which made his position all too clear.

Somebody rapped on the front door just as Althea reached the bottom step. She opened the door instead of waiting for Strensall to do the honors.

"Vicar Sorenson, good day."

The vicar wore riding attire well, though his smile was a bit anxious. "My lady, greetings. I apologize for calling on what I know must be a busy day, but I was hoping you could spare a moment of your time."

Jane watched this exchange rather than discreetly withdraw while murmuring about being needed in the nursery.

"Do come in," Althea said, "and allow me to perform an introduction. Your Grace, may I make known to you Dr. Pietr Sorenson, our vicar, and my conspirator in schemes to alleviate poverty. Vicar, may I present Jane, Duchess of Walden, my sister-by-marriage."

Sorenson handled the courtesies as if he met duchesses twice a week, and Althea was soon ringing for a tea tray and wondering what in all of creation could have inspired the vicar's call. Nothing good, of course. She was sure it was nothing good.

* * *

Pietr Sorenson baptized infants who wouldn't live out a week, he buried young people taken too soon, and he attended the final hours of much-loved elders. He handled the petty squabbles of the neighborhood without turning a hair and interceded with the magistrate's more zealous applications of the law.

In Nathaniel's experience, the vicar was not a man given to dramatics, but something had provoked him into calling at the Hall and pounding on the door until Thatcher admitted him.

"She's waltzing into an ambush," Sorenson said, striding into the estate office. "The parish's most zealous benefactor, the person who has done more to safeguard the well-being of our poor, the woman who has turned her sights on remedying poverty in all of York itself, is about to be publicly maligned by a gaggle of gossiping biddies in her own ballroom. All because of some pretty viscount who hasn't a clue he's become the spoils of a rural matchmaking war. I vow, Rothhaven, serving on the Peninsula was less vexation than tending a flock of English Christians."

Thatcher hovered at the door of the estate office looking all too interested in Vicar's tirade. "Shall I bring up a tray, Your Grace?"

"No, thank you. Brandy appears to be in order." Still Thatcher remained in the doorway. "You may be excused, Thatcher."

"Very good, sir." He shuffled out, leaving the door open.

When Nathaniel closed the door, Thatcher was peering at himself in the corridor's nearest mirror, licking his fingers and arranging the shocks of white hair that sprang from above his ears.

Nathaniel poured Vicar a generous drink and allowed himself a half-measure as well. Beyond the window, Robbie pushed a barrow along the bed of roses in the walled garden. He wore an old straw hat and a workman's garb, looking for all the world like an under-gardener rather than a duke.

But did he look happy?

"What has you in such a state?" Nathaniel asked, passing Sorenson his brandy.

"Not a what, a who—several whos. Lady Phoebe Philpot, the selfsame malicious meddler who happened upon you and Lady Althea in a harmless embrace, has taken it into her head that the entire shire should be apprised of the licentiousness she is certain she saw."

Nathaniel set down his drink untasted. "She saw a mere kiss on the cheek between two people she'd be hard put to identify at such a distance, particularly when she hasn't had a good look at me in years."

Vicar tossed back about a quarter of his brandy. "Not to hear her tell it. She saw you and Lady Althea all but ensuring the succession in broad daylight, and she means to trumpet news of that shocking behavior from here to York."

No profanity graced the English language sufficient to express Nathaniel's ire. "How do you know this?"

"My housekeeper heard Lady Phoebe and Mrs. Elspeth Weatherby scheming over the poor baskets. Lady Althea gave the housekeeper's nephew a half dozen pigs, use of Lynley Vale's bullocks, and two years' rent forgiveness on a little tenancy next to the moors. The lad longs to marry, and Lady Althea put that goal within his grasp. He's far from the only young person whom her ladyship has spared from the mines and slums. Lynley Vale has hired ample staff from the village and her ladyship pays well. My housekeeper could not keep silent."

"And neither can you. What do you expect me to do about this?" What *could* Nathaniel do? Warn Althea to absent herself from her own ball? "Both of Lady Althea's brothers are on hand, and they are not men to be trifled with."

Sorenson tossed back another quarter of his drink. "You are not a man to be trifled with. For five years, you've thwarted the whole shire's attempts to invade your privacy. You've managed a dukedom that prospers without the duke himself being in evidence. If you attended this ball, Lady Phoebe wouldn't dare spread her spite."

"She would spread it in the churchyard instead and likely already has." All of this over a kiss, over a simple, sweet *farewell* kiss. "I cannot attend this ball and you well know why, Pietr."

Sorenson joined Nathaniel at the window. "I've seen your brother out walking, Rothhaven. He's hale and whole, from what I can tell. Put some manners on him and introduce him as your long-lost second cousin. The old duke was known to be less than faithful to his duchess, and everybody would assume Robbie was just another by-blow. It's been done."

Robbie pushed his barrow full of thorny branches around to the far end of the rosebushes.

"By-blows have been passed off as long-lost cousins," Nathaniel said. "I grant you that, but dukes are not passed off as by-blows. If I agree to such a scheme, it only raises more questions—who is his mother, where has he been for years, why keep him secret until now? Besides, once presented as a by-blow, Robbie can never assume his rightful role as duke, not even when I die. He wants to leave, Pietr, to banish himself to some obscure manor on the moors, where I cannot protect him and all manner of trouble can find him."

"What does Her Grace say to that?"

Mama had arrived three days ago, settled in at the dower house, and begun looting its attics for paintings, porcelain, and other domestic touches. To Nathaniel's eye, Robbie's bed of irises was looking well thinned, the excess doubtless transplanted into borders at the dower house.

Too much change, far too quickly, and yet, despite the upheaval, despite Robbie's plan to banish himself, despite *everything*, Nathaniel still had time to miss Althea.

To wish for the impossible where Althea was concerned, and to worry for her.

"Her Grace is collecting intelligence," Nathaniel said. "In the manner of duchesses from time immemorial."

"A duchess sent me here, Rothhaven. I called at Lynley Vale, thinking to warn Lady Althea of the gantlet she will face at her own ball. Her Grace of Walden was present, and as the nominal hostess of the upcoming event, I felt she should also be made aware of the situation."

The door at the far end of the garden opened, and

Nathaniel's mother entered. She wore a plain day dress and a straw hat, and from a distance, could have been her younger self.

"That damned door was supposed to be locked," Nathaniel muttered.

"I beg your pardon?"

"Nothing. If the Duke and Duchess of Walden are on hand to protect Lady Althea from gossip, then I am not needed, am I?"

"After I had apprised Lady Althea and Her Grace of Walden of Lady Phoebe's intentions, the duchess walked me to my horse, Rothhaven. In the entire history of the realm, no Yorkshire vicar has ever before been walked to his horse by a duchess. Bishops and archbishops, perhaps, but not country parsons."

Pietr was not a country parson. He was a learned and well-connected man who should have been a bishop or an archbishop. That insight emerged in Nathaniel's awareness as Mama brandished a pair of secateurs and made a snip-snip motion in the direction of Robbie's roses. She and her firstborn went to work on the far end of the bed, looking like any companionable mother and son enjoying some fresh air.

"They may never work together in the garden again," Nathaniel said. "I hate that. In all the world, so few people know or love Robbie, and he's preparing to leave even those few behind. I have failed him, and I don't know how to make it right."

"You are failing Lady Althea as well. If Robbie's planning to leave, then you will be free—"

"*I will not be free.* If I marry Althea, and Robbie's existence becomes known, my vows will be worthless, our children illegitimate. Something as simple as leaving a lesser title off the marriage license can render the union invalid. If Robbie is found to be mentally incompetent, then he will be forbidden to marry, and the whole bloody mess will grow more complicated.

"Somebody already knows that Robbie yet lives," Nathaniel went on. "I've told you about the notes, and whoever wrote them would doubtless delight in thwarting any continuation of the succession."

And that probability was the real risk to any future with Althea. Nathaniel was simply not free to offer for her.

"I have a traitor here at the Hall," Nathaniel said, hating even to use the word aloud, "probably an unwitting traitor, and if I can silence the current threat, another one will doubtless emerge over time." Robbie had certainly puzzled that out as well, hence his recent inclination toward banishment on the moors.

"None of which is relevant to the current dilemma," Sorenson retorted. "Lady Althea's ball is tomorrow, and she has sent you an invitation."

Nathaniel slept with that invitation on his bedside table. He was so far gone with lovesickness that he wanted the comfort and torment of Althea's handwriting within sight as he fell asleep and as he awakened. Her little riding hat sat beside the invitation, all bright feathers and jaunty fashion.

"So she sent me an invitation. I have been rejecting courtesy invitations for years."

"Her Grace of Walden bid me to acquaint you with the particulars of the problem, Rothhaven, and she also asked me to convey a message."

Nathaniel mentally braced himself for a tongue-lashing, for the well-deserved setdown and sermon he was due.

"And?"

"The duchess told me to relay the following: If you give Lady Althea cause for tears, Phoebe Philpot's gossip will be the least of your worries. Guilt and shame will create more forbidding walls than you could ever erect on Rothhaven land, and you will be trapped behind them."

"A vicar bearing threats. What has the clergy come to?" Nathaniel managed the indifferent tone, the hint of amusement that his own father had so often claimed, and yet the duchess's message struck a severe blow to his resolve.

He had been seen kissing Althea—no matter that she'd kissed him too on occasion—and he was not an ogre. Not yet. If the lady was judged harshly because of his actions, he was honor-bound to make the situation right.

He was *also* honor-bound to keep his distance from her.

"I will consider the duchess's kind warning," Nathaniel said, "but now, if you'll excuse me, I feel the urge to do a spot of gardening with my family."

Sorenson stalked across the room and paused by the door. "I can call you out—you are as common as I am—except Lord Stephen deserves that privilege more than I do."

"Sorenson—Pietr—I would gladly call myself out, except that would also redound to her ladyship's discredit. I've already done far more damage to her reputation than any decent woman deserves, so we will have no calling anybody out."

Sorenson whipped open the estate office door, surprising Thatcher, who held a tea tray.

"Please take the tray to the garden, Thatcher," Nathaniel said. "I will see our guest out."

"Guest." Thatcher harrumphed. "We're not to have company here at the Hall, but it's good day Vicar, and here's the duchess, and how-do-you-do Lord Quarrymaster, and a tea tray for that Lady Althea with the splendid hogs. A body does wonder. That he does."

"The garden," Nathaniel said, sidling past the butler, "and then it's time you had a cup of tea yourself."

Nathaniel saw Sorenson on his way, changed into a pair of old riding breeches, and joined his mother and brother in the garden.

"Thatcher says the vicar came to call. What did Sorenson want?" Robbie asked, passing over a slice of lemon cake that looked to have been baked sometime before Yuletide.

"He wants me to go to Lady Althea's ball."

Mama glanced up from her battle with a bed of weeds. "What ball?"

* * *

"Jane tells me the local leading lights have taken you into dislike." Quinn passed Althea a glass of brandy, though the sun had not yet set and the ball was still hours away.

"One local leading light," Althea said, taking the reading chair by the fire, "and Lady Phoebe is within her rights. I have threatened her niece's prospects." Though Lady Phoebe's campaign had begun before Lord Ellenbrook had graced the shire with his presence.

"You? Threatening a local beauty?" Quinn settled into the seat opposite, though he looked out of place in Althea's private parlor in a way Nathaniel had not. "I mean you no insult, Althea, but I thought the finishing governesses had polished all threats right out of you."

Quinn made the years spent with all those tutors and finishing governesses sound like a lark. Fat lot the great and powerful duke knew. He'd been so busy building his

financial empire at the time, he might as well have still
been a footman in service on a distant estate.

"I have invited Lady Phoebe to tonight's gathering,"
Althea said, swirling the glass gently and holding it up
to admire its garnet color. "She can do her worst for
all I care."

"Then why have the ball, Althea?" Quinn sampled his
brandy without any preliminaries. "Why lure your enemy
into the open if you intend to cede the duel to her?"

"There will be no duel. We will reach a dignified understanding, and she will leave me in peace. That's why you
and Jane charged up from London, to ensure a truce. I still
haven't decided whether to disown Stephen for meddling
or commend him for trying to prevent the inevitable."

Quinn took another sip of his drink. "Lady Phoebe's
niece would be Miss Sybil Price?"

"Yes."

He brushed a glance in Althea's direction.

"Don't you dare, Quinn. Miss Price is innocent of her
aunt's schemes and will likely suit Lord Ellenbrook well."
Whatever Quinn was planning where Miss Price was concerned, it would be subtle and effective.

"Althea, you'd best worry less about what I might
get up to, and instead concern yourself with your own
deportment."

"I will behave," Althea said, breathing in the fragrance of
apples, cinnamon, and toffee along with the pungent scent
of the spirits. "This is one more ball. I'll get it over with,
and my neighbors can all have a good gossip at my expense.
Next year, somebody else's peccadilloes will be grist for the
mill, and I can hold my card parties and fêtes in peace."

Oddly enough, she no longer had any aspiration to hold
card parties or fêtes. Lady Phoebe was due for a setdown,

and Althea intended to deliver it. That Lady Phoebe would cast aspersion on Althea was to be expected—half of Mayfair had and with virtually no provocation—but her ladyship was also threatening Rothhaven, and that Althea could not allow.

"You will behave," Quinn said. "Why am I not reassured by that statement, Althea? Why am I more nervous about this ball than about any ball Jane has dragged me to?"

Althea took a considering sip of her brandy—mellow heat, a touch of oak and citrus—and was spared from making a reply by Millicent fluttering into the parlor, her complexion flushed.

"My lady, Your Grace, please do excuse me, but the duchess has asked that I fetch His Grace. She said I was not to alarm you, but I do believe Her Grace has a touch of dyspepsia."

"Bloody bedamned hell," Quinn muttered, tossing back the rest of his drink. "Not this again." He stalked out, Althea in his wake, for when Quinn reverted to foul language before his womenfolk, the matter was serious indeed.

* * *

The sun was making a leisurely progress toward the western horizon, and with its fading light, Nathaniel felt a sense of his own hopes dimming. Mama and Robbie were once again in the garden, bickering good-naturedly about whether to shade some pansies with burlap, while Nathaniel watched from St. Valentine's bench and pretended to read Treegum's latest report.

Something about the report nagged at him, a detail not quite on the page. Focusing on the same verbiage and figures he'd seen for years had grown difficult, though.

Robbie was making plans. In his apartment, boxes had started to fill with books. He'd inquired into use of the second coach and was having it fitted with heavy shades. He'd always been one to go after a goal once he'd made up his mind, a duke who charged forth fearlessly, however misguided his objective.

Stay where I can protect you. Nathaniel could not say that, could not impede his brother's plans in any way. The best he could do was maintain his silence and his privacy at Rothhaven Hall, and when word came that Robbie's venture had failed, intercede once again.

"Tell him he's wrong," Mama said, settling onto the bench. "The pansies want shade, and this garden hasn't much of that to offer."

Robbie was absolutely wrong. "You designed your garden to take advantage of the sun, Your Grace." When had Mama grown so diminutive? She'd always been a robust woman, but now her energy was the bustling, elderly variety, not the commanding consequence of a duchess.

"I wanted the sun, Nathaniel. I wanted fresh air and bright light. You should go to that ball. Dance with Lady Althea, lend her your consequence."

"And then turn my back on her? All that will do is fuel Lady Phoebe's gossip." Though to waltz with Althea would be divine.

"Robbie wants to set up his own household, and that makes sense to me. One of you needs to get on with being the duke."

A gentleman did not argue with a lady. "Duking is best undertaken by those who legitimately hold the title. If Lady Phoebe flies into the boughs over a spot of match-making competition, think what she'll do when she finds out my marriage lines are invalid." Assuming Althea was willing to marry him, which she ought not to be.

Robbie took off his hat and tossed it through the sunbeams to land at Nathaniel's feet.

"Good aim," Mama said. "He was a terror on the cricket pitch." She watched Robbie the way a parent watched a much younger child, one who could be carried off next week by a lung fever.

"He's not as sound as he thinks he is, Mama, or not the way he thinks he is. He could have drowned, walking by the river's edge, and then he was ill, and if it hadn't been for her ladyship—"

The door at the far end of the garden opened. Nathaniel expected to see Treegum, Elf, or a stray maid come through, taking a shortcut perhaps. The damned door was supposed to be kept locked during Mama's visit, but like many orders Nathaniel gave of late, that one had apparently been ignored.

Cousin Sarah bustled into the garden, a basket over her arm adding to her deceptively harmless appearance. She kept coming as Nathaniel rose and walked toward her, her every step deepening his dread.

She waved to Nathaniel as she approached Robbie, and Nathaniel saw the moment when she realized that the fellow without his hat was not an under-gardener or groundsman.

"Oh, dear," Mama muttered at Nathaniel's elbow. "I told her the dower house wanted flowers. I never thought she'd recall my little hobby."

Cousin Sarah dropped her basket, threw her arms around Robbie, and commenced to blubber and howl loudly enough to be heard as far away as London itself.

* * *

"I'm sorry," Jane said, aiming her apology at Althea. "Perhaps I can come down later, once the guests are through the receiving line."

Quinn scowled ferociously. "The scent of beeswax aggravates the condition, as I recall."

"What condition?" Althea asked, for nothing in this exchange made sense to her. Jane's belly was troubling her and her face was pale. Quinn looked ready to do violence to somebody, perhaps himself.

"You said you were past this part," he snapped. "You told me the worst of it was behind you."

"Is Jane ill?" Althea asked.

"No," Jane said, just as Quinn growled out, "Yes."

Jane smiled, while Quinn scrubbed a hand over his face. "The duchess and I are in anticipation of an interesting event. We have no son, which bothers me not at all when I have three daughters to love and spoil, as well as a brother and a cousin upon whom the dukedom can inflict itself. My wife nonetheless uses the lack of an heir to regularly and thoroughly—"

"Quinn." Jane's rebuke was gentle and amused. "Althea has no interest in those details."

Althea found those details fascinating. "Your digestion bothers you because you are expecting?"

"It shouldn't," Jane replied, aiming a puzzled glance at her stomach. "The midwives all claim that the belly settles down after the first few months. That was true with Bitty."

Quinn took the place beside Jane on the sofa and laced his fingers with hers. "And Bitty's sisters have refused to heed the midwife's guidance. Jane suffers for months with these babies. Contrary Wentworths, the lot of them."

Quinn suffered with these babies, a fascinating revelation. "What's to be done?" Althea asked. "Peppermint tea? Ginger and lemon? Lemon drops?"

"Lemon and ginger tea," Jane said, "and dry toast."

Quinn kissed Jane's knuckles, then rose and stalked toward the door, apparently intent on plundering the kitchen in person.

"Quinn, you cannot go belowstairs," Althea said. "The staff is in a near panic, the guests will start arriving in less than two hours, and Monsieur will have an apoplexy if you appear in his kitchen now."

"If my duchess is in want of damned lemon tea—"

"She's right," Jane said, rubbing a hand across her middle. "Use the bell pull, Quinn, but we have a larger problem to solve. If I am suffering a bout of dyspepsia, who will hostess this ball?"

For an instant, Althea considered that Jane's *bout of dyspepsia* might be manufactured, but the duchess's pallor and the real worry in Quinn's eyes argued for genuine bad luck.

"I will," Althea said. "I was originally planning to anyway."

Quinn yanked the bell pull so hard it came off in his hand. "That was before you aroused the ire of the local matchmakers."

"And if I am also suffering a bout of dyspepsia," Althea said, taking the bell pull from him, "what conclusion do you suppose Lady Phoebe will draw?" Althea dragged the chair from behind the escritoire to the place beside the hearth and used Quinn's shoulder to balance on as she climbed onto the chair. "She will imply that what she caught me doing was far more than kissing Rothhaven."

Althea retied the bell pull to the wire that dangled from the ceiling and climbed down.

"If Rothhaven presumed to that extent..." Quinn began.

"Nobody presumed," Althea retorted. "And I have a ball to prepare for."

She left Quinn draping a shawl around Jane's shoulders, a sight that did odd things to Althea's composure. Quinn was serious by nature, intensely focused on what he saw as his obligations, and not a man to be trifled with.

To see him dithering and fretting over Jane, worried to the point of storming the kitchen and breaking the bell pull, was reassuring. If Quinn Wentworth could be felled by Cupid's arrow, perhaps there was hope for Lord Nathaniel Rothmere.

Chapter Eighteen

"You're alive," Cousin Sarah said for the twentieth time.
"Oh, thank the benevolent hand of providence, you're
alive." Mama had managed to peel Sarah from Robbie's
neck, but then Cousin had cast herself against Nathaniel,
where further histrionics were in progress.

Robbie's gaze had a distant look, though he wasn't
having a staring spell. He peered around the garden as
if unable to determine where all the noise was coming
from.

"Robbie is hale and sound in many regards," Nathaniel
said, "but Mama and I didn't know that when I came of
age or when the former duke went to his reward. My father
perpetrated a great fraud on us all."

Sarah subsided onto the bench, Nathaniel's handkerchief
in her hand. "And you've only recently become aware of
Robbie's continued existence. That was the letter you sent
Cousin Wilhelmina before we departed. I knew something

was afoot, but I never considered it might be something
so, so..."

She looked at Robbie, the handkerchief held in a quiver-
ing grasp near her nose, and went off into a fresh display
of lachrymosity. Mama patted her back, Robbie paced, and
Nathaniel wanted to bellow profanities.

Another chink in the family armor, another inadvertent
tear in the secrecy cloaking the Rothhaven household.

"This is that awful man's fault, isn't it?" Sarah went on.
"He had fits, but he couldn't stand the thought of his own
son being similarly afflicted. If he weren't dead, I'd have
to kill him for that."

"*What?*" Nathaniel and Robbie had spoken at the
same time.

"Sarah, explain yourself," Mama said, sounding every
inch the duchess. "My late husband was obnoxiously
healthy."

Sarah ceased dabbing at her eyes. "No, he was not.
I saw him once in a shaking fit. He was Lord Alaric
Rothmere then, enjoying the favor of every matchmaker
in London. He never danced, except to partner a woman
in the evening's opening promenade. I thought that a ploy
to increase his consequence, but I later suspected he was
terrified of embarrassing himself."

Mama stared hard at the pruned roses. "Why didn't you
tell me? Why was this kept from me?"

"I thought you knew. How could you be married to
him and not...But then, yours was not a cordial union,
was it?"

In Nathaniel's opinion, his parents' marriage had been
one of fraught silences and tense distances. They had
occupied separate wings of the Hall, traveled separately,
and lived as near strangers.

"Perhaps now we understand why the union was so chilly," Nathaniel said to his mother. "What I'd like to know is how you allowed Papa to send Robbie away in the first place."

Mama's gaze went to Robbie, standing so still and tall in the lengthening shadows. "His Grace told me to choose. He could send one of my sons away or both. Nathaniel would go off to public school at far too young an age, and be banished in all but fact if I refused to accede to the duke's plans for Robbie. His Grace convinced me Robbie would be well cared for, the best care money and intimidation could buy, though he refused to tell me exactly where my son would be.

"Watching that coach disappear down the drive," she went on, "knowing my darling boy would be alone among strangers for the first time in his life, deceived, betrayed . . . I wanted to die. I very much wanted to die, but there was still you to consider, Nathaniel. There was always you, and I could not see you abandoned as well. The duke intimated, though he never quite threatened, that a mother too selfish to accommodate her sons' best interests was perhaps herself of unsound mind. One thwarted that blasted man at one's peril."

What in thirteen accursed purgatories was Nathaniel supposed to say to that? "I'm glad he's dead," came out of his mouth, an understatement for the ages.

"What sort of fits did he have?" Robbie asked quietly.

"I saw only the one," Sarah said. "I had torn the hem of my ballgown's underskirt—dresses weren't so practical decades ago—and sought an alcove to await my abigail. Lord Alaric already occupied the one nearest the terrace, though none of the candles had been lit."

"He likely blew them out," Robbie said, "the better to hide in the dark."

"He cursed at me," Sarah went on, "told me to take my damned self off immediately. I thought he was foxed, but then he fell to the floor and shook most violently." ·

"You saw this?" Mama asked, as Thatcher shuffled out of the house.

"With my own eyes, Wilhelmina."

Robbie took the place beside Mama on the bench. "Sometimes, I can tell when a seizure is about to descend."

"That is news to me," Nathaniel said. "I thought they struck like the proverbial bolts from the blue."

Thatcher stacked cups and saucers on the tea tray, for once not offering anybody any toast.

"Often there's no warning," Robbie said, "but sometimes odd sensations happen first, feelings that are hard to describe. A little dreadful, a little light-headed, like a touch of hashish only…different. Papa likely knew a fit was coming on, but he couldn't chase Cousin Sarah away in time."

Nathaniel pondered his father's coldness, his adherence to discipline and duty. His insistence that Nathaniel become some paragon of athletic and academic accomplishment, likely not because of the ducal succession, but out of fear that both sons would develop the falling sickness.

"Damn him," Mama said, softly. "Damn that wretched, awful, misguided man."

Thatcher was taking an inordinate amount of time to tidy the tea tray.

Because he was listening to every word.

Thatcher straightened slowly, not with the stiffness of an old fellow growing infirm, but with the wariness of a spy caught at his trade. Thatcher had been all but eavesdropping on Vicar Sorenson's recent call, he ever-so-helpfully *sorted the mail* for Robbie each day, and he'd allowed

Lord Stephen Wentworth access to the Hall despite strict orders to refuse all visitors. He'd also very likely left the garden door unlocked, and on purpose.

Nathaniel met Thatcher's gaze, saw the hint of defiance therein, and realized Thatcher had had an accomplice in these petty insurrections, perhaps an entire staff of accomplices. The handwriting Nathaniel had seen on the threatening notes—tidy, but not quite the same as what he'd been perusing each month for years—identified at least one other culprit.

Nathaniel had told Lady Althea to slightly disguise her handwriting when replying to Lady Phoebe's invitation, a ploy Treegum had taught him when pretending His Grace of Rothhaven was corresponding through a secretary or underling.

"Leave the damned tea, Thatcher," Nathaniel said, "and explain to us why Treegum sent those vile notes."

Thatcher stood straight, casting off the stooped posture of an elderly domestic. "I promised the old duke I'd look after you—we all did—promised him never to leave your service, but even the old duke can't keep a body from dying. Belowstairs, we discussed all the possibilities and decided that giving you and Master Robbie a nudge was the best way to go forward."

"*You* decided?" Robbie asked. "The lot of you below-stairs *decided*?"

Nathaniel hadn't seen Robbie in a temper for years. Though his voice was calm, his ire was unmistakable.

While Nathaniel was feeling everything from bewilderment—what other revelations were yet to come?— to relief—perhaps the old duke hadn't been a complete demon—to rage—the old duke had been demon enough— to concern for his mother and brother.

"We decided," Thatcher said, setting down the tea tray. "And it worked. Here's Her Grace and Miss Sarah, sorting out what needs sorting. You're not the same fella who came home from the moors, Master Robbie, and that's all to the good, but Rothhaven Hall needs for somebody to be the duke in truth. We can deceive everybody from the inn-keeper at the Drunken Goose to the king himself—*and we have*—but we cannot cheat death."

"He's right," Mama said. "The situation has grown untenable."

Robbie took to pacing before St. Valentine's statue, hands fisted at his sides. "If anybody, ever, calls me Master Robbie again, I will not answer for the consequences. I will be Lord Alaric Robert Rothmere, or Robert, or your perishing numbskull-ship, or the Damned Duke of Perpetual Twitching Darkness, but I am done being Master Robbie."

Mama sat up straighter. "Language, Robbie—er, my dear."

"Language?" Robbie shot her an incredulous look. "I have the falling sickness. Napoleon is rumored to have had seizures. Socrates had the falling sickness, Julius Caesar, *my own father*...they all managed rather competently despite their ailment, but I alone was relegated to a gothic horror of a life because of it. Now the servants have decided how my brother and I should be going on, as if Nathaniel has contracted some wretched infirmity of the wits too. I will *not* watch my bedamned perishing language, and I will not answer to a child's form of address."

About time. "Excellent notion," Nathaniel said. "But will you become Robert, Duke of Rothhaven?"

Robbie's gaze swiveled in the gathering gloom. "Don't ask that of me, Nathaniel. Ask anything of me but that."

"You said it yourself," Nathaniel replied. "Our own father managed adequately despite suffering the same affliction you do. He saw to the succession, he fooled everybody, including his own wife and children. We have a chance now to set aside a vast deception and escape from a prison of our own making. I want to take that chance."

Nathaniel wanted that chance for himself, but more than that, he wanted that chance for Althea, for Mama, for Robbie too, and for the staff that had served so loyally for so long.

"Nathaniel"—Robbie's gaze was once more that of the haunted wraith who'd come home five years ago—"it's too soon, it's too much. Someday, possibly, another year or two, but not—"

"You've taken yourself down to the river dozens of times, nobody the wiser. You handle the correspondence, you have long managed the investments. You work out here in the garden under bright summer sun. For God's sake, I'm not suggesting you give a three-hour speech in the Lords, I'm only asking you to be who you were always meant to be."

"I have fits," Robbie shot back. "I stare off into space like the veriest imbecile and don't even know I'm doing it. I dare not ride a damned horse, I dare not have more than a single glass of wine. You cannot ask this of me, not yet."

Nathaniel thought of Althea preparing to cross swords with a battle-hardened termagant who held the whole neighborhood in thrall. He thought of Mama, all but banished from her own home. He thought of the old men and women who'd served the Hall all their lives. They longed for the pensioners' cottages they'd well and truly earned, and he realized something about a small girl who'd been forced to beg for food.

Begging was not always failure of dignity. Sometimes begging was the triumph of love and courage over pride.

"Your Grace," Nathaniel said, meeting Robbie's gaze directly, "I am not asking you to take your rightful place as our duke, *I am begging you.*"

* * *

"Lady Phoebe is moving her infantry into place," Stephen said, beaming at Althea, despite the pain he had to be in. He'd not joined the receiving line, but for the past two hours, he'd flirted with anybody in a skirt while he leaned on a single cane.

"Must you be so indelicate," Millicent muttered from behind a gently fluttering fan.

"Her ladyship is merely visiting with our neighbors," Althea replied, and yet, after she'd danced the opening set with Lord Ellenbrook, nobody had asked Althea to stand up again. Quinn had tried, but to accept his partnering would have been too pathetic for words.

"You cannot know," Stephen said, "how I long to be able to dance. I'd ask Miss Price for her supper waltz, tear every hem she's wearing, spill my entire meal in her lap, and—"

"Stephen." Althea pretended to acknowledge a guest across the ballroom with a smile and nod, though nobody was attempting to gain her attention. Even in the receiving line, with Quinn at her side, she'd been the object of cold, curious stares, the occasional furtive sneer, and one or two pitying glances.

Millicent had begun the evening all but babbling her

good cheer. Now she stood at Althea's side, growling like Cerberus in a pink turban.

Only a few older women had offered Althea genuine smiles, while some of the younger men had risked dismemberment by visually inspecting her person until Quinn had noticed what was afoot.

None of it mattered. None of this mistreatment was new, and Althea bore it now with a sense of patient determination. Let Lady Phoebe attempt her sabotage, provided she aimed her malice at Althea rather than Nathaniel.

"It might be time to plead bad fish," Stephen said, taking a glass of champagne from a passing footman's tray. "Even Ellenbrook is looking uneasy, and I hadn't pegged him for a rotter."

"He danced with me," Althea said. "He's been put in an awkward situation."

"Bad fish is the least of what that Philpot woman deserves," Milly said, her fan moving more quickly.

Supper was typically not served until midnight, though Althea had moved the meal up considerably to accommodate an early moonset. She'd long since given up hope that Nathaniel would attend, but still, she stole the occasional glance at the main staircase.

The herald she'd hired from York remained at his post at the top of the steps, another fixture on the set of an evening that was descending into farce.

But not tragedy. She was done with tragedy.

"How can you allow Lady Phoebe to spread her poison while you stand by and do nothing?" Stephen muttered. "Bad enough Quinn had to dance with her, worse yet when she swans around as if this were her ballroom and her string quartet."

"If she confronts me, I will deal with her. If she's

merely gossiping, then I need not dignify her talk with a reply." Althea had landed on that strategy, knowing it for the compromise it was. She had wanted this ball to be the start of true acceptance by her neighbors, a gesture of goodwill and good intentions on her part.

But what mattered social acceptance from a lot of gossiping tabbies and tipsy squires? What mattered anybody's approval, if the whole of polite society stood between her and Nathaniel? Without him present, she would not be gaining entrée into the local community, but rather, hosting an expensive entertainment for the mean-spirited and small-minded.

A soft patter of applause signaled the end of the set. The couples wandered from the dance floor, and Althea gave Strensall the signal to open the doors to the buffet in the gallery.

"She's coming this way," Stephen said. "I'm off to fetch Quinn."

"Do not fetch Quinn," Althea replied, closing her fan with a snap. "I will deal with Lady Phoebe. You escort Milly to the buffet."

"But my lady…" Milly began.

Stephen took one look at Althea's face and winged his elbow at Millicent. "We have been dismissed from the dueling ground, and I, for one, need to sit down."

Stephen was being biddable, a first in Althea's experience. Perhaps she ought to have given up pining for anybody's acceptance years ago if that was one of the results. Milly took Stephen's arm—or offered hers in return—and they moved away toward the doors to the gallery.

Now that a confrontation with Lady Phoebe was at hand, Althea felt only calm. She had done nothing wrong, not even when she'd allowed Rothhaven to kiss her farewell.

Lady Phoebe's cruelty was wrong.

"My lady." Lady Phoebe nodded, when a deferential curtsy was called for. Perhaps she feared dislodging the plumes waving from her coiffure.

More likely she was being intentionally rude. "My lady," Althea replied, nodding as well.

"I bid you good night," Lady Phoebe said, loudly enough to stop the dancers from further progress toward the gallery. "I hope my neighbors soon see fit to depart as well. In future, perhaps your unfortunate upbringing will be less evident in your public conduct. I shall pray earnestly for your soul, though when a woman is lost to all discretion, when she flaunts her wantonness for any to see, I know my prayers will likely be in vain."

Mrs. Elspeth Weatherby, her two daughters at her side, stood behind Lady Phoebe.

"If you are determined to go," Althea said, "then I will wish you a safe journey home, but I must inquire what exactly you saw me doing that you now feel—after dancing with His Grace of Walden and spending the last two hours sampling my punch—it is imperative to quit my presence?"

One of the Weatherby sisters snickered, though her reaction was no consolation to Althea at all. More guests were gathering behind Lady Phoebe, doubtless intending to take an early leave of the ball, after offering Althea a final rude glance.

"What *exactly* did I see?" Lady Phoebe's pause was worthy of Mrs. Siddons. "At a shockingly early hour, I saw you in the intimate embrace of a man who is certainly not a member of your family. I saw you kiss that man where any passerby could gawk at the spectacle. I saw you strut off across the fields, a woman without shame, no better than she should be."

The ballroom acquired the hush of a rapt audience when the concertmaster held his bow aloft, and Althea was tempted to deliver the scathing rejoinder Lady Phoebe deserved. Miss Price stood off to the left, her hand wrapped around Lord Ellenbrook's arm. She of the dark hair and green eyes was the vulnerable point in Lady Phoebe's citadel of outraged propriety.

A veiled reference to glass houses, to even the best families having a few reasons to blush, would douse the flames of Lady Phoebe's righteousness.

And douse any chance Sybil had of making the match she so clearly desired with Lord Ellenbrook.

Worse, that tactic would reduce Althea to the same petty, vindictive plain on which Lady Phoebe dwelled and from which there was no return. Althea grasped the dilemma Nathaniel faced: two choices, equally wrong. For him the options were a life of deception or unacceptable risks to the people he loved. For Althea, the choices were to bully or be bullied.

And she rejected both of those options, in favor of the simple truth.

"What you saw, Lady Phoebe, was a parting kiss on the cheek between neighbors who'd shared a sickroom vigil, a vigil that ended in answered prayers, I might add. A friendly hug, nothing more. If the gentleman were here, he'd verify my version of events."

Steps sounded on the stairs behind Althea. Quinn, no doubt, coming to make Lady Phoebe regret her folly, though Althea's neighbors didn't know Quinn. He'd turned his back on his Yorkshire upbringing to bide in the south, and the best he could do was to end this skirmish before Lady Phoebe had the last word.

"But that gentleman is not here, is he?" Lady Phoebe

retorted. "He doesn't bother to show his face in public for the likes of you, a common, disgraceful—"

"Excuse me."

A hint of sandalwood gave Althea a moment's warning that the tread behind her did *not* belong to Quinn. Nathaniel took the place at her side. His height gave him presence, and in evening attire, his impact was magnificent. When he treated Lady Phoebe to an indifferent passing gaze, Elspeth Weatherby gasped.

Althea gestured to the herald gawking from the top of the steps. "Announce my latest guest, please." Her voice had been steady, for which there was no accounting. Her heart was thumping against her ribs, and a flock of butterflies had taken wing in her belly.

Two more latecomers appeared next to the herald, an older woman and...*Robbie*? What on earth could Nathaniel be about?

The lady passed a card to the herald, and Robbie murmured something inaudible to the woman, who conferred again with the herald.

"Do announce us, please," Nathaniel called. "Her ladyship's guests are doubtless awaiting their supper."

The herald cleared his throat and thumped his staff three times. "The Duke of Rothhaven, the Duchess of Rothhaven, and *Lord Nathaniel Rothmere*."

"Apologies for our tardiness," Nathaniel said, bowing over Althea's hand. "As a friend and neighbor, I hope you will overlook the fault, just as I expect Lady Phoebe to apologize for her *harsh*, *inaccurate*, and *immensely regrettable* words. If neighbors cannot hold in affection those who aid them in a time of need, then Yorkshire has become as backward as the capital, which I refuse to believe."

Somebody sighed. Lady Phoebe looked like she'd

swallowed a large bug. The whispering started before Nathaniel had finished speaking.

"One expects a duke and his family to be fashionably late," Althea said. "I must welcome Their Graces to the gathering. I am so very glad you all came."

Also so very surprised. Amazed, really.

"A token of apology for our tardiness." Nathaniel held out a little spray of violets, arranged in a wrist corsage. "I picked them myself. If I may?"

"Please." Althea held out her hand. "My gardenias have lost their fragrance." And she had lost her heart.

Nathaniel substituted the violets for the gardenias she'd been wearing and slipped the paler flowers into his pocket. Althea tucked her hand into the crook of his arm, in part to complete the display of cordial acquaintance he'd begun, and in part to ensure she remained upright. The crowd shifted to reveal Quinn and Stephen at the foot of the steps, chatting amiably with...

"The Duke and Duchess of Rothhaven," Althea murmured. "I can hardly credit it. At my ball."

"And Lord Nathaniel Rothmere," Nathaniel replied, bending close and covering Althea's hand with his own. "Did you know Socrates had the falling sickness? And Caesar?"

He smiled at her, the way a doting swain smiles at his lady love, and though Althea suspected the smile was half for show, she smiled back at him like a thoroughly smitten lady love.

"I was vaguely aware of those facts, my lord. Your brother cuts quite a figure, as do you."

"Robert is determined that he will not live down to our father's example, as am I."

Lady Phoebe remained in the middle of the dance floor,

the other guests drifting away from her, doubtless the better to gawk as Althea greeted *Their Graces of Rothhaven*. Before Althea reached the foot of the steps, she caught Vicar Sorenson's eye and subtly inclined her chin toward Lady Phoebe.

"She should be cast into the nearest moat," Nathaniel said. "What she was trying to do was the worst kind of evil. You meant her no harm and never have."

"I believe she has cast herself into a moat, and not a soul among us will toss her a rope, though Vicar will see to it that she's made to sit through supper for Miss Price's sake. Introduce me to your mama, please."

The introductions proceeded amid much smiling and bobbing. Stephen and Robbie were soon engaged in a lively discussion regarding the relative merits of Beethoven over Mozart. Quinn and the Duchess of Rothhaven went in to dinner arm in arm, and Althea was left with no choice but to do likewise with Nathaniel.

Though Althea was confident that, in the entire history of balls, no hostess had ever wished more fervently for her own entertainment to end. Something had changed at Rothhaven Hall, and Althea was dying to know exactly what.

Until she could have Nathaniel to herself, she'd play the part of the gracious hostess, right down to wishing Lady Phoebe a pleasant evening when her ladyship made an unsuccessful attempt to discreetly slink away immediately after supper.

* * *

A light glowed in the window of the second-floor corner suite at Lynley Vale. A more honorable man would have allowed the delight of his heart to get a few hours' sleep before he bothered her, but Nathaniel's gallantry was no match for the need to be private with his lady.

Dancing with half the giggling twits in the shire had sorely tried that gallantry. His Grace of Walden had doubtless stood up with the other half, while Robert had graciously kept Lord Stephen—and several fawning widows—company in the card room.

"My goodness." Althea came to a halt in the doorway between her sitting room and her bedroom. "You have graduated from lurking in gardens to housebreaking."

Nathaniel could not read her mood, could not tell if she was upset that he'd upstaged her at her own ball—though really, Robert had been the talk of the evening—or pleased to see him.

"If I waited to pay a proper call tomorrow, I'd have to fight my way past every callow boy and lonely widower in the shire." Nathaniel stalked across the room rather than shout. "And then your brothers would doubtless turn up troublesomely *congenial* in anticipation of watching your sister-in-law-the-duchess dissect my motives with her sewing scissors. How are you?"

Althea unpinned the rosebud on his lapel. "Tired. You?"

"The same, and glad to have this evening behind us."

They'd danced the good-night waltz with the entire neighborhood gawking at them. Althea had smiled pleasantly at Nathaniel's shoulder, while he'd aimed a fond gaze at the top of her head. His intention had been to let all and sundry know that a harsh word aimed at Althea Wentworth would have consequences.

He suspected Althea's motives had been the same where he was concerned, which left a former ducal impersonator all in a muddle.

"Tell me about Robbie," Althea said, pouring a glass of water at the sideboard and putting his boutonniere into it.

"Robert—he will no longer answer to Master Robbie— and I learned that our dear, dunderheaded father had the falling sickness too. He likely held Mama at arm's length to keep his condition a secret from her, though Mama thinks he was also simply difficult by nature."

Nathaniel took Althea's wrist and fiddled with the satin bow holding her corsage until the flowers came loose. He put the violets in the same glass of water as his boutonniere, added the wilted gardenias from his pocket, and led Althea into the bedroom.

"Might I assist you with your hooks?" He'd done that much before without completely losing his wits.

"I told my maid not to wait up for me." Althea gave him her back and swiped her hair off her nape. "She is doubtless in the kitchen, listening to all the after-gossip and flirting with Monsieur."

God bless Monsieur. "Monsieur's bill of fare was enough to make a grown man weep. I'd forgotten what a real quiche is supposed to taste like. Why does this blasted gown have so many hooks?"

"The better to stay on when I'm turning down the room with a friendly neighbor. Give me a moment."

I will cheerfully give you the rest of my life. Nathaniel didn't say that, but somehow, he'd find a way to convey his sentiments to Althea before this night ended.

She glided away on a rustle of silk and disappeared behind the privacy screen. "What does your father's situation have to do with you—and Robert—attending my ball?"

Nathaniel joined her behind the screen and took a few hairpins from her hand. "Papa regarded periodic seizures as a reason to shut his heir away, which resulted in Robert acquiring more complicated problems than the occasional staring spell or shaking fit. Papa did not shut himself away, though. The former duke voted his seat from time to time despite his infirmity. He rode to hounds, he had affairs and children, and the whole ducal bit. I pointed this out to my brother, knowing Robert has ever had a competitive streak."

Althea's coiffure was a complicated arrangement of several braids, the lot of it secured with scores of pins.

"Robert is not about to be out-duked by a man long dead," Nathaniel went on. "The matter will require time and determination, but when I challenged Robert to attend a neighborhood ball with me and Mama as a first step, he allowed himself to be persuaded—particularly because I told him I'd go with or without him, and I'd go as Lord Nathaniel Rothmere. I promised my brother I'd play the duke as long as he needed me to, not as long he fancied to putter in his garden. How did you stand all these pins? They cannot have been comfortable."

"How did you stand to walk into a ballroom full of people who have long believed you to be the duke? What of the deception, Nathaniel? Who are you now, and what made you change your mind?"

In the mirror over the washstand, Althea regarded him steadily. This question was doubtless the reason she'd allowed him to bear her company at such an hour, the reason he was not hiking home across the fields—yet.

"The deception is not entirely over."

Her shoulders sagged. "Then this conversation must be. I will not hide away—"

"Please hear me out. You once asked me to at least listen to a recounting of your situation, and I did you that courtesy. Cousin Sarah gave me a means to reconsider what you call the deception and I call the most well-intended, ill-fated series of unfortunate blunders a family could make."

Althea moved away from him and shimmied out of her dress. Her stays tied in front, and she wiggled out of those next.

Was she trying to drive him mad?

"Who is Cousin Sarah?" she asked, slipping into a blue velvet dressing gown and taking a seat on her vanity stool.

"I hardly know, when you disrobe so casually."

That earned him a small, feminine smile. "I am exhausted, Nathaniel, and you are stalling." She untied the ribbons securing her braids, while Nathaniel flailed about, trying to recall what in blazes—

Ah, yes. "Cousin Sarah is my mother's companion, and as it happens, the previous duke considered courting her. She learned of his malady, and he swiveled his gunsights to Mama. Both women were well dowered, having had the good sense to claim a wealthy grandfather among their antecedents. I could brush your hair for you."

Althea was winnowing her fingers through her unbound hair, erasing the evidence of the various braids and creating a riot of dark, cascading curls.

"If you don't finish this tale in the next five minutes, I will have my brothers toss you from the premises. I am weary, I am confused, and I want more than a waltz to scotch the neighbors' gossip. I refuse to accommodate any deception that paints me as merely your friendly neighbor or your, your"—she waved a hand toward the bed. "I am done with compromises and fictions and contorting myself for the approval of others. Finish your tale."

She was right to insist on a clearing of the air. Entirely

right. Also entirely luscious. "You were magnificent to-night, you know. Lady Phoebe was making a serious mistake. I could see you preparing to deliver her the cut direct."

"I was preparing to do no such thing. To deliver even that setdown would have been to imply that her games deserved my notice. Tell me how you mean to go on with Robert. He still has the falling sickness and he was still declared dead at one point."

"As to that, Cousin Sarah, like the rest of polite society, believed Robert dead. That's what Papa wanted them to believe, that's what both Mama and I believed for a time. Cousin Sarah came upon Robert in the walled garden, knew him instantly for who he was, and promptly went into strong hysterics."

"Oh, dear." Another hint of a smile. "How did Robert deal with that?"

"He was dismayed, I suppose, while Sarah was over-joyed. Lazarus risen from the dead did not meet with more sincere jubilation, and she assumed Robert had only recently rejoined the household at the Hall."

Althea took up a length of blue silk ribbon, then passed it to him and turned on the vanity stool to once again present Nathaniel with her back. "Why did she assume that?"

"Because it makes sense." He gathered Althea's hair into one thick skein. "Am I supposed to braid all of this?"

"Loosely. Sarah assumed that if you'd known Robert was alive, you would not have taken his place as duke. So where does she think Robert has been for the past five years?"

"She assumed he was enjoying a quiet, isolated existence unaware that he was needed at the family seat." He divided Althea's hair into three sections and began the braiding.

"We told her the truth," he went on, "but the crux of the matter becomes the death certificate and the old duke's deception. Fortunately, the doctor housing Robert for all those years has recently signed an affidavit attesting to the fact that the ducal heir was well known to him and was very much alive at the time of the funeral, though afflicted with a mild case of the falling sickness. Very fortunately, we are still within the seven years when missing heirs can come forward."

"But *you* knew Robert was alive for the past five years."

"Therein lies the difficult part, the part that will require some creativity."

Fine dark brows drew down. "You will claim Robert only recently came to live at the Hall?"

"We will be vague and allow others to draw that conclusion. For a time after Papa's death, Robert did not know he'd been declared dead—that much is quite true—and I did not know my brother was alive—also true. The only element of discretion we will apply to the facts regards the timing of Robert's return."

"Discretion." Althea remained silent while Nathaniel tied the ribbon at the bottom of her braid. "And what of the Crown? What becomes of the title?"

Nathaniel went down on one knee, the better to look Althea in the eye as they had this difficult discussion.

"The more secluded Robert's life is, the more he's at risk to be taken advantage of. You made me see that. You refused to allow Lady Phoebe to send you into exile, though that would have been the easier course. She would either reveal herself before the entire shire for the spiteful creature she is, or she'd learn to behave decently toward her neighbors.

"You called the tune," Nathaniel said, taking Althea's

hand, "because you chose the battleground not of public opinion, but of simple decency. A duke who's never seen, who eschews good society, has far more to fear from public opinion than a duke who goes about his business taking a few precautions to accommodate a quirk of his health."

"And you think Robert can be that duke?" She brushed her hand over his lapel, smoothing the slight wrinkle where his boutonniere had been. "The duke whose mental and physical competence is regularly on display?"

"Not immediately, but he can strive toward that goal. He attended your ball, and that was a leap away from the role of the cowering invalid. He cannot return to the fiction of death. I won't allow it."

The compulsion to be more than Althea's lady's maid had been growing since she'd appeared in the doorway, a tired vision in bronze silk. This discussion was important, but Nathaniel was increasingly distracted by the sheer need to touch her.

"How does your brother know my sister?" Althea asked, drawing the pin from Nathaniel's cravat. "Robert and Constance were having a conversation that was intended to look cordial, but I know my sister. She was clinging to her composure by a slender thread."

Althea set aside the cravat pin and drew the signet ring from Nathaniel's finger. She was *undressing him*, and that had to bode well for a former false duke on bended knee in a lady's boudoir.

"At this moment, Althea, I am clinging to my composure by force of will alone. I have no idea how Constance and Robert might have met, but he has ever had private correspondence into which I do not pry. You want more than a neighborly connection with me, Althea, and I want more than that from you too. Much more."

She untied his neckcloth and piled it with his cravat pin and ring on the vanity. "Our situation will be complicated. We cannot abandon Robert, but he must make his own way. My family will try to meddle."

Our situation. How Nathaniel loved the sound of that.

Next, she started on the buttons of his evening coat, which was difficult when he knelt before her, so he stood and offered her a hand.

"I was hoping the Wentworth family would add their support to Mama's efforts when it comes to managing the gossip. Robert should eventually present himself at court, there are writs to sort out, letters patent that might require re-issuance. His Grace of Walden mentioned an acquaintance at the College of Arms who could be helpful."

None of which Nathaniel cared two groats about at the moment. He was in Althea's bedroom, her hand in his, and she was apparently undaunted by all that lay ahead. Truly, he had given his heart to the right woman.

Althea rose and looped her arms around Nathaniel's waist. "This will be challenging, to navigate the whispers, deal with family, and aid Robert."

Her embrace wasn't seductive so much as weary, which Nathaniel could well understand. "I welcome the challenge, Althea, provided you welcome it too. You were right that the deception had served its purpose, and right that Robert was capable of more. So am I. I am capable of loving both you and my brother, and I want more too."

She sighed, relaxing against him. "More?"

"My mother's company at frequent intervals. The occasional winter spent someplace other than Yorkshire. Mostly, though, I want you, and I am willing to beg you for the honor of your hand in marriage." He prepared to go down on one knee again, but Althea stopped him.

"Beg me, Nathaniel? Beg me for the honor of my hand?"

"I'm certainly not going to beg any other woman for that honor."

"But *beg* me, Nathaniel?"

He'd bewildered his lady and put a touch of wariness back in her eyes. An explanation was in order—a *brief* explanation.

"My late father was so afflicted with pride that he refused to allow even his wife to know of his illness. He was so worried about what the world would think of him that the welfare of his own young son was sacrificed to his arrogance. I could have become him, Althea. Organizing my strange little fiefdom to suit my narrow version of order, telling myself the whole arrangement was done for the benefit of others, when in fact, I was simply being a martinet. I never was the Duke of Rothhaven, nor do I wish to be that man. I am Lord Nathaniel Rothmere, and not too proud to beg for what really matters."

Althea bundled close. "You need not beg me for the heart I have already given you. I have puzzled out that when a child has to beg for food, any shame attaches to those who pretend not to see her or those who scorn to help her. When a well-established hostess must be begged for common courtesies, so too is she the party deserving of shame. I do have a few demands of you."

"Anything, provided we can get into that bed in the next five minutes."

"I want circulating schools in the slums, I want goats to go with my pigs, for goats give milk that can be made into cheese and butter but they don't require half the grazing a cow does. Goats can live on alley weeds and table scraps. I want—"

Nathaniel kissed her, because she wanted all good things, and because he wanted *her*. "You want?"

Her smile was slow and sweet, then a bit naughty. "To take you to bed."

Thank God. "I intend to court you properly for all the world to see."

She slid his coat from his shoulders. "Must you?"

"For the three weeks necessary to cry the banns, I will be a pattern card of swainly devotion. I will walk you home from services, endure meals with your bothersome family and even be somewhat polite to Lord Stephen, drive out with you..."

His waistcoat went next, casually draped over her vanity stool. "You were saying, *my lord*?"

"Something about making passionate love until the sun comes up."

"That's in a mere hour or two."

He let her pull his shirt over his head, then eased her dressing gown off. "We won't have an easy time of it, Althea, not at first."

"I don't want easy. I want honest and meaningful, and I want *you*."

"We are in accord."

"Let's be in accord in bed, shall we?"

They were, gloriously so, and when Nathaniel came down to breakfast hand in hand with Althea, not even her brothers dared offer a remark, though they, Millicent, and Her Grace of Walden did smile. Both Quinn and Stephen passed the duchess a coin, while Nathaniel passed Althea the teapot and the entire basket of cinnamon buns.

Author's Note

How likely is it that wealthy late-Georgian families would stash an inconvenient or mentally infirm relation in a "private madhouse"? To answer that question, we need some context.

Most readers will be familiar with the infamous Bethlehem Royal Hospital, an institution established in 1337 that by Regency days was notorious for its inhumane confinement of the (allegedly) mentally ill. Bethlehem, or Bedlam, as it came to be known, was a paupers' hospital. People with means were not generally admitted, and people with any compassion didn't want to see their relatives in such a place. Until the Madhouse Act of 1774, admission to any place of confinement on mental illness grounds was mostly based on the common law tenet that allowed a relative to "confine a person disordered in mind, who seems disposed to do mischief to himself, or another person." [Unsworth, Clive (1991). "Mental Disorder and the Tutelary Relationship: From Pre- to Post-Carceral Legal Order." *Journal of Law and Society*. 18 (2): 254–278. doi:10.2307/1410140. JSTOR 1410140.]

If the family could not keep the patient at home, the private madhouse—using the terminology of the day—was the only alternative. For a sum, the patient was housed and cared for by somebody who professed to have relevant knowledge and ability. Two problems arose. First, sane people were warehoused against their will, and second, conditions in these private institutions varied greatly. (Note the euphemism.)

The Madhouse Act of 1774 came about in part because of what is known as the Hawley case, which transpired in 1762. A Mrs. Hawley had been confined in a madhouse and a friend sought her release on the grounds that she was not, in fact, mad. The case was initially dismissed because the friend had no standing to bring the petition for a writ of habeas corpus (which would have required Mrs. Hawley to appear in person before the judge). The judge instead sent a physician to visit with Mrs. Hawley, who was apparently quite sane.

She had been incarcerated at the madhouse on the word of her husband alone, could not leave the place, and was to be kept there, no questions asked, as long as the husband paid the monthly fee. Further investigation revealed that the madhouse where she'd been confined hadn't admitted a truly mentally ill person for years. No one who could pay was turned away.

When a House of Commons committee investigated this case in 1763, they reported that the situation Mrs. Hawley found herself in was typical of many such institutions. No physicians attended the patients, they were refused all communication with people outside the institution walls, and they were treated as if insane without anybody in authority finding them so.

It took a few false starts, but in 1774 Parliament passed an act requiring that any place holding more than one allegedly insane person had to be licensed by a committee of the Royal College of Physicians, all such private madhouses were to be inspected annually, and the Royal College would keep a register of who was housed where. Outside of London, the task of ensuring an annual inspection of these facilities fell to the judges presiding at the Quarter Sessions.

All better, right?

Well, not exactly. The Madhouse Act of 1774 made no reforms as to how patients were to be treated or the rigor of the admissions process, and—typical of much Georgian and Victorian reform legislation—made no provision for funding enforcement of the law. Various subsequent acts chipped away at the inhumane and over-use of restraints, isolation, and "lowering regimens" (subsistence diets or worse), but no legal process could address the fact that Georgian and Regency mental health care, generally, was by modern standards terrible.

Dr. Benjamin Rush, known to some readers as a signer of the Declaration of Independence, was also an Edinburgh-educated physician and social reformer based mostly in the Philadelphia area. He is considered a founder of American psychiatric medicine, and corresponded extensively with physicians all over the United States, the United Kingdom, and Europe. In 1813, he published "Medical Inquiries and Observations Upon Diseases of the Mind," and therein enumerated the treatments he had found most effective over decades of dealing with the mentally infirm.

Those were, in order: bloodletting, laxatives (usually

mercury-based), emetics, a starvation diet ("food and drink that contain but little nourishment...combined with the three remedies above..."). This regimen (assuming the patient survived it, which many did not) was to be followed by stimulating aliment, drink, and medicine (meaning spirits); warm baths; cold baths; friction to the trunk of the body; the excitement of pain (yeah, he went there); salivation; blisters; exercise; and "terror," among other approaches.

Rush also developed a chair that prohibited the patient any movement, even turning the head, and he was also comfortable with using a spinning chair, which twirled the patient into prolonged vertigo and nausea.

And this guy was considered a humane, enlightened, educated, well-intended, highly knowledgeable authority on treatment of the insane.

So, the chances of Robert ending up in a private mad-house were pretty good. That he was from a ducal family with a martinet of a father might have mitigated against the more severe treatments inflicted on the powerless else-where, but also would have assured that any physician or judge making an annual inspection of Dr. Soames's estab-lishment would have been reluctant to question Robert's confinement.

On a cheerier note, it's worth mentioning that York, United Kingdom, became the site of significant mental health care reform under the aegis of the Society of Friends. The York Asylum was one of the licensed madhouses established pursuant to applicable law. A Quaker widow, Hannah Mills, was admitted to this institution in 1790 and died shortly thereafter. She'd been denied any contact with friends or family while at the institution and had been in good physical health when admitted. The Quaker community became suspicious regarding the circumstances of her death, but could do nothing at the time.

When Quaker philanthropist William Tuke visited a London mental hospital following Hannah's death, he found the conditions there predictably deplorable, and he became determined to create a better option. In 1796, with the aid of charitable supporters, he opened the York Retreat. The building featured spacious, airy corridors where patients could wander at will even if they could not go outside. Other reforms included what we would call occupational therapy (arts and crafts, gardening, board games), line-of-sight supervision, minimal use of restraints and the straitjacket vastly preferred to chains, and an abandonment of the "heroic medicine" favored by Dr. Rush.

The residents were encouraged to read books and to write, and to interact with the domestic animals kept in the Retreat's various yards and gardens.

In 1813, Tuke wrote a treatise on the methods used at the Retreat, and initial reactions included much derision and criticism. His approach, though, was simultaneously being developed and adopted by forward-thinkers in France, Italy, and elsewhere, and came to be influential throughout the English-speaking world.

So, yes, Robert could have easily been packed off to a house of horrors masquerading as a mental hospital. He would have kept company there with people whom we wouldn't regard as insane, while putting up with "medical" interventions that would have killed a lesser man.

Fortunately, he also ran into a very young Constance Wentworth, but that is a tale for another time....

LOOK FOR ROBERT AND CONSTANCE'S STORY IN
THE TRUTH ABOUT DUKES

KEEP READING FOR A PREVIEW.

Chapter One

Constance Wentworth sidled along the edge of the ball-room, trying to look like a forgettably plain woman making a discreet exit. This should have been a simple challenge, because she was forgettably plain and she desperately needed to make a discreet exit.

When she was two yards shy of the archway, Robert, Duke of Rothhaven, turned his gaze in her direction.

Bollocks and bedamned, he *recognized* her. Surprise flashed in his green eyes, as fleeting as distant lightning on a summer night, and then he lifted his glass of punch in a gesture of acknowledgment.

More than ten years later, and still he knew her at sight, as she'd known him. His height was striking, but so was his sense of focusing utterly on the object of his attention. Rothhaven came to a still point, then aimed every sense exclusively and intensely at who or what had caught his notice.

He was worth noticing too. Deep-set emerald eyes, dramatic brows that gave him a slight air of inquisitiveness at all times. High forehead, dark hair pulled back in an old-fashioned queue. Features that blended Nordic power and Celtic ruggedness with just enough Gallic refinement that his portraits would be stunning, even into old age.

Once upon a time, Constance had contented herself with sketching his hands. Given the opportunity, she would not make that mistake again.

She inclined her head, for it would not do to snub a duke, much less one who held sizeable acreage in the neighborhood. That he'd completely misrepresented himself to her, that he'd at one time been a friend, that he was hale and whole and not five yards away made her steps as she wove through the crowd more urgent.

Which is why she nearly ploughed into him, though his reflexes, as always, were uncannily quick.

"Lady Constance." He bowed correctly.

With the whole ballroom watching, Constance could only curtsy in return. "Your Grace."

"You are looking well." No emotion colored that observation, and Constance *was* looking well compared to when he'd known her previously. She had made it a point to look well and dress well since then, but not too well.

"Thank you, and Your Grace appears to be in good health too." When she'd first met him, he'd been a wraith, pale, mute, watchful, and bitter.

"I have my dear brother to thank for my improved health. Shall we enjoy the evening air?"

He offered his arm and Constance had no choice but to take it. Her very own sister, Lady Althea Wentworth, was the hostess at this gathering. Her brothers, Quinn and

Stephen, were on hand, and as far as the family knew, Constance and Rothhaven were strangers.

Would that it were so.

The goggling crowd that hadn't allowed Constance to pass only a moment before parted like sheep for Rothhaven. His pace was leisurely, and he rested a gloved hand over hers, as if he knew she struggled not to flee.

"The quartet is in good form," he said. "I do fancy Mozart done well."

"Do you still play the violin?"

"Rarely. Do you still paint?"

"Every chance I get." He'd taught her to paint, though all he'd had at the time were oils, which ladies were dissuaded from attempting.

"I rejoice to know that something of lasting value came from our association, my lady."

They reached the doorway to the back terrace. "May I slap you now, Your Grace?"

"Best not. Your sister as hostess deserves to command all attention this evening. Then too, your brother might take a notion to remedy any insult done to you, making me a very dead duke."

"Again."

"Let's step outside, shall we?"

Constance allowed that, because she loved to look at the night sky. Rather than lead her to the balustrade overlooking the garden, His Grace escorted her to a bench along the outside wall of the house. Music and conversation spilled through open windows, and torches flickered in the evening breeze. The terrace, though, was blessedly deserted.

"How are you?" Rothhaven asked, taking the place beside her. He sat a bit too close for propriety, but his proximity meant Constance could speak quietly.

"I am well. I paint, I attend the gatherings I'm told to attend. I dance, I drop French phrases into my conversation, I read but not too much. I have become a portrait of a lady. And what of you?"

"The tale is complicated, and I will happily regale you with it at another time. For the present, might we agree to behave as if we are two cordial people acquiring a family connection through our siblings?"

"We *are* acquiring a family connection through our siblings, more's the pity. Your brother and my sister are clearly in the advanced stages of besottedness." How had that happened, when Althea had given up on polite society, and Nathaniel Rothmere had famously shunned company of every description? That he even had an older brother sharing Rothhaven Hall with him was quite the revelation.

"Can we manage the cordial part?" Rothhaven asked. "I would like to try."

He sounded sincere. He had always sounded sincere. "I don't know what I can manage where you are concerned."

"Honest, as ever. Your forthright nature is one of your most appealing qualities."

"As if I give a hearty heigh-ho for your good opinion of me or of anybody else." Constance rose, abruptly at the limit of her patience. "I wish you a pleasant evening."

Before she'd taken a single step, Rothhaven had risen and manacled her wrist in a firm grip. He did not hurt her—he was the last person to inflict physical harm on another, she trusted him that much—but neither could she leave.

"You must not abandon me to the darkness, my lady."

"Why not? You are a duke, of sound mind, in good health, and the worst that can befall you on this terrace is that one of the Weatherby sisters will try to get herself compromised with you."

He changed his hold, so his fingers interlaced with Constance's. "You must not leave me alone out here because I am generally terrified of the out of doors."

Constance's first inclination was to laugh, scornfully, because Rothhaven's comment was a pathetic attempt at flirtation, but the quality of his grip on her hand stopped her.

"You are serious."

"I am entirely in earnest. If you would assist me to return to the ballroom, I would be much obliged. I should never have assumed I was up to the challenge of wandering about an unwalled terrace under an open sky, even at night."

Constance had been angry with this man for half of her life, but that tirade could keep for another time. He was entitled to his fears, and she liked the notion of having Rothhaven obligated to her. She took his arm and rejoined the crowd in the ballroom, and before her thinking mind could stop her, she agreed to partner His Grace through the ordeal of the supper buffet as well.

About the Author

Grace Burrowes grew up in central Pennsylvania and is the sixth of seven children. She discovered romance novels in junior high and has been reading them voraciously ever since. Grace has a bachelor's degree in political science, a bachelor of music in music history (both from the Pennsylvania State University), a master's degree in conflict transformation from Eastern Mennonite University, and a juris doctor from the National Law Center at George Washington University.

Grace is a *New York Times* and *USA Today* bestselling author who writes Georgian, Regency, Scottish Victorian, and contemporary romances in both novella and novel lengths. She's a member of Romance Writers of America and Novelist, Inc., and enjoys giving workshops and speaking at writers' conferences.

You can learn more at:
GraceBurrowes.com
Bookbub:
https://www.bookbub.com/authors/grace-burrowes
Twitter @GraceBurrowes
Facebook.com/Grace.Burrowes

Don't miss Grace Burrowes'
My One and Only Duke, the first book
in the Rogues to Riches series

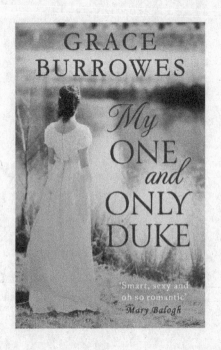

Also includes the bonus novella
Once Upon a Christmas Eve from *New York Times*
bestselling author Elizabeth Hoyt!

Discover more Grace Burrowes with her bestselling
Windham Brides series

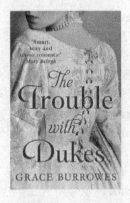

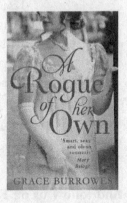

'Sexy heroes, strong heroines, intelligent plots, enchanting
love stories … Grace Burrowes's romances have them all'
Mary Balogh, *New York Times* bestselling author

Do you love historical fiction?

Want the chance to hear news about your favourite
authors (and the chance to win free books)?

Mary Balogh
Lenora Bell
Charlotte Betts
Jessica Blair
Frances Brody
Grace Burrowes
Evie Dunmore
Pamela Hart
Elizabeth Hoyt
Eloisa James
Lisa Kleypas
Stephanie Laurens
Sarah MacLean
Amanda Quick
Julia Quinn

Then visit the Piatkus website
www.yourswithlove.co.uk

And follow us on Facebook and Instagram
www.facebook.com/yourswithlovex | @yourswithlovex